INTO THE HEARTLAND

JACK CASEY

DIAMONDS BIG AS RADISHES, LLC

Published by
Diamonds Big as Radishes, LLC
3956 Bentley Bridge Road
Raleigh, NC 27612

ISBN: 9781734366624

Cover photo: Lee Avison/Trevillion Images

Earlier versions of this novel were published
as *A Land Beyond the River* by Bantam Books, NY (1988)
and Diamond Rock Publishing Co. (2005)

Dedicated to my wife

VICTORIA

whose faith and love fill

my life with surpassing beauty

FOREWORD

In today's digital world, why a novel about a slow, plodding, muddy canal?

The Erie Canal was America's first information highway, and it proved to the world that American ingenuity could conquer time and space. In its day, the canal sped communication, transported goods from the Midwest to New York Harbor, and ushered in an age of commerce and new concepts of wealth.

Long before railroads and internal combustion engines, visionaries dreamed of penetrating the vast wilderness of New York State to reach the Great Lakes and America's heartland. Europe boasted intricate canal systems, and ancient Egypt, Babylon and Sumer used canals to irrigate their farmland and transport produce and livestock. But this canal would be different.

First, the land was largely unexplored. George Washington had only recently banished the Iroquois from their homeland for siding with the British. A route needed to be mapped and surveyed through uncharted forest. Rugged cliffs and wide river valleys posed engineering challenges unknown in the much flatter Old World. Streams and rivers needed to be crossed with aqueducts, cliffs scaled with locks, and feeder canals dug to keep the main artery filled with water. Most importantly, who would pay for it?

DeWitt Clinton took up the cause of the canal full-time during a brief hiatus as New York City mayor. He knew this slender ribbon of water would make New York City the financial capital of the nation, and so he looked everywhere for funds to build it. Many scoffed at him, dubbed the project "Clinton's Ditch" and "Clinton's Folly."

When Martin Van Buren opposed him in the state legislature and James Madison and Congress denied him federal funds, Clinton took his case directly to the people and convinced energetic New Yorkers to invest in their future. After eight intense years of digging, the canal opened to wild celebrations, and immediately reaped handsome dividends.

Not only did the canal pay for itself in nine years, it also gave birth to American geology and civil engineering, sciences that would eventually tap coal and oil reserves, and erect railroads, skyscrapers, highways and suspension bridges. As technology advanced, the old canal was superseded by the New York Central and then the New York State Thruway.

Although it is now long obsolete, the Erie Canal hearkens back to a more innocent age when America began to flex its muscles. I wrote this novel because I wanted to visit and temporarily dwell in that simpler time. I envisioned this tale as a love story in which an heiress from the landed gentry, Eleanora, casts off the strictures of her class to join an enterprising westerner, Daniel, in a colossal work that feeds their growing love, and changes them as it changes the world.

Two centuries ago the Erie Canal called forth the best in our American character, and launched our nation's westward expansion. Given the dire challenges we face today, it's refreshing to see how our push into the West began, and how lovers struggled on the frontier to create a better tomorrow. And who doesn't enjoy a happy ending?

Bantam Books first published this work in 1988, and I revised it in a deluxe edition with illustrations in 2005. Now, with yet another advance in technology, I present this newly edited digital edition to a wider audience. A year ago I married my incomparable Victoria, and so I want to share a fresh vision of how love conquers all, and how we can build a life of joy and harmony if we work together to make our world a better place.

JACK CASEY
Troy, NY
January 5, 2021

BOOK I
THE LANDED GENTRY

CHAPTER 1

"*L*ove?" Lady Eleanora turned and frowned at her maid. "Did you say you were in love?"

Again, Kate's idle tongue had betrayed her. Her face flushed and her nimble fingers, braiding her ladyship's hair, darted and wove more quickly. "Yes, mum," Kate thrust her chin up heroically. "Leastways, I believe I'm in . . . in love."

"And what, poor lamb, would you know of love?" Lady Eleanora's eyes gleamed with mirth. The maid stepped behind the chair to avoid her gaze, but Eleanora turned fully around. "Well?"

Kate pulled the braid and her ladyship winced. "P'rhaps it weren't that neither."

"But you said you were in love! I heard you!"

Kate's eyes welled with tears. She longed to be away, out in the cool evening river breeze. "Well, to me, mum, it is!" Her breath came short and quick. "And it mayn't be so grand as you knew, neither, but it's the best I can ever hope for!" Now she dared to look into her mistress' eyes and saw her smile. When Lady Eleanora smiled it was like the sun beaming on a summer morn. Only now her dark eyes held a gleam of ridicule, so Kate concentrated mightily on her work.

"Who is he?"

Kate threw up her hands and the braid fell, slowly untwining. "You mock me, mum! It's not as though we'll be setting up a household and scrapin' the ground for a few bushels of corn, and raisin' brats and growin' mean and sour to each other! But if he should pr'pose, and mind you I believe he will, then I must think on it hard, and if I accept, as I'm not saying I won't, then I'll be his wife."

Lady Eleanora spoke softly, "Who is he?"

"A groom of the stables here at the general's manor. I'll fetch the wig so's you can descend the stairs to the ball. I can hear them fiddles now."

Indeed, the strains of a Viennese waltz lilted up the stairs above the low rumble of men's laughter.

"Let them wait, pet." Eleanora turned to face her reflection in the mirror. She wore a low-cut sapphire gown with a lace bodice, and though her rich dark hair usually hung freely, tonight it would be tightly pinned under the heavy old-fashioned powdered wig. "Tell me more about him."

"Why, he's ever so nice. Joel Kipp's his name. From Connetty-cut. He's tall, mum, and lean, and he has such happy gray eyes. He can ride the most spirited of the general's steeds with ease and skill. I bet he could ride your Hecate first time."

"How does this, this *love* make you feel?"

Kate blushed. "It's ever so wonderful, mum! When he speaks my name, I quiver, . . . though I'd never compromise my virtue! Never!" She shook her head seriously, then her eyes widened. "But I did kiss him once, and it stole my very breath away." Kate pinned up the braid. "A-course it's nothing, like you must've felt with Master Jacob . . . "

The mention of her late husband stung Eleanora.

"Them poems he switched from Latin, why, mum, I never

made much sense of the meaning of them, but they sounded so lofty and wondrous even in American, and you made the happiest couple!"

Kate brought the powdered wig and placed it like a high crown on Eleanora's head. Eleanora frowned. "Poor Master Jacob! The accident and all. What a horrible loss!"

"Yes," Eleanora said. She inclined her head and listened to the bright violins and the melancholy cello. Tonight would be as always, witty young men after her hand and her lands, making fools of themselves; and aging beaux, whispering they understood a widow's plight. At twenty-two, it was over. There would be no new love. She scowled at her powdered, perfumed, bejeweled reflection, like an actress burlesquing the vanities of her class.

Kate deftly combed the wig. As Eleanora watched her in the looking glass, she predicted Kate's sad future. The stable hand would have his way, then leave the girl, grieving and bitter, hopefully with no bastard in her arms. Eleanora considered giving advice, then thought better. Each woman must make her own mistakes. Tragic but true. She stood and the gown rustled elegantly about her.

"Oh, mum, you'll steal every heart!"

"If only, my pet, there were one worth the taking."

Then Eleanora brightened and touched Kate's cheek. "But I'll not need you till midnight, so after you finish here, run along. And see you put your time to good use."

Kate curtseyed. "Yes, mum." She didn't hide her joy. As she opened the door, music wafted into the room like sweet perfume. Lady Eleanora pulled herself up to regal height, touched Kate's cheek fondly and then glided along the hallway to the stair. The laughter and talk of the men suddenly stopped. The maid dared not look over the bannister. She quietly closed the bedroom door, darted to the dressing table and dabbed rouge on her cheek and a puff of powder on her nose. Quickly straightening the clothing and lingerie strewn on the bed and chairs, Kate checked her appearance in the mirror, flounced her skirts, then scampered down the back stairs to the kitchen, and the yard and the stables beyond.

Descending with queenly grace, Eleanora Van Rensselaer was met by a room of admiring men. She bowed slightly, took the arms of two escorts, and then entered the high, deep ballroom. Cherry paneling glowed in the soft candlelight from the ceiling candelabras and wall sconces and resonated with sweet violin and with the laughter of the periwigged legislators celebrating the end of their 1810 session.

Eleanora glided to a handsome, white-haired man and extended both her gloved hands. "You look radiant, my dear," the general said. Stephen Van Rensselaer, her late husband's uncle and her host for the weekend, had tonight assembled the best and brightest of New York society at his elegant manor house.

"I'm so happy to attend, General."

"Not nearly so happy as we." He bowed. "You remember Mr. Irving, I'm sure." He moved her along gracefully so he might greet his next guest.

"Dear Eleanora." The tall man bent to brush her hand with a kiss. "It's been far too long."

"And since we last met you've become our literary lion. I so enjoyed your *Knickerbocker's History!* "

"London and Paris do rave about it too!" Washington Irving admitted, then added more modestly, "They enjoy ridiculing Americans as a primitive race and I fear I may have encouraged such unkind portraiture."

"Well, then, you must correct it by writing our national epic!"

"Actually, I have returned to undertake something of the sort," the author mused, then his expression grew sad. "But since my exquisite Matilda passed, I have no heart to write at all." Gently he touched her hand. "Yet you have had your hardship, too. Jacob was my dear friend." The author dropped his eyes and smiled with effort. "But I must introduce you to Theodosia!"

He led her through the crowd to a striking young woman whose dark eyes were quick and suspicious, and whose prominent nose seemed poised to smell danger. She wore no outdated powdered wig, no brocade gown, no whalebone stays. She wore a loose-fitting sheath of gold tissue with an Empire waist in the latest Parisian style. Her raven black hair hung in luxuriant ringlets and her lips curled as if she were enjoying a private joke.

"I've heard so much about you," Eleanora said evenly as Irving introduced them. Theodosia's eyes glittered.

"Yes, there are many stories, so very many stories." Theodosia affected boredom. Her ringlets shimmered. "People could spend time far more productively than in spreading gossip."

"I agree," Eleanora said, "unless they are generating it."

Miss Burr narrowed her eyes like a cat, then her lips curled again. "I so enjoy meeting Washington's friends. They're so disarming. Like the characters he creates with his pen."

"Dear me!" said Irving.

"Why, Eleanora!" It was Eleanora's cousin Harriet. "Let me steal you away. Come over and greet Rob! He's been working extremely hard, and only left the boat tonight to talk with some of the legislators."

"It was so nice to see you again, Washington." Eleanora gave him her hand, and she smiled and inclined her head slightly. "And to meet you, Miss Burr."

Harriet, a flighty redhead, took Eleanora's arm and rolled her eyes as they moved through the statesmen, soldiers, and aristocrats. "Oh, what they say about her!" Harriet whispered. "That scoundrel father of hers in exile, penniless, while she runs from state to state, scraping

together shillings and pence to send him! I don't trust her!
Never have!"

"Oh, I do," Eleanora said lightly, "I trust her conduct to
always be impeachable."

"Quite. Quite."

They approached a cluster of men. Harriet's husband,
Robert Fulton, and her uncle, Chancellor Robert Livingston,
were talking to two other men. By their dress, these men were
from the west. Instead of wigs, sequined waistcoats, breeches
and stockings, they were bare-headed and wore trousers and
black frock coats. One man had dark features and piercing
eyes, the other had curly, sandy hair, bright blue eyes, and
against all dictates of fashion, a shaggy moustache.

"Who are they?" Eleanora asked derisively. "Quakers?"
"They're from the west!"

"Perhaps we shouldn't interrupt." Eleanora looked elsewhere for someone to greet.

"Oh, let's invade! Let's do!" Harriet took her arm and
boldly approached the group. "Now there, Rob, this is a ball,
not the legislature or your captain's bridge! We're here to celebrate the end to all your political haggling."

"As if it will ever end," Fulton sighed, then bowed to
Eleanora. "So good to see you again, my dear."

She inclined her head in greeting to Fulton and to her
uncle the chancellor. Then she looked with unabashed
curiosity at the tall, balding westerner. He dropped his eyes
respectfully and bowed.

"This is Joseph Ellicott," Fulton said. Ellicott reached to
kiss her hand, and as she yielded it to him, she looked toward
the man at his side. He did not bow. He stared directly into
her eyes, and he stood leaning easily backward with a cup of
punch resting on his folded arms.

"And this is Daniel Hedges."

She tilted her head curiously. He was neither impressed
nor subservient. A broad smile broke beneath his moustache.

"Pleased. Pleased." But his relaxed impertinence confounded her when, instead of kissing her offered hand, he shook it! This had never happened to her.

"We've been discussing the canal proposal," Fulton explained.

"These men are from the frontier, from a hamlet called Buffaloe Creek on Lake Erie. They incorporated their township with the legislature this session, and Mr. Hedges has done some surveying for a proposed canal route."

"So, Mr. Hedges," Eleanora turned to him, "do you think such a major undertaking is humanly possible?"

"Well, now," he grinned, "I sure hope so." He nodded and stared keenly at her until she looked away. "I'd sure like to get down to these parts more often."

Eleanora was affronted and looked at him as if to ask, "Do you know who you're talking to?" At that precise moment, as if reading her mind, Hedges grinned and nodded. It shocked her, though she didn't want him to see. Instead, she joined the conversation about the canal, and found herself striving to demonstrate how informed and involved she was. She looked for a reaction. He didn't seem impressed.

The chancellor's wife was suddenly there. "We must dance, dear. It's the general's waltz."

In desperation Eleanora looked about for her escorts. She did not want to dance with the frontiersmen, and all the others seemed to be paired.

"Why, it's a real shame I don't dance that way," Hedges shrugged. "I'd take you out there myself." Eleanora glared at him. "And yet, you're in luck." He slapped Ellicott on the back. "My friend here is as good a dancer as we have west of Schenectady."

"How comforting." She attempted a smile.

"Madame," Ellicott gave a polished bow. She nodded, took his hand and glided out on the dance floor. When the music began, she found Ellicott was indeed accomplished.

"Your friend is impertinent," she observed as they danced. "That's just Daniel's way. He doesn't let much bother him. He's different, sure, but he's the most capable man I know."

"What is his, his *occupation?*" She asked this with a distaste for the notion that people had to work.

"A little bit of everything. He owns a brig on Lake Erie. He plies a trade from Buffaloe Creek and Black Rock out to Cleveland."

"Oh," she grimaced. "A merchant."

Ellicott frowned. The word wasn't sufficient. "Partly. But understand that out west we don't fit neatly into Eastern conceptions. He trades, yes, but he's a ship captain of considerable skill. He accompanied me to Albany because he is the best surveyor we have. His knowledge of lands west of Oswego is second only to the Iroquois."

"So he is to help on Mr. Clinton's canal survey?"

"When we meet with the commissioners Wednesday, he will file a preliminary report."

"I see." Her eyes indicated the matter was over, but she stole a look at the tall ship captain. He was watching her.

Each time they spun, she looked again, and Hedges' relaxed posture and smile irritated her. He was so different from anyone she had ever seen at a ball, and when the violins ceased, she thanked Ellicott and crossed the ballroom in the other direction.

Lady Eleanora danced through the evening with many dashing young men. Her grace and skill in the quadrille, the minuet and the waltz were greatly admired by her partners. Occasionally she glanced over to the corner where the impertinent frontiersman stood. He still watched her and while this unnerved her, it excited her too, and she found herself dancing more animatedly to impress him. It was with a pang of disappointment, then, that she looked over after a rather difficult pirouette and saw he was not there. She scanned the room as she continued to dance, but in vain. She told herself he must have left, and she made up her mind to forget him altogether. When the orchestra ceased playing, Eleanora wanted to take some air alone, so she walked out unescorted on the broad front lawn.

A fat, honey-colored moon hung in the June haze, and the dark, untroubled river glided by the boat slips, beneath the hanging willows. She took a deep breath. The night was warm and close, perfumed with jasmine from the general's gardens. Here and there on the lawn, couples strolled and talked in the soft darkness. The quiet soothed her. Eleanora walked down a graded path to a grove of tall willows. Stretching luxuriantly, she turned to look at the mansion, majestic on its knoll.

How comforting was the enjoyment of property! From a prosperous estate all else flowed: prestige, status, the pursuit of elegance and excellence, one's very identity. The general, perhaps the wealthiest man in America, kept a superb house. She had visited before, but had never stayed overnight. The general's capable, fatherly management of his vast lands produced this luxury, this splendor. He was master of Rensselaerwyck just as she was mistress of Claverack, and although the general surrounded himself with military men, bankers, land speculators, artists, inventors, governors and judges, the source of his wealth and power were the thousands of tenant farmers, blowing to warm their chapped, filthy hands as they waited on wagons each January 2 to pay their ground rent with wheat and fat hens.

Eleanora loved her estate too, but it extracted a heavy price from her. Betrothed at sixteen to the general's nephew Jacob, married at eighteen, her dowry and Jacob's patrimony were joined by their families to form a large, comfortable estate called "Claverack." But soon its metes and bounds had closed in on her, constricting, deadening her spirit. No more did the gracious Claverack mansion host such balls as these. True, Jacob had enjoyed his circle of young literary men who reveled at secluded hunting lodges, but the translations and poetry that had charmed her as a girl did little to satisfy the strong desire that surprised and confused her a year after their wedding.

Eleanora scanned the tall French windows, glimmering with candlelight. She watched dancing forms whirl to the faint strains of violin. Like a wondrous abbey she'd read and dreamt about in French romance, Van Rensselaer's seat of wealth and grace and power seemed tonight how things should always be. She shivered and sighed. Though her marriage had never bloomed, and widowhood proved nagging and lonely, Claverack was now her comfort. She must be satisfied with her station and her lands. Suddenly she smelled a cigar and turned. Not eight feet from her stood the tall ship captain.

"Evening, Mrs. Van Rensselaer." His voice was deep and serene.

"I wasn't aware I was being observed."

"Didn't want to interrupt. I was watching the river." When he puffed the cigar it lit his features. "Tide's coming in." He turned away. He was forcing her to decide whether she'd approach or leave.

"Mr. Ellicott informs me you are meeting with the canal commission Wednesday."

"Yes." He faced her.

"And beyond your survey, will you be involved?"

"Too early to say. . . . Very ambitious project, though." His voice was inviting.

"Yes." She took a step toward him. "Your friend told me you own a boat on Lake Erie."

"I do." He smiled warmly as the topic pleased him. "A brig, two-masted, hundred and ten tons. Draws five feet of water full-loaded." He puffed from the cigar and gave an easy laugh. "A lively ship she is, and old Lake Erie's mighty rough in a squall. It's then my *Silver Pearl* shows her pluck." He turned to face her fully. "She's a sight to see under full sail."

Eleanora took another step forward. "We hear such fabulous tales of your western reaches: native scalpings, black bears, panthers, impossible blizzards. It's a wonder anyone chooses to live so far from civilization."

Hedges laughed. "Why, it's my home." He flicked an ash and looked at her. You should see it for yourself, form your own opinion."

He was ridiculing her notions about the west! Eleanora cleared her throat. "Is this your first visit to Albany?"

"Yes it is. This place seems to have its benefits, too." He held up his cigar and winked. He was including her as a "benefit"!

She fumed. "Well, I hope your report is well-received, Mr. Hedges. Good night." Abruptly she lifted the hem of her skirts and moved smoothly toward the mansion.

Daniel Hedges watched her sweep across the lawn, nodded and turned to enjoy the remainder of his cigar.

"She was asking all manner of questions about you," Joseph Ellicott said as they walked into the city after the ball. "I think she's smitten."

"I'll wager that underneath the wig and jewelry she's a handsome woman. Odd notions about the West, though. Got a mite shrewish at one point." Hedges smiled to himself. "Does she have a lover?"

Half a mile before them the roofs of Albany lay in sleepy repose, and the cupola of the state Capitol gleamed in the moonlight.

"It's best to ignore the personal lives of the landed gentry," Ellicott cautioned. "They own everything, and they rule everything, and that is their sole objective. You see how quickly factions form and dissolve in the legislature!"

"My, she is a handsome woman."

Ellicott scoffed. "Did you tell her you were married?"

"No."

"She'll find out. If she has taken the least notice, she will inquire."

"Why do you always see the dark side of things?"

"Never underestimate these aristocrats," Ellicott advised. "Sure, they prattle on about republicanism and equality, but they are very adept at controlling men and events. Eleanora Van Rensselaer is quite a worldly lady, and she's a confidante of Mayor Clinton, prime sponsor of the canal project. She helped get the needed votes in the legislature last spring to keep the project alive. She'll have you as her lap dog until she tires of you. Then you'll exist no more for her."

"Maybe so," Daniel said, "but my, she is a handsome woman!"

"Yes, Kate," Eleanora said pensively as the maid removed her wig, "surprisingly so, I did have a good time. I used to dread the end of session, and the long muggy months of inactivity. Albany is a forlorn enough place in summer. But there was a certain excitement about next month's expedition to the west, about the survey and the canal project."

"Anyone of partic'lar interest?"

Eleanora frowned in the mirror. "Why, yes, there was."

"Tell me, mum, what was he like?"

"At first I thought he was a Quaker in that long black coat and trousers. He was different . . . very different. He had composure, a self-possession, a relaxed quality. Not a pretense, but a true serenity. And such impertinence! He used no form of address. He spoke to me as if to one of his men. And he shook my hand!"

"Wealthy, mum?" Kate clearly found this far more important than manners.

"He owns a small freehold in the west, but I daresay he's not as wealthy as Cox or Peterson who hold tenancies of me.

He's a merchant too. He captains a ship on Lake Erie, evidently a remarkable feat for those who live there. I suppose it is from this that he derives his air of command."

"And his looks, mum, what are the cuts of him?"

Lady Eleanora smiled warmly. "You might call him handsome, though in a rugged way. His face is weathered and brown. His hair is sandy and he wears a moustache! But his eyes, Kate, his eyes! Deep blue, penetrating, wise. You can imagine them scanning the water for shoals and the western horizon for storms."

"It's always in the eyes, mum."

"I suppose it is."

With her hair loosened for sleep, Eleanora stood and Kate unlaced the corset. Although slender, Eleanora had been so tightly laced into her whalebone corset that she emitted a deep groan when it was released. She stroked the marks on her sides, then rubbed her palms over her breasts. She turned sideways in the mirror and stood on tiptoe to flex her legs. Then, sighing loudly, Eleanora placed her hand in the small of her back and arched backward, pushing her shoulder blades together until they nearly touched. "Ahhhh!"

Kate returned the corset to the traveling trunk, and pulled out Eleanora's nightgown.

"Oh," Eleanora groaned, "I despise Federalist fashion. I wish the general would finally notice the French."

As she removed her camisole and slipped into her nightgown, she remembered Theodosia Burr in her French gown. What disgrace she had lived through; what dark passions she must know. Eleanora nodded to herself. Reputation must be guarded carefully and always and everywhere. Yet she had lived more carelessly before, and she remembered it tonight.

"On summer nights such as these, Kate, when I was a girl, I would steal out of my father's house and go galloping along the high road, galloping in the moonlight. Oh, if we could only do that tonight! Yet that would not be proper for a respectable widow, would it?"

"No, mum. We must sleep."

Eleanora slid between the starched linen sheets of the four-poster bed. A cot had been set up for Kate to share this guest room. Kate stepped out of her dress and in her chemise, blew out the whale oil lamps.

"Pleasant dreams, mum," she whispered, wondering how soon her mistress would be asleep and she might escape to her tryst.

"You too, my pet," Eleanora said tenderly, and she reached over and stroked Kate's cheek. Then she snuggled into the pillows and let the steady gaze of the westerner come into her mind. His mellow intoning of her name had reminded her of someone else, and now she realized it reminded her of her father's voice. How new and different was his manner! As she drifted off to sleep, hugging her pillow, she imagined Daniel Hedges piloting his *Silver Pearl* on the rolling, moonlit breast of Lake Erie so very far away.

CHAPTER 2

*S*ince the Revolution, classical columns, pediments and domes, hallmarks of the New England Yankee, had been rising above the stepped Dutch gables of Albany. As a thriving Hudson River port and the capital of New York State, Albany also served as a gateway to fertile western river valleys. Three gravel turnpikes radiated westward over the gentle hills, and accommodating Albany merchants sold dry goods and tools to the thousands of Connecticut and Hampshire Yankees who left their steep, rocky hillsides for the loamy bottom lands of the Mohawk, Susquehanna, Oswego and Genesee.

Enterprising Yankees in warehouses and chandler shops traded along the waterfront where Robert Fulton's steamboat belched sparks and smoke coming and going from Manhattan. To the Yankee, no invention was too outlandish, no project too big. They knew no word "impossible." A canal three hundred and fifty miles through the wilderness? Why not?

On a pleasant Monday morning, two days after the general's ball, Washington Irving encountered a dapper, fair-haired young man on the State Street hill. The author had first met Martin Van Buren, surrogate judge for Columbia

County, while collecting folk tales of the Hudson River Dutch. Van Buren's parents were innkeepers in Kinderhook and Irving stayed with them. Young Van Buren lacked a formal education, wealth and family connections, but had nevertheless fared well in law and politics due to his quick mind and engaging smile, not to mention the mentoring of Aaron Burr.

Van Buren praised Irving's recent *Knickerbocker's History*. "A wonderful, hilarious work!" Although he had only skimmed the satire, Van Buren knew the value of flattery. "It is destined to lift you among the literary immortals."

Irving thanked him, and as they talked, happened to mention he was traveling with Theodosia Burr. When Irving explained she was visiting her father's old friends, including Joseph Ellicott, to ask for money, Van Buren rubbed his chin thoughtfully. "Interesting, most interesting."

"The poor man is penniless in Paris just now," Irving explained.

"The Madison Administration adamantly refuses to issue him a passport. Poor Theo despairs of ever seeing her papa again."

"Brilliant man, absolutely brilliant. I idolized him. He should have been president." Van Buren nodded. "But he will never be forgiven for shooting Hamilton, it cost him the price of his public career."

"Public regard is damnably fickle," Irving agreed, "and not only toward authors."

Van Buren's eyes brightened. "I say, Irving, may I call on Theodosia? I'd certainly make a donation."

"She would be honored." And Irving gave him the address.

After his noonday meal, Judge Van Buren slipped into a fresh ruffled shirt, buffed his shoes, inscribed a banknote, "Miss Theodosia Burr," and presented his card to the servant at Mrs. Elden's Boarding House for Young Women. Van

Buren affected an aristocratic air, and though short of stature, he walked erect and proudly into the waiting parlor.

"I'm so very happy to meet you, Judge."

Van Buren turned to see a striking young woman with black ringlets offering him her hand. He bestowed a kiss on the outstretched hand. "It is so kind of you to come."

"Not at all, not at all." They sat. "When I learned you were in Albany, I wanted to call personally. I was an ardent admirer of your father, and I know many others among the Sons of Tammany. Politics has dealt him evil cards." Van Buren reached inside his waistcoat.

"I hope this will in some small way ease his situation." He handed her the folded banknote. Theodosia's eyes brightened. She inclined her head and smiled with pressed her lips.

"My father will be most grateful. Above all else, he regrets losing the devotion of all the young men who nearly made him president." She touched Van Buren's hand. "If there is anything I can do in return . . ."

Van Buren flashed his engaging smile, and his pale blue eyes sparkled. "There is, Miss Burr, though it is merely a trifle."

"Name it, sir."

"Mr. Irving informs me you will meet soon with Mr. Ellicott of Batavia."

"This afternoon. Yes."

"I wonder if perhaps you might sound him out on a delicate matter." Van Buren pressed his fingers together and pursed his lips. She nodded. "The canal project greatly intrigues me and I must know two things. First, are the canal commissioners planning a series of locks merely to augment existing streams and lakes, or do they propose an entirely separate ditch three hundred miles long? Secondly, financing. Will they give franchises to private corporations, or do they look to the government for capital?" He smiled pleasantly. "I'm sure you understand the delicacy of this matter."

19

"Of course. I shall notify you directly when I return."

Van Buren stood, took her hands and kissed them both. He bowed respectfully, opened the door and departed with a flourish of his walking stick.

Theodosia dashed up to an oval window on the landing. "A most charming man, indeed." She watched his small form in a swallowtail coat and three-cornered hat pass through the narrow street where pigs and chickens rooted and pecked. She noted how the noise and the squalor did not affect his smooth gait. Then she unfolded the check. "Twenty-five dollars!" She looked up as he disappeared around the corner. "A most worthy friend." Then she smiled because she realized how important the information must be to him.

Daniel Hedges and Joseph Ellicott shared a suite of rooms at Mrs. Pratt's Boarding House two blocks away.

"Unprecedented!" Ellicott exclaimed. Hedges had just received a note from Mrs. Van Rensselaer. "Suitors and hopeful suitors wait for months to get the smallest glimpse of her, and she invites you to call after one encounter!"

"Strictly business, I'm sure." Hedges held the note in the air. "'Mr. Hedges,'" he read aloud, "'I should be pleased to speak with you regarding some matters of our mutual interest. I hope four o'clock will be convenient for you. Until then, I am respectfully yours, Eleanora Van Rensselaer.' Nice ring to that, 'matters of our mutual interest.'"

"Take my advice and don't presume anything with her," Ellicott warned. "I am certain she has some ulterior motive, and it won't be 'mutual interest.'"

"Care to accompany me?" Daniel ribbed him. "Might need some help."

"No, I'll be seeing Miss Burr then."

"Want me to cancel and chaperone?"

"Hardly," Ellicott frowned. "I cannot forget that scoundrel father of hers. Aaron Burr twisted legislative arms for me to get the Holland Land Company charter passed years ago, and that's the only reason I agreed to see her. But she worries me. Thank heavens that traitor's safely across the sea." "No love lost between her and Eleanora Van Rensselaer if I'm any observer of women." "Women!" Ellicott threw up his hands. "If only they'd stay out of our affairs!" "Don't know about that," Hedges held the fragrant note to his nose.

At four o'clock, Theodosia Burr paced in the parlor, wringing her handkerchief, waiting for the serving girl's return. Agitation showed in her face. Now and again she checked it in the mantel mirror to assure herself it showed well enough.

When ushered into a spacious third-floor living room, Theodosia turned a woeful look to Mr. Ellicott. He registered no emotion. Theo cleared her throat. "It's very kind of you to see me, sir."

He motioned her to a settee. "I hope I can be of service."

"I'm sure you can." For an awkward moment she sat with a trembling lower lip. Then, "It's my father, sir, my poor papa. I realize you and he are men of the world, and you know how cruel and harsh it can be. Yet it defies my simple understanding of things to see how a man's best and closest friends can turn on him when he is wrongfully disgraced, how people he helped now prey on his property and reputation."

"Your father was a man of great ability."

"He firmly believed in developing our west, and he secured the grant your Dutch investors needed. Everyone involved has benefitted from the Holland Land Company, and when the canal is dug, you will all be very wealthy."

"He was a man of great foresight."

"Men's fortunes change so rapidly," she sighed. "Today my poor father sits penniless in Paris, exiled from the America he fought to free, banished from the British Empire, the whole of the English-speaking world. And I, I have come to you today," she applied the handkerchief to her eye, "to implore you, his old friend, whether you might find it in your heart to . . . "

"To extend him a loan?"

"Oh," she clasped her hands together, "could you? Would you?" She burst into sobs, covering her face with her handkerchief. "Oh, he'd be so grateful for any consideration whatsoever."

Ellicott looked at her with contempt, critiquing her performance. Aaron Burr was now a criminal, an outcast. Though it had been handy once to know him, helping him now might carry a stigma. Caution was required. And yet, having two nieces at home himself, Ellicott sympathized with Theo's plight and even admired her courage.

"I can be of service, yes, in a small way, but I must impose one condition."

"Oh, name it, sir!"

"I wish my gift – not a loan, mind you – to remain anonymous."

"You are a true Christian, sir." She bowed her head, humbled by Ellicott's Christian generosity.

As he arose to write a bank draft, Theo set her lip. How to get Van Buren's information? Flattery usually worked in getting people to talk about themselves.

"Why, it is a grand enterprise you're engaged in, sir," she said casually. He harrumphed from the desk. Theodosia stood, dried her eyes and walked to the window. "I once rode west with my papa. We had holdings in the lands of the Oneida. Remarkably green and fertile."

"Yes," Ellicott said, sprinkling sand on the bank draft and setting his quill by the ink pot, "and land farther west becomes even flatter and richer."

"It staggers the imagination, Mr. Ellicott, to consider that these waters of the Hudson," she waved at the waterfront out the window, "will someday teem with boats sailing all the way from Lake Erie."

"Few undertakings can boast such audacity, I'll grant you." He stood. Theo tilted her head slightly so her black curls bobbed.

"There already exists a canal company, sir, near Rome. I saw that small canal once. I know so little about such things. Will your canals also allow boats to avoid the rapids?"

Ellicott held the bank draft between his thumbs and forefingers. "No, young lady. Ours is a far greater plan. We will avoid streams altogether. We'll cut a ditch clear across the wilderness to the lake. No flood or ice jam or spring freshet will hinder the boats. A ribbon of water in all seasons but winter." He held out the draft. She accepted and folded it without looking.

"Your Dutch principals must be very wealthy and bold." Ellicott frowned. "They are wealthy, but not often bold. Why?"

"By underwriting such a vast . . ."

A smile played, then broke on Ellicott's lips. "They? Oh, now there is a thought." He began to chuckle. "That indeed is a droll notion." After years of listening to the stingy land company's principals complain, the thought they'd pay for such a canal was hilarious. "Oh, pardon me, miss," Ellicott laughed out loud. "I do not mock you. It's just the idea is so novel."

"Well, then?" she asked with simplicity, "Who is to pay for it?"

"Ah, ha! You'd like to know, would you now?"

Theodosia formed an expression of perfect innocence and slowly nodded her head.

"Well, being as you're not involved, I'll share our secret if you promise to keep it." She nodded and placed the check in her bag. "Everyone!" he exclaimed, waving his arms in the air. "Everyone will pay for it, and everyone will benefit from it!"

Theo looked puzzled.

"The government," Ellicott explained. "This great state of New York, and the United States Government, together. That, anyway, is Mr. Clinton's plan." He smiled paternally. "Now be off with you before the banks close for the evening, and remember, this is to be an anonymous gift."

"Oh, thank you! Thank you, sir!" She curtseyed. "You're so kind and Christian to remember my poor papa in his adversity. If he, if he can ever help you, just let me know. Only then will I number you by name among his benefactors."

Ellicott held the door for her, then re-entered his rooms. He mused how such a scoundrel could sire such a forthright, intelligent, caring daughter. His thoughts turned to his nieces, and he longed to wrap up his business in the capital so he might return home.

Around the corner, Theodosia unfolded the bank draft – ten dollars. She slapped it against her palm. Her father had bullied and bribed Ellicott's charter and land grant through the legislature, and his return? Ten dollars! And she had groveled before him! Her poor father, most excellent of men, starving and friendless in Paris. Ten dollars was infuriating, and even that begrudged! At least she had Judge Van Buren's information.

First Theo cashed the draft, then she called on Van Buren.

"You are most kind to return so soon."

"The very least I can do." She relayed what she had found out – the canal would cut through three hundred and fifty miles of farmland, swamp, mountain spurs, virgin forest, cliffs and torrents, much of the land still unexplored, and it would be publicly funded.

"Excellent." Van Buren smiled radiantly. "Precisely what I needed to know. If I can be of further service, please, Miss Burr, do not hesitate to call." He motioned for her to stand.

"Judge Van Buren," she looked at the floor, "there is one thing." She sighed. "I have been rebuffed countless times trying to secure a passport for my father. The Madison Administration refuses even to hear my requests. If you might intercede?"

"I'll most certainly try. I know some people in Washington who hold your father in the greatest esteem. I'd be more than happy to ask. Promise me you'll call on your next visit to Albany. I can be reached here at the Mansion House if I'm in town, and if not, they relay my mail. Just leave a note."

She smiled and nodded. "I most certainly will."

Van Buren took her hands and kissed them, then he showed her out the door. He watched for a moment as she swayed down the stairs to the street. Closing the door, he quickly calculated where this new information best fit in his plans.

CHAPTER 3

*P*lasterers, painters, carpenters and masons were busily refurbishing the gabled brick townhouse as Daniel Hedges approached.

He climbed up the stairs and hammered the brass knocker of the open door. Down the dim hall a butler approached with a silver tray.

"Good day, sir. May I help you?"

"Mrs. Van Rensselaer asked me to call."

"Have you a card?" The butler held out the tray.

"No. Just this." Hedges placed Eleanora's note on the tray. The butler pursed his lips disapprovingly, but was back in two minutes smiling.

"Please step this way, sir." Guiding Daniel through plaster dust and wood shavings, he opened a high door to a sitting room. It was furnished with a German pianoforte, a wide set of bookcases, a Louis XIV writing desk, four sturdy Dutch chairs and an elegant chaise lounge. When the butler left, Hedges catalogued the haphazard furnishings. The wallpaper was faded, the drapes antique and dusty. A threadbare carpet curled on the floorboards. Hedges admired four canvases, one an idealized landscape of the Alps, another a view of the

Hudson, and two stiff portraits of a husband and wife. He was inspecting an old Dutch clock when the door opened. Eleanora Van Rensselaer entered in a white, empire-waisted sheath. Her dark hair was only loosely gathered and fell well past her shoulders.

"Please forgive the chaos, Mr. Hedges." She was all business. "We hadn't opened this house for a decade. Now, after a year of mourning, I've decided to sweep away the cobwebs and re-enter the life of our capital city. Won't you have a seat?" Eleanora rang a little golden bell. The butler answered. "You may serve the tea now, Edward." He bowed and closed the door.

Daniel sat in one of the sturdy Dutch chairs, hooked a boot heel on a rung to lift up his leg, then leaned his elbow on his knee and regarded her with interest.

"I was intrigued Saturday night by our conversation. I don't believe I've ever met anyone from the frontier, let alone the captain of a trading vessel so far from civilization. Have you lived your whole life there, Mr. Hedges?"

"As much as I remember."

"Your parents, were they westerners as well?"

"Don't really know." He was puzzled – what interest could his past possibly hold for her? "They were massacred near Cherry Valley during the Revolution. I was among the Iroquois for two years until Sullivan's army burned the village. After being exchanged for a prisoner of war on the Niagara frontier, I was apprenticed to a ship captain in the lake trade."

"How fascinating."

They stared awkwardly at each other.

"And Mr. Ellicott then secured your services as a surveyor?"

"Yes. I helped him lay out the tract of the Holland Land Company about ten years back, and I know the area well. He wants the canal to come west through his lands to increase their value. He chuckled. Last year, some of the villagers insisted Ellicot straighten out a curve in the road over his lot, so he abandoned his building plans and moved inland to Batavia. I'm about the only friend he has left in Buffaloe Creek. He asked me to help, so I left the brig with my first mate and came east."

"I hear that you're meeting with the canal commission Wednesday?"

"Yes." He narrowed his eyes. Her interest in his life did not quite square with her businesslike manner.

"So you will discuss the survey you have undertaken?"

"As much as they wish to."

Eleanora reclined slightly. "As you know the territory so well, do you believe such a canal can be dug?"

Daniel extended his arms candidly. "I'd like to help, ma'am, but won't you first tell me what all your questions are for?"

She was momentarily flustered and tried to hide it by leaning farther away on the sofa. The butler entered with a silver tea service – teapot, sugar bowl and tongs, cream urn, spoons – and a delicate pair of porcelain cups and saucers. Placing the service on a table, he left.

"Shall I pour?" she asked. Daniel shrugged and nodded. He watched how gracefully she poured the two steaming cups of tea. "Milk or lemon?"

"Lemon."

"Sugar?"

"No, no thank you." He accepted the cup, stirred it and took a sip. He couldn't remember having had tea before, preferring whiskey and ale late in the afternoon. It was pleasantly fragrant, hot and tart. Eleanora drank and Daniel watched her pale lips sip delicately from the cup.

"You were about to say whether you believed such a canal could be built."

"Well, sure, sure it can. I don't believe there's a thing men can't do when they put their minds to it."

"But we understand the terrain to Lake Erie is quite rugged."

Daniel nodded. "It is that. Land west of here looks like a great claw gouged it from south to north, with long narrow lakes and swamps in the low places, great heaps of boulders and gravel in the long, narrow mounds."

"Then it's possible to bridge those low places?"

Again he nodded. "You'll have to lay culverts and bridges and aqueducts over the gullies and valleys, and you'll have to blast through the mountains. It's not a project you'd plan if you wanted an immediate profit. It'll take years, and men will die."

"But you have walked it? What are the most serious obstacles?"

Daniel gave a low, ironic laugh. Although she presented a pleasing appearance, lounging with her teacup in the sun, he was suspicious. "Still haven't told me what all this is about. You're asking more than the commissioners will."

Eleanora pursed her lips. "Let's just say, Mr. Hedges, that I'm extremely interested in this project, and that I want to see it through to completion. I can help both you and the project if you'll cooperate, and things that I am not at liberty to discuss just now will become more apparent as soon as they need to."

"Fair enough." He nodded and set down his cup. "Mind you, I haven't looked at the easternmost sections, and I understand there's a substantial cascade at Cohoes, but from Utica west there are three major obstacles. First, near Salina, there's the Montezuma swamp, a hellish land breathing malaria and plagues. Second, two great valleys must be bridged, the Irondequoit Creek and the Genesee River. They'll require stone breastworks to carry the canal over the water, aqueducts strong enough to withstand the spring ice floes."

"And the third?"

"A great cliff must be scaled by the canal, the same cliff

the Niagara cascade plunges over. We'll need to get up and over it to reach the altitude of Lake Erie. Much blasting will be required, and many locks. Men will die."

She nodded, satisfied.

"But those are only the prime obstacles." Daniel regarded her. "There are problems the entire length of the project, trees as old as time, streams to be dammed and forded, boulders and cliffs to be blasted away. Least of all the worries, a smaller network of canals must be built to keep the main ditch filled. An army of men will be needed, and of course that will bring labor problems."

She nodded. "Are you aware of the essays written by Jesse Hawley?"

"No."

She set down her cup, stood, crossed the room, and returned with an envelope of newspaper clippings. "While serving a jail sentence for debt, Mr. Hawley wrote these four-teen pieces about digging just such a canal. You should read them as they will help you with the commissioners."

"I'll do that."

She leaned over him and as Daniel accepted the envelope, he looked up. Her face hovered briefly above his. She quickly retrieved her tea and hid her mouth behind the teacup.

"I should like to meet with you after you speak with the commissioners, and I hope you will consider me a confidante. I cannot tell you my role just now, but I can carry your concerns to a level where most difficulties may be overcome."

"Well, then," Hedges stood, "if we're to be working so closely, you call me Daniel, and I'll call you Eleanora." He put out his hand to shake. "Out west folks don't simper around with 'mister' and 'missus.' It wastes time."

She backed away slightly, unsettled by his frank demeanor and surprised by his sudden height. She reached to place her tea down but missed her mark. Cup and saucer fell to the floor and the cup shattered. She yielded to her first nervous instinct:

instead of calling the butler, she knelt and placed the broken porcelain in her left palm. Daniel retrieved a piece that had flown across the floor, and joined her. Side by side, they picked up the smallest particles.

"There," he said, "I think we got it all."

Eleanora turned and looked in his eyes. She paused, her eyes opening wider, and Daniel gazed deeply into them. He saw there a loneliness that shocked and surprised him. She had let her guard down and now inclined her head ever so slightly, looking from his eyes to his lips and back again.

She wanted to be kissed, he sensed, but he held back. He looked from her wide clear forehead, down her long brown tresses, then returned to her eyes again. Yet it was as if her eyes closed to him; no longer could he look into them. She sighed and shivered ever so slightly, pressed her lips together with impatience. The moment had passed. "Thank you, Mr. Hedges. That was clumsy of me."

"Not at all." He climbed to his feet and reached down and as she placed her hand in his palm, he felt it trembling.

"And thank you, also, for sharing your observations with me." A tremor was in her voice. She turned away and walked toward the door.

"I'll call Thursday before I leave for home."

The mention of his leaving did not please her. She opened the door and suddenly the reality of plastering and sawing was on them.

"Good day, Mrs. Van Rensselaer."

"Good day, Mr. Hedges." She stood in the doorway watching him pass through the workmen. He turned once before he stepped into the outside light and looked back, but did not wave. She raised her hand, then closed the door. She turned down the hall and entered a rear sitting room. Looking into a mirror she could see the rebellion in her eyes. Eleanora went upstairs to get a bonnet and shawl. She left by the back door, passed through the empty stables behind her townhouse and walked up the alley to a cross street. She went directly to Gregory's Inn, where she hurried past the open door of the taproom and upstairs to a private room. When she knocked, the door was opened by a handsome, dark-haired man of forty. Neither spoke as she entered and sat down. Books, charts, and papers lay strewn about the writing desk and floor. A closed portmanteau rested in the doorway to the bedroom. DeWitt Clinton had just arrived that morning and immediately plunged into his work. He was a tall man, as tall as Daniel Hedges, but massive, bulky. A restless energy burned in his intense blue eyes, at variance with the deliberately slow and patrician cadence of his speech.

"I sent Carr away. What news do you bring?"

Eleanora gave an account of her interview with Hedges, conveying the surveyor's opinion about the project, the three most difficult obstacles, and his daring sense of enterprise. As he listened, Clinton's penetrating eyes appeared to weigh each piece of information.

As Eleanora finished, Clinton fixed her with an imperious look. "All you have said marks this fellow as a valuable asset. Can he be trusted?"

For a moment, Eleanora tried to separate her personal attraction to Hedges from her assessment of his character. "I believe he can."

"I defer to your judgment then." Clinton turned to look out the window. "Your instincts are infallible, so they are invaluable to me." Eleanora winced at the high-handedness of the compliment.

Clinton's chief flaw, she felt, was an inability to understand normal human emotions.

"You can work with him then, and you will be my intermediary until I choose to work with him directly."

"Yes, DeWitt. It would be a pleasure. He's refreshingly

different from the men I have known here in Albany and New York."

The big man scrutinized her. "Is there any personal interest?" His suspicion unsettled Eleanora and she faltered.

"I find him amiable and talented . . . yet certainly unsophisticated in the ways of public men. He knows much about the western lands, more, probably, than any other white man. But be assured, DeWitt, I am ever mindful of my station and the decorum required of widows." Still he stared at her. She sought refuge in a platitude: "Reason must always govern passion." Then she gave a half-hearted laugh, "Not that I could ever feel passion for such a son of the forests and lakes."

"Very well," Clinton nodded abruptly. "But I trust you will inform me if your feelings change. We all are, unfortunately, susceptible to such emotions. And they can prove very dangerous to our undertaking."

"Of course." Eleanora suppressed her annoyance. "I have asked him to read Jesse Hawley's essays, as you suggested, and he will meet with me after the full commission sits. I will, of course, convey his impression of the other commissioners to you."

Clinton crossed to her and held out his hand to raise her up from her seat. "I will call for you Thursday, Eleanora. Until then, farewell. Your services, as always, are deeply appreciated." He smiled affably as he escorted her to the door. "How does work progress on the townhouse?"

"Very well."

"Spare no expense. We will establish a salon where the necessary votes can be cajoled, bought or forced next session. It will be the talk of New York and Washington. Send Carr the bills as they come in." He opened the door. "You look well, Eleanora. Returning to the world of politics and society has put some color in your cheek."

She smiled and touched his hand with hers. He began to close the door, then he opened it again. "Eleanora?" She turned, adjusting her shawl. "Did that fellow Hedges happen to mention he's married?"

"Yes," she lied, and she smiled at him. "Why, yes, he did."

Clinton nodded approval, then closed the door. Eleanora turned away, her mind stunned by the news. Married? The thought infuriated her. Blindly she descended the stairway, passed through the parlor and out into the sunshine. Her quick reflexes had just saved her from humiliation in Clinton's eyes as a lonely, impressionable widow. Clinton had deliberately saved that tidbit for her departure to throw her off guard. Tears pressed at her eyes. How would he know Hedges was married? But Clinton always knew everything.

Eleanora dined that evening in a private room of Foley's Chop House with Kate. She steered the talk away from love. When she went to bed that night in a makeshift boudoir in the townhouse filled with the smells of drying plaster and reawakened wood, her mind was in a hot confusion. She tossed and turned, plotting how she might confront Hedges with her knowledge, how she might let him know she was not to be trifled with, how she might accuse him of . . . of what? Of being married? Of raising her expectations? Yet beyond the events of the day, one image kept arising out of the tumult of anger and doubt and desire. She saw a helpless baby boy ripped from the arms of his mother as she was being attacked behind a burning cabin, and then carried off into the forest in the swarthy arms of his captors.

CHAPTER 4

A recent political upheaval had stripped DeWitt Clinton of his New York City mayor's office, so he adopted the canal project to broaden his political base. With a statewide presence he might emulate his uncle George Clinton, New York State's first governor and now vice president, to grasp at national laurels. The slim waterway held strategic potential. Not only would it tap into those vast inland seas, the Great Lakes, for shipping goods and produce, but Britain wanted her errant colonies back. The waterway would provide swifter deployment of troops and ordnance in case of an attack from Canada, just as ancient stone roads secured the *pax Romanum* in Rome's far-flung empire. On paper, General Stephen Van Rensselaer chaired the canal commission, but Clinton's foresight and energy guided the group and he actually presided over the meetings.

"Motion!" Mr. Eddy, a thin fiery zealot, stood up. "That the New York State Canal Commission christen the two flatboats on its upcoming westward exploration as the *Argo* and the *Cosmo.*"

"Mr. Eddy's motion is on the floor. Discussion?" Silence.

"Very well," Clinton said, "Call the vote. All those in favor of the motion?"

"Aye," said Mr. Eddy alone.

"All those opposed?"

"Nay." Everyone but Mr. Eddy. "Next item: Mr. Morris."

Plump Gouverneur Morris rose.

"As General Van Rensselaer and myself will employ his coach-and-four to propel us westward, I move that we split the sum granted us by the legislature in half." In that room, Morris' wealth was second only to Van Rensselaer's.

"Point of order!"

"The chair recognizes Mr. Eddy."

"Mr. President. The fund appropriated by the legislature is for the express purpose of viewing these wild lands, and not to provide fine Madeira for two commissioners." This caused a stir. Eddy's garrulity and temperance were widely known, as was his dislike of Morris.

"I suggest therefore that thou divide the fund into six equal parts," Eddy said. "Disburse them and let each commissioner be accountable, even as he is to his Maker. Thy proposal, Mr. Morris, is avaricious."

"Order. Order." Clinton tried to remain patient. Joseph Ellicott frowned impatiently. He was sitting with Daniel Hedges along the wall of Simeon DeWitt's dusty office watching the proceedings. Mr. DeWitt held the post of surveyor general to the state of New York, and his office was strewn with maps and charts, quadrants, an astrolabe, sextants and telescopes.

"Many of our expenses will be communal," Clinton tried compromise. "It would be premature to make a disbursement at this juncture. But the matter is open for discussion."

The discussion lasted twenty minutes and at times became very heated. During it, Clinton seemed very much a god gazing down at the petty squabbling of mortals. Finally he intervened. "The chair recognizes Mr. DeWitt who will call the vote."

His first cousin dutifully took the cue, called a vote and Morris' motion to split the fund in half was approved five-to-one.

"Next item: The survey. Mr. Daniel Hedges joins us this morning to inform us about the survey he has conducted in our western reaches, and to answer questions as to what we should be looking for on our expedition. The chair recognizes Mr. Ellicott for purposes of an introduction."

"Gentlemen," Ellicott stood and spoke with utmost formality, "I have known Daniel Hedges for fifteen years. He supervised a crew on the survey of the Holland Land Company's grant and he has been invaluable to me on many, many occasions. At my behest, he left his mercantile pursuit in plying the waters of Lake Erie to lend us his talents on a survey of the hills and ridges, the lakes and streams and cliffs that now separate the Hudson from the distant western lakes. Mr. Hedges."

"Morning, gentlemen." Daniel stood. "Joe here is right. I've walked much of the land between Lake Erie and your river and it's a rugged forest with cliffs and outcrops and swift rivers . . ."

"Young man!" harrumphed Mr. Morris. "Do you believe locks will be necessary for this canal?"

Daniel looked to Joseph Ellicot and Joseph winked.

"Haven't seen a better way to raise and lower a boat. Be a mighty lot of that going on from here to Buffaloe Creek."

Morris laughed derisively. "Does it not strike you, sir, that Lake Erie being six hundred feet above the Hudson at Troy, an easier method might be employed?"

"I have an open mind."

Morris scanned the table with a superior attitude. "We start at Troy," he held his hand high in the air with the fingers sloped upward, "and we incline the canal half a foot every mile up to the lake." He demonstrated with his hand. "Thus the water of Lake Erie will pour by gravity into the Hudson, forming a natural, man-made river, and we may thus avoid the annoyance of building locks."

Daniel looked to the chair for a reaction. Clinton's eyes bored into his, trying to read his opinion of Morris. "Well, I will admit that thought never occurred to me."

"No, young man, I suppose it never did!" Testily Morris folded his arms across his chest and proceeded to look out the window.

Clinton spoke: "The surveyor general has asked Mr. Hedges to join our expedition at Utica. We will have ample time along the route to question him about engineering possibilities." Clinton nodded to Hedges and Hedges resumed his seat.

The remainder of the meeting was devoted to discussing what to bring along in terms of clothes, fowling pieces, boots, sketch pads, wines and cheeses, conjecture about the ferocity of the natives and wild beasts they would encounter, and how they would locate taverns to put up for the night. Ellicott, the western expert on the commission, diplomatically addressed each of these concerns.

General Van Rensselaer then delivered a lofty speech about the trust placed in them by the people of New York State, the high purpose of their expedition, and the tremendous benefits they would bring home for the legislature to consider, both in knowledge and expanded opportunity.

As they left the Capitol, Joseph asked Daniel, "What did you think?"

"Good they live along the Hudson. Good that they're all wealthy and have servants. If they lived where we come from, they'd starve." Joseph clapped him on the back and Daniel shook his head sadly. "Be a fine afternoon's enjoyment watching them design and build a boat . . . after a year they might get a raft . . . and then it wouldn't float."

"Yes, you did well to hold your tongue. Van Rensselaer is well-intentioned, though. North and Eddy are useless. Morris is senile. There's our majority. But we have Peter Porter from Niagara who wasn't able to attend the meeting. Do you know him?"

Hedges nodded.

"And there's myself."

"Two shining stars."

"Don't overlook Clinton. You didn't see him at his best. He has a first rate mind and extraordinary political talents and connections. He's some sort of high-priest in the Free Masons and his uncle, of course, is vice president. He's related to half the aristocracy in New York, including your Lady Van Rensselaer. Today he was laying back, playing mediator, letting all of them prattle on and feel as though they were making decisions and participating. He can't afford to alienate any of them because they have the influence and the votes he needs. He was observing you, too."

"But ain't the pretense silly, Joe? Clinton is the whole commission and the rest of them are just along for a jaunt."

"Yes, but it's the way it has to be. Here in Albany, the secret in getting what you want is not antagonizing anyone needlessly. Here's Mrs. Pratt's. Let's start packing. I'd like to leave this afternoon."

"I'll join you in an hour. I have a visit to make."

"Eleanora?"

Hedges nodded.

"Be careful what you say. Clinton's man, Edgar Carr, was asking questions about you yesterday."

"Questions?"

"One of them regarded your marital status."

Daniel grinned widely. "So I'm walking into an ambush."

Joseph slapped him on the back. "Yeah, but a pretty one to be sure."

"See you later."

41

~

As Hedges walked, he observed the townhouses, carriages, horsemen, women carrying baskets, shopkeepers and boys with wooden pails from the well. Looking up the muddy lane that was State Street to the tower, cupola and statue atop the state Capitol, Daniel took a deep breath. In that building decisions were made that affected every phase of life here in the street. He understood better now. Before, Albany had seemed vague and strange to him. Stealth, gossip, feints and fakes were how things were done here, much like hunting in the forest. Only here the rules were made by men in power. That commission could no more build a canal than it could raise a house or dam a stream or build a wagon, yet it was vested with the authority to determine the fate of the canal issue and keep it in play. Without the commission, there wouldn't even be curiosity.

The workmen were nearly finished in the hallway of Eleanora's townhouse. The butler showed Hedges into the same parlor as a few days before. Drastic changes had been made nearly overnight: a new carpet, graciously upholstered chairs, a settee and new drapes. The walls, the ceiling and the floor needed more work, and the furniture seemed to be on display so Eleanora might approve it. She entered briskly in a loose green gown, her hair pinned up. She looked pale.

"You've done much work since the other day," Daniel observed.

"Yes. I'm returning to Claverack tonight and I wanted to be sure the furniture would be acceptable." She motioned him to a chair and she sat on the settee. "How was the meeting?"

His smile spread his bushy moustache broadly and made Eleanora smile in spite of her serious purpose. "Got to get those boys out west and teach them a few things."

She inclined her head quizzically. "Yes?"

"Well, I can draw a line across a map and say this is where

a canal will go, but nature, why, she might have a different notion." He shook his head. "They're smart enough, those boys, so I'm sure they'll learn when they actually see the land they're up against."

"What if there are disagreements?"

"Always are. Best you can hope for is to show them the meadow, let them graze for a while, and then get Clinton to pull them into a team."

She gave a small start at the mention of Clinton's name. Daniel noticed.

"What did you think of Mr. Clinton?"

"He has the knowledge and sees it all and he's reserved, don't show his cards. I'm leaving Albany first thing tomorrow, overland, and I'll meet up with them in Utica. When I can get his ear alone, I'm sure we'll get things sorted out. He has a chore convincing the rest of them boys to see his way, but he's equal to it. He'll be all right."

Eleanora relaxed. "You must understand Mr. Clinton. Often only he knows why he does certain things. Those around him must trust him. Support and loyalty are the principal qualities he demands."

Daniel nodded. "I look forward to showing him the West."

"Will you attend him during the entire month?"

"No. I can only spare two weeks. Obligations."

"Business?"

"Yes, business and family. My wife is very tolerant, but I don't like to leave her with the little ones for more than a month at a time."

"Oh," she said, feigning surprise, "you have children?"

"Didn't I tell you? A son and a daughter."

"I had no idea."

"Make a difference?"

"No," she said quickly, "of course not. Not at all." Daniel scrutinized her. She returned his gaze. There was a strong animal attraction between them. Daniel had passed her test, and he now sensed the need for her caution: her widowhood and station made her vulnerable.

"Will you want to participate in the building of the canal, or will your business and family absorb your time?"

"Business could run itself awhile." He didn't tell her his current business interest included smuggling pelts, wood, rum, potash and salt to the British across the lake in defiance of Madison's embargo. "Salary attached?"

"Of course, of course." Now she saw danger. She could not very well offer him a position, yet she was supposed to test his willingness to accept one.

"Don't know what I could do. The project does intrigue me, though. That fellow Clinton's a bold one, ain't he?"

"How so?"

"Why, who else would set sail on so long a voyage with such a crew?"

The image pleased her. She envisioned staid General Van Rensselaer climbing the rigging with portly Gouverneur Morris at the wheel. General North would be in the crow's nest, and garrulous Mr. Eddy spouting "thee's" and "thou's" as boatswain.

"Perhaps Mr. Clinton has other plans," she suggested. "And he'll need another hand aboard."

Daniel nodded. She had just confirmed the identity of her patron.

Daniel stood. "Well, ma'am, my journey has been most rewarding. I'm thankful Joseph asked me along." He extended his hand and shook hers. She was getting used to this custom of his. "I'm happy we met, and hope I can get east again soon." He started for the door.

She watched him dourly. She wanted to hold him back, keep him here longer, blurt out something. She hesitated, the opportunity was being lost.

Daniel turned, drew himself up to his full height and

leaned his head back in an air of relaxation. "Won't you see me out?"

Eleanora smiled and pulled herself from the settee.

"Of course." She pressed her lips together and narrowed her eyes in anticipation as she approached him. For once in her life she couldn't predict what she would do.

She walked very close to him, so close he might have encircled her with his arms. She looked up into his eyes, daring him to embrace her. For a long moment, he looked from her lips, into her eyes, up to the mass of dark curls on her head, then down past her eyes, her lips, down her long white neck. His eyes returned to hers and acknowledged the desire.

Gently, ever so gently, he reached down and placed his hands on her hips, then he bent down and brushed his lips over hers. His moustache tickled her upper lip, and she faintly felt his lips touch hers. She reached up, and with the room falling away, circled her arms around his neck and pressed her open lips to his. They kissed hungrily, delight and pleasure and discovery drawing them together. Their fingers grasped each other, their arms, now strong and fearless, tightly clinging.

When they parted, it was as if they had just surfaced together from underwater. They both gasped at the air, while their smoldering eyes remained locked. Again they came together in a kiss, more passionately than before. She felt the tremendous power of his shoulders and arms, the firmness of his jaw, the tenderness of his lips. She pulled herself away and caught her breath, felt her lip with her fingertips. A thousand voices within her spoke about what she should not, could not, must not do, and she knew those scruples were correct even while she ached for him.

"Have to go," he said. He suddenly felt thirsty. He saw the battle within her so he leaned over and kissed her gently on the cheek. "I'll miss you. But I'll be back."

This soft intimacy made her shudder. She took his hands

and held them up. Large, strong hands, calloused and scarred from work, the nails split and jagged. She held them to her lips and gently kissed them. When she looked up at him, the faintest moisture was in her eye. "Good-bye," she whispered, and she opened the door so he might leave. Daniel looked longingly into her eyes, then dropped her hand, turned and was gone.

She didn't watch him walk away. She slowly closed the drawing room door, and the sound seemed that of a tomb. She leaned back against the door, and breathed heavily to slow her beating heart. She bit her lip. She wanted to explode in rage. She wanted to weep. She wanted to purge herself, to feel clean and whole and pure. "Kate!" she cried, "Kate!" There were footfalls on the steps up from the kitchen, and the small door by the chimney opened.

"Mum?"

"Have Guy ready Hecate. We will ride."

"Hecate, mum, are you sure? She's so wild." Eleanora glared at her. "Yes, mum. Hecate it'll be, mum."

"And not the side saddle either."

"No, mum." The maid left for the livery stable in the next street to deliver the orders.

Eleanora stormed into her bedroom and tore off her clothes. She stood naked in the afternoon sunlight, and the sun felt warm and pleasing. Thankfully she'd packed the riding trousers she wore at home in the country. She opened her wardrobe and, thrust aside the gowns and lingerie to pull out her riding attire and boots. She changed quickly and put her hair up under a three-cornered hat so passing horsemen would not recognize a woman riding as a man. Soon the horses were clattering on the stones at the vacant stable behind the townhouse. Hecate, a spirited black mare, pawed impatiently until Eleanora leapt from the mounting stone into the saddle. Then the horse reared up, and Eleanora pulled at the reins, the horse whinnying, snorting and protesting the weight. Eleanora kicked the horse and it sprinted up the hill.

When they'd gained the top of the hill by the capitol, Eleanora whipped Hecate into a gallop, and continued to kick and whip the horse toward the distant blue escarpment of the Helderbergs. Her thighs clasped the horse tightly as she bent far forward, shortened up on the reins and rode hard, as hard as she'd ever ridden. She felt the exhilaration of the wind in her face, the horse's pounding hooves, the churning, heaving rhythm of the horse's back arching then straightening, arching then straightening. She thrust herself down into the saddle, losing herself in the pounding, furious rhythm of the ride until she was panting to catch her breath and slightly dizzy. On and on and on she rode, the sky burst with sunlight, and a bird screamed across the blue in a mad flight and she closed her eyes. The sun splashed into her mind as she opened her eyes, and she was gulping deeply of the clean summer wind.

When at last Eleanora reined in the mare, Hecate resisted and rose up, forehooves in the air. Eleanora was perspiring, exhilarated, bright-eyed and happy. She cried out in joy, and it was like a musical note as it hung in the air between herself and the slumbering blue mountains. Then she turned in the saddle. Far behind her, a mere speck in the road, Kate was striving to keep up. Eleanora threw her head back and laughed at the sky. She was in love! She could admit it! She could call it out in the bright afternoon: "I am in love!" She felt weightless and free. How extraordinarily simple! And such a man! Such an unusual man. She patted Hecate's long black muscular neck, perspiring now from the gallop. "Come on, girl," Eleanora whispered. "Let's collect Kate."

Eleanora suggested they graze the horses and sit on a knoll overlooking Albany and the Hudson and the knobby silhouette of Rensselaer County across the river. They tethered the horses to graze on the sweet grass, and sat looking eastward.

"How is your young man?" Eleanora asked.

"Fine enough, mum. But too polite. 'Tis a bad sign."

"Why?"

"I don't know if I like it or I don't, mum." Kate pouted. "What with all the 'by your leave's' and 'with your permission's.' It's not like him." She regarded her mistress. "And the gentleman from the West?"

"Oh," Eleanora smiled and a shiver passed through her. "A fine man, a very fine man. Married. Yes, but a fine man nonetheless." She slapped the riding crop twice on her thigh.

"Married?" Kate cried in horror. "Oh, mum, I'm so sorry!"

"That's his affair, not mine," Eleanora said, more to herself than to Kate. She pointed to a farmhouse, then swept the riding crop in a semicircle in the air. "See these lands, my pet? Do you know how they're held, how they're owned and transferred?" Kate frowned, not understanding. "They're owned by the general, and they descend eldest son to eldest son, forever . . . forever. The farmers never own the land they work. They only have the right to plant and harvest so long as they pay rent. And so it is at Claverack. Who made it that way? Someone long ago and far away. Someone we've never met. Yet someone, even though he's dead, controls all their lives with his dead hand, general and farmer alike. The 'dead hand' is what the law calls it, and the dead hand's shadow falls over me and you today even as we sit in the warm sun. Our dead ancestors steer the course of our lives, allowing us property or freedom as they saw fit long ago, or else taking it away. They don't know us today. They can't know what we feel, yet they run our lives."

Kate nodded, but did not understand. The clouds passed and she watched their shadows sweep over the fields and the river and the forests.

"But it must not be that way, Kate. It must not!" Again, Eleanora slapped her thigh with the riding crop. "We must summon all our courage and it will not be so. The dead hand

48

must not control us, and it *shall* not! This day, this sun, this sky, this world belong only to the living, Kate, only to us who breathe and walk and see and . . . and love. Come, my girl, let us return."

"Can't keep up with yourself and that mare, mum."

Eleanora smiled fondly and patted Kate's shoulder. "Then we shall proceed more slowly, and we'll stop and pick some flowers along the way. And tonight, why tonight we'll sleep in the house again, and we'll have a hearty meal sent from Hawley's Pilot House and return to Claverack tomorrow."

"I'd like that, mum." Oysters and ale were Kate's favorite fare. Eleanora helped Kate into her saddle, then vaulted into her own, and they rode leisurely back toward Albany as the sun set behind the escarpment of deepening blue.

CHAPTER 5

a black coach clattered through Albany's rutted streets at sunrise the next morning. The coach bore an ornate golden monogram, "SVR," and through the morning fog its four plumed white horses led a procession of two open carriages, a baggage dray, and two men on horseback.

The party paused at the toll keeper's gate just west of the city, and when the driver leaned down with coins to pay the toll, the gatekeeper turned his pike to allow entrance to the private gravel highway. "Heee- ya!" the driver called, snapping his whip, and the four plumed horses jerked the coach into motion, and soon were galloping west.

The two horsemen, Ellicott and Hedges, trotted briskly behind, discussing how soon the commissioners' pride would be dampened by corduroy roads, waterfalls, slippery portages, mosquitoes, the rain and mud and humid sun, by drunken Yankee frontiersmen, surly boatmen, flea-infested inns, rancid meat and butter, and flat ale served by tavern wenches.

"They do have their notions," Ellicott was laughing.

"Oh, they'll love the West," Hedges observed.

The procession reached Schenectady by noon and split

into three. Ellicott and Hedges rode directly out of town on the Utica turnpike. The gentlemen of the coach, General Van Rensselaer and Gouverneur Morris, enjoyed a sumptuous luncheon and then selected a case of Madeira to ride with them inside. Uncorking a bottle, the general knocked on the ceiling trapdoor: "Onward, Joel!" And the coach lurched forward.

"Fine vintage, General."

"Imported, Morris. Does it remind you of Paris?"

"Why, yes. Of course. The day they stormed the Bastille!"

"Just the thing to cut the dust." The general held up his glass and smacked his lips while the four horses stepped high on the gravel turnpike as the coach attained a breakneck speed of nine miles an hour.

The leader of the third group, DeWitt Clinton, found he could not leave Schenectady that day. The boats were still being caulked and painted because Mr. Eddy had commissioned their preparation only the day before. To keep up spirits, Clinton suggested they elect Mr. Eddy "Commodore" of the expedition, and that they name the baggage boat after him. But Clinton was not amused. He instructed the workmen to erect an awning and curtains to shield out the sun, something Eddy had overlooked, and he delivered two flags for the passenger boat, an American flag with fifteen stars and fifteen red and white stripes, and a New York State flag with the state seal on a royal blue background.

The small party awoke the next day to Independence Day fireworks. Realizing they had a dignitary among them, the citizens of Schenectady asked Clinton to address an assembly in the old stockade. Clinton discussed the need for internal improvements in an impromptu speech, and he urged that the nation avoid war with Britain at all costs. Immediately afterward he visited the boatyard, to find that the two boats were ready.

The entire village followed the expedition party to the river. Baggage filled the *Eddy*, and the men took their seats in the *Morris*. An eight-piece band played, and the crowd cheered as the boatmen cast off, planted their long poles in the river bottom and propelled the long, flat boats into the current.

Progress upstream was slow. A sail did not help as the boats had little ballast and no keel. Their undersides were smooth and shallow so they might be dragged over portages. Clinton stood in his leather slouch hat hour after hour for three days, smoking cigars and gazing moodily into the wind. The others seemed festive, but Clinton was restless. This was no Sunday outing. At each bend or shoal or creek that spilled into the river, he checked Wright's map for its accuracy. He questioned the boatmen incessantly about the river's depth and currents, what goods were shipped each way, the prices and quantities, the length of the shipping season and the number of boats in active trade.

Clinton yearned to emulate the great leaders who had opened new trade routes – Henry the Navigator of Portugal, Ferdinand and Isabella of Spain, Peter the Great of Russia – and wealth poured into their treasuries. The estates of the eastern landed gentry now slumbered in pastoral bliss along the Hudson, but Clinton, a devotee of Adam Smith's *Wealth of Nations* and the principles of Freemasonry, saw that trade was the new path to both personal and public wealth. The canal he envisioned would allow New York State to open an inland route to connect the virgin territories of the Great Lakes with New York harbor, diverting streams of goods from the Mississippi and the St. Lawrence down the Hudson, and making New York arise as the financial center of America.

In five days, they ascended the Mohawk to its source at Rome, and their boats passed into a channel constructed by a private canal company. The wooden locks that lifted boats over the hill and into Wood Creek were rotting. Bridges were so low that their awnings and flagpoles had to be removed. The locks were so slow and cumbersome, many boaters simply affixed dolly wheels to their bateaux, contraptions that carried the boats in the dry season down to where Wood Creek was navigable, and bypassed the canal altogether. As the boatmen poled the boats into the first lock, Clinton jumped ashore to survey the western slope and Wood Creek. He scanned the terrain with the eye of a general. The Mohawk, downstream broad and placid, had recently become swift and narrow near its source. On the other side of the hill, Wood Creek meandered westward through the willows into salt marshes, swamps and shallow lakes – a foreboding land.

Clinton was sitting beneath a tree with his journal and pencil when he heard a harness jingle, and Van Rensselaer's coach rolled into view.

"Hey-ho!" Morris deposited his bulk on the roadway and the general stepped out behind. "You made it, Clinton!" Morris called in high spirits. Clinton slapped his journal shut; they had clearly been drinking all morning.

"We heard from a chap who saw you at Engster's Tavern last night," Van Rensselaer called. "We took the liberty of preparing breakfast. Come!"

The general led them down an embankment to a cool brook where a table was set beneath tall pines. They ate a breakfast of fried pork, ham, bologna sausages, Oswego bread, biscuits, coffee and tea, old and new cheese, partridge, duck, boiled eggs, perch, salmon and bass. A keg of strong ale was tapped, and in the shade they regaled each other with humorous anecdotes of their discomforts. The boats would be another hour in passing through the locks. Growing impatient again, Clinton wandered off to inspect the primitive locks.

The Inland Navigation Company that had built them was nearly bankrupt and only kept solvent with state funds. Poor design, lax management and far too little trade taught harsh lessons, Clinton reflected as he measured and considered the locks, and watched other boats wheeling along the dirt portage road.

"Had an eventful week?" he heard at his elbow, and it was the surveyor, Daniel Hedges.

"We've seen much." He squinted at the horizon.

"I was through here in April when all the streams were swollen with rain," Hedges observed. "This is the tamest segment from the Hudson to Buffaloe. I'd begin construction here and continue westward." Clinton searched Hedges' eyes. Often his penetrating gaze intimidated men, but Hedges simply smiled good-naturedly and nodded. "That's what I'd do."

"Why?" Clinton asked.

Hedges looked to the west. "Two reasons. First, it will be the easiest leg to construct – only a dozen locks in ninety miles. The rapid progress will let the public see success quickly and gather support for the canal. Second, if the project is stalled or abandoned afterward, this portion will still benefit the people hereabouts by linking them directly with the Mohawk. The effort won't be wasted."

Clinton nodded. These were the first sensible observations he'd heard all week.

"What is your impression of the locks operated by this company?"

"Dismal. Their use and demand greatly exceed their engineering. Certainly they ease the loading and unloading of goods, but they are too wide, and so require too much time and water to fill." Hedges pointed to the rotting beams. "Also, they're made of wood and will need to be replaced in three years. The greatest cost of a canal lock is labor, not materials."

"What would you use?"

Hedges pointed south. "There's an outcropping of granite not half a mile from here. The land will supply all the materials if you know what to look for. With proper maintenance, a stone lock lasts forever."

The boatman's cry interrupted them. With flags fluttering and awnings re-erected, the two boats had passed from the eastern waters of the Mohawk into the western waters of Wood Creek, and were ready for boarding.

"Are you accompanying us now, Mr. Hedges?"

"I'd planned on it, sir."

"Sit with me, then." Clinton led him to the waiting boats.

As the boatmen poled with the current down the winding course of Wood Creek, the stifling, mosquito-ridden air closed in on them. Nevertheless, Clinton felt refreshed because he found Hedges not only knowledgeable about the land, the beasts and fish and trees and plants, but also about inland trade routes, products shipped and prices per hundredweight. Hedges knew distances between towns both by horse path and by water, and he related all he knew with the practical good sense of a backwoodsman.

True to Hedges' account, the land westward was flat, and the creeks wound around and back on themselves so a distance by water route was often twice or thrice of that by land. Shallow lakes filled with bass and pike stretched into marshes choked with seagrass, cattails, cranberry and scrub pine. Homesteaders were slowly clearing patches on the bordering hills.

They paused for the night at Cicero near the mouth of Oneida Lake. As the sun set and darkness sifted in, Hedges and Clinton walked the ruined battlements of Fort Brewster which brooded over the lake.

"You have an admirable knowledge of this land," Clinton said.

"I've lived here all my life."

"Yes, but so have many others." Clinton squinted ahead to see bare-chested men paddling bark canoes on the placid breast of the lake. Sparks from flint and iron lit flames in the canoes on the water. "What are they doing?"

"Fishing. They're Onondagas. They set braziers up in

their canoes and light fires of pine knots. The light draws the salmon up to the surface of the water for spearing."

Both men watched the canoes glide to and fro, flames reflecting eerily in the water. The soft, mournful complaint of a loon edged the evening with melancholy.

"It's pagan sorcery," Clinton whispered. "Quite pleasing to watch how they fish." The loon persisted and bats flitted over the water. "We who live in the cities consider this land wild, yet it possesses a quiet and a mystery we lack." He produced two cigars and handed one to Hedges.

They lit them, then leaned against the abandoned ramparts and watched the canoes and the reflected firelight move peacefully back and forth.

The next morning they poled down from the lake into the Oneida River, reaching the Oswego River by evening, and they poled down that river the next day. After twelve miles of slippery portages and waterfalls, they finally drifted into Lake Ontario. The village of Oswego was a cluster of fourteen houses and six log cabins.

"You would think you were on the shores of the Atlantic," Clinton observed in the stiff breeze that raised surf.

"Ontario never freezes," Hedges remarked. "Erie does. Erie is not nearly as deep."

"It's been proposed, Mr. Hedges, to end the canal here. What are your thoughts?"

"It would defeat the purpose."

"Why?" Clinton gave a rare involuntary smile as he regarded the surveyor.

"The falls at Niagara pose the principle obstacle to shipping east. Once goods reach Oswego, they can easily continue down the St. Lawrence to Montreal so there would be little benefit to entering the canal and going down to the Hudson and New York. But if a canal can connect Albany to Lake Erie and bypass the Niagara cataract, all trade will descend through New York to the sea. Besides, Salina's salt springs produce great quantities of salt that require a ready route to market. The canal should pass through Salina and below the Finger Lakes. The canal should steer away from Oswego. Oswego can continue as a lake port, certainly, but not as a terminus to the canal."

"I agree with your thinking on the subject. I should like next to visit the salt springs at Salina."

For two days they toiled back upstream to Onondaga Lake. They visited the Galen Salt Works at Salina where thousands of gallons of brine were pumped from the earth, boiled night and day over cordwood fires in rows of enormous black cauldrons until the thick salt residue was dried and packed into oak casks. The endless boiling muted all sound, so Hedges waited until they were returning to the boats. He showed on his survey map how the canal could be routed directly by the salt refineries in order to ship tens of thousands of barrels annually both east and west. "It will foster the industry of these men," he reasoned, "and provide money in tolls."

After detouring from the proposed canal route for a week to view the Finger Lakes, they set out to meet Van Rensselaer and Morris at the comfortable Powell Hotel in Geneva. A note awaited them there:

July 20, 1810

My dear Clinton:

The general and myself, finding our port and Madeira supply dangerously low, have repaired to Batavia where, we're told, Mr. Ellicott keeps an admirable cellar. We shall meet you at the Niagara cataract August 2nd, instant.

Your most obt. svt.

G. Morris

"I pity Ellicott," Clinton remarked.

"Not at all," Hedges said. "Joe is shrewd. He'll enlist

Morris and the general to support some bill or other for his Dutch principals. And if the digging begins next summer as we all hope, his reputation will be greatly enhanced."

The expedition feasted that evening on venison steaks, trout, bass, salmon, wheat and corn bread, and squash and tomatoes from the hotel garden, and plums, peaches and apples from its orchards. All agreed it was a very fine stopping place. They relaxed this night since having completed all but ninety miles of the route, they would continue the next day by land. "Many canal supporters propose that the canal follow the Genesee River into Lake Ontario," Clinton mused as they lingered over brandy and cigars in the candlelight of the grape arbor. "They say the remaining mileage to Lake Erie is a needless expense." Clinton looked to Hedges for the response he'd heard a week before. Clinton wanted the other commissioners and scientists to hear Hedges bear out what he himself had told them.

"That would be a mistake," Hedges said. "As I've been telling Mr. Clinton, it must begin at Lake Erie, since the greatest expense in shipping goods east from the Great Lakes is to get them around Niagara Falls. Once on Lake Ontario, they can easily sail down the St. Lawrence, and the trade will enrich Montreal instead of us."

The others nodded in the candlelight.

"Western farmers and traders don't really care whether their goods go to Canada or to New York City. They will ship to the readiest market. What is a treacherous portage and an obstacle to trade will really be a boon to our enterprise. Niagara Falls poses such an obstacle to shipping that we can use it to divert all inland trade to New York. We must go all the way to Lake Erie or not bother at all."

"How difficult will the dig be from the Genesee to Buffaloe?" Mr. Eddy asked. Hedges unrolled a map and traced a line roughly parallel to the south shore of Lake Ontario.

"West of the Genesee there is a level ridge over seventy miles long. It rises fifty-five feet above the lower land and if we can route the canal along it, we won't need a lock for seventy-five miles."

"Preposterous!" Eddy sputtered. "After we have struggled up and down rapids and falls, climbed tortuous portages, dost thou mean the rest of the course is level?"

"Exactly," Hedges said. The others at the table were amused by Eddy who had become something of a blustering mascot of the expedition. "This was originally the shore of the lake when it was higher than now. I have taken the level and the ridge is four hundred eighty feet above the level of the sea – only eighty feet below Lake Erie. If we use this ridge, gentlemen, we need only scale one cliff afterward with locks and the canal will be a straight dig to Buffaloe Creek."

"So the whole of the canal is divided into three parts," Clinton nodded. "From Schenectady to Rome, a river valley; after Rome, swamps and lakes; from the Genesee westward, a level ridge. Thus the construction should be divided into three parts which will require different engineering skills."

"I don't see why," Hedges said facetiously. The entire table looked to him, now the acknowledged expert, to see why he was challenging Clinton. "What skill is needed to grade an inclined plane?"

It took a moment for his joke to register, then as they all recalled the ruggedness and variety of the land they had explored, they laughed at Morris' original plan for a gently sloping man-made river. "Mr. Morris, no doubt, is enjoying Ellicott's wine and designing new engineering feats," Clinton said. "We shall hear them presently."

They set off at daybreak on a turnpike graded by the Holland Land Company for its settlers. The horses galloped along as if on a racetrack, and though the party could not see the lake ten miles north, they could smell the clean wind blowing as if from the sea. Clinton ordered the driver to stop after five miles, and he emerged bareheaded from the coach to climb and observe the height and width and surface of the ridge above them. Fifty-five feet higher, the ridge ran parallel and as level as the road itself.

"It most certainly was the lake's shore in some ancient time just as the road is a more recent shoreline." Clinton bent down and felt the sand. "Imagine, Hedges, the upheaval when this lake burst its natural dam and the waters went crashing down the St. Lawrence Valley to the sea! These ridges show it happened twice. Ah, this mocks our human vanity in digging a canal. These shorelines have lain here for thousands of years, evidence of untold violence and upheaval, and we look on them as if they were formed for our convenience. But enough of that." And he smiled up at Hedges. "A glimpse at the eternal is enough for practical men, eh? The convenience this ridge affords can hardly be believed after so much rugged country. Let's continue, I have much to discuss with the commissioners."

Below Niagara Falls, the port of Lewiston bustled with traders and teamsters and stevedores. Barrels of salt and potash were loaded and hauled on sleds by snorting teams of oxen up the steep Niagara gorge to the level of Lake Erie. A team could haul a mere twelve barrels a day. The slow plodding of the beasts was matched for inconvenience only by the danger of the trail.

The party visited Fort Niagara the afternoon they arrived, and the red-faced, sputtering American captain discussed Canadian politics.

"The Brits use Canada as they did our states before the Revolution. They bleed the province of men and materials. Compare our fair state with the land across the river, just across, there! Look! Same land, only different governments.

Here we have farms and orchards. There it's nearly barren. Last year, eighteen thousand barrels of salt were lifted up the American side of the falls, and only four thousand on the Canadian. I can tell you, the Canadians are disgruntled. They secretly promise that if America declares war, they will side with us and run the Brits out and declare their freedom."

"Interesting perception," Clinton observed. Later, as he and Hedges walked the battlements high above the river, Clinton asked if this were true, if the Canadians were so dissatisfied.

"He's half right," Hedges said. "The Canadians are upset with the British; yet I doubt they'd join us. Too much to lose. In any event, a war would be disastrous for both sides."

"It always is." Clinton scowled. "Always and everywhere."

Morris and Van Rensselaer arrived as promised on August 2. Three of their original four horses had been traded at tavern yards along the route, and the remaining one had lost its plume. The two gentlemen stepped stiffly from the coach. After a rousing evening in Batavia, they needed sleep, but Clinton insisted they view Niagara Falls together that day.

Hedges was an able guide. Pointing out abandoned cranes and sleds used by the French fifty years before to haul goods up the escarpment, he compared the old portage with the modern teams and oxen for safety and convenience. He shared anecdotes of pets and cattle who'd plummeted over the falls and survived.

"An interesting legend is told about going over the falls," Hedges said when the band collected to hike along the brink of the cliff. "An Indian chief moored his canoe at the shore near Chippewa and fell asleep. A British soldier loosened the rope, and the current carried the canoe away. Drifting along, the chief awoke to the roar of the rapids, and he tried to

62

paddle first to one bank and then to the other. But the current held him fast in its grip. At last he wrapped himself in his blanket and met his death, singing his death song in defiance." Clinton brooded as Hedges told this legend, and gazed at the whitewater thoughtfully.

"I say, Hedges, that tale would make an admirable topic for one of our poets if properly rendered."

"How so, Clinton, how so?" asked Van Rensselaer.

"Think on it, General, the pagan stoic meeting his death. No folderol about heaven or funerals or wills. A man and this cataract. Ahh," he breathed deeply, "the mortal loses to the immortal falls. This land is inspiring. I shall recommend the story to our own Mr. Irving when I return to New York. He should shun those European capitals, and visit this land for his subject matter. It has far more heart."

As they approached the thundering cataract, froth from the rapids pitched over the edges, and beyond, a great billowing cloud of spray rose into a glorious rainbow. No one spoke. Beneath them the earth rumbled. They picked their way along in single file until suddenly, one by one, they emerged from the dim forest to view the spectacle of the falls.

Before them in a gentle horseshoe crescent, a full mile of water spilled over the lip of the falls in a luminous green until whipped into foam by the air, falling, falling, then dashing itself on the dislodged rubble, clouds of spray ascending into the air, into the sun, blushing with colors of the rainbow.

The commissioners gazed silently at the majestic spectacle for a quarter of an hour. The vastness of the sight defied words: The wide semicircle of rock; the freefall height from the sharp brink to the enormous stone blocks torn and plunged and mercilessly pounded below; yet above all, the immense volume of water that poured over second by second, day and night, year by year, century after century.

"Makes our concerns seem rather small, don't it?" Hedges asked Clinton.

"It is magnificent." Clinton's eyes burned intensely. "The land this river drains rivals the size of all Europe. And our canal will join those lands, those lakes and river valleys, with the sea." He placed his hand on Hedges' shoulder. "If only we could stand every legislator and congressman here, we'd never want for funds."

Unfortunately the legislators couldn't share Clinton's lofty vantage point. Other business now kept them in the lowlands, and their own shortsightedness and sluggishness would always keep them there. Martin Van Buren knew this. Clinton was such a visionary that the Democratic-Republican Party could hardly keep track of his whereabouts, much less keep pace, so Van Buren seized his chance to lead. The Tammany Society was dead set against the canal because it feared cheap produce from the West would abolish downstate markets and their trade.

Van Buren saw he might move to the forefront of the party by openly opposing the canal. Added to the political issue, Van Buren believed the canal was a physical impossibility and, therefore, politically suicidal. Posturing himself as a voice of reason and caution, he met in Albany with Tammany legislators from New York City while Clinton was scouting in the hinterlands.

The Tammany sachems loathed Clinton. They frowned on spending tax money upstate and feared any progress that could threaten workingmen's jobs. The party leaders agreed that a three-hundred-fifty mile ditch was foolhardy, wasteful and impossible, but they didn't quite trust Van Buren. Why was a judge meddling in legislative and executive matters? Recognizing that he had valuable information and a quick and persuasive manner, they urged him to meet with the great chief of the Tammany Society, Brody O'Hanlon. "Talk with him," they advised, "he'll know what he wants and he's never shy about telling us how to vote."

Van Buren was encouraged. He had tapped into a large

and powerful political organization and was immediately directed to its leader. If he persuaded O'Hanlon, the Tammany boys in Albany would begin to look to him for guidance. Van Buren planned to run for state senate from Columbia County when the seat came vacant in 1812 and he believed he could organize canal resistance upstate, marry it to Tammany's votes, and thus lay a foundation wide and deep enough for his own ambitious statewide political future. Martin Van Buren, an upstart who left school at fourteen, would force the patrician Clinton, nephew of the vice president, to deal with him, and thus rise in public esteem to stature equal to the great man. Let Clinton explore the state's wilderness and appeal to men's hopes and dreams for the future, Van Buren knew where fear lurked in men's hearts, and he knew how to harness it. Van Buren's only regret, as he girded his loins for his own David and Goliath contest, was that his brilliant strategy must be kept secret. Sharing it would ruin it, and bearing such a burden in private would be lonely and tiring work until such time as it began to succeed.

DeWitt Clinton had discussed the appointment of a surveyor to the canal project individually with each of the commissioners to make each man believe the appointment had been his idea. When they met at the small village of Chippewa, Clinton diplomatically allowed General Van Rensselaer to chair the meeting.

"We have, in the past four weeks, traversed the entire course of our proposed canal," the general began grandiosely. "We know now firsthand what difficulties lie in our path. Inland navigation today is rough and primitive," he held up his tankard of ale, "so rough and primitive that Mr. Morris and I chose the turnpikes and corduroy roads rather than the portages and Durham boats you suffered in." This brought cheers. He stopped them and looked about the tavern. "Not too far in the future we will build the longest, smoothest, most efficient waterway the world has ever seen."

The commissioners applauded heartily. "I have spoken with Mr. DeWitt. I have asked him to survey and lay out the isle of Manhattan in a grid of streets and avenues. His duties as surveyor general for Manhattan will keep him busy as our great state of New York continues laying out townships, setting boundaries and settling land disputes. Today we have the task, and the privilege of naming someone to survey the actual course the canal will take, a thorough survey that will allow our august legislature to make an informed decision about appropriating funds. Therefore, it greatly pleases me to nominate Mr. Daniel Hedges of Buffaloe Creek as chief surveyor for the Grand Canal."

This took Hedges completely by surprise. Joseph Ellicott, his usual informant, had not attended. Hedges looked about the tavern at the pleased, congratulating faces, and he nodded. Duly seconded by Clinton, Van Rensselaer called the vote.

"Aye!" rang out from all.

"It's unanimous, then. Mr. Hedges is our chief surveyor. Congratulations, Mr. Hedges. I see no reason to be stingy, so let us affix a salary of five hundred dollars per annum, and we shall secure this appropriation from the legislature when it convenes. Edna, my good lass," he called to the buxom barmaid, "more ale, please."

Applause and laughter filled the room, and the barmaid brought each man a full tankard. Daniel stood to accept a list of places the commissioners wanted surveyed in greater detail.

"Gentlemen," he stood easily and spoke slowly, "I'm mighty thankful for the honor you give me today, and I will work as hard and as well as I can to get the survey completed for next January. Mr. Clinton and I have been together for three weeks discussing any number of things – plants, birds, beasts, rock formations, clouds, even some ancient Indian mounds I never explored before. His questions have been constant and not always easy to answer. Now, I'd like to put one to him here and now, just one. You see," he slouched a bit and grinned, "I ain't a political man by nature, and I don't understand much of what goes on in Albany. But as we've traveled three hundred miles to view the wildest reaches of this state, I'd like to know, Mr. Clinton, just what does all this mean to an ex-mayor of New York City?"

The taproom erupted in laughter, men crying, "Clinton for governor! Clinton for president!"

DeWitt Clinton stood before them with a benign smile, calming the applause. "Gentlemen, gentlemen . . . as Mr. Hedges asks, I must respond. Don't ever believe anyone who tells you I'm not just another concerned citizen." Again, laughter and resounding applause.

"Seriously, though, we have walked this land together, you and I, and we have just appointed a most capable surveyor. The only obstacle to construction now is money. If I may, I'd like to leave today with something you can give me." The listened attentively. "I move, as a member of this commission, that we petition the United States Congress for funds to help the people of New York undertake this great endeavor. With a favorable vote on my motion, I will personally travel to Washington and lobby strenuously for federal dollars. We believe this canal will serve not only our national goals, but even as we sit today in Chippewa, in British territory, it will serve our international interests and national defense as well."

Gouverneur Morris had been flirting with the barmaid. Anxious to participate in the meeting, he clumsily stood and wiped a moustache of foam from his lip. "Not only do I second the motion," the old Federalist blustered, "but I will accompany you to Washington, Clinton, and I'll twist a few arms of my Revolutionary comrades who are now sitting in Congress. Jemmy Madison won't keep all the federal money for Virginia."

"The motion is on the floor," Van Rensselaer called. "All those in favor?"

"Aye!"

"Opposed?" Silence.

"Mr. Clinton's motion carries. Let us adjourn this meeting," the general held up his tankard, "with a toast. I raise my glass to the people of the State of New York and the great destiny that awaits them."

CHAPTER 6

*D*aniel Hedges stood on the packet ship's deck as the wind pushed it from Chippewa, scanning the shoreline past Black Rock for the sandbar and mouth of Buffaloe Creek. It was as if he were seeing the shore for the first time. He longed to pace the deck of his *Silver Pearl,* and to feel her sails swell in the wind.

As packet ship entered the sparkling mouth of Buffaloe Creek and Daniel looked both fondly and critically at his brig. Her lines were true and sure, and riding at anchor, she seemed anxious to be out on the lake. But he had other obligations. A rowboat brought him to shore, he walked along the dock, then up a rise into town, and then he paused. He scanned the forty-odd buildings clustered together on the shore of the lake: the new stone courthouse and jail, the one-story customs house, and Cook's Tavern, Buffaloe Creek's gathering place. Although he was glad after eight weeks to be home, to see Carrie and the children, after Albany, the village seemed dismally small and quiet. The town fathers had shown themselves to be unwisely petty the year before when, insisting on straightening a road, they bisected a curve on Joseph Ellicott's property where he had collected building stone to build a stately mansion overlooking the lake. Resentful and bitter by this unwarranted intrusion into his land, Ellicott canceled his plan, sold the stone to the Holland Land Company to be used for the courthouse and jail, and returned to Batavia. What would these same town fathers think of the ambitious canal project?

Smoke trailed up through the shade of virgin pines where log cabins nestled, their frontier slumber unbroken. Daniel and Carrie lived in such a cabin, but earlier that year Daniel had dug a cellar and laid a fieldstone foundation on his large lot on Washington Street, and he had secured lumber, window glass and roofing shakes. He'd planned to build a large frame house for his family until Ellicott and the canal project intervened. Hedges passed the site and inspected the sail canvas protecting the lumber from rain and sun. The foundation lay ready for floor beams and walls. The commissioners wanted their surveying done by October, and he wanted the house ready for the first snow. Many plans needed to be made.

He passed along the path south and east, sea bag over his shoulder. As he turned a corner, he saw Carrie, and he stopped to watch her scold Eli who'd been teasing his sister. The scene was so domestic and familiar, yet so new. Clothes hung on a line between two trees, and the cabin seemed so very small, yet far more comforting than he remembered.

"Carrie!" he called. She turned, squinted into the shade, then her mouth opened, her eyes widened.

"Danny? Oh, Danny!" and she ran to embrace him.

"Papa's home!" squealed Rachel and she bolted up. Eli dropped his toy musket and dashed after her.

"Oh, you're home!" Carrie cried, and she hugged him and kissed him on the neck and the lips. "It's been so long!" She pulled back to look at him and he smiled down at her.

"You look wonderful!" he cried, then he lifted her up and spun her around. By now the children had reached him and were hugging his legs.

"Wait, wait, I have presents for you." Daniel pulled away from Carrie, opened his sea bag and produced a doll with a ceramic head and a wooden ship, a brig like the *Silver Pearl*. The children squealed and thanked him for the gifts.

"Ah, Carrie," he slipped his arm about her waist. "It is a grand enterprise Ellicott's involved me in, but I so hate being away from you."

She kissed him again and rested her head on his shoulder as they walked together. "Things have been well here. Lester completed eight voyages – four to Presque Isle and the Pittsburgh Road, two to Cleveland, and one each to Port Colborne and Detroit. We have wanted for nothing, and I have kept the account books."

"I'll see Lester in the morning." He hugged her again and viewed the cabin as if seeing it for the first time. "Must get reacquainted with you and home first."

They sat together on a bench, and through a clearing in the trees they could see the buildings of town, the creek and the lake sparkling in the sun out beyond the sandbar.

"So the trip overland was good?"

"Yes. Mr. Clinton is a capital fellow and it was with him that I returned. But politics! I don't know how he stomachs it. Everybody squawking like crows in a tree. The canal has become his personal ambition and he wants to build New York State into the foremost state of the nation. He is wise, and his questions and comments brought the land alive in ways I'd never seen." He paused. "I'll be working with him again. That's the news. They have appointed me chief surveyor."

"Oh, that's wonderful! What an honor." Then her expression clouded. "Will it require you to be away from home often?"

"Can't tell yet. I have another survey to do before winter, but that should take only three weeks."

She nodded soberly. "I see." Then she brightened. "But you're home now, that's what's important."

They talked together for an hour, then Carrie prepared a dinner of venison backstrap, cornbread, baked beans and bass fried with onions and potatoes. Daniel brought a pail of beer from Cook's Tavern and they dined under the pines as sunset burnished the lake beyond. Before they went to bed, Daniel held his children, and told them stories about the great city he'd visited and the queen with deep brown eyes and long dark hair who ruled there.

"Is she a beautiful queen?" Rachel asked.

"Yes, the most beautiful in all the land. But not as beautiful as you." The little girl looked up at her father, searching his eyes.

"As beautiful as Mama?"

"No, not as beautiful as Mama."

"Let him finish the story," Eli protested.

"It's wonderful to be home," Daniel said, returning to Carrie from putting the children to bed. She was sitting by the hearth. He placed his hand on hers and sat beside her. "Often as we lay down for the night, I'd think of you and the children, and you'd seem so very far away. I'd ache to be here with you, and I'd gaze up into the stars as I do when navigating at night and wonder how long it would be."

"I know, I know."

"It's difficult when I'm away."

"I wish you could always be here, but . . ."

"Someday," he patted her hand and nodded, "and the work I do will make all our lives so very much better."

She agreed, and Daniel suggested they lay on the bearskin rug before the hearth. Together they gazed into the fire and talked. Daniel told her about the aristocrats he had met at the general's ball and the wonders of the expedition. He neglected mentioning Eleanora Van Rensselaer, however. As the embers burned low, a soft wind played through the pines outside, crickets chirped and the moon cast its light in through the doorway. Nestled in Daniel's arms, Carrie drifted into a deep slumber. He held her, soothed and comforted to feel her breathing once again in his arms, and he watched the embers burn like rubies and the cool moonlight spilling into the room.

"Hey, ho, Lester!" Daniel called next morning as his rowboat pulled alongside the anchored brig. Lester Frye, a burly, whiskered, sunburnt fellow in his mid-forties, peered over the rail, squinting into the sun.

"Danny? That you?" He ran to the stern and heaved over a rope ladder. "Come aboard."

Daniel clambered up the ladder and vaulted the rail.

He scrutinized the masts, the furled sails, the rigging and the deck. "Everything appears shipshape," and he thrust out his hand for his first mate to shake.

"You didn't doubt me, did you?" Lester asked suspiciously. "I'm sure your beautiful bride informed you of the good news? The runs we've made in your absence?" Daniel nodded. "Well, then, how was your trip?"

"Long. And I leave again the tenth of September."

"So soon? But they must value your services, eh?"

"Yes. And we have our work cut out until then. It's time to make some quick money, Lester. What's in the wind?"

Lester looked comically shocked. "Oh, ho, ho! Danny! Not me, says you, never again will I turn to smuggling, says you, once the embargo is lifted, it's by the book, says you. Ho, ho, ho. By the book!"

"We all need to make sacrifices." Hedges shrugged. "For a worthy cause, mind you. I must hire some men to help raise the house in town and finish it while I'm away. Otherwise Carrie will make good her threat and move onto the Seneca reservation. With two little ones in that cabin, we can't be snowed in there again this winter."

"Well," Lester licked his lips, "I hear tell there's six hunnerd barrels of corn liquor from Ohio arriving at Presque Isle in a fortnight, and that the man's seeking transportation, name of Sims. He wants to walk away clean."

"Buy-and-sell?" Daniel scowled.

Lester nodded. "Cash on the barrel head."

"But why? They never do that. What's the price?"

"Ten-fifty a barrel."

"Is it quality at that price?"

Lester nodded. "Only hitch is whoever takes it must take all."

"That's sixty-three hundred, twice the value of the *Pearl*."

"Yes," said Lester, "but worth ten thousand in the right hands."

"Does this Sims have a customer?"

"A merchant in Port Colborne, name of McFarland. He'll pay ten thousand, maybe an additional five hunnerd for timely delivery."

"But why?" Daniel asked. "It's only a thirty-hour sail."

"Customs. Since the embargo's been lifted, the new agent Wiley takes it as his personal mission to collect every penny in duty."

"Well, then," Daniel peered over toward the customs house, "we'll have a little fun at Wiley's expense. Tell Sims we'll be there." He went below to inspect the condition of the ship. It was as orderly and as clean as he left it, and he returned to the deck satisfied. "Did you have any plans today?"

"No, sir, Cap'n."

"Well, let's hang some sail and take her out. Those Durham boats I've been on lately are cramped and plodding craft. Call the lads!"

The first mate called two boys who were splicing cable at

the bow. They sprang to the masts and unfurled the topsails. Lester cast off from the mooring, and Daniel carefully steered the *Silver Pearl* over the sandbar and onto the lake. The boys then unfurled the top gallants and the mainsail.

Pregnant with wind, the sleek ship responded, and soon the prow was slicing through the pale blue waves. With the wind in his hair, his blue eyes keen and happy, Daniel Hedges steered away from land.

This was what he lived for, a feeling of freedom, freedom from the concerns of land, from money and prestige and power and all the things Albany represented. The day was bright and sunny, huge cumulus clouds piled in the sky. Gulls screamed and dipped behind the ship.

He tacked back and forth, examining things from both sides. What had Ellicott enmeshed him in? He considered the maneuvers and strategies of Albany. The contortions those people went through! Like the dancers at the general's ball moving in patterns of the quadrille and minuet, they all knew the steps, and they enjoyed the ritual, but he did not belong to that world, among those people. He belonged here with Carrie trading on the lake. And yet the grand enterprise of the canal lured him. It was more ambitious and wonderful than anything he had ever done, ever attempted, indeed ever thought about.

Then he remembered Eleanora. She had somehow worked things out with Clinton, and perhaps knew about his appointment before he left Albany. Had she sighed him? Perhaps. Yet the hunger in her eye, the nervous tension in her smile, the energy coiled in her limbs even as she reclined, her passion awakened a need in him stronger than he knew he possessed. He contrasted Eleanora and Carrie.

Carrie's bright, candid green eyes and impish smile summoned him to a haven where life was sedate and happy and complete. Her tenderness and sensuality satisfied him, made him feel whole and domestic and fulfilled. Her black curls, luxuriant as the flowering vines on their cabin, her sweet laughter, the grace of her step, her calm acceptance all embodied innocence, health and well-being. Her maternal instincts and the patience she put in nurturing their children awakened him to the voice of the future, of a new generation that must be guided and provided for. An orphan himself, Daniel took fatherhood most seriously.

He thought back to their wedding day eight years before. That sunny afternoon Carrie had stepped out of the shadows in a dress of white buckskin with beaded designs a Seneca woman had sewn. The ceremony by the local justice was held in a glade, and with white moccasins and her hair braided with white flowers, Carrie was so beautiful. After the vows, her lively nature spurred others to dance to the fiddles, to eat heartily from the tables of game and vegetables and fruit, to drink from jugs of cider and corn liquor. Last night Carrie had again lavished on him such joy and peace. He didn't want to leave again. Then he thought of Eleanora.

How different was Lady Van Rensselaer! Some deep sadness, deeper than a widow's grief for her husband, burned with a subdued flame, a flame of outrage deep within her. He felt that. Insulated by her position and her wealth, she dared not express that rage, but though she held it in, it burned and rebelled. Clearly, Eleanora knew a loneliness Daniel himself hadn't felt since childhood. Amid the social whirl and political intrigues and escapades of aristocrats, she knew how horribly alone she was, and this knowledge tormented her.

Why such interest in the canal? He saw and he knew. She longed for a grand passion to sweep her up, to engage her energies and talents in an intense communion with something that would take her out of herself. Something that might convince her, even if just for a day, that she was wrong about life, wrong about desire, and wrong about love. Daniel hated to see suffering, yet he wondered what he could do. Ellicott didn't understand. Eleanora wasn't using him. She was simply curious as to whether he saw into the source of her despair, and if he saw, what he would do about it. He couldn't do much. His life was settled here on the frontier, with his wife and two beautiful children, with his beloved ship, in his village. And then he remembered her sweet kiss and was enticed by the thought of gazing for hours into her deep eyes, of feeling the slim lines of her body, the passion pent up within –

"Danny!! Hey, Danny!" Lester cried. Daniel shook himself awake. "Ye've been too long on land, lad. We're luffing!" Startled, Daniel looked up at the sails snapping idly in the wind. "Decide which side you want the wind on, lad, and keep to your course."

"Sure, old man!" Daniel yelled to cover his embarrassment. "My ship's been too long under your care and forgot its master's hand."

And Daniel vowed then and there to forget the grand lady and whenever they should meet again, to concentrate solely on his role as surveyor.

CHAPTER 7

*E*leanora returned to her Claverack estate. Her crops were planted, her foals, lambs and calves grazed in her pastures, and her mills ground winter wheat and sawed her lumber. All was in order, but she felt strangely unsettled and restless. The outward appearance of everything was the same, but its essence had changed. She wandered through her mansion at all times of day and night. She gazed distantly out the window as her foremen discussed business. She sat before portraits of her ancestors and Jacob's ancestors wishing she might ask them questions. Most disturbing, though, she awoke from dark dreams, tangled in the sheets, dreams that she'd been disgraced, dispossessed and turned out of her home.

Daniel Hedges occupied more of her thoughts and dreams than she cared to admit. She admonished herself not to think of him, and she felt foolish when she did. What was he, a merchant? A surveyor? There were yeomen and tradesmen all about her more accomplished in their callings. He had calloused hands with jagged nails. He ignored the most fundamental of the social graces – he shook her hand! Yet in moments when she least expected it, his smile and his mellow voice were with her.

Worst of all, she allowed herself to remember his kiss. Other than her husband, he was the only man she had allowed to kiss her. But the difference!

By late August the workmen had finished the Albany townhouse so Eleanora left her Claverack estate to wait for Clinton in Albany. She admired the culmination of all she'd directed to be done, and she walked from room to handsomely appointed room. There was a dining room where eight could dine in intimacy discussing delicate matters of state; the drawing room where brandy and cigars might be enjoyed and where she would play the newest Parisian and Viennese compositions on the pianoforte; the library stocked with the classics and with Locke, Rousseau, Hume and Hobbes and the comfortable parlor with a Chippendale sofa, love seat and parlor chairs, and canvases of classical groves and wood nymphs.

Upstairs were three bedrooms: hers, the master bedroom with a four-poster bed, full-length mirror, vanity table and spacious closet, and two guest rooms simply but tastefully furnished. Servants' quarters were in the attic, a kitchen and wine cellar in the basement. The stable likewise was complete, and a flower garden planted in the back. After a week, Eleanora felt strangely more at home here than in Claverack.

Clinton called on his return from the West and he viewed the furniture, paintings and arrangement of the first floor rooms with approval. "You've done an admirable job."

"I'll show you the upstairs."

"No need, no need."

"Please sit," she motioned him to one of the chairs. "How was your expedition?"

Clinton was excited, and he paced, ignoring the chair. "Inspiring, inspiring. We saw lands I never dreamt existed. You have seen the coastal cities, Boston, New York, Philadelphia. But our nation now only hugs the edge of this continent. There is so very much land to the interior! These cities along the coast are mere shadows of what will spring up when the West is developed."

He walked to the window, then back again. "After so much forest, so many rapids and mountain lakes, we traveled along a ridge nearly eighty miles long and perfectly flat. A marvel. And just when we considered we'd beheld all the wonders of the country, we were shown the Niagara cataract. Why, Eleanora, I felt as Moses must have on Mount Nebo, when Jehovah allowed him to view, but not enter the Promised Land."

She smiled at the allusion.

"Vast empires lie to the West waiting to be developed. If my reappointment as mayor were not imminent, I would undertake a journey such as Lewis and Clark did for Jefferson. The West, Eleanora, holds our future, but so few of us along this coast can see it."

"Then we should begin work to secure funds?"

"Absolutely. It is imperative now to connect those lands with our seaboard."

Edward the butler brought tea, and Eleanora poured and handed Clinton a cup. "How were the rigors of camp life?"

He smiled, then sat down. "We stayed in some true hell-holes: mosquitoes, drunken yeomen, bed-bugs, moths, even a snake in one elegant hostelry. The land is very primitive, mere clusters of sheds they call towns. But there is ample wood and stone for building. I spent most of the time with Hedges, the surveyor. A capital fellow."

Eleanora shifted her position. "Oh?"

"Yes. The others looked at the surface of everything. Hedges helped me look through much of it. We discussed elevations, rock formations, methods to circumvent the rougher land with locks. He was a salvation to me, trapped as I was in the company of Eddy, Morris and North. We elected him chief surveyor of the canal project. Simeon DeWitt grows old and has many other tasks to perform. Hedges will be taking a second, more intensive look at some places we viewed."

"And he'll report his findings to the commission?" She tried to hide the hope in her voice, but Clinton heard it. He raised an eyebrow. "We expect him to deliver a report early in October." He watched. She nodded and stared into the tea leaves in her cup and said nothing.

"So, Eleanora, I have come today to enlist your help."

She peered up and smiled. "You know I'll do anything I can."

"Yes. And this might even be a bit of fun. I'd like you to accompany Morris and me to Washington where we will ask Congress for funds to help us begin the work. Now is a good time to force the issue since a bill for a mountain road in Cumberland, Virginia, is before the lawmakers. But beyond the finances, federal money would give our project a boost in the public eye."

"When do we leave?"

"As soon as Hedges delivers his report. Sometime in October, I should think. If I cannot make it here, then you should bring his report to New York. We'll set out together from there."

"I look forward to it."

Clinton nodded and stood. "I must return this afternoon to New York. I expect my reappointment as mayor any day, and I must immerse myself in city council matters."

"Have a safe trip in Fulton's boat. Frankly, I prefer coaches. The sparks and noise frighten me and it always seems on the verge of exploding."

"Progress, Eleanora, progress."

That night Clinton stood at the railing aboard Fulton's North River Steamboat, enjoying a cigar and the moonlight on the waves. He thought of the expedition and he thought in particular about the ancient mounds Hedges had showed him just south of the level ridge. They were forts built along the ancient shoreline, surely before Rome was sacked, before the Greeks sailed to wage war on Troy.

The civilization that built the mounds was now extinct. Clinton had wondered, gazing at the surrounding countryside, who the mound builders were and where they went. How did they live, by hunting or planting? What gods did they worship? What were their boats like? Did fierce invaders, perhaps ancestors of the Iroquois, conquer and disperse them?

Clinton saw in the mounds exactly what he now was pursuing with New Yorkers, work for the common good. The mounds were ancient public works, now mute and ruined. Directed by chiefs and priests, the thousands of laborers had built them basket by basket of earth. Clinton considered himself such a leader of multitudes. "Nothing makes a leader so admired as the undertaking of great enterprises." Machiavelli, but so be it. He would construct this vast canal for the common good. He'd persuade, cajole, intimidate and force New Yorkers to see its value, vote for its funds, engineer and dig it. Its completion could very well lift him into the presidency.

Clinton was suddenly aware of someone nearby. A small man with reddish blond hair, a man he knew but couldn't immediately place. "You seemed so absorbed in thought, I didn't want to interrupt," the man said. He was a lawyer, no, a judge . . . a judge in an upstate county. He had a Dutch name.

"It is a fine evening," Clinton stalled.

"Have you been long in the West, Mr. Clinton?"

"Yes." Van Buren, Matthew? No, Martin, they called him Matty. Martin Van Buren, surrogate judge of Columbia County, Eleanora's county. "Why, yes, Judge Van Buren, I have."

The small man preened at being recognized and addressed by his title. "And how fares our canal project?"

"Well, sir, well."

Van Buren nodded. Clinton said no more but Van Buren was not dissuaded by the pause.

"I have business in the city," he announced with a certain self-importance.

"Business is an honorable pursuit," Clinton patronized him.

"No, no, no," Van Buren grinned. "Political business."

"There is surely much of that these days."

"I am upset our noble party is being torn in two by a war faction and a peace faction."

"And to which do you belong?"

Van Buren smiled quickly. "I do not think factions accomplish much, Mr. Clinton. I believe we all stand or fall together."

Clinton agreed with him. "And your errand?"

"Hardly an errand, sir. More of a mission." Van Buren knit his fingers together. "I am hoping to help bind the two viewpoints together."

"Well, then, sir, I hope your efforts have success." The sarcasm was imperceptible.

"Perhaps we might meet in New York and discuss where you stand on the war question."

Clinton was surprised at the young upstart's impudence. "Contact my man Carr for an appointment."

"Very good." Van Buren nodded, smiling at the subtlety of the cut.

"I am sorry sir, I hope you will forgive me. I simply must repair to my cabin and rest."

Van Buren bowed. "Good night, Mr. Clinton."

Clinton returned the bow and departed for his berth.

"Yes," Van Buren muttered, "I'll forgive you. Sleep well." And he grinned, pleased with the informal encounter. Men were approachable when met unexpectedly, and though Clinton had brushed him off, that slight would soon be avenged. "Ah, my fine aristocrat, soon you'll have to reckon with me." Van Buren stretched and gazed at the moonlight on the water. It was indeed a lovely night to be on the river.

Fulton's steamboat, dwarfed by the tangle of masts and spars of clipper ships, docked at dawn. Impeccably dressed and groomed, Van Buren marched along the wharf and into the streets of the metropolis. He knew New York City well. As a penniless law clerk seven years before, he had heeled votes in the rougher wards, his boyish physique jostled by the thick, rough Tammany blacklegs and thugs. Thanks to the canal proposal, he now had an appointment with the Tammany chief. Better than venting the resentment and envy he felt for Clinton's pedigree – indeed, Clinton had been serving as United States senator from New York back in 1803 when Van Buren was struggling to find voters and clients – Van Buren now saw his opportunity to grapple that power away from Clinton. If he could ally the interests of Clinton's upstate opponents with the Sons of Tammany, he could get himself elected to the state senate, single-handedly bring Clinton down, and build his own political temple on the ruins.

Brody O'Hanlon, boss of the Tammany Society, ran a foundry on the East River. His "office" was a small cluttered backroom whose cold hearth served as a spittoon.

"What can I do for ye, sir?" O'Hanlon had a thick brogue.

"It's more what I can do for you." Van Buren flashed a ready smile, rubbed his hands together. "I've been discussing sensitive matters regarding Clinton's canal project with your legislators in Albany. They suggested I share this information directly with you. I know there's no love lost between the Loyal Sons of Tammany and Mayor Clinton . . ."

"Silk-stockinged bastard!" O'Hanlon spat and nodded his white bushy head.

"And yet the council of appointment is about to reinstate him as your mayor?"

"Aye, the boys go back on their word. But they'll reap what they been sowing, sure enough."

"Clinton is posturing himself to run either for governor or president. He believes the canal project will bring him the recognition he needs. Clinton is very shrewd, but his arrogance will be his undoing. We must attack where he is vulnerable." Van Buren raised his eyebrows and O'Hanlon nodded for him to continue. "With his education and his connections, he believes office should be conferred on him rather than earned. He despises the political process."

"Aye, until the bleedin' Federalists acknowledge him, then he jumps into bed with 'em." O'Hanlon grew testy. "What is it, Van Buren? I'm not one for theories or p'rhapses. What have ye come for?" He spat a line of tobacco juice into the fireplace.

Seeing that delicacy was futile, Van Buren grew more direct. "I'm running for state senate next election and I want to offer my services to the Sons of Tammany."

"What district?"

"Columbia County,"

"Why, we own half the legislature now, and we can't get out the vote away up there." O'Hanlon squinted. "What can you offer us?"

"Clinton." Van Buren let the word register.

"Well, that would be grand, sir, but better men than you and me have tried to bring him down."

"Don't misunderstand me. I won't topple him. At least not yet. Good enemies are scarce, and therefore valuable. I suggest we use him as our adversary to strengthen the party. We minimize his accomplishments by taking credit for them ourselves, and we blame all of our misfortunes on him."

"Aye, we've been trying to do that, but ain't as easy as it sounds. He always seems to rise above the donnybrook. What will you claim for yourself, sir?"

"Your undying friendship." This made the Irishman smile. Van Buren continued: "As a preliminary matter, I've made some inquiries about Clinton and the canal project."

"Have you now?"

"Yes, and I offer my information not for general circulation, but to indicate how we may work together, what sort of benefit I can provide."

"Let's hear." Again O'Hanlon spat a line of brown juice at the fireplace, and clasped his hands together.

"First of all, it is not merely an improvement of existing watercourses he's proposing. It's digging a ditch from Albany clear across the wilderness to Lake Erie. Sheer madness! He'll need immigrant labor to do it, and the foreigners will need work when the project falls through, flooding the labor market and driving Tammany members from jobs." The Tammany leader nodded gravely. "Second, and more importantly, Clinton is trying to finance the thing publicly."

O'Hanlon scowled. "The whole thing?" Van Buren nodded. "But who's to own and run it?"

"The State of New York."

"The State?" O'Hanlon nearly choked on his tobacco wad and without warning he hawked it into the fireplace, coughed and struggled to regain his breath. "Since when does a government go into business building canals?"

"Never, if we're successful. The whole scheme is preposterous. Clinton's arrogance will undo him. Why, if his plan were widely known, and cast in the proper editorial light," he winked, "you do have friends who are editors?"

"We own two newspapers, man. Don't you know that?"

Van Buren dodged the question. "Well, when this becomes public, the outpouring of scorn will make it impossible for

Clinton to hold his head up. Think of it! A four-hundred mile ditch."

"Aye, and it baffles me what our dandy mayor wants with farmers and trappers and woodsmen and Injuns."

Van Buren leaned across the table. "Would it surprise you to hear that Mr. Clinton is planning to go to Washington to seek federal money for the project? He will tout his recent expedition westward as a personal quest in the interests of the nation."

"And so, what do you recommend?"

"If you have any access to Madison or his cabinet, forestall the federal funds. Clinton wants to run for president and the suggestion that he'll be Madison's opponent in 1812 should sabotage any federal help. The public, I think, may enjoy learning of Clinton's Washington trip, too. They may like to know when their mayor is out of town and how he's spending his time. Perhaps the notion of a publicly owned ditch through the forests upstate might stimulate some interest here in the city." Van Buren opened his arms in candor. "I will leave all of this in your capable hands."

"Aye," O'Hanlon's expression grew sly. "Have you talked with any of the lawmakers about the canal specifically?"

"Only the Loyal Sons and three of my closest allies. If I may count on Tammany's opposition, I shall begin working with other legislators. Your say-so must come first, of course."

O'Hanlon tapped his temple and winked. "Wise, Van Buren, very wise."

"Of course, my name in no way must be connected—"

"Never, sir, never. We have never met."

Van Buren stood and extended his hand. "The accounts I have heard of you and the Loyal Sons were not exaggerations."

"We do our best." O'Hanlon shook Van Buren's hand and dismissed him from the office, and the judge strutted through the grimy, clanging foundry wearing a broad smile.

CHAPTER 8

*U*nder the nose of Wiley, the new customs agent, Daniel Hedges and Lester Frye carried on their shipping business as usual until, late one September night, they quietly cast off and were away. The *Silver Pearl* could reach fourteen knots in a good wind.

Presque Isle rose into sight on the evening of the second day. Two miles to the west of the Pittsburgh road smugglers had built a port during Jefferson's embargo. It was reached through a narrow channel that the proprietors camouflaged with evergreen trees so the shore appeared unbroken. In the lagoon stood six log warehouses and eight docks.

While his crew moored the ship, Hedges went to negotiate with Emmanuel Kraab. Hedges had borrowed two thousand dollars, Lester had put up two hundred, and Daniel had staked forty-five hundred of his own money – every penny he possessed – on this venture. The fat, bearded liquor dealer sat behind a counting table, a jug of whiskey and a glass in reach.

"Sims sent me." Daniel threw down a leather satchel. "There's the price, six thousand in gold. We can be loaded and gone by morning."

"Price is seven thousand." Kraab did not look up.

"Too bad." Daniel picked up the satchel. "I won't waste your time." He walked out of the office and back to the ship.

"All set to load?" Lester asked.

"No. Cast off."

"Cast off? But our investment!" Daniel glared at him until Lester hurried about his business. Just as they had loosened the lines and were beginning to leave the lagoon, the fat man appeared in the doorway.

"Hey, horse trader! Want to sample my wares?" He held up the jug.

"Tie up," Daniel said.

In exasperation, Lester shouted orders to the two lads.

"What are you about?"

"That little antic just cost the son of a whore three hundred."

Daniel took his five hundred in bargaining money from his pocket, and handed it to Lester. "Hold this."

He hopped to the dock, walked up the path and again entered the counting room. He sat and accepted a glass of whiskey from Kraab, and though it was smooth and well-blended, he spat it on the floor. "That's the best you can peddle? The farmers should keep it as corn."

The fat man tried not to seem disturbed. He extended his hands. "I'm going to do you a favor. Sixty-eight hundred, take it all."

"Do me a real favor," Daniel spat the bad taste out of his mouth. "Don't waste my time. Sims said six thousand and that's what I brought, no more, no less. That's ten dollars a barrel and I take all the risks."

"That liquor would fetch twenty-two at Montreal."

"Good. You get it there. You want the six or you want the liquor? I don't exactly see sloops lining up." Again he tossed the satchel on the rough plank table. The fat man licked his lips, poured another drink and swallowed it.

"Six thousand it is," he slapped his fat palm on the table, "but you leave me fifty barrels."

"I leave you ten." Daniel stood and walked through the door. He turned outside. "Count the money. We'll be loaded and gone before sunrise."

Back at the ship, Daniel ordered the lads and Lester to begin loading. Oil lamps were lit, hatches opened, and all night long they sweated, stacking the barrels in the hold. "Smell each one," Daniel cautioned. "I'm not paying for Cuyahoga water."

By sunrise, they had loaded five hundred and ninety barrels. The six hundred barrel cargo had been two barrels short. Kraab had appropriated two for himself. He was now sleeping on a heap of gunnysacks in the corner of his counting house so Hedges did not disturb him. Because the farmers who preferred to ship a few barrels of liquor rather than wagonloads of corn wanted to avoid paying a whiskey tax, no bill of lading was supplied. As the sun rose above the treetops, Hedges cast off, and slowly made his way through the narrow channel to the lake.

"Will we run straight across?" Lester asked.

"Not today. The lads are tired and I'd prefer to set out at dark. I know a cove to the east. We'll anchor there and take on some drinking water."

They sailed around an island to a hidden cove with a sandy beach and a clear brook and ferns beneath the tall pine. A boulder at the waterline offered them mooring. Daniel, Lester and the lads stripped off their clothes and plunged into the water to wash away the night's sweat. One of the lads cooked salt pork and beans and with a dram of whiskey and some biscuit they had breakfast. The youngest lad, Jim, who'd worked the least was sent aloft for the first watch, and the rest strung their hammocks between the masts and the railing. Soon Lester was snoring.

Daniel folded his hands on his chest and gazed up into the

rigging. The boat rocked gently like a cradle. He thought of Eleanora. He had tried to forget her many times, but her image came to him again and again. Perhaps when he was in Albany next, he'd visit her. He tried to imagine her on the ship, her hair in the wind, but he couldn't. Their worlds were too different. But thinking of her was still pleasant.

He was awakened by the lad Jim whispering excitedly: "A cruiser, sir."

Hedges sprang up the rigging with his telescope. Half a mile off shore he spied a two-masted schooner tacking back and forth aimlessly. He looked for her colors, but the schooner was flying none. Very odd. "This is more than coincidence," he muttered, and he told Jim to get some sleep. Hedges stood watch and when he was high in the crow's nest, he observed the ship pass back and forth, back and forth. He felt safer at sunset when it stopped patrolling and sailed north.

A gentle September night came on. The moon wouldn't rise until daybreak. They blew out all lamps, cast off, then out on the lake they hung every square inch of sail. With a stiff westerly, they began the wide tacking that would take them to Canada. All night and all the next day Hedges manned the wheel, and the lad in the crow's nest warily scanned the horizon for any sign of a sail. None appeared. Near evening, the lad shouted, "Land off the starboard bow."

Hedges sighed with relief, his fortune was secure. But his relief was short-lived, because soon the boy announced, "Ship off the port bow, approaching fast."

"What are her colors?"

The lad squinted through the glass and said nothing. The sun was sliding down the western sky, back-lighting the ship.

"A two-masted schooner?" Daniel called up. "Aye, sir, but I can't see no colors."

Hedges ripped out his own telescope and looked across the waves. "It's the schooner I saw yesterday." This set them all buzzing.

"Will we outrun her, Danny?" Lester asked anxiously.

"We'll try, loaded down as we are." He fired off orders to his crew.

"Approaching quickly on the port side!" called the boy. Hedges looked anxiously for land through his glass. It was too far to run. He looked to the west praying for a heaven sent bank of fog to roll in, but the night was clear.

"They have no right to stop us!" Lester cried.

"And we have no right to be smuggling liquor," Daniel said quietly.

"They can't catch us!"

Hedges looked grimly ahead.

Soon the schooner was within shouting distance. "Ahoy there!" a large bearded man called through a megaphone. "Slack your sail. I'm coming aboard."

"Who are you?" Daniel demanded.

"His Majesty's customs."

Hedges swallowed hard. It all flashed before him, the end. Arrested, tried, imprisoned, his family destitute – but there was nothing he could do nothing but obey. He gave orders to slacken sail.

"I've got two hunnerd dollars invested!" Lester cried. "Do something, Danny!"

"Let's hear him out. Throw down a ladder and a line."

The schooner pulled alongside and waves rocked the two boats together, then away, together, then away as the red sunset was reflected double in the water. The Canadian fastened a line, then clambered up the ladder.

"Customs," he announced gaining the deck. "I need your bills of lading, a view of your cargo and your log."

"We're hauling potash. We've come from Erie and are bound for Port Colborne."

"I need to see your bills, your log and the cargo."

Hedges whistled and one of the lads swung down from the rigging. "Take this man to the hold. I'll get the paperwork."

The lad escorted the man, and Daniel looked to the schooner and saw three raffish, barefoot sailors on deck. That was unusual for a British customs ship.

"What do we do?" Lester groaned.

"See what happens. They look more like pirates than customs agents to me."

"But my two hunnerd dollars!"

"Quiet. Here he comes."

"Mr. Hedges," the Canadian said, but the boy aloft interrupted him with a cry of – "Sail off the port bow, closing quick." All faces turned eastward where the ship was lit by the dying sun.

"Her colors?"

"United States."

"Mr. Hedges, you are transporting liquor into Canada. I demand to see your bills of lading or I will immediately impound your ship and cargo."

"Of course," Daniel nodded, "but I need to see your commission first."

The man got angry. "Those documents will be in my hands inside of two minutes or you'll be in the brig aboard my ship."

"All right. Lester, help me."

They went down into Daniel's cabin and Lester was wailing, "My two hunnerd dollars."

"Quiet!" Daniel whispered. "The American ship is probably Wiley looking for us. We have to stall until he arrives."

"But if that Canadian feller don't impound us, Wiley will."

"Stall him," Daniel ordered. He thrust a pistol into Lester's hand. "Hide this in the companionway."

"Ahoy, there!" was called from the American ship, "Name yourself!"

"The *Silver Pearl* of Buffaloe Creek," Jim from the crow's nest called. Daniel rummaged through his desk and collected all the papers he could find. Arming himself with the other pistol, he put on his coat to hide it, then carried the papers up to the deck.

"Ah," the Canadian reached for the papers, but just as he touched them, Daniel dropped them to the deck and they scattered in the wind. The Canadian looked alarmed, then raised his eyes to behold Daniel's pistol pointed at his heart.

"You're not a customs officer, friend. You and the boys look like pirates to me. So we'll just wait a few minutes together."

"Amos!" the Canadian called to his crew and there was suddenly the sound of men clambering up the rope ladder boarding the *Silver Pearl*.

"Lester!" Daniel cried, but the first mate was brandishing a belaying pin club at the top of the rope ladder. A shot was fired from the schooner's deck, and the boy in the crow's nest cried and fell forty-five feet to the deck. The Canadian grappled with Daniel, trying to wrest away the pistol. As the pistol fired into the sails, Daniel kneed the man in the groin, punched him squarely in the face and sent him reeling backward. With his one pistol shot spent, Daniel grabbed for a belaying pin, as the man hit the mast, shook his head, then lumbered forward.

"We're coming aboard!" the American officer cried.

Lester was busy keeping the Canadian pirates from climbing over the railing. The other lad threw a ladder over the port side as Daniel wrestled again with the big Canadian. A third gunshot sounded and all eyes turned toward a man in uniform, Wiley, standing at the rail. This distracted the Canadian and Daniel dealt him a blow to the side of the head that sent him sprawling to the deck.

"In the name of the United States government, cease and desist!"

"Yes, sir," Daniel said.

Lester had sent one of the sailors into the lake and two

others back to the ship. "They're casting off," he cried. Wiley approached.

"We heard shots, Captain Hedges. What is going on here?"

"They're getting away!" Lester cried, pointing toward the west where the horizon was aglow with dying light.

Daniel paused, then nodded. "This fellow here says he's a British customs officer, but he is a pirate. His ship is escaping, leaving him behind."

"Can I trust you to put him in irons and produce him at Buffaloe Creek?"

"Yes, sir."

Wiley turned, vaulted the railing and ordered his craft to chase the escaping pirate ship. Bleeding and sore, Hedges went to the boy who lay lifeless on the deck.

"My God!" the other lad cried, cradling the lifeless head. "Jimmy! Jimmy!" Hedges looked down, and by the angle of the boy's neck he knew that if the shot hadn't killed him the fall had. He turned and walked to Lester.

"What the hell just happened?" Lester asked with terrified eyes.

"Don't know, mate. Help me haul that blackguard below."

Together they went over and dragged the Canadian moaning down the companionway and tied him to the mainmast 'tween decks.

"What now?" Lester asked.

"Your two hundred dollars."

"Don't joke, Danny. What now?"

"We'll look to the boy, then deliver our cargo."

The boy was dead. They brought him to Daniel's cabin and lay him in the bunk, then Daniel took a reading to see how far off course they had drifted. He consulted his charts, then set a new course to Port Colborne.

They delivered the corn liquor to the McFarland warehouse in Port Colborne late that night, and received seventeen and a quarter dollars per barrel. A stiff westerly wind allowed the *Silver Pearl* to clear the sand bar at Buffaloe Creek two days after the lad had died. His body was beginning to putrify, so Daniel and Lester and the other lad immediately carried him to the barber who also served as the village doctor and undertaker, and they notified Jim's mother. As she was a widow, her son her sole support, Daniel gave her five hundred dollars of his profit. Returning to the brig, they untied the Canadian pirate, who staunchly refused to identify himself, and they delivered him to the sheriff.

Daniel reserved a thousand dollars for his backers to give them the promised fifty percent return, and he computed Lester's share to be eighty-three dollars, twenty cents, plus his original two hundred. Because of his heroics, though, Daniel gave him an extra hundred. He gave the other lad a hundred, and he kept almost nineteen hundred clear profit. Added to his investment, this gave him sixty-two hundred dollars, and he considered himself damned lucky not to be in shackles facing a long prison sentence.

The story unfolded in Cook's Tavern four days later. Daniel and Lester had not told a soul, but when the customs pilot boat returned, they were celebrated heroes. The schooner belonged not to British customs, but to the pirate Jack Layland. During the embargo, Layland preyed on American smugglers who, if they survived Layland's men, would not be likely to report the theft. Layland hadn't ventured out since the embargo ended in July, and when he finally went out in early September, Daniel Hedges and Lester Frye had captured him. Happening on the scene, the American customs packet gave chase. A gun battle ensued and Customs Agent Wiley was slain. The three surviving inspectors subdued the pirate crew, and brought them before the federal circuit judge in Buffaloe Creek to be tried with Layland on charges of piracy and murdering a customs officer. In all the excitement, no one thought to ask what the *Silver Pearl* had been shipping.

Characteristically Hedges shied from any publicity. He credited his ship's hand who perished, Jimmy Dougal, as the true hero of the incident. Lester, though, reveled in his newfound importance, and the tale improved each time he told it in the taproom of Cook's.

"Danny, Danny, I can't buy a dram no more," Lester bragged when Daniel met him a week later. "The folks love me."

"Ain't good to get your head up too high, mate. That's when it gets shot off."

"Ah, loosen up, Danny. We're heroes."

"Yeah, Lester, sure we are. We could have been true heroes in federal prison. Those barrels weren't stamped."

"What's happened to you, Danny? You ain't been the same since you went to Albany with Ellicott. What difference does it make? It come out our way. Remember the good old days of the embargo, what we used to do? This was nothing compared."

"You're right, Lester. Let's have a drink. You can buy today."

"Sure, Danny, sure."

CHAPTER 9

*D*aniel departed in September, the day after the pirates were hanged. He was not happy about leaving. His new house was framed and roofed and he wanted to finish it before heavy snows flew. True, it would be good to complete the survey, fulfill his duty to the commission and get paid, but a certain dread attended the leaving. The last nights with Carrie had been lovely and tender, and he did not want to leave her. The children, so bright and lively running in the sun, needed to be protected, he felt, from some vague threat.

And yet, as he set about surveying and mapping, camping alone in the evening, he had much time to think, and he enjoyed the solitude. The survey took him three weeks, and he reached Albany as the leaves were mellowing. In those long nights alone, he had vowed to keep away from Eleanora, not for anything she had done, but because he wanted his life to remain simple. He reviewed his findings with the commissioners, and then Simeon DeWitt made a surprising request:

"Mr. Clinton is unable to be here, so he asked that you deliver your maps and observations to Mrs. Eleanora Van Rensselaer."

The old surveyor fumbled among his papers to find her

address, and Daniel allowed him to search. He took the address offered him as an instrument of fate, and dispatched a young boy with a note to Eleanora's townhouse announcing he would call that afternoon. He vowed, too, to leave Albany the next day and return to his family as quickly as possible.

Before he went to see her, though, he bathed and clipped his moustache, shaved, combed his hair, put on clean linen and had the boy brush his suit and blacken his boots. He regarded himself with approval in the mirror, and gazed into his eyes for a long moment trying to read something there.

Meanwhile, Eleanora was running Kate in circles as she tried various gowns and hairstyles to achieve some ill-defined effect. She wanted to be casual, yet she wanted to impress.

"The green gown, Kate. Bring it back. And the peach shawl. Yes, it has a certain rustic look. The kid slippers? Yes, I think they will do. Now, shall we weave flowers in my hair? No, I agree. A ribbon, yes, but green or white? Peach to match the shawl. Jewelry. The gold chain, and perhaps the emerald ring. No, too gaudy, just the chain. The pearl earrings, though, yes."

At the appointed hour, Daniel knocked and was shown into the drawing room. He watched the pendulum of the old Dutch clock swing back and forth, back and forth like an instrument of fate. After ten long minutes, the door opened and slowly he turned. Eleanora stood in the doorway in a diaphanous pale green gown with an empire waisted bodice of darker green, a peach colored shawl loosely around her white arms and shoulders and a delicate peach ribbon threaded into her hair. Her smile, the gleam in her eye made him gulp for breath.

"So nice to see you again." She swept into the room.

Hedges looked down to the yellowed roll of maps and parchments in his hand. "Mr. DeWitt asked if I'd deliver these to you for Mr. Clinton."

"Have you a moment, or must you rush off?"

"I'm not leaving until tomorrow."

"Well, then." She motioned him to an upholstered chair and she reclined on the love seat. "Mr. Clinton told me of your expedition into the wilds and the unanimous choice of the commissioners to name you chief surveyor."

"It's an honor to work with them." He held up the papers. "I hope these will be helpful." He stared at her until she dropped her eyes. "Why was I asked to bring them to you?"

"I'm to accompany Mr. Clinton and Mr. Morris to Washington.

We're seeking federal money for the project."

Daniel nodded. "Tell me, how do you get money in Washington?"

"You begin by losing all your illusions." That was flippant and it annoyed him. "They call it 'lobbying' because you must wait in lobbies for hours to talk with the congressmen. Greed and power are the only motives for going to Washington, so if you can show them what they will gain in their purse or in power, they'll give you what you want."

"Sounds simple enough."

"All the groundwork must be done on one's bill before it comes to a vote on the floor. Then, if you get a favorable vote, you go to the president and try to show him how he will benefit, and if he agrees, he will sign it and you have the money."

"He and Mr. Clinton are in the same party."

"That means nothing. President Madison sees DeWitt as a threat in 1812, so convincing him to help will be no small feat. And there are other agitators. The Tammany Society, for example. But surely you didn't come here to speak about politics. How are things in Buffaloe Creek?" Daniel described the town, his brig, his cabin and his new house, and he related a few anecdotes about the townspeople, but did not speak of Carrie or the children.

"Sometimes I envy you and the people out West. Everything seems so straightforward and simple."

"Envy?" Daniel frowned. "People in the West are working to get what you already have."

"Yes, I know." There was a weariness in her voice. "But they don't see what I see. They don't see what wealth does or how it comes to own the person who has it."

Daniel shifted uncomfortably in his chair, wondering why she was telling him this.

"Of course I didn't always feel so." She leaned her head back and looked at the ceiling. "When I was a girl, I discovered the poet Rabelais. Do you know of him?" Daniel shook his head. She grew animate. "Oh, he was a revelation to me at sixteen! His elegance, his crudeness, his flights of fancy, his genteel amusement with the world. He wrote of the Abbey of Thélème founded for men and women of elegant taste, set apart from the rest of the world to allow the poetic and the sensual to bloom, a place where greed and power and other vulgar passions were forbidden and unknown.

"For a time I dreamed the abbey existed somewhere, and fine ladies danced and were courted by elegant men. They'd walk in tapestried halls, with music always playing, and with good taste and humor they'd follow the abbey's one commandment: 'Do what you wish.' No gluttony, no lechery, no greed or lust for power."

She smiled, amused by her naiveté. "And so, even with wealth and comfort, I hated my life. I despised the provincial world about me because it could never reach the poet's ideal. Our income came not from some heavenly unnamed source, but from crude men and women, tenant farmers who sowed the fields and bred cattle. Where were the fine people? Our houses were drafty, our carriages squeaked, and we entertained ourselves with churlish songs and doggerel."

Daniel frowned and shifted again in his chair.

"And so I married to escape," she said as if admitting a frailty. "I married a man who saw more than the crude people, whose devotion to poetry elevated him, I thought, into a sublime realm. Ours was to be a communion of souls, and together we were to have what no man and woman dared to have on this continent. Platonic love."

"What's that?"

Eleanora winced. "Love without physical passion."

"And he was your husband?" Daniel asked in disbelief.

"Silly, wasn't it? Yet he lived up to our pledge."

"Why?"

"He preferred his circle of young poets who drank and visited hunting lodges together, recited poetry and dedicated their lives to art. But I found that I," she looked down wistfully, "I needed more. After Jacob died, men approached me," she nodded, "whispered in my ear, passed me notes, insisted they knew a widow's plight, but I despised how their eyes shifted, how their breath came more quickly." She sighed. "Perhaps that is the impression I gave; or perhaps they lusted after my lands. My lands," she shook her head and gave a short laugh, "but of course they are mine."

"And no doubt very valuable."

She nodded. "Yes, and undoubtedly worth the price I pay every single hour of every single day." Daniel knit his brow at her sudden bitterness. He didn't understand what she was trying to say. "But then I met DeWitt." Her expression cleared. "DeWitt replaced all that nonsense about abbeys and genteel folk with practical concerns. Instead of pining for what could not be, I looked instead to see what I could do to improve what was. And I found, much to my surprise, that I was good at it, at politics, able to find values behind the rhetoric, willing to work for things I believed in."

Eleanora stared at him for a long moment. The purpose of her revelation was unclear, and Daniel was uneasy.

"I have worked with DeWitt on establishing free schools in New York City, on advancing history and literature in New York, on getting Mr. Fulton a monopoly for steam navigation, and on chartering turnpike companies to build roads. And now the canal, a culmination of much of our effort. DeWitt is a natural leader. He uses his position and his wealth to better the lot of all. Surely he will be president someday. Since working with him, I've found new meaning in my life," her voice dropped, "and widowhood bothers me far less."

Daniel winced and shifted in his seat. "But canals and turnpikes? They hardly seem worthy of your attention."

Eleanora nodded, thought, then answered. "It does seem odd to the women friends I have, or used to have. They fill up their days with floral arrangements and dinner invitations and their evenings with drawing room music or needlepoint. Yet I see so much happening just now. You should hear DeWitt speak on this point. A new order is struggling to be born, Daniel. Commerce, manufacturing, these right now are redefining everything we once knew. Observe how Fulton's steamboat has altered travel between here and New York – thirty-six hours! Read Adam Smith. Soon trade will supplant land as the basis of our wealth. You make your living by trading goods, not in land holdings. DeWitt believes that by helping commerce to prosper, he will help build and strengthen our state and ultimately our nation." She shrugged and waved at the maps in his hand. "And so now we go to Washington."

"You say a new age is being born, yet you hold an estate as old fashioned as an English manor."

She shrugged. "Of course I see that, but how else shall I live? I have no husband. I have no other way to gain the means to live. I am reaching out for the new, yes, but I must cling to the old. Helping DeWitt gives my life a purpose. He is so remarkable. You should be happy he has seen fit to favor you."

Daniel bristled. "I hope it's mutual."

Eleanora laughed. "Yes, of course. Absolutely. Sometimes I get carried away in my admiration of him. He is pleased with your work, your commitment. Very pleased."

"And so, what now?" Daniel was visibly annoyed.

"We see how we fare in Washington. That will determine our next move."

"So I should wait to be summoned?"

"I'm afraid so." Eleanora frowned. She heard the off-note in his voice.

"Well, then," Daniel handed the papers to her, "I will wait at home.

"Daniel?" she asked softly, "would you care to stay for dinner?" He searched her expression for some ulterior motive.

"No, no thank you. I've made other plans."

Eleanora was stunned, and she retreated behind formality. "Well, thank you for delivering your report. I am sure it'll be most helpful in Washington."

"That's what matters after all," he said curtly. He walked to the door, opened it, then turned to look at her for a last time. "Good-bye."

She attempted a smile and held up her hand in a wave. He closed the door behind him. She tapped her fingers on the table beside the love seat and looked down at the green gown, as open and fragile as tender new sprouts in the spring. She heard the front door close. She had fussed over details with the cook. She had flowers picked for the table, and he had walked out. She hurled the maps and parchments to the floor, and bit her knuckles. Her eyes lurched about the room as if looking for an escape, but there was none.

"Did Mr. Hedges leave?" Kate asked as Eleanora stormed down the hallway. The look she received in answer quieted her. "Oh, mum, I'm so sorry."

"I don't need your pity! Take this ridiculous gown off me."

"Yes, mum." Kate obediently followed her upstairs, removed the dress and hung it in the closet.

"Tell Rufus to make the coach ready. We'll return to Claverack tonight."

"Yes, mum." Eleanora brusquely donned a dressing gown

from a hook in the closet, picked up a novel and lounged on the bed to spend the afternoon vicariously enjoying the passions of fictional people. It was Walter Scott, and it was about ladies and knights. What went wrong? The Abbey of Thélème! What idiocy! As if her girlish fancies mattered to this practical man! Now Walter Scott's knights and ladies fair! She hurled the book across the room.

Kate returned in a few minutes with a hangdog expression. "Mum, I'm sorry to trouble you, but Rufus found the coach's axle bent and he's working to repair it but says it won't be ready till mornin'. Would you like me to go 'round to the livery stable?" Kate picked up the novel.

"And your groom, where is he?" Eleanora asked suspiciously.

"He's tending to his chores at the general's, I'd be thinking."

"And there's not the slightest possibility you have planned a tryst for tonight?"

Kate's eyes opened in shock. She placed the book gently on the nightstand. "Oh, mum, you don't suspeck me of lyin' do ye?"

"I wouldn't be surprised by anything today!"

"Oh, mum!" Kate cried, holding her apron up to her eyes, "How can you say such horrible things?"

"Take yourself away! Go meet your groom! Do whatever it is you do with him. Just leave me alone!"

Kate set her jaw in defiance. "I'd be thinking that's not the way I'd speak to my poor girl even if a gentleman upset me as badly as he musta done. And, mum, you may do with me what you wish, for that is your right, but servants ain't dogs to kick, neither. That's what I'd be thinking were our places to be reversed somehow." Kate abruptly spun around and left, shutting the door harder than necessary, and clomping loudly down the back stairs.

Eleanora grit her teeth and tried to focus again on the

words of the novel. She read the same sentence four times. The words danced on the page. Tears of rage filled her eyes. She shook the book as if commanding the words to stand still, yet they still danced and mocked her. She slammed the book shut, stood and paced. Looking out the window, she saw the flower beds were in an autumn bloom, and the fragrance of roses wafted up. She slammed the window shut angrily and pressed her fist hard against her mouth so she wouldn't weep. She loved him, she loved him desperately and without reason. She had told him things she never told anyone else, and because of one slip of the tongue, he had left. He had left! How could he leave?

Now the tears came hot and cleansing. Eleanora leaned her forehead against the cool windowpane and sobbed uncontrollably. Her profound loneliness poured out in violent sobs. She saw her vanity and it disgusted her. He was a married man so why should she expect anything else? But oh, how she loved him! The sight of him and his tales of the West excited her. Her body had tingled this afternoon when she heard his deep mellow voice and looked into his eyes, a true man's man. She had wanted to open up her heart to him again, but she must sound incredibly vain to him. His face would not leave her mind. She bit her lip, hard. "What a mess, what a perfect mess."

She stumbled to the bed and threw herself across it, embraced her pillow and curled her knees up with the pillow pressed into her stomach.

There was no end to it. She conducted herself exactly as everyone expected, with perfect virtue. But her virtue and her wealth were no consolation for this profound emptiness! Why couldn't she be selfish just once, and just once do something forbidden, shocking, even wicked? But that would lose her this gilded cage. Eleanora rolled onto her back and looked up through her tears at the frilled canopy, buoyant with afternoon sunlight. She stared at it for a very long time.

As he left, Daniel burned with anger. The nine blocks to his rooming house flew past. Ellicott, damn him, had been right. Eleanora was playing games with him. Not only must he carry out Clinton's orders, he must feel privileged to do so. These aristocrats! He remembered Joseph's warning. Yes, he had imagined sharing her bed, and the conflict within him had keyed him up for the past three weeks. He did not want to betray Carrie, but Eleanora was so elegant, so sublimely enticing. Then she subjected him to half an hour of nonsense extolling Clinton's virtues! Though he had paid Mrs. Pratt in advance, as he hastened along the street, he decided to leave Albany immediately. A cool ride through the pine bush country west of Albany would be welcome, and perhaps a bed at a Schenectady inn. But when he reached Mrs. Pratt's, a note awaited him that Simeon DeWitt wanted him to call in the morning. Daniel nodded and his lip curled in disgust. "Now I'm completely at their beck and call."

He dined at Mulligan's Oyster House on oysters, steak and lager, and he read the newspapers the house offered. He tried not to think about Eleanora or Clinton. After dinner, he walked along the river with a cigar. He studied the lines of Fulton's steamboat. It was a grotesque craft compared to his *Silver Pearl*, with its ugly smokestacks and paddlewheel, but no doubt there'd be one on Lake Erie soon. Progress.

He passed by riverfront bars, boisterous on this Saturday night, but he had no desire to drink. He threw his cigar in the river and walked back up to his rooming house. "A young woman is waiting for ye," the serving girl told him.

"A lady?"

"No lady, sir, neither by her dress nor by her conduct. You're aware of the house rules about visitors?"

"Yes, yes, thank you."

"Said she'd wait no matter how late you were." The girl raised her eyebrows.

"Yes, thank you."

"She was crying!" the girl said accusingly. "Must be someone has wronged her."

"Thank you!"

Daniel climbed the stairs and opened his door. A plain young woman sat sobbing in his chair. "Miss, can I help you?"

"If you can't, then maybe there's no one can. You are Mr. Hedges. I'm Kate McCarthy, Miz Van Rensselaer's girl."

"Eleanora?"

Kate nodded and started to sob.

"Has something happened to her?"

"She's . . . she's not well," Kate said. "She . . . she . . . she yelled at me today and accused me of the most horrible crimes. She has never, ever yelled at me so, sir. But today, she lit into me because she had to flog someone so great is her pain." Kate turned away to wipe her tears. "To see the change in her from the time she was dressing to meet yourself till she came storming upstairs, 'twas a different woman altogether."

Daniel scowled. "Has she sent you here?"

"No! Oh, no, sir, no, no, no. If she knew I come, why, that'd be the end of me, sir." Kate gulped. "Whilst I was picking up the papers she strewed through the drawing room, why, I come across-t a note with this address, and I think to myself, I think, p'rhaps I should ask the gentleman's advice on what to do."

"I don't see how I can help."

"It's you, sir, she pines for. Oh, to see how excited she was before you came! Like a lass waiting for Kris Kringle. Then, like day and night when you departed! Oh, sir, if you'd come round to see her tonight, I know 'twould have the most pleasing effect."

Daniel frown again. "You say I should call uninvited? At this time of night?"

"Oh, yes, sir, and unannounced. Otherwise, she'd thrust you away from her out of pride. Just go to her. I heard such terrible sounds from her room just before I departed."

"And she knows nothing of this?"

"Cross my heart and hope to die she don't, sir, no." Kate crossed her heart and held her hand up.

"I make no promises," he was wary. "Your mistress is a very powerful lady."

"Yes, sir," Kate said, looking up imploringly, "but above all else she's a woman."

Hedges opened the door and led Kate down the stairs and out into the street. They walked the nine blocks in silence. Daniel's nerves raced with anticipation. Beneath the oil lamp outside the townhouse Kate took him by the sleeve. "Her room is up the stairs and to the end of the hall, overlooking the garden, sir. If there's even a sniff of disgrace, she will flee from it, but knock at her door, sir, and announce yourself. Tell her I'm away from the house and that you were concerned about her. Go, sir, go to her."

Daniel clenched his teeth and climbed the steps. He turned once to look at Kate, and she urged him on with a flick of her hand. He lifted the latch.

Three candles burned in a hallway sconce. Daniel took one as he walked quietly down the hall. The house was silent and the shadow cast by the candle caused him to squint. Down the hall, at the last door, he paused and listened. He heard nothing. Gently he knocked. No answer. The candle trembled in his hand. He pinched it out, knocked again, louder.

"Yes?" The voice was weary, despondent. Hedges swallowed, but said nothing. He lifted the latch and opened the door. The room was dark and fragrant and cool with autumn air. Dimly the white canopy of the bed materialized out of the gloom. "What is it, Kate?" Again, weary, despondent.

"Eleanora?" His voice was deep. She whirled in the bed, her white gown luminescent in the pale moonlight. She started to climb from the bed, but stopped, her hair hanging long, undone for sleep. "You've come!"

Slowly, like an apparition, she rose from the bed and approached him, her feet bare on the wide boards. Her eyes gleamed in the faint light and her lips were pale, like a child's. She stood on tiptoes, wrapped her arms about his back and neck and drew him down to her in a kiss. Gently, ever so gently she kissed him, just brushing his lips with hers, then, parting her lips, she kissed him again.

"I was concerned . . ." he began. She put her finger to his lips as if words would break the spell. She helped him remove his coat, then led him to the bed. She lay down, her dark hair spilling across the pillow in the moonlight, and she beckoned him with outstretched arms.

He removed his boots and lay next to her, gently smoothing her hair, awed by her beauty, her youth, her vulnerability here, undressed for bed in her chamber.

"It is like a dream!" she whispered and arched her back, closed her eyes and drew him to her in a kiss. The kiss was long and slow and gentle. She kissed as a girl kisses, chaste, inexperienced, but her young body quivered. "Hold me," she whispered in his ear and he encircled her with his strong arms, "Please hold me, Daniel," she said, trembling against him. She closed her eyes and swallowed as she felt a strange and powerful passion.

He thought of his wife and his children and of the forest cabin and the unfinished house, and he thought of the *Silver Pearl* under full sail in the moonlight on the heaving waves of the inland sea. "Oh, Daniel," she whispered and now she was above him, holding his face between her hands, draping her long fragrant hair over him. "I've dreamed of you, of this, this moment with you . . . but . . . but . . ." she moaned and fell on him and he caressed her. She was shaking against him and suddenly he realized she was weeping.

"Are you all right?"

"Yes, yes."

"What is it?"

"I've . . . I've never . . ."

"You. . . ?"

"But I want to!" She raised up her head and tears streamed down her face and her breasts were heaving beneath the sheer camisole.

"But you were married."

"But we never . . ."

"I'm sorry. But I am married."

"I know. I've tried to overlook that," she confessed. "Other men never seem to give it a second thought. I've heard they call it 'wenching.'"

"I'm not another man. And you're certainly not a wench."

She began to laugh.

"What's funny?"

"We are a fine couple! A virgin and a married man."

"It surprises me, too," he said, holding her. "What are we to do?"

"Just lay here together. Hold me, Daniel, please hold me."

He pulled the counterpane up, and they kissed and she put her head on his chest and they slept.

Light crept into the room and found them slumbering peacefully. Eleanora stirred first. She nuzzled into him and sighed contentedly. He awoke and looked about the elegant room, taking in the stenciled plaster, the frills of the four-poster bed, the washstand.

"Good morning," he said.

"Good morning."

"I must be away."

"Yes. And this shall be our secret."

"You've never . . ."

"That's what I was trying to tell you yesterday afternoon." She raised up her head. "I mixed it all up. I went on and on and never got to the point. I was doomed to live my life as a spinster and now I have fallen in love with a married man." She looked at him. "I wanted children. Beautiful little ones running about, climbing into my lap. Your wife is a lucky woman."

"You're young, a beautiful young woman. It's all before you! You can have your pick of the men."

"No," she whispered, "I can't."

"But why?"

"Trust me, I just can't."

"I'm sorry."

"Oh, Daniel! I shall think of you often aboard your ship in the winds and storms of the vast lake, and I will believe that perhaps when you look into the sun and mists you'll think of me."

He held her and whispered: "When the lake runs wild and free, I'll think of you," he lifted her chin and peered into her eyes, "and I'll look toward resuming my duties for Clinton as a chance to be near you."

Her face showed momentary alarm, then she smiled. "We must, though, we must keep our . . . our . . . this a secret. You are married, and I have other reasons, good reasons, unfortunately, that compel me to hide this."

"Yes."

"Therefore you must not be surprised if I don't acknowledge you, or sometimes don't acknowledge *this*, even when we're alone." She put two fingers gently to his lip.

"I understand."

"It is customary for a lover leaving his lady at dawn to sing her a song, an *aubade*."

He laughed. "My singing would not please you." He sat on the edge of the bed and held both of her hands in his, "But know that you will be in my thoughts until we meet again."

"Daniel!" She kissed him.

"I must go."

"Yes, before Kate is stirring. She must know nothing of this."

"Kate?"

"My maid."

Daniel nodded and kissed her again. Then he tiptoed from the room, turned for a last look at her and closed the door to descend the back stair. The sun was fully up as he passed through the garden, walked up the alley and proceeded down the street. He felt clean and whole and happy.

Eleanora lay back on her pillow and savored the warm delicious glow that infused her. "What a distinctive man, an unusual man," she murmured. "An absolutely wonderful man!"

BOOK II
THE BATTLE OF LAKE ERIE

CHAPTER 10

On parchment maps, as surveyed by Ellicott's brother, Washington, D.C. was a magnificent city where the streets formed the spokes of a wheel. But in 1810, it was little more than wilderness. Few streets were wider than paths and some were not yet located through the brush and woods. Besides a few public buildings of white sandstone and the twelve homes that cabinet members and other Virginians had built, the landscape was dominated by boarding houses. Clinton, Eleanora and Morris took rooms at Quinn's.

They immediately set to work lobbying. The Capitol dome existed only in an architect's drawing, and the Senate and House were connected by a wooden walkway, dark and narrow as a covered bridge. Back and forth the three passed day by day, showing the war hawks the canal's strategic use as a defense against the British, while touting its benefits to commerce and manufacturing to the doves.

Each evening they dined together and tallied up the favorable, the wavering and the unfavorable votes. If a legislator was fence-sitting and Clinton considered him ready to fall their way, he dispatched Eleanora to charm him. Her Livingston maiden name stood her well with Democratic-

117

Republicans and her Van Rensselaer married name appealed to Federalists. Her beauty, wit, logic, and feminine appeal to their "better sense" won many votes, especially from chivalric southerners who saw no better reason to divert federal money to the north than having a beautiful woman ask for it. Yet Eleanora chafed at this ploy.

"What difference should it make whether it's me or you or Mr. Morris asking? The soundness of argument, the reasons and the benefits in each case are the same."

"Ah," Clinton replied, "but the results are not."

In three weeks they secured the necessary votes, and while drafting the congressional intent, they were all invited to the executive mansion for a gathering of the New York Congressional delegation. They were greatly encouraged that President Madison seemed disposed at least to discuss the project.

The executive mansion had been extensively changed since George Clinton's swearing in as vice-president six years before. Dolley Madison had decorated the huge barn-like rooms, insistent on transforming the public building into a home following Jefferson's long bachelor stay. Staircases were completed and mantels were set over open chimneys while draperies, furniture, carpets, china, silver, crystal, chandeliers and candelabra purchased in Baltimore, New York and Philadelphia were tastefully arrayed.

The First Lady received them in the Oval Room. She sat on a settee in a gown of yellow satin and a white Parisian turban offset with colorful plumage against her dark locks.

"Delightful of you to come," she nodded to Clinton, and "So nice to meet you, my dear," to Eleanora. For Morris she had a fond handshake – Morris and Madison had become intimate friends while drafting the Constitution. A fire burned in the grate and punch and pastries were set out on tables. Clinton led Morris and Eleanora among the assembled, introducing them to New York's congressmen, as well as merchants and manufacturers who were in Washington to push their trade and tariff bills.

Eleanora wore a flimsy sheath of silver batiste with an Empire waist. With the appropriate nude-colored undergarments, her figure was subtlety and enticingly revealed as she walked. Instead of cropped hair *a la guillotine* as was high style this season, she had collected her tresses in a jeweled headband with peacock feathers.

"Eleanora? You look absolutely ravishing!" She was startled with a hand on her elbow. It was Washington Irving.

"Why, our literary lion! What a pleasant surprise. What brings you to the capital? Have you turned to satire?"

Irving grinned broadly. "Alas, I'm lured here, moth to candle flame, by self-interest." He scanned the room. "The same animating emotion that draws every other soul, except yourself, of course." He bowed. "I'm seeking an appointment."

"How wonderful! A cabinet post? Do tell me! You're to become secretary of literature!"

"Oh, no, no, my dear, nothing that would anchor me in this wilderness. A foreign ministry, an exotic port of call – Paris, Lisbon, Barcelona, London."

"Who could better represent America than her foremost man of letters?" Her eyes gleamed with mirth. Their recent success with Congress had raised her spirits, and she enjoyed ribbing the rather sad and serious author.

"I agree, but literary fame and politics are strange bedfellows."

"Optimism, Mr. Irving, optimism. And our good friend Miss Burr? How is she faring?"

"She's in Charleston with her husband and son. I see little of her, but her letters are filled with pining for her father, poor heart." Irving pointed across the room and Eleanora turned to see a smart little man with strawberry blond hair and bright blue eyes, amiably addressing a circle of ladies. "Have you met Judge Van Buren?"

"I don't think I've had the pleasure, though I believe he's some county functionary where my beloved Claverack lies."

"He and I have taken lodging together in Lynch's. Among other matters he seeks a passport for Theo's poor papa. He expects to have better luck when Mr. Monroe becomes secretary of state, as is rumored."

"Rumor certainly thrives in this place."

"And what may I convey about you? Why are you here?"

"Our canal project. DeWitt, Mr. Morris and I have been lobbying for federal money. We believe we now have the necessary votes in Congress, and we hope the president will be persuaded."

Irving nodded to the far side of the oval room where Clinton had Madison backed against the wall. Towering over the little Virginian, Clinton seemed to be energetically explaining the need and correctness of spending federal money on internal improvements.

"Ah, Mr. Clinton and the lure of the wilderness. He sought me out in New York to write an epic, prose or verse, he said it didn't matter, about some native chief swept over the Niagara cataract." Irving shook his head.

"When may we expect it?"

Irving rolled his eyes. "I prefer more, shall we say, civilized subjects. Who wants to read about natives and trappers? For his surpassing intellect, Clinton certainly displays peculiar tastes."

"He has vision, Washington. Soon the canal will open up our frontier and will alter the way we think about the West. Who knows? Indians and frontiersmen may then become popular subjects of romance."

Irving laughed. "I should like to speak with Walter Scott on that score! But as to the canal, Clinton must get past Madison, and Madison is spoiling for war. That's where he wants to spend his federal money. It is ironic and sad that Jefferson the titan avoided war with Britain, but poor little Jemmy will be the one to fight."

"Excuse me, Mr. Irving. DeWitt summons me." She bowed and smiled. "Best of luck on the appointment." She squeezed his hand farewell.

"Lovely to see you again."

As she glided across the room, Eleanora turned many heads.

"Mr. President, allow me to present Eleanora Livingston Van Rensselaer. Eleanora, President Madison."

She curtseyed with impeccable posture. The small, scholarly man had a pale complexion and nervous, shifting eyes. He wore his hair in a simple Democrat queue tied with a black ribbon, and seemed quite ill at ease in his own drawing room.

"I was just informing the president of the immense national benefits to be gained with a federal subsidy, and that the necessary votes will soon land our proposal on his desk."

"I'm sure the president would prefer discussing less weighty matters at a social gathering." Eleanora smiled. He made a grimace that seemed to thank her.

"The plan has merit," he said noncommittally. "If nothing else, it has the advantage of being wildly ambitious."

Clinton nodded confidently. "With Congressional approval I hope we can rely on the president's gracious support."

Eleanora looked directly at Madison. "I have every confidence the president will act in the best interests of the nation."

Approving of her tact and diplomacy, the president bowed, and muttered, "Thank you for saying so." With that, he fled across the room, held a hurried, whispered conference with his secretary of war, then escaped.

Dolley Madison circulated through the crowd like a mother hen, urging everyone to eat and drink. "You'd never guess she was a Quaker," Clinton said. "Often times I think she is the president and he is her advisor. Let's find Morris. There's no advantage in staying now that Jemmy's left."

Over dinner the New Yorkers discussed their campaign and agreed that other than monitor the vote, they had done all they could. "After Thursday's vote in the House, it'll be completely up to Madison. We'll know in two weeks."

"He didn't seem overly receptive," Eleanora observed. "He's got as much charisma as a coat of whitewash."

"Ah, but he's a shrewd one." Morris observed. "He reads men as critically as he reads books. Though he looks careworn and ill-at-ease, he's ruthless and tyrannical when crossed. That Tammany crowd has no doubt informed him of your ultimate personal ambition, DeWitt."

"Yes," Clinton frown, "I saw Van Buren today. Odd that an upstate judge would be at the executive mansion. Perhaps he has some connection with Tammany, though I can't imagine how or why."

"With Congress on our side," Eleanora said, "I don't see how Madison can simply ignore us."

Clinton agreed. "Furthermore, I don't believe Madison has the backbone to veto this. On our side we have both houses of Congress, with a hearty majority in the House where it counts, we have Uncle George, the people of New York, and even a precedent. Madison just signed a bill giving funds to build the Cumberland Road. He *must* sign our bill."

"Well," Eleanora said, "all we can do is wait and see." She raised her glass and they toasted to their success.

With great rhetoric and fanfare, a half-million dollar canal appropriation for fiscal 1811-1812 passed Congress and went to Madison for his signature. Clinton, Morris and Eleanora were ecstatic. Only Madison stood in their way now, and to defeat them at this juncture, he would have to veto a popular bill that was supported by both the war and the peace factions.

On the strength of his Tammany connection, Judge Martin Van Buren met with Madison. The president anxiously put questions to Van Buren about the project in New York State.

"Not more than a third of the population supports the ditch," Van Buren informed him with a ready smile. The president seemed troubled and Van Buren enjoyed augmenting his distress. "One-third actively opposes it, the Tammany Society in the forefront. They don't believe it is possible, and even if it is, the flood of new labor entering New York will starve workers out of their jobs. You may rely on Tammany's support, of course, if you veto this bill, and those votes will more than compensate for what you lose upstate."

Then Van Buren described moves Clinton had made to position himself as a candidate for the presidency. "On the other hand, sir, approval of this bill will fuel Clinton's ambitions to oppose you next year. And as much as New York would like to be rid of him, we realize we need you, Mr. President, to lead us to victory over Great Britain."

Madison nodded and stood to end the interview. "Thank you, Judge. I'll inquire about that passport for Mr. Burr. He has known enough disgrace, I should think. Both the nation and the times have changed so that his brand of political machinations will no longer be tolerated, and he'll be but a harmless old man."

Van Buren left the executive mansion quite pleased. He had taken three decisive steps to further his ambitions: he'd given Madison good cause to veto Clinton's bill; he'd strengthened his position as an ambassador for Tammany; and he'd seen firsthand how a president acted in office under pressure. He knew he could do a better job. He formulated two strategies for the future: He must get himself elected to the state senate from Columbia County so he could begin organizing there; and he must stay out of the war. Let others fight battles with muskets and cannon and sword. He would work behind the scenes to consolidate his power so when the war ended, the returning leaders would have to deal with him in re-establishing peace. Van Buren left Washington the next day, before Madison took any official action on the canal bill.

During the week they waited for Madison's action, a shred of news from the Washington gossip mills diverted Eleanora's attention from the canal. The president was moving the customs house for Lake Erie from Buffaloe Creek to the more easily fortified Black Rock because a customs officer had been murdered last summer. She heard also that a heroic ship captain named Hedges had brought the criminals to justice and they were hanged for piracy. Among the prattling, gossiping politicians, Eleanora thrilled to such an account of her man of action, and she daydreamed about him at the helm of his *Silver Pearl*. "And he never mentioned this!" she thought to herself.

While they waited for the vote, Eleanora busied herself with reading and correspondence and returning visits each day, and with long dinners each evening. She was surprised then when she entered the parlor of Quinn's after an energetic ramble through town to find Clinton sitting, staring into the fire. He offered a wan smile. She leaned against the armrest of the sofa.

"What is it, DeWitt?"

"Madison vetoed our bill."

"How could he?"

Clinton shrugged. "Said he had 'Constitutional scruples' about signing it, confusing federal and state obligations. Tenth Amendment or some such drivel."

"Oh, I'm so sorry."

Clinton set his lip stoically. "Everything is clear now. We're destined for war."

She winced. "How soon?"

"Six months. Perhaps a year. Instead of financing

improvements to strengthen our nation, Madison will rush headlong into a war to chastise the British Empire. This could very well plunge our continent into the dark ages, return us to the subservience of colonists. Our little scholar believes the world is his personal chessboard. His vainglory will reduce us to a smoking ruin." Clinton shook his head sadly. "If only men would think beyond themselves! Jefferson's embargo paralyzed us for two years, but that will seem like a bankers' holiday compared to this."

"So, what are we to do?"

Clinton fixed her with a stare showing sadness and regret. "Two things for the present. First, if the national government won't underwrite the canal, we must turn to the people of New York. We'll need to plead our case well. If New York builds and owns the canal exclusively, then New York alone will reap the benefits. Secondly, I will immediately put my name before our committee as a presidential contender. I'll offer the voters a clear choice: Peace instead of war." He opened his hands and raised his eyebrows. "In either case, let the people decide."

CHAPTER 11

*E*ach Sunday that summer, instead of attending the new church with the other villagers, Daniel took Carrie, Eli and Rachel on outings: rowing on the lake, hiking in the forest and visiting friends on the Seneca reservation. One night, as they lay in bed, Carrie remarked about a change in him, how quiet, how pensive, how joyful he had become.

"You take such pleasure in being home."

"I'm just waking up to it, is all."

"You must tell me what Albany is like. Each time you go there, you come back changed. Happier, more thoughtful."

"It's a fine enough place, far different from here. Yet I see everything through new eyes when I return. I appreciate what I've got here more keenly. What we've got here together."

"It's a good change."

"Yes, but Cook's not pleased. He's complaining I don't spend my money in his tavern anymore."

But this new happiness lasted only through the summer. One bright September morning when Daniel rowed out to the brig, Lester met him at the ladder. He was obviously shaken and had been drinking.

"They been here, Danny! They was asking all manner of questions about the *Pearl*." He licked his whiskered lip. "Then they went away." His eyes lurched around. "Just like that. They . . . went away."

"Who?"

"Federal marshals." Lester shook his head. "This can't be good."

"They want to talk with us?"

"Don't know. You seen them fellers operate before. Tight lips they got till all the evidence is collected."

"I told you not to go around bragging and to keep your head down! Did they ask at all about Sims or Kraab or the liquor?"

"No."

"Good. Best thing to do now is to go meet them."

"Us? Meet them?"

"Sure. Ask them what's on their minds. Worst thing to do is show fear. Come on." He and Lester rowed to shore, walked to the customs house in the post office and knocked. Shown into a room cluttered with maps and papers, Daniel introduced himself. "My first mate says you fellows were at the *Silver Pearl* this morning. Something I can help you with?"

One of the marshals looked to the other. "Maybe there is." They motioned Hedges and Lester to chairs. "We're handling a matter that requires the utmost secrecy." Daniel nodded that he understood. "You captured Jack Layland last summer?" Daniel nodded again, but Lester began to fidget. "We understand you know much about smuggling hereabouts, the coves and trade routes."

"Much as anyone," Hedges said. Lester continued to fidget and nervously chewed his lip.

"By this time next year we will be at war with Britain. We have come to begin preparations, and we need your help."

"We looked over your ship this morning," the other said, "and we understand you built her." Daniel nodded. "We've just bought four schooners from Mr. Ellicott, and we wish to reinforce their hulls and arm them as gunboats to patrol the lake. We have leased land for a shipyard near Black Rock, and a hundred carpenters will soon arrive overland from the Brooklyn Navy Yard. In order to avoid suspicion, it would be better if a civilian supervises the work."

Daniel smiled broadly at Lester. "We could use employment for the winter, eh, mate?"

"Yes. Why, yes, that'd be damned decent!"

After they discussed salary and other details, they shook hands and Daniel and Lester adjourned to Cook's Tavern for a tankard of ale to calm Lester's nerves.

Daniel soon got his first taste of working for the government. Ellicott pocketed a tidy profit for his sale of the boats, but the sloops were cast-offs, filled with dry rot and carpenter ants, hardly salvageable. The hulls needed to be re-ribbed and re-planked. The promised carpenters didn't arrive until November, and they spent three weeks building ramshackle sheds to live in, using for their housing all the lumber Daniel had collected. The fierce December and January snows prevented any work beyond stripping the hulls. Over the men's complaints, Daniel had them cut, haul and kiln-dry lumber for spring construction. Other needed supplies were in short supply – canvas for sails, cordage for rigging, tar, and cannon and powder and shot, as well as food for the men.

Although Daniel wore a path to the customs house, demanding, cajoling, even threatening the officials, supplies only trickled into the workers' camp. And not the least of his worries, his promised salary was never paid. By late May the hulls had been strengthened and fitted with bulwarks to repel enemy cannon-balls, but the masts lay on the ground nearby for want of rigging. Now came a new threat: Congress officially declared war June 12, 1812. Directly across the steely gray Niagara River the British threw open the gun ports of Fort Erie, and muzzles of cannon thrust out and shelled the shipyard. The guns would roar unpredictably, causing docks to splinter and sink and sheds to be blown to slivers. The ships were just beyond cannon range and Daniel had the men move the workers' camp to safety. During periods of calm and quiet he kept work progressing, but the men howled and ran for cover when a bombardment again began. After an apprentice carpenter was killed sitting in the outhouse, the carpenters deserted and began the long trek back to Brooklyn.

When the two marshals returned to inspect Hedges' progress, Daniel had local farmers working on the ships. He responded to the marshals' criticism about the slow progress with a demand for pay. They assured him the command would soon be assumed by a military man, that he would be paid and relieved of responsibility. Yet when Naval Lieutenant Jesse Elliott reached Buffaloe Creek in July, he asked that Daniel remain at work commanding the locals in building the fleet.

"We cannot continue at this site," Daniel told Elliott. "The shelling makes work impossible."

"But it is the only harbor where British cruisers can't destroy our work before it reaches the lake." Indeed, the small customs boat was the only American vessel on the lake while the British had three cruisers under sail and three more under construction.

"I know a sheltered port near the Pittsburgh Road," Hedges said.

"I am not authorized —"

"Who is?"

"You'll have to speak with the secretary of the navy."

"Can he speed up payment of my salary?"

"If he can't, no one can."

"Very well."

During the dogdays of August when malaria and lake fever prostrated many of his workers, Daniel and Lester sailed to Presque Isle, and rode rented horses toward Washington,

D.C. As they traveled along the dusty roads of Pennsylvania dressed in buckskin, they looked more like two backwoods peddlers than architects of the American navy.

Hedges had never seen the Atlantic. Though he captained a proud vessel on the fresh water sea of Lake Erie, the low sandy coastal lands were new to him. His keen eye made a quick study of the river deltas, estuaries, dunes and outcroppings of rock as he journeyed along the coast from Philadelphia. The nation's capital was a wretched enough place – clusters of rooming houses and public buildings at odd intervals among the swamps of the Potomac. Its dismal prospect was heightened by a swollen, oppressive sky, unbearable humidity and swamp fever. Though government officials usually retreated to the cooler Virginia hills in August, this year the war kept them in town.

With no letter of introduction, no commission and no recognizable name, Daniel Hedges was rebuffed by the offices of the secretaries of war and the navy. The town was crawling with ambitious soldiers and sailors anxious for commissions along with merchants and manufacturers greedy for lucrative war contracts. Daniel was just one more voice in the general clamor.

He sought an appointment in vain. About to leave in disgust, he fell into conversation with a fellow New Yorker in the sitting room of his boarding house. This gentleman, Washington Irving, of whom Hedges had never heard, had just been named *aide de camp* to New York Governor Tompkins. Daniel was pleased to learn from Irving that DeWitt Clinton was also in town and, dressed in his buckskins, he went the next morning to Clinton's boarding house. The serving girl told him to wait in the parlor.

As he entered the room, Hedges saw Eleanora Van Rensselaer sitting in a long gown reading a newspaper. She looked up momentarily, did not recognize him and returned to her reading. Hedges gazed at her white morning gown with its bright blue bodice and a blue ribbon in her hair.

"Eleanora?"

She looked up in surprise. She tilted her head and tried to place the voice. "Daniel?" She put aside the newspaper, her expression changing from surprise to joy. She stood and walked to him. "Look at you!" He took her outstretched hands. "You look like a Kentuckian! What are you doing here?"

"Trying to win the war."

She laughed, and her laughter pleased him. "I heard about your capture of the pirates. You're quite a hero."

He grinned. "Don't know about that, but I think we'd all benefit from fewer professional soldiers. They seem to enjoy their rank and their uniforms and have little stomach for fighting."

"Clinton and I are here asking for money again – this time to fortify the city. We expect the British will attack New York harbor first." She dropped her eyes, then looked up uncertainly. "The canal is forgotten with all this saber-rattling. This war is so ill-advised. It will accomplish nothing, and may do very great harm."

Daniel nodded. "How does Clinton's presidential campaign go?"

Eleanora sighed. "As well as can be expected for a peace candidate in these times. Unfortunately everyone's in a war frenzy. Clinton and I and a handful of energetic people have been forming political coalitions to wrest the federal government away from these Virginians. Half of New England wants to secede. It's weary, frustrating work. How are things with you?"

Daniel frowned. "The war hits us very hard in Buffaloe Creek. We're the first line of defense. Joseph Ellicott's warehouse is just beyond the range of British cannon. They have already destroyed his docks. I'm helping build and arm ships to win control of the lake."

"All this effort, . . ." she sighed, "just to show might makes right."

The door opened then and DeWitt Clinton entered. Eleanora went to him. "You remember Daniel Hedges."

"Of course, Mr. Hedges! How kind of you to call!" His familiarity was excessive. Clinton looked from Daniel to Eleanora, then back again.

"I trust all is well with you."

"Actually, I've come to ask for your help," Daniel said. Clinton, who acquired power by trading favors, showed concern. "I need to talk with the navy secretary about a very important matter, and he has refused to see me. Probably thinks I'm just another open palm looking for a dollar." Daniel outlined his plan to move the shipyard to Presque Isle to build larger, stronger warships.

"It has merit," Clinton said. "I am meeting with Secretary Jones this afternoon to discuss the British blockade of New York harbor. You are welcome to attend if . . ." and he looked down at Daniel's buckskins.

"Of course."

"Very well, then, meet me here at two o'clock. I have business that calls me away just now."

"Will you be needing me?" Eleanora asked.

Clinton looked from her to Daniel, then back to her. "No, not for the present."

"Very well. I will show our surveyor what there is to see in this forlorn place."

The slightest annoyance passed over Clinton's features, and he bowed and bustled from the room. Eleanora's eyes burned with mischief. "Come," she whispered, "let us make you presentable."

They walked arm-in-arm along the dirt streets in the close muggy air, visiting shops, talking animatedly, buying the necessary clothes and generally enjoying the morning despite somber discussions of war. They returned with the clothes to Daniel's lodging. Eleanora waited in the parlor while he bathed and shaved and changed, and he emerged clean and civilized. Eleanora surveyed him with a gloved hand to her mouth and a twinkle of approval in her eye.

They ordered lunch at a tavern, but were so intent on one another that they hardly tasted the food. Eleanora complained about the stalled canal effort and the hysteria of New York City under the threat of invasion. They discussed Washington Irving's appointment, his attraction to Theodosia Burr and war along the Niagara frontier. But it was not the topics or the words, it was the tone of their voices and their eyes that communicated. With a shock Eleanora realized that two o'clock had arrived and Clinton would be waiting.

She insisted on billing the meal to Clinton's account and they hustled along the street to the boarding house. Clinton was just emerging as they reached the front door. Not looking at Eleanora, he said simply, "Come along," to Hedges and Daniel fell in step without bidding farewell to her. All the way to the naval secretary's office Daniel felt Clinton talked too energetically about New York's fortifications in order to avoid discussing something else.

The meeting was half success, half disappointment. Daniel, whose strategic plan required no outlay of government funds, was given approval, and was assured the order would reach Lieutenant Elliott authorizing the shipyard move. Clinton, who was challenging the Madison Administration at the polls and whose plan required three hundred thousand dollars, was told the citizens of New York must fortify their own city as best they could. At a street corner where their ways parted, Hedges said: "I'm much obliged for your help."

Clinton brusquely said, "Happy I could be of service," then he shook hands and hurried off. Daniel stood on the corner, watching him walk away with an unsettling feeling that Clinton was jealous of him, jealous because of Eleanora!

But that was not the only unsettling thought. At the interview, William Jones, secretary of the navy, asked him if he knew Emmanuel Kraab. Daniel said he knew of him, knew he'd conducted a great deal of smuggling on the lake during Jefferson's embargo. No further questions were asked, but Daniel felt the whole affair with the pirate and his liquor smuggling might not be over.

A note arrived early the next morning from Eleanora. "The campaign summons us to Philadelphia, and so I must bid adieu this way." Daniel suspected Clinton had intentionally removed her to prevent their seeing each other. He pulled on his comfortable buckskins and set out with Lester for home.

CHAPTER 12

*E*leanora returned to Claverack in September. War was a distant rumble along the Canadian frontier two hundred miles away.

Harvest season was nearing and the weather had mellowed. During an Indian summer afternoon, she gazed out the window admiring her lands. She listened to the groom sing as he combed her black mare, Hecate. She idly paged through a book Washington Irving had sent her years before from Scotland, but her thoughts were on Daniel Hedges, pleasant thoughts as she remembered civilizing the backwoodsman in Washington. Suddenly she heard Kate.

"Oh, my lady!" Kate dashed up the stairs and burst into Eleanora's room. "He's gone and done it! He's done it, and there's no undoing it!" She threw herself on the bed, weeping inconsolably. Lady Eleanora marked her place in *The Lady of the Lake* and went to her. "Who did what, my pet?"

"Joel!" she cried. "He enlisted!" Her despair could not have been greater if he were dead. "Some of them was talking 'bout the war, mum, and Master Solomon and the general are conscriptin' reggy-mints out of the tenants, and they work up one another's pride till they're all struttin' and puffin' like cocks in the henyard, and so it gets to workin' 'round in Joel's head that he'll be left behind whilst there's glory to be won, so he visits Master Solomon's office and makes his mark on the paper, and that's it. I'm ruined!" She wailed and kicked the bed.

"When do they leave?"

"Two weeks. Two *weeks!*"

"Well, my pet, you can be excused from your duties till then.

Spend time with him. I'll get by with Allie and Lynn."

"But that's the worstest part!" she cried. "He pr'posed!" Kate buried her face in the pillow.

"Why, that's wonderful!"

"Oh, mum, it ain't sposta be this way. Ain't sposta be this way a-tall. Two weeks is all we have, then he'll be gone for heaven knows how long and I'll be a widder, truth to tell, and what could be worse than that?" She looked up at her mistress, then her mouth dropped, her eyes widened as she realized what she had said. "Oh, I'm sorry, mum! I'm so sorry."

"Yes, Kate," Eleanora said quietly, "but at least you will have those two weeks, and Joel will come back. I'm sure he will."

"Then you believe I ought to say yes?"

"Of course! We'll make arrangements. We'll get you a house – the Preston place is vacant now, and it's lovely there with gardens and walks. You and Joel may live there until the regiments march."

"Oh, mum, you're so kind!" She pressed her lips to her mistress' hand and smiled through her tears. "May I tell him?"

"Of course. Tell him today, right now. We'll have the wedding Saturday, and you'll have ten wonderful days together, all your own."

Kate began to sob, and fell into her mistress' arms. "Oh,

thank you, mum! P'rhaps some good may come out of this state of affairs!"

"Now, my pet, stop that. Up with you now and face this. Dry your eyes, freshen up, find Joel. Where is he working now?"

"Master Solomon's forge, across the river at Mount Hope."

"Send word. Don't fret about the preparations. I'll make all the arrangements. We'll have the service downstairs in my drawing room."

Kate sobbed again. "It's happening too fast! It ain't sposta happen like this."

"My pet," Eleanora helped her up from the bed, "it happens as it happens. Accept it."

In two days, the cooks prepared roasts and pastries, a tall elegant wedding cake and vegetables and garnishes and great arrangements of apples, pears, plums and grapes. Eleanora's seamstress fashioned a white wedding dress with a modest train. Eleanora supplied hard cider, wine and a cask of ale from her cellars. The minister of the Dutch Reformed Church arrived in his buggy and the tenant farmers and their wives clustered about the yard in Sunday clothes and talked in hushed whispers as they waited in the large rooms of the mansion.

"You're very beautiful today, Kate." Eleanora handed her a small box.

"Oh, mum, I'm so a'feared something will go wrong!" She opened the box and drew out a small sapphire pendant on a silver chain. "Oh, it's beautiful!" She looked up and tears welled in her eyes. "Oh, thank you, mum, thank you for everything." She kissed her mistress' hand.

Kate moved smoothly down the graceful staircase to music from a violin, bass and cello. In ill-fitting clothes the ruddy tenant farmers and their plump wives stood uneasily in the grand parlors. Abel, the gangly ancient gardener who seemed to converse only with plants, had unexpectedly offered to give Kate away, and he took her hand as she reached the bottom of the stair. He led her into the drawing room. Joel stood tall, dignified and serious in breeches and cotton stockings, his ruffled shirt tied with a black ribbon.

Eleanora watched from the back of the room in order to be inconspicuous, and she remembered her own wedding with mixed emotions. It had been a lavish affair at the Livingston's Clermont estate. Although her father's death a year before still saddened her, she knew that he would have been happy and proud. The joining of two aristocratic lines, the creation of a new estate as the Van Rensselaer Claverack property was doubled by her dowry. Hundreds of relatives and friends had attended. Jacob had been nervous, and his hand trembled as he tried to slip on the wedding band. She had been so young and foolish and happy. A tear slipped from her eye and rolled down her cheek. Today, by contrast, Kate and Joel seemed so young, so poor and frightened, yet so very happy. She prayed that even in the face of Joel's going off to war, their blind love and innocence would bless them.

Two young farmer's daughters stood in front of Eleanora, whispering comments about the wedding.

"She's so pretty."

"And he, so tall and handsome. Janey used to walk with him, till Kate spied him and flounced herself around."

"I'll be the one to catch the bouquet, Mary, and next year 'twill be Billy and me."

"No, you won't. I'll catch it."

"But you don't have a beau."

"Never you mind."

"You don't, you have no one. You'll be a dried-up old maid!" And she laughed, and as she did, she turned about and saw Lady Eleanora. She gasped and the other turned about and gasped too. There was no question as to their thoughts.

Eleanora gently lifted her skirts, turned and hurried from

the room just as the vows were being exchanged. Her face burned and she needed to be alone. She climbed the stairs and noticed the narrow staircase that led to the cupola on top of the mansion. She had a sudden impulse to go up there and she climbed to the glassed tower. Closing the trap door, she sat on the bench and looked around her. It was quiet and she was alone.

Eleanora scanned her fertile fields rolling toward the horizon in all directions, her forests and creeks, and the cattle lowing in the pastures. She held her head up proudly. She mustn't listen to the prattle of such foolish young girls. These lands prospered under her hand. Claverack gave her her living, her identity. What matter if her farmers' daughters thought of her as an old maid? The lands she now viewed were comfort, comfort indeed when the loss of them was considered. Her mother had died so young that Eleanora had always been the mistress of her family land. She had lived her life as a solitary only child, so that being orphaned and child-less seemed merely a continuation of her lone existence. She had dreamt of something more with Jacob. The comfort of her land was not that of human warmth. Now, as the music rose faintly from far below in the house, Eleanora realized that today she could not even call Kate for comfort. She folded her hands in her lap and listened to the bridal song. She must not think of the westerner. She must not think of romance. Claverack must be her comfort, and it would be, even if there was no husband to share it, nor children to inherit it. She would do nothing to jeopardize this life, even if it was infuriatingly tidy and dull.

CHAPTER 13

*P*anic swept through Buffaloe Creek in October. The British anchored two warships, the *Caledonia* and the *Detroit*, below the escarpment of Fort Erie, ready to sink any craft issuing from the Black Rock shipyard. Citizens of Buffaloe Creek and Black Rock constantly glanced north-ward, fearing an attack. Every day Daniel Hedges walked the shipyard in his leather apron, encouraging his workers not to worry. Then a daring idea struck him, and he sought out Lieutenant Elliott.

"We been moving about hangdog for weeks, as if we're already scuttled. Whyn't we come about hard-to-lee and attack?"

"Attack the British?" Elliott shook his head in disbelief.

"Sure. Attack and capture them."

"Capture them?" Elliott rose and looked at the warships through his spyglass. "Could we?"

"Only way I see to even things up." Hedges took the telescope and looked out over the lake. "Those two craft would sure be welcome in our navy."

"They'd never believe we have the sand to do it! The

mighty British!" Elliott spat. A broad smile spread across his face. "Let's do it, and catch them on the two-seater."

Before setting out, Elliott needed permission from his commander, General Smyth. The gruff old general balked.

"Soldiers and carpenters? They'll be helpless, dangerous on the water."

"But, sir, our spies tell us there are only thirty-six sailors aboard the *Detroit* holding thirty American prisoners, and only a dozen are manning the *Caledonia* with ten American prisoners."

Still the general seemed to hesitate. But the next afternoon a messenger announced that a hundred sailors sent up from New York by the war department were only a day's march away. Smyth summoned Elliott back to inform him of the reinforcements.

"Give me those sailors," Elliott promised, "and I will add two seaworthy ships to our navy."

Smyth agreed. The sailors arrived the following morning, ragged and dog-tired from the five hundred mile forced march. Elliott ordered that they be fed and rest well for battle that evening. Meanwhile, Hedges and Lester collected every weapon they could find in the villages and Elliott planned his surprise attack. The *Caledonia* carried eight six-pound guns, and Elliott assigned fifty seamen under Daniel Hedges to attempt its capture. He reserved as his own prize the bigger ship, the *Detroit*, with fourteen guns. Hedges and Lester returned after sunset with twenty pistols and an assortment of axes, cutlasses, knives and bayonets.

As Elliott instructed, the men muffled the oarlocks of the two large scows, and after eating supper and resting a few hours, they boarded the boats just after midnight and rowed silently on the placid lake. For an hour the men strained at the oars, Elliott piloting one scow, Hedges the other. Slowly the ships loomed larger until the scows were illuminated by the ships' stern lanterns. Drunken laughter drifted from open portholes. They rowed into the shadows, then the men stealthily sprang to their tasks.

Five men in each party were deployed to cut the anchor cables and the rest readied to board. Hedges secured a rope ladder to the scow, and as the small detachment began hacking through the anchor cables, he motioned to his men. Hedges quietly swung out of the boat and climbed up the ladder, his men behind him. When he reached the deck, he spied two sailors of the watch playing cards on a barrel head by the light of a lantern. Crouching in the shadows, he led a file of men toward the card game, and they watched and waited for Hedges' signal. Suddenly a shout sounded from across the water aboard the *Detroit*, and shots were exchanged – Elliott had encountered trouble. The watchmen sprang to the railing. "Now!" Hedges whispered. His men rushed forward and wrestled the two sailors to the deck, clamping hands over their mouths. Then others went forward and secured the forecastle hatch so none of the men below could emerge.

Hedges seized one of the captured watchmen by the hair, pulled back his throat and touched his keen blade to the man's skin. "Where's your captain?"

"Ashore."

Daniel pressed the knife deeper into his flesh and a slim trickle of blood appeared. "Where does he sleep?"

"Amidships, sir."

"And the first mate?"

"The same – across the companionway."

Daniel shoved the sailor toward the others to be tied up and motioned to Lester. The two descended through the hatchway. A lone whale oil lamp burned and the air smelled of greasy fried pork. A small brass plate marked one room "CAPTAIN" and the other "FIRST MATE." Daniel signaled to Lester, and they kicked in the doors. Indeed the captain was not ashore, but lay in his narrow berth with a young woman.

Hedges placed his pistol to the captain's temple and said, "In the name of the United States of America, I take possession of the *Caledonia*. Get up."

The woman shrieked and bolted up. Hedges threw her a shirt to cover herself and he manhandled the naked captain to his feet. The woman cowered with terrified eyes. "Get dressed," he told her, and he shoved a nightshirt into the captain's hand and led him into the companionway. Just then Lester emerged, roughly pushing the groggy first mate. "Take these two up on deck," Hedges said. "I'll be up presently."

Lester bustled them along the narrow passage, then up the steps and through the hatch. Shots rang out across the water aboard the *Detroit*, but Hedges' capture of the *Caledonia* was clean. Again he opened the captain's door, and the woman had quickly pulled on her dress. She was sitting on the edge of the berth, her hair disheveled and panic in her eyes.

"Who are you?"

She looked up at him defiantly. "Don't you remember me? I worked in the tavern in Chippewa. You were there with other men a year or so back." He did remember then. She was the barmaid who had served ale to the canal commissioners. Her name was Edna McKay.

"You are our prisoner," he said.

Her lip trembled and she hid her face and began to sob.

Hedges took pity on her. "Now, now. This is no business for civilians, so if you follow my instructions, I'll see you are quietly returned to Canada."

"Oh, please, sir!"

"Remain here below. The blood of my men is hot, and I'll not answer for what happens if you come on deck. Place the captain's sea chest in front of the door, and don't open it for anyone but me. When I identify myself, open the door and step smartly. You mustn't be seen by anyone or there'll be all sorts of questions. Now do not move from the cabin as we're in for some stormy weather. Stay below no matter what you hear."

She nodded. Hedges turned and left, closing the door behind him. On deck, his men were busy in the rigging, unfurling sails. But there was no wind. Suddenly a roar was heard to the right, and fire leapt from a gunport of Fort Erie. The cannonball passed over the bowsprit of the *Caledonia* and threw up a great splash of water.

"Return fire!" Hedges commanded. Four of the carronades pointed out the starboard side, and his sailors sprang to them, loaded them and touched them off with a flame from the lantern. At intervals the four carronades spoke and their shots slammed into the wooden palisade of the fort high on the cliff, splintering the logs. Still the lack of wind damned them. The sails hung limp and with the anchor cables cut, the current of the Niagara River drew the ships downstream, closer beneath the fort.

"Man the oars!" Hedges called, and those men not firing cannon or guarding the crew in the forecastle climbed down into the scow. Lester threw them a line, and the men began rowing, trying to tow the ship upstream. Again the guns of the fort flared, and this time one of the shots squarely hit the *Detroit* where Elliott's men were fighting. That ship reeled, and the current, pulling more strongly as it entered the river, drew it just beneath the fort.

"She'll run aground!" Lester cried from the rail.

"There's nothing we can do," Daniel said coolly. He paced up and down his battery of guns, urging the sweating men on. Two guns fired in unison and the balls hit the top of the battlements, severing the tips of pointed logs. Three flames sprang again from the gunports, then, three clouds of smoke rolled out and the mainmast of the *Detroit* groaned and twisted and fell in a tangle of rigging.

"Again! Fire again!" Daniel ordered, hoping they might draw the fort's guns away from the foundering ship. Sweating men loaded the cannon with powder and shot, positioned it and sparked it off. The deafening explosion rocked the ship.

"The crew is busting through!" a sailor screamed, pulling on Hedge's sleeve. Daniel walked along the deck to the forecastle hatchway where the trapdoor groaned and buckled each time a heavy object rammed it. He aimed his pistol at the door and fired. A scream issued from inside and the battering stopped. Suddenly he remembered the American prisoners below.

"Go down into the hold and free the Americans!" he hollered to Lester. As the cannon blazed above his head, Lester crept down through the ship with an oil lamp, then he descended into the fetid hold. He heard the rattle of chains, and thrusting the light into the pit that smelled of mold and excrement, he saw a pitiful sight – ten emaciated men, nearly naked, their hair and beards matted, their glazed eyes staring blankly up at the light.

"The key!" he cried. "Where's the key?"

One of the men pointed to a far corner. Lester shone the light and saw a long iron key on a ring hanging near the ceiling. He stepped down into the bilge and nearly vomited. Wading across the hold shin deep he took the key and unlocked the padlock on the chain that ran through the rings in their leg irons. He shouted for them to pull and free themselves. They did so, despondently, and Lester hauled them to their feet one by one and led them to the deck.

The eastern sky was blushing with morning, and the reds and golds of fall foliage greeted Lester as he gulped for clean air. The men in the scow strained every muscle, pulling the *Caledonia* to safety as all the fort's guns were trained on the foundering *Detroit*. Barely a hundred yards from the fort, Elliott had dropped the remaining anchor to prevent the ship from drifting any closer and the ship took a terrible battering.

"They'll be captured," Lester cried, greatly affected by what he'd just experienced in the hold.

"There's nothing we can do," Hedges said.

They watched as a red-coated British officer ascended the ramparts of the fort, cupped his hands and called: "Surrender, or we'll sink you where you sit!"

Elliott mounted the rail, but they couldn't hear what he replied. Suddenly four rounds were fired from the fort's battery, and the hull reeled under the impact. The *Detroit* drifted toward the river and the raging cataract beyond.

"They're gone!" Lester groaned.

"Yes, but we're not. We're out of range, so there's no use firing. Take these men and relieve them at the oars." Daniel watched as the *Detroit* foundered helplessly closer to shore. But soon Elliott found a cross-current, and the *Detroit* entered shallow rapids, gained speed and then grounded on Squaw Island, tipping over precariously. As the sun rose and the oarsmen towed the *Caledonia* past the point of Black Rock, Elliott lowered his boats, abandoned the battered hulk and ferried his British prisoners and the freed Americans to safety.

"They attacked us as soon as we boarded," Elliott explained as he and Daniel stood together on the dock later that morning. "We were fighting, and no one watched where we drifted. The ship's done, but there's plenty of guns and fittings and shot and powder to salvage if we can get in under those guns."

Elliott ordered the sailors to get some sleep. Then he, Hedges, Lester Frye and a contingent of soldiers rowed out to the hulk. Harassed by British fire, they salvaged what they could, then spread pitch over the *Detroit* and set it afire.

Back at Black Rock, Daniel boarded the *Caledonia*. It contained a cargo of furs worth more than a hundred and fifty thousand dollars. Hedges had no claim to the plunder because he was not a registered privateer. He notified the customs official of the cargo, then boarded the ship and went to the captain's cabin. When he announced himself, the woman opened the door. Daniel transferred her to his *Silver Pearl* before she was discovered and numbered among the British prisoners and sent to a prisoner-of-war camp. In Buffaloe Creek he made arrangements for her passage over to Chippewa.

"I thank you, sir. May God bless you for the risk you took. If ever I may return the favor . . ." They stood together on the dock.

"Just keep it quiet." Daniel held her hand as she stepped into the packet boat. Then Hedges turned toward the village, his night's ordeal over.

As he opened the door to his new home, Eli and Rachel cried, "Papa!" and ran to hug him. Laughing, he lifted them high and hugged and kissed them. "Where's your mother?"

"Upstairs in the loft," Rachel said sadly.

"Now, what's the matter with you two?" He jostled them and they both tried to laugh, but Rachel asked to be put down. "Rachel, what is wrong?"

"Mama's crying."

"Oh," he said with a nod. "Well, we can't have Mama crying, can we? Wait just outside the door and when I need your help, I'll call. Then come running upstairs just as fast as you can."

He deposited them on the floor and ascended the steep ladder stairs to the loft where the children usually slept. Carrie was in one of the narrow beds staring despondently at the rafters.

"Is something wrong?"

"No."

"Tell me. The children are upset. They said you were crying."

"Why didn't you tell me?" she blurted. Then she rolled away from him, hugged the pillow and sobbed. "Why did I have to find out through others?"

Daniel said nothing. He suspected this had something to do with Lady Eleanora, and he was shamed. "What is it?"

"I don't care if you go to Albany for the entire summer. I don't care if you sail from here to Sandusky every week. I don't care if you survey for a canal or get into politics, or hobnob with the fine rich folks, only you didn't tell me!"

"I'm sorry." His words sounded weak and hollow.

"I was so worried."

"Why would you worry? I love you, Carrie. I have always loved you! I always will."

"I never doubted that." She lifted her head. "It's just that you should have told me you were going."

"Going?"

"Yes, on that foolish mission to capture the British ships. I was so worried."

Daniel smiled broadly. "It wasn't foolish! We captured one, destroyed another, freed American and took forty prisoners and a rich cargo of furs."

"But you might have been killed!"

"I'm too smart for that," Daniel said with bravado.

"Or taken prisoner to some camp in the forest and we wouldn't see you for ten years."

"But that didn't happen."

She looked up at him, her eyes brimming with tears. "Not this time." Her eyes this morning were large and imploring. Daniel could not remember seeing them more luminous, more beautiful. He sat on the narrow bed and held her.

"Oh, Danny! Oh, Danny!" she whispered in his ear. "I was so worried! When they told me where you'd gone, I was frantic. I can't imagine life without you. Please, please don't do anything like that again."

He pulled away. "But I must help the cause!"

"Why?" She was indignant. "What have they ever done for you? For us? You used to smuggle under their very noses. You mocked them. You traded with the same British you're now fighting and you never cared before. The government doesn't understand how we live out here, what we face all the time. They'll use you as far as they can, then discard you. You yourself said that."

"I did." He looked away, considering. "But now things are different. Times are changing. Our future, the future for Rachel and Eli depends on winning this war. If we lose, we lose our home, everything."

"But there are soldiers and sailors to fight!"

"Yes, but they don't know the lake as I do. They're strangers and they'll retreat when it suits them. This is our home. I must defend it. I can't just pretend things are not the way they are. We must beat the British or the British will beat us, and if they do, we'll have nothing. We'll be just like the Seneca, cleared from our land, wanderers."

"But if the British win, you'll be punished. Executed. And where will that leave us?"

"They'll never catch me. You, you're the only one who ever caught me." And he held her. "You're all I have in this world, Carrie, and . . ." he tilted up her chin and looked deeply into her eyes, "and all I truly want."

"Oh, Danny," she said, hugging him fiercely. "I'm so glad you're safe."

"Watch this!" he said mysteriously, and he tiptoed to the doorway, and called, "Eli, Rachel, come help me!"

Clambering feet sounded on the ladder stairs and the two children burst into the room. They paused, looking back and forth with alarm. "Come on!" Daniel called playfully. With a squeal of delight they dashed across the room and bounced into the bed, burying their faces in the bedclothes.

"Don't ever go away again, Papa!" Rachel demanded.

"All right, Miss Silliness! It's time for the tickling fingers!"

"No, Papa! No!" she squealed, and as Daniel's rough hands began to tickle her, she wriggled and laughed and struggled to get free: "Help me, Mama! Help!"

∾

For a second time, Daniel Hedges was known as a hero to the people of Buffaloe Creek, and for the second time he shunned the attention. But the American flush of pride over the capture of the ships was short-lived.

Commander of all the New York frontier militia, Major-General Stephen Van Rensselaer saw a surge of recruits swell his ranks to six thousand strong. He, too, believed a surprise attack would gain America a needed foothold in Canada. Stationed below Niagara Falls, he planned to cross the Niagara River and attack the British emplacement on Queenstown Heights. The morning of the attack, October 13, his cousin, Colonel Solomon Van Rensselaer ordered three hundred men to cross the river and scale the escarpment. In hand-to-hand combat, they drove the British flank back into the fort. General Van Rensselaer then ordered all of his troops to cross the river. Seven hundred followed in the first wave, but the remaining troops refused.

"Blast it all!" he fumed, "What is the matter with them?" The adjutant gave the order again and again there was no response.

"Sir," a captain cried, running up to the general, "the men say that being state militia, they can't invade a foreign country. They'll only defend their own state."

Van Rensselaer gave the order again, but in vain. Seeing such hesitation, the British opened their fort, charged down on the stranded American troops and captured nearly a thousand men. In disgust, General Van Rensselaer resigned his commission and returned to his estate on the Hudson along the same route he and Morris had traveled in happier days. The British bustled the prisoners off to a camp in the Canadian wilds to winter in bark huts, waiting to be ransomed. Among the men that the British marched into the snowbound forests was the Good Patroon's coachman, Kate's husband, Joel Kipp.

Meanwhile, votes of the Electoral College were cast November 21. Results came to Washington in saddlebags over rutted roads and river ferries. The results were officially announced December 12: Clinton, 89 votes; Madison, 128.

"So the nation prefers war," Clinton mused to Eleanora. "Our quest to fortify the country with internal improvements and to avert the disaster of war with Britain has failed. Yet we must not give up. We must work now to see that New York repels the British invasion which Madison's vainglory will surely bring upon us. Thank Providence that Britain is preoccupied with Napoleon just now. I shudder to think how we would oppose the full might of its wrath."

Granted a passport soon after Van Buren met with President Madison, Aaron Burr left Paris for America, but his ship was captured by the British and he was detained nine months for questioning about the massing American forces and about the new nation's politics. Burr reached Boston in May, 1812, and disembarked wearing a disguise. In a hired coach, he traveled the post road to New York City and immediately wrote to Theodosia.

Although Theo rejoiced that her father was again on American soil, a fever prevented her departure for New York. When the autumn months brought cooler weather, she recuperated and took the *Patriot* out of Charleston harbor and disembarked December 12. But the ship never reached New York. Aaron Burr, Washington Irving and a dozen friends scanned the gray waters from the Battery in vain. They anxiously awaited news of her arrival, but Christmas came and went, the bright decorations in the City Hotel mocking Burr's fear that his daughter was lost. Burr's old Tammany crowd threw a New Year's party to acquaint friends with his return and help stimulate his law business. Burr hid his distress under excessive charm, but at night he grieved that cruel fate, which had punished him so severely for the duel with Hamilton, had taken away the only person he cherished in the world. He read and reread a letter he had carried next to his breast since receiving it one foul autumn day in Paris:

"You appear to me so superior, so elevated above other men; I contemplate you with such a strange mixture of humility, admiration, reverence, love and pride, that very little superstition would be necessary to make me worship you as a god, and I had not rather live than not be the daughter of such a man."

Did she still live? Fatherly worry dogged him in those midnight hours. Would he ever see her again, she who single-handedly kept him alive in exile? By mid-January the New York owners of the *Patriot* petitioned their underwriters for recovery; the ship was lost at sea. Rumor abounded: It had been captured and scuttled by the British; it had been seized by pirates, its passengers forced to walk the plank; it had foundered and beached on the Carolina coast and was then plundered by looters who murdered all survivors. Aaron Burr went about his daily litigating, walking the streets of Manhattan, and sardonically reflecting that this land was now as lonely and unfamiliar to him as any capital of Europe.

In the months that passed, Burr cast about for a protégé, a young man or woman whom he might guide and thus ease the pain of losing his dear Theodosia. Speaking with Washington Irving, Burr was reminded that a young judge from upstate, exactly Theo's age, had met with her and had given her a donation for his living expenses in Paris. Burr made inquiries among Tammany people and discovered that Judge Martin Van Buren had risen from obscurity as the son of Kinderhook innkeepers. He now manifested surprising political skills and had helped in securing Burr's passport with the Madison Administration. "I should like to meet this young man," Burr told O'Hanlon. "If I can no longer lead our Tammany efforts, perhaps I may guide those who help you."

Life must go on, fraught as it is with sorrow, Burr mused in those dark hours. This lad showed promise and perhaps he might impart to him some of the more delicate lessons of power and persuasion. Burr didn't tell O'Hanlon or Irving, but he dimly remembered an inn in the Village of Kinderhook, Columbia County, where he usually stopped when riding with the circuit court. There had been numerous indiscretions with tavern wenches, and though he generally refrained from dishonoring married women, and didn't remember any specific liaison in Kinderhook, there was a chance this upstart genius could be the result of a casual tryst. Had the innkeeper's wife come to him? The lad showed a brilliance that far outstripped the abilities of his Dutch yeoman parents. Perhaps there'd be physical similarities?

CHAPTER 14

$\mathcal{T}$he fledgling United States Navy offered Daniel Hedges the title of "sailing master," a civilian commission, because of his journey to Washington and his capture of the *Caledonia*. He accepted and despite Carrie's concerns and his children's tears, he left immediately for Presque Isle to build two warships. Since the lake trade had halted, Hedges volunteered his *Silver Pearl* as a neutral cartel ship to carry wounded soldiers and trade prisoners between the belligerent forces in the area, from Mackinaw and Fort Malden to Sandusky and Cleveland. As a result, he obtained valuable information from the men who were transported.

The hills and forests around Presque Isle bristled with rumors of British scouting parties. Residents expected a squadron of redcoats to fall on the shipyard any day or night. The work proceeded. Hundred-foot keels were laid, two of them, and the rib work was rising. The peril Daniel feared most was arson by a British spy. He insisted on personally screening each man who came to work, and he slept in a cabin between the two ship keels.

After a few sabotage episodes – stolen materials, three

suspicious fires and the disappearance of two lumberjacks as they searched for trees suitable for masts, Hedges summoned the federal marshal. Lester Frye learned from a Cleveland merchant about a British agent operating near Presque Isle. Hedges told the federal marshal, "His name is Emmanuel Kraab."

"We've been searching for him for two years," the marshal said. "One of Jack Layland's crew confessed that Kraab was conspiring with with the British."

When Hedges told Lester this, he added, "Nice people you do business with."

They planned a surprise attack. Early one evening, Hedges showed the agent how to enter Kraab's cove, and they hauled the fat man down through the mists to face the circuit court in Pittsburgh on espionage charges. Kraab's arrest and execution ended the sabotage.

A young naval officer arrived in March to command the shipbuilding. When the officer appeared, Daniel's leather apron was covered with sawdust and he was holding a hammer. The officer, accompanied by his teenage brother, was holding a blonde cocker spaniel in his arms.

"How do you like our navy?" Hedges asked.

"You have worked swiftly," the officer said curtly. Oliver Hazard Perry had requested active duty on the western frontier, and was assigned to supersede Lt. Elliott with the title of "commander." He was meticulous and unyielding in his bearing. He barely looked at Hedges. "But we'll need much more than lumber and muscle." He scanned the sand bar blocking the harbor's entrance to the lake. "There has been much concern that once built these vessels can't enter the lake. There's only five feet clearance for a ten-foot draught. How will we get the ships out?"

Hedges nodded with confidence. "The bar only keeps the British out, sir. It allows us to work in peace, something we didn't enjoy with the shelling at Black Rock. As for getting the ships out, they're shallow-drafted. We'll buoy them up unloaded, then rig and outfit them in the bay." Daniel winked. "When men say something can't be done, they're only saying they can't do it."

"As you say," Perry replied. He looked up into the sky as if he envisioned masts, rigging, sails and ensign flags fluttering above the pitch and lumber. "We'll need those vessels from Black Rock as well, and all the cannon we can find, powder, shot, cordage, canvas, galley stoves." He stared directly into Daniel's eyes. "Above all, we need men."

"The Navy Department ignores my requests."

"The Navy Department is not fighting this battle. I am," Perry snapped. He inspected the hulls and Daniel followed him. "I see no iron bolts. Why?"

"No iron to spare, sir." Hedges shrugged. "As I tell the men, slipshod work will not do, yet we want to spend no extra care for the sake of time. These ships will be needed for one battle only. If we win, they've performed their service; if not, they're good enough to be scuttled."

Perry squinted incisively. "I see you are a practical man."

Daniel frowned as the small man walked away with his dog and his brother, unable to fathom whether it was a compliment or a criticism.

The work proceeded rapidly. While Hedges supervised the men in the shipyard, Perry worked tirelessly to secure equipment that would transform the empty hulls into battleships. He traveled to Pittsburgh to hurry the workmen along the road, and to speed the shipment of canvas, cables, anchors, swords, muskets, pistols and powder. He met with an army officer and arranged for carronades and shot to be cast. A call went out through the countryside and every frontier village collected scrap iron – nails, harnesses, kettles, and horseshoes and farming implements. Hedges shipped a team of oxen to

Buffaloe Creek, and despite spring freshets that washed away bridges, he hauled two twelve-pound cannon overland to the shipyard.

The ruins of an ancient French fort and three English blockhouses were refurbished above the bay, and Perry mounted the cannon there to protect the building and the launching of his fleet. When the major construction of the hulls was completed, and only the planking, masts, spars and weaponry remained to be mounted, Hedges returned to Buffaloe Creek for more cannon. Transporting these taxed his ingenuity. Shipped up from Lake Ontario and hauled past Niagara Falls by sled and oxen, they were monstrous thirty-two pounders weighing two tons each. Hedges strengthened an old Durham salt boat, loaded the cannon with a makeshift crane, and set out, keeping the boat, water lapping over its gunwales, close to shore as his men rowed furiously.

At midnight a storm rose on a stiff dark wind, and the heavy rolling of the seas carried away their rudder and mast. The weight of the cannon had so warped the boat's bottom planks that water rushed in. Men were screaming in the rain that the boat would sink. Despite their fear that the cannon and possibly lives would be lost, Hedges wound a coil of rope about the boat, and turning it like a tourniquet with a gunner's handspike, with all the men bailing and rowing at once, he managed to keep the craft afloat. Thirty hours later they reached the shipyard.

The villagers of Presque Isle also helped. Resenting the arrogance of British cruisers, many camped at the American shipyard, laborers by day, watchmen by night. Women stitched heavy canvas and the community donated its largest building, the courthouse, to serve as a sail loft.

Toward the end of May, the hulls of two large ships were nearly finished and four smaller gunboats were begun. Commander Perry was called down to Lake Ontario to help command a ship in the siege of Fort George and Hedges sailed with him as far as Buffaloe Creek. The two had developed a mutual respect, and while Hedges would say of the young officer, "He ain't the sort you'd share a mug of ale with," he admired Perry's ability to command men, how sharply his orders were given and how quickly criticism, blame and punishment were doled out.

When Perry left to fight on Lake Ontario, Daniel cherished spending a few days with his family. Both he and Carrie knew this might be the last time they'd see each other, but neither mentioned it. They lay in each other's arms, talking in low voices, caressing as they hadn't done since courtship.

"Why does Papa have to go?" Rachel wailed.

"Hush now," Carrie said as she hugged him and kissed him good-bye.

"I'll be fine," Hedges said. He lifted his daughter up and smiled at her. "You mind your mama, and look out over the lake at night and maybe you'll see the lights we make."

"What lights, Papa?"

"We'll be dancing with the British soon, and there'll be grand red and yellow lights at the party."

"Can you come home after the party?"

"I'll come home then, and I'll stay for the rest of the winter."

Eli was sullen, standing off to the side with his toy boat under his arm. Daniel went to him and tousled his head. "You're the man of the house now. You protect your mama and your sister."

"I will, Papa."

Instead of kissing his small son, he shook his hand and then embraced him.

News reached Buffaloe Creek that morning of an American victory. Fort George had fallen the night before, and now the British withdrew their forces from Fort Erie to regroup down in Lake Ontario.

As he passed through Buffaloe Creek, Perry himself did

not talk about the battle, but his men regaled the patrons of Cook's Tavern with accounts of his bravery, how he had walked untouched through the rain of bullets and shells. Hedges joined his entourage.

Now, with the British gone from Fort Erie, Perry ordered Hedges to run the five ships out of Black Rock at night to join the fleet at Presque Isle. Only the *Caledonia* could sail under her own power. Hedges' men fixed oars to the others and, hitching a team of oxen to pull against the Niagara's current, one-by-one the ships cleared the sand bar. At daybreak, linked with cables, the five ships hugged the coastline, wary of British cruisers, and proceeded toward Pennsylvania.

They arrived in two days and joined the two new ships, Perry's flagship, the *Lawrence*, named for his mentor Captain James Lawrence, killed off Boston earlier that year, and her sister ship, the *Niagara*. By late July four additional smaller boats had been built and armed with carronades and cannon to guard the launching of the bigger ships.

From time to time British patrols hove into sight along the horizon, sailing just out of range of the guns in the fort. Each time the Brits appeared, a palpable shudder of fear ran through the navy yard, but Hedges, with a pleasantry here and a shout there, maintained discipline and kept the men working. At the end of July, the squadron was ready to sail. Perry planned to float the smaller boats of shallow draft over the bar unequipped, and he did so in two days. He anchored them just beyond the reef and his men hurriedly ferried out their guns and fixtures. Soon the seven smaller ships, bristling with guns, stood as sentinels to guard the emerging flagship and her sister.

The big ships drew eight feet of water even before they were loaded with guns, equipment and provisions. Daniel used an ingenious method to lift them over the bar where the water ran five feet deep – "cameling." First he sank long scows and attached them to either side of the *Lawrence*, then, pumping and bailing furiously the scows were raised. The extra buoyancy as the scows were emptied lifted the big ship up the needed three feet so it could scrape over the sand bar. The first day, with rowboats tugging and men pushing from behind, the *Lawrence* sat grounded on the sandbar. The next day, all eyes to the north fearing the British, the camels were again attached, the ship's hull raised and it slid unceremoniously into the lake. The villagers shouted and applauded at the proceeding. But just as Hedges was ordering his men to bring the *Niagara* into place to repeat the lifting operation, a shout went up. On the northern horizon a sail had appeared, then another behind it.

Perry gave his prearranged signal and the sentinel boats massed below the guns of the fort and fired warning shots. The British ship sailed closer. Perry sent the sentinel boats out and he instructed the drummer boy to beat a tattoo as if marshaling men to their posts. "If they attack us now, we're finished," Hedges muttered. He hammered on an iron bar to get the attention of his own men. "Leave it for the gunners to watch the Brits, lads. Come on, we've got work to do."

Again they positioned the hull near the sand bar, sank the scows, attached them, plugged the holes and pumped and bailed until the *Niagara*, too, rose up and scraped into the lake. Watching through telescopes, the British waited until the operation was complete, then inexplicably sailed away. Perry feared the entire British squadron would return in the morning. There was no time to rest. If caught unaware, the American ships could be quickly sunk before they ever sallied forth into battle. All night by the light of pitch torches, Perry and Hedges and the men ferried the cannon, equipment and barrels of water, salt pork and biscuit, coils of rigging and great bundles of sail canvas. Makeshift cranes lifted the goods and swung them aboard and down into the holds, then raised the masts where they were quickly secured with stays. Crews

strung ladders and rigging, hauled up and affixed the spars
and then unfurled the sails.

The men worked for two full days without rest. When they
were done, Perry ordered them to sling their hammocks and
get twelve hours' sleep. Except for the men in the crow's nests,
all that could be heard for those twelve hours was snoring.

But Perry allowed himself only four hours' sleep. After the
herculean effort of building his fleet in five months, only one
component was lacking – men. He had constantly petitioned
his superiors for shipbuilders and sailors. Groups of fifty, sixty,
or ninety men had been sent him from time to time so Perry
now had enough men to sail the ships, but he needed more to
fight. He dispatched a messenger to his superior asking for a
hundred and fifty men immediately.

Later that afternoon, the *Silver Pearl* arrived and Lester
rowed to the *Lawrence* in great excitement to impart news:

"We was tacking north-northeast past Isle du Plat when we
saw something red. Turned out to be three Yanks escaped
from the prison camp far to the north. Horrors they told
would make a man prefer death, I tell ya, Danny. They are
nearly starved there, and they told, too, the British provisions
are running low because the prisoners and the thousands of
natives and their squaws and families must also eat. Now
being there's no route from Detroit overland to Hamilton or
York, the Brits will need to make a run down the lake soon for
provisions."

Though he didn't show it, this news greatly pleased Perry.
A desperate enemy made mistakes. He put a few questions to
Lester, then dismissed him. Using the *Silver Pearl*, with the
neutral cartel ship flag flying, Perry and Hedges sailed to
Sandusky to seek troops from Brigadier General William
Henry Harrison. Realizing the importance of a naval victory
to support his land forces, Harrison offered Hedges seventy
Kentucky riflemen.

When Daniel conveyed the offer, Perry grew impatient.

"We want sailors, not riflemen! Doesn't he have any sailors from lake towns?"

Hedges had a suggestion. "These sharpshooters can hit a silver dollar at a hundred paces. If we put them high in the rigging, they could pick off men at two hundred yards. The Brits like to vaunt their rank, so we could instruct the riflemen to snipe only at the cocks with the plumage. Without officers, they'll break." Daniel shrugged.

Perry accepted Harrison's offer and set a date to take them aboard. He didn't want to feed them until he could use them. In addition, a hundred sailors had been sent up from Lake Ontario, and with the Kentuckians, Perry's command would swell to five hundred strong. Excitement and anticipation ran high and Perry staged wrestling matches ashore to spur their combative spirit.

On August 12, the fleet weighed anchor and moved out smartly. Colored ensigns had been distributed along with coded signal keys. Perry's flagship, the *Lawrence*, led the fleet and the green or white or red flag that Perry hoisted signaled the ships following to tack, to close in, to form the order of battle or to sail within calling distance.

At first Daniel had been given command of the *Ohio*, the smallest ship of the line. But Perry decided to leave the smallest two ships behind because he hadn't enough sailors to man them properly. He invited Hedges to join him on the quarterdeck of the *Lawrence*, to give advice on the lake's winds and currents.

The enemy was nowhere on the lake, so Perry used the buoyant August days to drill his commanders and their crews. He stood on the bridge with his cocker spaniel and his brother, giving orders to run up the signal flags. Back and forth they tacked, like a flock of great white birds in the wind on the water, forming a battle line, running before the wind, drawing up into attack formation, falling away to regroup. Aboard the ships, the commanders ceaselessly drilled the sailors and gunners. By repetition and trial and error the men soon came to know their tasks and to perform them flawlessly.

Hedges was fascinated by Perry's tactics in commanding men. He saw how Perry simplified procedures so that individual judgment was minimized, and how through repetition the men came to act without thinking. Daniel saw that his own friendly, paternal attitude aboard the *Silver Pearl* would never work on such a large operation. One moment's hesitation could ruin the entire enterprise.

Day by expectant day, the men grew impatient for battle. Hedges marveled how calm and benevolent the lake seemed. He often daydreamed of his smuggling days, and the evenings so long ago when he courted Carrie. He thought occasionally of Eleanora and imagined her regally insulated from all threat of war.

They sailed at last to Sandusky to meet with General Harrison and to take on the Kentucky riflemen. Harrison brought twenty native chiefs down to the lake to view the "big canoes," and they panicked when Perry ordered his men to fire a salute. "Tell your brothers," Harrison spoke to the chiefs, "that these canoes will make war on them if they give aid to the men in red coats."

Harrison sent the Kentucky "marines" to Perry, and the commodore drilled them for two days on clambering up rope ladders with rifles and powder horns. Twice Perry sailed his squadron to the mouth of the river to lure the British fleet out from Detroit, but the British would not accept his challenge. Anchored at Put-in-Bay, the American fleet drilled and rested and checked and re-checked that all was in order for battle.

Then early on the sunny morning of September 10, the cry of "Sail ho!" snapped the fleet awake.

"Where away?"

"North'ard," cried the lad, "from the Detroit River." Men sprang to their battle stations and the bosuns' whistles sounded.

On his quarterdeck, Perry looked into the sky and there he saw an eagle.

"What do you make of that, Hedges?"

"Fine wingspan."

"The national bird, man! It is a good omen."

All eyes were looking to the masts of the flagship for the signal flags. A blue flag followed by a white flag was run up the mizzenmast to summon all commanding officers for a hasty council of war. They all rowed over and climbed up the rope ladder. Nervous anticipation filled the cabin, but Perry seemed remarkably cool and calm.

"We will form in a line with the *Lawrence* leading."

Daniel Hedges handed out copies of the secret code describing the colors of the flags and what they signified. The men, farmers, frontiersmen, blacksmiths and cobblers, nodded and stroked their beards. "We will join with the enemy when this," Perry unrolled a blue banner with white letters, "is run up the mainmast." The flag had been sewn by the women of Presque Isle to immortalize Captain Lawrence's final words:

DON'T GIVE UP THE SHIP

Perry ordered the captains to feed their men at eleven, just before battle would be joined. "Men fight better on a full stomach, and the grog will settle their nerves." When there were no questions, Perry gave them encouragement: "Do your utmost today, gentlemen, and victory will be ours." With a handshake to each, he dismissed them.

Back at their ships the commanders weighed anchor, and with sails unfurling and fluttering in the late summer breeze, they followed the *Lawrence* on a tack around Rattlesnake Island. By eleven o'clock, the full British squadron was in view eight miles to the north. The hulls were freshly painted and their white sails were dazzling in the sun. Aloft, the Union Jack and red ensign flags snapped and fluttered.

"What is your impression?" Perry asked Hedges, lowering his spyglass.

"The wind will die within an hour."

"No. I meant the Brits."

"Strong, sir. Very strong."

Perry ordered the midday meal distributed with a fifth gill of rum. He himself took no food. He dressed in a plain blue coat to afford no target to the enemy, and he locked his cocker spaniel in a china cabinet where it yipped and barked in protest. True to Hedges' prediction, the wind fell to three knots, and slowly the two fleets drifted nearer. When he could see the enemy standing in its rigging, moving along the rails, Perry produced his signal flag.

"What say you, men?" he cried over the railing of the bridge. "Shall I hoist it?"

A resounding cheer sounded from the sailors and gunners and sharpshooters, all anxious for battle. Perry handed it to his bosun who clipped it to a line and ran it up the mainmast. It unfurled and the white letters blazed:

DON'T GIVE UP THE SHIP

Now Perry went on a final tour, inspecting the gun and chatting amiably with the men. He instructed that sand be spread on the deck to give traction when blood started to flow. He had left the bridge to Hedges, and Daniel peered through the telescope at the British squadron. His nerves tingled and his blood raced. Only the midnight raid with Elliott compared to this sensation. A bugle rang out in the British fleet, then a full brass band played, "Rule, Britannia!" Perry climbed back up on the bridge.

"Ready, Mr. Hedges?"

"Aye, sir."

The signal flag was run up the mainmast and the American ships clustered near the *Lawrence*. Once assembled, with the men roaring chanties, they bore down on the British line. The first shots from the British flagship fell short, sending up high streams of water. Yet with adjusted sights, the second volley from the long guns slammed into the *Lawrence*, tearing sailcloth and rigging. Men on the foredeck screamed in pain. The guns of the *Lawrence* spoke, and clouds of black smoke enveloped the deck, but they were not within range. Another volley exploded from the British gun ports, and men amidships screamed and fell. One was helped, his left arm mangled, to the hatchway door and Surgeon Parsons below.

"We have a light but favorable wind," Perry told Hedges, as if he couldn't hear the screams nor even his dog barking below. Hedges scrutinized the commander's face, astonished how cool and calm he remained with such chaos all around.

Now the two British ships drew near one another, and three British gunboats reinforced the *Queen Charlotte*. Jesse Elliott, who commanded the *Niagara*, was inexplicably hanging back, and the *Lawrence* took the punishment alone. Explosion after explosion rocked the *Lawrence*. As Hedges attempted to read the wind and plot a course, he could not tell which ship was firing.

The cannonballs flew relentlessly. Spars fell to the deck, the rigging tore from the masts, and sails hung in shreds. Gaping holes were opened in the planking, and the deck was engulfed in the stench of gun smoke and the screams of wounded men. Arms, legs and heads had been carried away by enemy cannonballs. Blood flowed freely, staining the deck red, running into the scuppers.

"We're losing men quickly," Perry cried above the screams and explosions. "Go to the hatchway and order the surgeon to send up any man who can walk."

Hedges leapt from the captain's bridge to the deck, and slipping on the blood and stepping over bodies in gruesome positions, he reached the hatch and threw it open. His gorge rose in a thick clot and he turned aside and vomited. Below, men with bones sticking through their flesh, horrible head wounds, legs missing and abdomens riddled by shrapnel screamed, moaned, writhed and shook in horrible pain. The smell of open bowels was stronger than the stench of gunpowder. Among them the surgeon and two men moved with a saw and hatchet, amputating limbs, setting broken bones, applying splints and administering what opium they had to ease pain.

"Dr. Parsons!" he cried above the din, "Send up any man who can walk!" Hedges wiped his mouth on his sleeve. A dozen bloody, bandaged sailors slowly climbed the ladder and Hedges pointed them to the guns where their mates had been carried off. High in the spars the Kentucky riflemen were firing, aiming at the British officers' plumage, but cannon balls carried away the rigging and spars and in twisted tangles of rope, timber and canvas, the Kentuckians fell to the deck.

"Mr. Hedges!" Daniel looked up toward Perry. "Man the helm. Our helmsman's gone."

Hedges rushed to the wheel, and grappled to bring the ship back on course. The helmsman had just been carried overboard by a cannonball. Relentlessly the punishment continued. Hedges looked over the port railing and to his surprise he saw the rest of the American fleet standing idly and safely away from the battle. The *Lawrence* had taken the severe punishment alone and was nearly disabled. The tangled rigging and sailcloth hardly caught a breeze, and gaping holes in its sides flooded the hold with lake water, drawing the ship clumsily down.

Men stumbled about the deck, fainting with fatigue, but still loading and firing by instinct the one cannon that had not been dismounted. Again the call went down to the surgeon to send up any man who could haul a line, and eight men, unable to walk, crawled out of the hatch and took the ropes handed to them. Suddenly all grew very quiet on deck. All eyes turned to watch the signal flag descending:

DON'T GIVE UP THE SHIP

"We're surrendering!" one man cried, yet others quieted him. As the flag reached the deck, Perry draped it around his body so it wouldn't be dragged through the blood, and he walked across the deck to the railing and climbed down the rope ladder into a waiting boat. The British, also thinking he was surrendering, held their fire. The boat cast away its line, and the oarsmen rowed him toward the *Niagara*, Perry standing in the bow wrapped in his blue signal flag. When the Brits saw he was merely transferring to another ship, they poured rifle fire and grapeshot on him, but Perry glided through the battle smoke untouched.

As soon as he boarded the other ship to relieve Captain Elliott of his command, the signal flag was run up the main-mast. A shout of exultation rang out through the American navy, and the *Niagara* moved up to join battle.

Try as he might, Hedges could not get the *Lawrence* to respond to its rudder. Heavy and listing, it fell away from the engagement, the stars and stripes still fluttering above. As the Lawrence drifted away, the sounds of battle far away were soon muffled by the screams of the dying men aboard, and by Perry's dog, who kept up an energetic protest. Hedges scanned the deck where the wreckage and carnage of a mere two hours lay. Then he looked out at the continuing battle. Across the calm water, Perry boldly maneuvered the *Niagara* to shoot through the British line. Both port and starboard guns blazed as he flew through, cutting the squadron in half, the fire raking the decks, Kentucky riflemen picking off officers. The move was bold and calculated to send the British into confusion. Daniel turned away from the battle in disgust. For ten months he had worked day in, day out to build these ships. They had searched and hunted, bought and begged the materials to outfit the fleet from all quarters, and enlisted men to fight. In two hours all his work was undone. Men lay everywhere crying and screaming, and the stench was sickening.

An annoying pain announced itself in his shoulder. Daniel was surprised to see blood flowing from an open shoulder wound. He'd been hit during the battle, but hadn't noticed. Since steering the disabled wreck was useless, he let her drift, and he went below for a bandage, and to help the surgeon minister to the wounded.

From the deck of the *Lawrence*, it was unclear how the battle went. But two British ships became entangled in each other's rigging and, punished by American fire, they clutched each other in a death embrace. Soon a feeble cheer went up: the British colors had been struck. Those able to see did not believe what their eyes told them: The Brits had surrendered!

All afternoon Daniel Hedges helped stitch the bodies of the dead into their hammocks along with cannonballs for weights. Twenty-two men had been killed, sixty-one wounded. They lined the hammocks of the men along the deck. Officers would be buried ashore, a privilege of rank. Late that afternoon, Perry's rowboat pulled alongside. He climbed up to the deck, read a perfunctory prayer over the corpses, and down a plank, one by one, the bodies slid, splashing to a watery grave. Perry went down to the captain's cabin and on a torn envelope he scribbled a note in pencil to William Henry Harrison:

> Dear Gen'l:
>   We have met the enemy and they are ours; two ships, two brigs, one schooner and one sloop.
>   Yours with great respect and esteem,
>   O.H. Perry.

He retrieved his yelping dog, and emerged with the cocker spaniel nuzzled in the crook of his arm.

"Return the *Lawrence* to Put-in-Bay," Perry ordered

Hedges. "Make such repairs as necessary. We shall patrol the lake now that it is ours."

And that was all. Perry, curt and military in his bearing, snappy and flushed with victory, departed from his flagship. He sailed that very night to Presque Isle to arrange parole for the British commander, and to see about his own immediate promotion.

CHAPTER 15

*H*edges refused to discuss the battle. Though townspeople dogged him for details, all he would say was, "We won." This time they whispered that his heroism had made him conceited. He heard this but he didn't care. He felt cheapened by the battle. Perry sailed away unscathed after he had used everyone and everything to win. Perry got a promotion and sailed west to fight with General Harrison at the Battle of Thames River, but everyone else was devastated. The image of the *Lawrence* haunted him: the disabled ship, crippled, listing away from the guns, limbs and corpses and groaning men strewn in gore and splintered wood, men killed, men crippled for life.

He would only discuss the battle with Carrie, and only then after she told him about his violent tossing in bed, his crying out and his retching sounds.

"What were you dreaming about?"

"The battle. It was horrible! Horrible!"

"I didn't want you to go. I was so worried. You were wounded, and you might have been killed. Then where would we be?"

"It was foolish," he admitted. "It seemed honorable, but it

was shocking to see how quickly Perry left us all behind. He used us, came here and used us, then moved on. He won the battle, and the battle was crucial, and there probably isn't another man who could have done it. But at such a price!"

"Well, I have news that may help you to forget." Carrie embraced him and leaned her head on his shoulder. "Do you remember back in August when you came to fetch the cannon, and we were together? Oh, Danny, we're going to have a baby!"

"Oh, that's wonderful! Wonderful!" Tears welled up in Daniel's eyes. "After all the destruction and death." He held her. "Ever since the battle, I've been thinking that there really ain't much a man can count on beyond his family."

Tears were flowing down her cheeks as she pulled away, and she smiled through them. "All will be well now and we'll be so happy."

"There won't be any other missions, any other causes. I promise. Just you and me, and the children."

In the next few weeks Hedges came to see that a sense of challenge and adventure had been stimulated by his first journey to Albany, and that instead of smuggling against the embargo, he had looked toward Albany and serving the common good as a worthy enterprise. Now, when the common effort proved so destructive, he saw things differently. He might have been killed with no provision for his family. So Hedges vowed to learn a lesson from the battle, that in a gamble, whether for the money in smuggling, prestige in serving the canal commissioners, heroics in daring missions, or for the love of beautiful Eleanora, it was so extraordinarily easy to lose all.

Winter swept over the lake and by December a crust of ice burned red and orange in the early sunsets. In past winters, wolves came out of the forests to forage among the settlements, but now a worse danger was ever-present as British raiding parties descended on dogsleds and snowshoes to attack the Americans.

The Brits mounted a strong offensive early in December. Attacking Fort George below Niagara Falls, they drove the Americans back. As he retreated, American General Samuel McClure burned the village of Newark and murdered Canadian women and children on the pretext of depriving the British army of lodging. This outraged the British command and McClure's massacre became a rallying cry. The Brits crossed the river and marched on Black Rock, and as they came, panic seized the Americans. No leader could muster troops. Joseph Ellicott sent three hundred settlers from Batavia, and they formed a battleline outside Black Rock, but when the British loomed out of a gray Christmas Day blizzard, the Americans broke and fled into the woods. The British streamed into Black Rock and burned the customs house, wharves, warehouses and the ships in drydock. Then for three days they hunted settlers and turned them over to bloodthirsty Iroquois who tomahawked and scalped them.

The Batavia contingent fell back to Buffaloe Creek, attempting to regroup. A stormy meeting at the courthouse was held December 28, and wild tales of the depredations of Black Rock only fanned the flames of panic. No one was thinking clearly.

"Please!" Daniel Hedges cried, rising to face the clamor. "Hear me!" He waited, staring at the more vocal in the crowd until they fell silent. "The British will be here tomorrow or the next day. Their blood is hot and they want revenge. We could stand and fight, but they'd soon overpower and kill us too. I say we organize a retreat inland to Batavia, that we collect all our food and ammunition, our women and children, and set out tonight together."

"Coward!" someone screamed.

"We must face facts!" Daniel protested. "They will burn

our homes but there is no reason for us to be in them when they do!"

"We must meet them and fight! You have fought them. You know that!" cried a young man. "Victory will be ours if only we have courage."

"No," Daniel cried, "we'll be overrun!"

"They said you was a hero!"

"Sit down!"

"Coward!"

Hedges left the meeting and walked home in the falling snow. The American army had long ago confiscated all the horses, so Daniel made up packs for himself, Carrie and the two children holding their valuables, some clothes and food. Thirty miles east, they could reach Batavia by midnight the next day. Joseph Ellicott would give them shelter and food, and his sister-in-law Marian would comfort Carrie and the children while they waited to see who would hold the shore-line of Lake Erie.

They set out at sunset. The children sensed the danger and were silent. They were dressed in their warmest furs and leggings and Daniel had made their packs as light as possible, only blankets and food. Yet after seven hours, the biting wind had Eli whimpering, and Rachel was stoic but faint.

"How's my girl?" he asked, and her little face peered up in the fur hood.

"Fine, Papa!"

"I think we should rest," Carrie said. She was nearly five months pregnant, and the trek had exhausted her.

"Can't we try for another mile or so?"

"I'm afraid not," Carrie said.

Daniel did not want to stop because they might be over-taken, but he saw how weary she was. "All right, but we must get away from the road."

For an excruciating half hour the refugees trudged on. By now little Eli was sobbing quietly, his fingers and toes frostbitten. It was midnight when Daniel spied a thick clump of pine across a snowy field a hundred yards from the road. They waded through four-foot drifts and made camp. Carrie began breaking off dead branches, but Daniel stopped her.

"No, we can't risk a fire. I'm sorry." He had Eli's leggings off and was rubbing blood back into his frostbitten toes. "Brits and Indians are everywhere."

She nodded grimly and spread a blanket on the snow. She took Rachel to her, and covered her with the bearskin robe. Daniel heard them sobbing. "It'll be all right," he said. "We'll be with Joseph and Marian tomorrow." He wrapped a bear robe about himself and his son, and he lay down and went to sleep.

He awoke to muffled voices. He pulled back the robe and peered out. It was gray dawn and a biting lake wind blew from the West. On the road was a scouting party of three English soldiers and eight Iroquois in fur tunics. Carrie heard them too, and she peered out.

"They've seen our tracks," Daniel whispered. "I should have covered them. Maybe they'll keep on."

One of the Iroquois grunted, pointed a warclub directly at them, and they all started through the snow drifts.

"I'll go and meet them. I'll bribe them and they'll go away. Don't make any noise." Daniel pulled back the robe. "It'll be all right." His legs were asleep and it took great effort for him to stand. He clenched his fist as a sign he would prevail, and flashed her a grim smile. Carrie looked weary, frightened and pale, shivering in the cold light. Rachel slept curled in her lap.

As Daniel emerged from the thicket, the Iroquois cried out, the British regulars pointed their rifles at him and were about to fire when Daniel threw up his hands and called: "Don't shoot! I'm a friend!" He waded through the deep snow toward them. The corporal ordered them to keep their rifles trained on him.

"Gentlemen," Daniel approached the group, "I'm a

tradesman of Buffaloe and only my family is with me. We're making our way toward Batavia, and have nothing but food and blankets. However," he tried to seem casual in the gaze of the soldiers and the natives in war paint, "I have a thousand dollars in gold, and you may have it in return for our freedom."

This made the corporal grin. "Yes?"

"Yes," Daniel still held his hands high in the air. "If you'll allow me to get it."

"Step closer." Daniel approached the group. Slowly they surrounded him, training their muskets on his head. "Let's see the money."

With his left hand Daniel reached cautiously into his coat, and he pulled out a pouch and handed it to the corporal. The Englishman opened it, looked inside, and nodded with approval. "You say it is only your family? How many?"

"My wife, my son and my daughter."

"Very well," the corporal smiled and nodded, and the words echoed and the voice sounded far away, "Very well, very well, very. . . well . . . very . . ." and suddenly a searing white pain filled Daniel's head, and he felt disembodied, floating. Something was tremendously funny, wonderfully ironic and funny, and the cool darkness was pleasant and he laughed as "Very well, very well, very well," echoed as if down a dark well with black water at the bottom of the hole.

"Danny?" A voice came from very far away. The cool darkness was so pleasant he did not want to wake up. Why were they trying to wake him up? He was so very tired. It was cold and dark and pleasant. His fatigue made even the act of hearing painful. "Daniel?" It was a man's voice, a familiar voice. "Danny!"

With great effort he opened his eyes and looked up into the painful light of the sun dazzling on the snow. He squinted and suddenly the pain exploded in his head. Joseph Ellicott stood above him. "Daniel!"

"Joe?" he whispered hoarsely. A tremendous thirst made his tongue thick and sluggish.

"Lie still, Dan."

"What are you doing here . . ."

"Lie still."

"Carrie? Where is Carrie?" He raised himself up on his elbow, but the pain exploded and he nearly blacked out again. He lay back down, gasping. "Where're Carrie and the children?"

Ellicott said nothing. Slowly the world pieced itself back together and Daniel looked suspiciously around. He was lying in the snow and his blood had melted and stained it all around his head. "Where's Carrie?" he cried, bolting up, feeling faint and dizzy. "The children?" And then, looking in Joseph's face, and in the pity of the others, he knew. He sat up and looked toward the road, and buried his head in his hands. "No! No! No!" he groaned. Then he looked toward the clump of fir trees. "I must go to her!"

"No, Danny."

Daniel closed his eyes and his mouth worked with agony. "No!" he whispered, "No!" he said breathlessly. Then he screamed, "No!! Nooooo!! Tell me!" He looked up at the others, his mouth trying to form words. "They didn't! They couldn't! Oh, Carrie! She's going to have a baby! Joseph, we're going to have a baby!"

"I'm sorry," Joseph said, and he helped Hedges to his feet.

By then other men of Batavia were dragging bundles wrapped in bearskin robes from the trees. Daniel rose to his feet and started toward them bellowing like a wounded animal. Joseph grabbed him and wrestled him by the shoulders. "Don't look, Danny! Don't look. You mustn't!"

"Noooo!"

"Come with me. We'll return to Batavia."

"No! We're going to have a baby! A baby!"

Hugging Joseph, Hedges stumbled through the snow

toward the roadway. He looked back toward the clump of trees, and saw two men in red uniforms face down in the snow.

At Joseph's house in Batavia, Daniel lapsed into a delirium for two weeks. A fever shook him night and day, and alternately burning and sweating, then shivering and chattering. He babbled incoherently. When the fever broke, Daniel remained convalescent for a month. Joseph's sister-in-law Marian and her girls sat at his bedside, nursing him, talking pleasantly, and avoiding the one topic he most wanted to discuss.

It wasn't until February that Joseph told him. Marching with two hundred men to defend Buffaloe Creek, they had happened on Daniel face down in the snow. Turning him over, they saw he was still breathing, but had suffered a violent blow to the head from a war club. Tracks led into the woods, and suddenly they heard Carrie scream. Rushing toward the clump of trees, they found the Englishmen and the Iroquois holding her captive. The children had been murdered – Ellicott didn't tell Daniel his daughter had been raped – and the men were raping Carrie. First they tried to use her as a hostage to buy their freedom from Joseph and his men, but one of the Iroquois lost his temper and clubbed her dead with one blow. Joseph and his men then opened fire.

Daniel heard all this in grim silence. Three days later he left Joseph's house. The thirty-mile walk to Buffaloe Creek gave him time to think. How empty and still everything was in the village, how overcast and dismal and dead. The courthouse was burned, the black skeletons of ships were frozen into the ice and the ice was littered with charred masts and spars. He knew he couldn't live in the new house without Carrie and the children, but that choice had been made for him. Only a blackened roofless shell remained. Daniel walked about the deserted streets as if in a nightmare. Every home had been burned, Clark's Hotel, Cook's Tavern, everything destroyed. The few people he encountered did not seem to recognize him, everyone was numb, disoriented and suspicious. Daniel walked to the harbor, and there he gazed for half an hour at the charred hulk of his *Silver Pearl.* Then he looked past her, out over the lake. The western sky was the color of iron and the stiff wind assaulted him. There was nothing but a blank and frigid expanse of snow. "And men have suffered like this before!" he murmured, fighting sobs.

He clenched his fists, his face twisted with agony, "Everything . . . everything is lost."

CHAPTER 16

*A*s Napoleon Bonaparte fled in defeat from the gates of Moscow, Britain now turned her full attention to the war in North America. Mayor DeWitt Clinton feared an invasion of New York. He built fortifications in Harlem and along the East River in the spring of 1814, to protect the northern reaches of the island, and he reinforced the Battery at the tip of Manhattan to protect the south. He set up bonfire signal stations on Governor's and Staten Islands to warn of an approaching fleet. He planned forts for either side of the Narrows with big guns to blow any advancing squadron into driftwood. But for this, he needed money, and undeterred he again looked to Washington.

When Clinton's invitation came, Eleanora asked Kate along instead of one of her other girls. Kate had become so despondent with the news of Joel's capture and Eleanora believed the journey would cheer her. They went to New York in Fulton's steamboat and then overland by stage coach to the capital.

The entourage arrived in mid-August as the small town sweltered in the muggy Potomac heat. Clinton had brought Edward Carr, his secretary, and the party of four took a suite of rooms at the Washington Hotel, across from the federal treasury. Their timing was bad. Reports that the British fleet was patrolling up and down the Atlantic coast caused President Madison and his cabinet considerably more concern about Washington than far-off New York City. Day by weary day, Clinton and Eleanora called on senators and representatives in the twin buildings of the Capitol, but so much confusion reigned under the threat of war that they accomplished nothing. After a week of no success, Clinton was ready to turn homeward.

"Denied funds again," he said. They were dining at Mason's Gardens. "All our efforts in Washington seem doomed. I suppose we should remain up north and rely on our own resources and let the Virginians have their sway down here. But it galls me how they're destroying the country. Jemmy Madison is riding out to inspect the troops himself tomorrow, as if some presidential derring-do will rectify all the death and injury and destruction of property he has caused. He can start a war well enough, but he certainly doesn't know how to wage it."

"And the British get closer each day." Eleanora sipped her tea. "As you know, poor Kate has come down with the fear and in her state Kate she fears she'll be taken prisoner like her husband."

Clinton smiled reassuringly. "They'll never get that close. At the last moment American soldiers will come rallying to defend their homes."

"It is rather tantalizing to wait here and see what happens."

"Yes, but after I complete my meetings tomorrow we should start for home. Hopefully this will be the last time we return home empty-handed from this God-forsaken city."

"Yes, and I must think of Kate. I need to get her home."

The next day, Eleanora conducted the packing and made arrangements for their transportation. But they arose the following morning to startling news: British troops had crossed the Potomac at Bladensburg, and were fighting hastily-summoned American forces.

"It's useless for you to go north," Clinton said to Eleanora at breakfast. She had managed to hire a coach-and-four. "Better to take the ferry to Maryland and head directly for Baltimore."

"You're not coming?"

"I'm not. There are a few services I can render here in the capital if the British reach it."

Eleanora scowled. "Services?"

"Yes. Madison and his cabinet are rushing pell-mell around the countryside. No one shows a cool head. If I can speak with the British commander, perhaps I might negotiate terms. It is in times such as these, my dear, that reputations are made."

"Well, then, I am staying with you," she said firmly. "I can find a means for Kate to be taken home."

"No, you must leave. A woman such as yourself – there's no telling what barbarity . . ."

"I can care for myself well enough."

"I'll make arrangements for your passage."

As the morning wore on, dust and smoke filled the northern sky. Toward noon, the dust clouds on the road loomed higher, presaging the invasion. Many horsemen, apparently, were riding hard toward the city. The anxious populace strained out of windows to see and hear news of the battle.

Just after noon, a hatless rider dashed through the streets. "Flee! The British have broken through our lines! They're attacking! Flee!" His sweating, frothing horse spun in the middle of the street, rearing high. Clinton grasped the bridle, then hauled the man out of the saddle.

"Why do you throw us into such a panic?" He shook the man by the collar.

The man was angry at this treatment. "The British have smashed our line! Three times we fell back and three times we regrouped. And still they came on. There's no stopping them. They'll be here by afternoon. No one opposes them now. Look!" And he waved his arm up the road and a hundred men were running toward the center of the city. The man broke Clinton's grip, vaulted onto his horse and galloped off, screaming, "Flee! Flee!"

"Eleanora," Clinton pleaded when he found her in the hotel garden. "You must leave the city at once. The British will be here by nightfall. The looting and destruction will be horrible. No one will be safe."

"I cannot," she said. "We are all packed, but the coach you hired has been gone for two hours. Someone stole it."

"Then we must get you another." Clinton called his secretary and told him to find any sort of vehicle. By now the streets were mobbed with fleeing soldiers and frightened bureaucrats. Many of the wealthier folk buried their silver and jewelry and banknotes in the boarding house yards, and a line of refugees streamed from the city toward Alexandria. President Madison himself drove back from viewing the battle through the clamoring streets to his executive mansion, and citizens hurled insults and mud clods at his coach.

Carr returned in an hour with a hay wagon and two old horses. The din of panic was loud in the streets. "Leave as soon as possible," Clinton instructed. "Dress as farmers and take the road to the navy yard."

Kate and Eleanora dressed in the most ordinary clothes Kate had packed. Carr had a hotel porter load the trunks of gowns and jewelry onto the wagon, then covered the cargo with hay. Eleanora and Carr climbed up into the seat as two men gently lifted Kate into the hay. She was very ill and was moaning softly.

"I leave under protest," Eleanora said, clasping Clinton's hand.

"The bridge by the navy yard is still up, and you may make good time. The road that way is deserted."

"And if we encounter the enemy?"

"You won't. They're marching in from the north. Make haste. When the British enter, the marines will explode the navy yard and burn the bridge so you'd better be going."

"Shall we wait for you in Baltimore?" Carr asked.

"No," Clinton handed her a packet of letters. "Leave a note that you're safe at the Eldridge Hotel. Stop there overnight if you're tired. But if the British are successful here, they'll move up the coast. Get back to New York as soon as you can, and deliver these letters to the common council. I'll follow in a few days."

Clinton motioned them onward. Carr snapped the whip and the old horses plodded east toward the Capitol and the river beyond. The road was filled with refugees fleeing westward, and they made slow progress against this human current. Past the Capitol, the throngs disappeared and Carr urged the horses into a trot. They paid their toll and crossed the rickety bridge, and then all breathed a sigh of relief for being in Maryland.

"I'll keep to the main road," Carr said, "and so avoid getting lost." The level turnpike offered speed and comfort. Kate lay quietly, prostrate with fever. They traveled all afternoon, and as the sun set they discussed whether to camp for the night or continue.

"Are you all right to keep on, Kate?"

"I'll be just as sick anywhere, mum."

"Then let us continue. We'll reach Baltimore by noon tomorrow."

As the night thickened, a red glare filled the western sky.

"Washington is burning," Eleanora said. "I hope DeWitt is all right."

"He'll be all right," Carr assured her. "When the smoke

clears, he'll stand head and shoulders above that coward Madison who fled like a doe before the advancing hunters."

They drove for two more hours, and Carr finally persuaded Eleanora to climb up into the hay with Kate. The hay was soft and fragrant, and the night moonless and starry. Eleanora had never ridden on a hay wagon. She lay back, gazing into the heavens, looked from star to star and remembered Daniel Hedges. He could chart a course by reading these stars. How often must he look up into the heavens and feel secure.

"Halt!" The command startled her awake. She felt she had been sleeping for a very long time. "Who goes there?"

"Why, say, what's that?" Edward Carr spoke in a foolish accent. Eleanora raised her head and looked down to see the blue uniform of a British marine. Behind him stood four others, and they held rifles and bayonets.

"Step down from the wagon," the marine ordered.

"Well, sure, sure thing."

"What are you hauling?" The officer's voice was soft, but menacing.

"Hay. I'm hauling hay. Goin' yonder to Nottingham with it."

"Who's with you?"

"Why, my wife and her sister, and they're both asleep up there in the wagon. It'd be such a shame to wake them as Kate's quite ill."

Two of the marines advanced, and they searched Carr, one pulling a pistol out from under his coat, the other drawing out a thick packet of letters.

"Bring a torch," the officer snapped. One of his men ran for the torch and scanning the addresses on the dispatches, he broke the seal and remarked: "Fortifying New York harbor." He turned to his men. "Spies. Search the wagon."

Three of the marines jumped up and roused Eleanora and Kate. They swept back the hay to uncover the trunks, then hauled them down, broke the locks with the butts of their rifles, and threw them open.

Eleanora watched indignantly. Kate, weak and sick, leaned on her mumbling incoherently.

"Identify yourselves."

"We're private citizens trying to return home."

"Take them," the officer ordered, and they were seized and bound and roughly heaved back up into the wagon. The soldiers pawed through the gowns and lingerie and jewelry until their officer instructed them to close the trunks and drive the wagon toward the coastal town of Benedict. One marine sat facing them as a guard and the other drove. The journey seemed endless. Kate was mumbling deliriously when the eastern sky grew light. Eleanora was despondent. It was futile to say anything or move so she sat and watched like a cornered animal. She only hoped that Kate would be all right.

The marine drove them down to Pig Point, a small bay on the Patuxent River. Another sweltering day had dawned. A crowd of three hundred prisoners stood along the muddy shoreline. A British officer at a table with a ledger and a quill took information from prisoners in a single file, after which they were led off to eight mastless ships, hulks that fleeing Americans had left to block the river.

"Oh, mum," Kate groaned, "whatever are we to do?"

"We must bear up, my pet," Eleanora said, but the weariness in her voice belied her words. She held Kate to her and urged her forward when the line moved.

Clinton believed the British would march into the capital in orderly rank and file, their officers in firm control of the troops, and would then occupy the Capitol and the executive mansion, and garrison the city until receiving further orders. Such was his grandiosity that he saw himself as an envoy, and since the president and the entire cabinet had fled, that he alone would negotiate with the occupying force on behalf of the nation. Thus, he thought he would vindicate his loss at the polls by saving the capital from "Jemmy's" botched war. But Clinton completely misjudged the situation. After a deathly quiet of four hours, the first British troops and marines poured into town, a vanguard for the main force. They moved aggressively through the streets, weapons aimed and bayonets fixed, calling out for all citizens to stay indoors.

Clinton was sitting on the veranda of Samuel Blodgett's Hotel. He had been discussing the war with some acquaintances and, seeing a British officer, he stepped into the street and tipped his hat.

"Permit me, sir. I am DeWitt Clinton, mayor of New York City and lieutenant governor of New York State."

"We're searching for the president." The soldier pushed him back with his rifle.

"President and Mrs. Madison have fled. If you'd be so kind as to take me to your commanding officer."

"Return to the hotel and you won't be shot." The soldier began to move up the street. Rebuffed in front of his acquaintances, Clinton docilely returned to his chair.

"We must wait until they take formal occupation," he explained with a shrug. "The commanders have not yet arrived." But the rebuff surprised him. He had an unsettling suspicion then that the afternoon and evening might not turn out as he'd expected.

The tide of British regulars and marines swelled. When shots were fired from Robert Sewall's house on two officers, the mansion was immediately searched, looted and torched. It burned high and violently, an example of what any resistance would bring. Soldiers broke windows along the street and yelling and cursing filled the city. The British officers attempted with some success to restrain their men with threats that looters would be shot. They tried to limit the destruction to public property, and tried to make it methodical.

As a thick, humid dusk descended, a chorus of voices in the street rang out: "The Capitol! The Capitol!" Clinton looked toward Capitol Hill and saw the wooden passageway connecting the House to the Senate was ablaze and flames licked out of the windows of each chamber, blackening the white limestone facades. The people watched in disbelief. Soon fire burst through the roofs, and the blaze spat and sparked, rolling high against swelling rain clouds, turning the lower portion of the city into an inferno.

Very shortly the navy yard was touched off by the American commander to keep ships and supplies from falling into enemy hands. Flames flew out along the spars and sails and tarred rigging and barrels of tar exploded. As if the back-lighting on a stage, it theatrically lit the sky behind the burning Capitol.

"The British commander is at the president's house," a man whispered to Clinton as they watched the fire from the porch.

"Will they make their headquarters there?"

"Don't know, sir."

"Very well," he said and rose to walk to the mansion. The burning Capitol imposed an ominous silence in the streets. As he approached the wrought iron fence, two British sentries called: "Who goes there?"

"DeWitt Clinton, an American citizen, lieutenant governor of the State of New York."

One sentry went inside. Returning, he said, "The admiral requests the pleasure of your company at table." This greatly pleased Clinton. He acquiesced to a search and then accompanied the sentry.

Admiral Cockburn reclined in the president's chair at the head of a table set for forty, his muddy boots on the fresh linen.

"Wonderful Madeira, wonderful bouquet." He held his glass to the light and smacked his lips, concentrating on the wine's color and ignoring Clinton.

Clinton gaped at an incredible scene. In the presence of

their commanding officer, British soldiers were stuffing their pockets with silver plate and utensils. Paintings had been ripped from the walls, clocks, lamps, firedogs from the hearth were scattered, and upholstery was torn in a mad search for valuables and money. A British officer came down the stairs boasting as he buttoned one of President Madison's frilled shirts.

"Drink!" Cockburn yelled and slapped a plump little man who sat near him, a small bookish fellow who appeared very ill at ease. "Drink to Jemmy and Dolley! They set this fine table for us. Drink!" The admiral turned to Clinton.

"You, there! Speak!"

"I've come to ask for your terms." Clinton used as haughty and commanding a voice as he could muster.

"Terms?" Cockburn quaffed off a glass of the Madeira and threw the crystal goblet into the wall. He turned and smiled. "Private citizens and private property will not be touched if no resistance is met. Any house with guns or powder will be burned immediately, and anyone offering resistance will be shot."

"And public property, sir?"

The admiral sneered, picked up a china plate and by way of an answer hurled it into the wall. He motioned the soldiers to take Clinton out, and they led him roughly by the arms and deposited him on the east lawn. He listened a moment to smashing plate and glassware and struggled to control his breath. The British were deliberately defacing and destroying the seat of government, obliterating Americans' faith in their public institutions. Madison had allowed this to happen! If only Pennsylvania had voted sensibly! Twenty electoral votes would have won him the presidency and this outrage never would have occurred. Clinton brushed his sleeves off, adjusted his collar and cravat, and walked away as calmly as possible. Now all would be burned – the libraries, the patent office, the courtrooms, the newspaper. Certainly they would not touch the houses of worship! Yet they acted like barbarians. Clinton shook his head, barbarians who claimed to serve a Christian king!

The Capitol smoldered like an expended pyre, and the navy yard still blazed. Furious but powerless, Clinton watched the spectacle silently. It would be this way all up the coast. Baltimore would be next, then Philadelphia, then New York. New York. He had come to the capital to get funds for two redoubts at the Narrows, and Madison had rebuffed him. Madison was now in hiding. Now Clinton clearly saw where his duty lay. He could accomplish nothing here. He must find the funds and build the forts immediately. He would not allow New York to be conquered.

As he approached the Washington Hotel to pack, someone cried: "The president's house!" Clinton turned to see flames erupting inside the windows as British marines, done plundering, touched off their black powder and rockets. Room by room, the great white stone mansion glowed like a giant lantern until the windows exploded, the roof blew upward with a hot rush of wind, and a brilliant volcano of flame exploded into the sky. Clinton pushed disgustedly through the fascinated crowd.

Kate was too ill to weep. The light was dim below the deck of the prison ship where they had been thrust the first day, and the cowering fear she saw in the eyes of the other prisoners caused Eleanora to despair. She must not give in to such feelings, she told herself, she must stay strong to nurse and comfort Kate. Kate's fever worsened. The British had not separated men and women, so for modesty the prisoners hung blankets up at either end of the fetid hold to hide the holes in the floor that served as latrines. Kate vomited until nothing remained, then, exhausted, she alternately slept and retched.

All the first day, Eleanora escorted her to the latrine. Children cowered in their mothers' arms complaining and whimpering dejectedly. Toward midnight on that first day a gentleman who had been wounded by a British musket ball died, and his two little daughters wailed and slumped over his corpse until someone called a guard and they dragged the body up from the hold, its eyes and tongue lolling, the head banging on each rung of the companionway ladder.

That night, Eleanora sat in mute terror, one whale oil lamp illuminating the clusters of prisoners. She stroked Kate's forehead, and tried her best to provide comfort. But by morning, her fear had turned to rage. She was incensed.

"Where are you going?" an older man asked as she climbed up to the hatchway.

"I'm going to talk with our captors." Her boldness sparked a faint hope in the others. She rapped on the hatchway, and it opened. The guard was shocked to see a woman, and Eleanora climbed out.

"My maid is ill and she needs a doctor."

Fearing one of his superiors might see he'd let a prisoner on deck, the guard stood at attention looking directly ahead.

"I said, my maid is ill, and she requires the attention of a physician," Eleanora repeated. "I demand to be released to find a doctor."

The guard stared blankly ahead.

"I refuse to remain down there and watch my girl die," Eleanora cried, and she turned away from the sentry and started for the railing of the hulk. He grabbed her roughly. She resisted, her eyes on fire with rage. "You can't let her die! All I ask is a doctor to look after her!"

The guard forcefully dragged her back. Now Eleanora's anger took over. She beat on his chest with her fists. "You can't do this! You can't!" Hardly looking at her, the guard led her to the hatch and threw her down. Her foot struggled to find a hold on a rung of the ladder, her hands lurched out at the lip of the opening, but she hit her arm, spun halfway in the air and landed in a heap at the bottom. The other prisoners gasped and cried out as the hatchway slammed shut, and Eleanora lay dazed on the floor, bleeding from a cut in her scalp.

Reaching Baltimore late the next day, Clinton looked in vain for a message at the Eldridge Hotel that Carr and Eleanora Van Rensselaer had arrived safely, or indeed had passed through.

He inquired at other hotels, but learned nothing. Frantically he retraced his steps, hoping that in his haste he had neglected to ask someone, to see or hear something. For three days, Clinton tried to locate them with no success. He considered returning to New York and searching for them there, but the British were now moving on Baltimore, and if she were still in the area, she would be in peril. The dead ends maddened him. On the fourth day of his search, Clinton learned that a cartel boat had reached Fort McHenry, and he rode south from Baltimore and asked the burly old captain whether he knew of any prison camps.

"Sartinly do, sir, 'tis prison hulks at Pig Point where they're keepin' 'em."

Clinton slipped him a five dollar gold piece. "And how would I make inquiry of a lady who may have been captured?"

The fat old man licked his whiskered lip. "Why, I can pass through the line."

Clinton considered embarking with the fellow, then realized he would make better time overland. The British would deem him a prime prisoner if he were caught, but he disregarded all caution, determined to take the chance. That afternoon, in a warm summer shower, he pulled his hat low and set out on a rented horse.

When she awoke on the fifth morning in the prison ship, Eleanora didn't want to stir. Kate had slept soundly through the night for the first time, and even now was slumbering. Eleanora looked on Kate's features. She felt responsible for this predicament. She should have insisted they stay with DeWitt. She vowed she would lease a large farm to Kate and Joel on minimal terms when she returned to her estate. Good, kind, supportive Kate, her confidante for years. Eleanora reached over to brush a strand of her hair aside and was startled by Kate's white, waxen color, the chill of her skin. She pulled her hand back involuntarily. "No," she moaned, "No!" A sob welled up as she realized she was holding a corpse. "Oh, Kate," she cried, "what have I done?"

Some of the other prisoners rose and walked over. Eleanora fell weeping on her maid's lifeless breast. "Oh, Kate! Oh, my Kate! I'm so sorry!" She looked up, but didn't know which way to turn.

~

After talking his way through three sets of sentries, Clinton bribed an officer to secure Eleanora's release. He paid half again as much for her maid and his private secretary.

The sight of the prison hulks depressed him, high-ribbed ships beached on the shore of the swamp. He had sent the three away to this, and he had stayed behind for false heroics. He presented his papers to the officer in command and a marine was dispatched. Clinton learned then that Edward Carr had been hanged as a spy carrying enemy dispatches. Shocked and pained, Clinton did his best to control his rage in front of the British. Better to get Eleanora and Kate out safely.

The hatch opened on a despondent throng of prisoners, each man, woman and child staring blankly ahead. For an entire week they had dragged on a dire existence, eating thin soup and moldy bread. No sunshine pierced the gloom. When the sentry called her name, Eleanora stared blankly ahead. She hardly heard him.

"Pardon me, ma'am," a boy said, "but I think he's a-calling for ye." She looked up and squinted into the dusty rays of sunshine. "Yes?"

"Come with me," and the sentry escaped back up to fresh air.

Stiffly Eleanora rose to her feet, her dress in rags, and she felt her way among the stretched-out bodies on the floor. She climbed stiffly up, and peered, squinting over the edge of the hatchway. When she reached the deck she saw DeWitt Clinton standing below, waving his hat.

"You came!" Her cracked lips formed the words, but her voice failed. "You came!" Tears flowed down her cheeks.

"Eleanora!" DeWitt sighed as she was helped out into the fresh air, then down to the muddy shore. He waded into the water, knee-deep, waist-deep, and he lifted her up, and she clasped him around the neck and buried her face in his chest.

"Isn't Kate coming?"

"Kate's dead," she said hollowly.

"Oh, Eleanora, Eleanora, I'm so sorry, so very, very sorry. My heroics . . ."

"No, DeWitt!" Eleanora pulled back. "If only . . . if only . . ." she broke down then, "Oh, DeWitt," she sobbed convulsively, "if only it had been me!"

"You mustn't say that. You must never say that!"

"I mean it! I am so weary, so very weary of it all! Kate had so much to live for, and I have nothing. If only she had been spared, and it had been me! Oh, this world!" and she fell against his breast weeping bitterly.

"Bear up, Eleanora."

"Oh, DeWitt," she sobbed, "take me away from here, please. Take me away from this awful place."

"Bear up. Be strong." And Clinton let her down on the shore so she could walk on her own.

BOOK III
INTRIGUE IN THE STATE
CAPITOL

East View of the Capitol at Albany.

CHAPTER 17

As war clouds hung over the western frontier, the inept American military command offered no defense. The battle of Lake Erie cured Daniel Hedges. He had no stomach for fighting, and with his family gone, he could no longer remain in Buffaloe Creek. Packing a bedroll, shot and powder, an axe and frying pan, a week's provisions and five pounds of salt, he took up his musket and set off toward the shaggy wilderness of Cattaraugus and Allegany.

For days he climbed into the mountains seeking solitude. On the south face of a nameless peak he set up camp. Two boulders had come to rest above a stream forming a shelter between. In front of the boulders Hedges built an entrance and behind, a hearth of stone and a chimney of clay and sticks. From the door and from the wide ledge where virgin pine protected his camp from the buffeting winds, he watched storm clouds gather and sweep up the mountain slopes, shivering the leaves, obscuring the peaks, then passing eastward toward Philadelphia and New York.

Although Hedges had abandoned his Iroquois identity, "Eye of Bright Water," and had taken the surname carved in a leather satchel the chief carried – perhaps the name of his father, or perhaps a tomahawked Yankee peddler – his theology was decidedly Iroquois. An old Seneca chief, quietly smoking his pipe in the winter lodge, once murmured: "To walk among the mountains, a man needs long legs." Sorrow for the loss of his family and the memory of the battle now gave him the "long legs" the chief had described. He looked down on the world and saw so much he hadn't seen before.

A family of otter built its barrow in a pool directly below his camp soon after the spring thaw. When their home was finished, the otters found a rock slide that fell fifteen feet into a pool. For entire mornings Hedges sat on the lip of rock and watched them playing, sleek and quick, they plucked and carried fish from the water. A profound sadness filled him when he watched the otters. His life had once been just as simple and happy. He now bitterly regretted the time he'd spent away from home, trading and smuggling on the lake and surveying for the canal. The memory of Eleanora Van Rensselaer stung him, too. Only those long winter afternoons, listening to Carrie sing, and the children play, their nursery rhymes, their songs, only those nights in the cabin in the pines seemed worth remembering now.

Spring brought swarms of black flies which shut him up in his smoky den for days. Swarms of mosquitoes laid him low with a fever that he treated with bark tea. Weak and shivering, he lay on his bed of skins listening to water race and boil in the creek, the birds chirping, the thunderstorms rolling up the mountains, owls screeching and wolves howling in the forest. At last he recovered, sallow-skinned and weak. He did not know how long he had been sick, only that the summer nights had lengthened and a scent of autumn was in the air. His beard was long, and shaggy, and his reflection in the water showed him thin and wild-eyed. He noticed the otters had departed, and this saddened him. But he also saw his sentimentality, and knew it was an indulgence for which there was no time. He dragged his wasted form about the mountain, trapping hares, chopping wood and preparing to meet the winter, while trying not to listen to a voice that whispered its indifference as to whether he lived or died.

Eleanora returned to Claverack chastened by the war and Kate's death. Although family and friends tried to shake her from despondency, she shut herself up in her mansion, wrapped her lands about her as a cloak and vowed to bear her hardship alone.

She peered out of her window each day feeling numbed and indifferent. Late summer bloomed, then mellowed into a rich harvest, and she almost despised the fruitfulness of her lands. When she heard of a farmer's family welcoming a new son or daughter, she fought to control her envy. The creeks ran and the millwheels turned, sawmill, gristmill, linseed oil mill, squeaking and grinding. Her barns swelled with hay and fodder and winter wheat. It was the order of things. The sheep grew heavy with wool; the beams of smokehouses and milk houses groaned with the weight of smoked pork and beef and cheese. All that she did not need was sold and the profits banked.

Her lands and the fortune they produced insulated her from the buffets of war and politics, but Eleanora saw them as a prison. It was the wrong way around, she believed. The estate owned her, fixed her identity in the eyes of others, and didn't even have the grace to be as barren as its mistress. All was wretched and ugly. She refused all invitations to balls and parties, even to the customary Harvest Home celebrated by her tenants. She bit her pillow in the night and wept. An enormous aching emptiness engulfed her.

She was not even cheered by the Christmas time news that America won the war and the fighting was over. The great matters of state she had championed seemed now, in retrospect, so much wasted effort. What did it matter that America with its tiny army and fledgling navy had vanquished the most powerful empire on earth? What did it matter that universal celebrations of the treaty heralded a new era for the nation? She was alone, and she'd seen how cruel and indifferent the world was, and how vulnerable she could be. She locked herself in her room for days at a time, hardly eating meals from the tray that Hilda, her new maid, carried up from the kitchen. Eleanora began to have ailments. Dr. Edwinston could only prescribe rest and herbal tea, though out of earshot he confided to the medical student who accompanied him, "What she requires most only a man could administer, and the dose should be liberal. She's a high-spirited one."

The young man, smitten by the beautiful aristocrat, agreed: "It's always the highest apples that go unplucked."

In the prison ship, Eleanora had seen how cheap life was. She longed to challenge that revelation, but she couldn't. Although her lot was pre-ordained, she blamed herself and her naiveté. She had never dreamt that a man could prefer to love other men as her husband had. Jacob Van Rensselaer's revels in various hunting lodges up and down the Atlantic seaboard must indeed have startled the beasts of the forest. And that damnable condition in the deed to Claverack! Mistakes, all mistakes, and the dead hand would continue to guide every decision. She was powerless in its shadow, doomed to live alone.

Two months after the Treaty of Ghent, a ragged, bearded stranger presented himself at her Claverack mansion, inquiring about Katherine Kipp. To replace Kate, Eleanora had selected Hilda Bruen, daughter of a German Palatine. Hilda conveyed this news to her mistress who was playing a minor-keyed prelude in the drawing room.

"What is his name?"

The girl bashfully stared at the floor. "I didn't ask, ma'am, but he's nothing more than a wanderer. Shall I feed him some scraps and send him along?"

Eleanora glared at her for her lack of sense. Kate never would think this way. "No, Hilda. Show him in." The flustered girl left and returned in a few moments with a bent, haggard man in rags.

"What is your business, sir, and how do you know of Katherine Kipp?"

The man looked up and his penetrating blue eyes fixed Eleanora with their sadness. "She is my wife, Lady Van Rensselaer."

"Joel?" Eleanora was startled. "Joel Kipp?" He looked down and nodded slowly. "We thought you died in the prison camp."

"And I nearly did, ma'am. Is Kate still working here?"

"I'm sorry, Joel," Eleanora said quietly. "She died in my arms. We too were captured by the British, held in a prison hulk. The fever took her."

Joel lowered his head until his chin rested on his breast, then he turned and started to leave.

"Please wait." Eleanora was on her feet, and she took his arm. "You'll need a position now, and, and a *home*." This word sounded queer to her even as she uttered it. "New tenants have taken over the farm you and Kate shared after your wedding, but we shall find you a house and a station." Quickly, before he refused, Eleanora instructed Hilda to take him to the kitchen for a meal, then to Edward to be barbered and fitted with clothes. Hilda nodded and took Joel by the hand.

That evening, Eleanora summoned him: "I have inquired about where we may locate you." She smiled kindly. A startling transformation had taken place. Shaven and dressed, rested and fed, he seemed nearly as vigorous as before. He certainly was as handsome and the sadness in his eye made him even more so. "I have decided, if you find it satisfactory, to employ you as a member of my household."

Joel was visibly surprised. "And what will I do? Serve your meals?"

Eleanora laughed softly. "No, not as a servant. I shall need someone to supervise the stables and to recommend what sort of improvements should be made to the house and barns and fences. I am in need of someone to collect the rent, someone with tact and diplomacy. You are highly regarded among our people. And, Joel, I should like someone to travel with me."

Already, Eleanora had instructed that an apartment above the stables be readied for him. He shared a glass of claret with her, discussing his new position, then he stood. "Lady Eleanora," he said, "I deeply appreciate this kindness. I shall do my best to earn it."

She took both his hands. "Your courage speaks for itself. It will be Kate's memory that binds us."

She watched as he left, then sat again and sipped the wine. Joel's reappearance had changed things for her. He had suffered far more than she. He had seen battle, mutilation, death and starvation. She had lost a servant, but he had lost a wife. His return shook her out of her despond and self-pity. He had always been energetic, helpful and affable. As she thought about him, she realized why she had acted so quickly – Joel Kipp reminded her of Daniel Hedges. Joel was younger and not nearly as capable, but he had the qualities of quiet strength, competence and resilience that she remembered in Hedges. She wondered what Daniel was doing now. Perhaps he had grown rich on war contracts. Perry's fleet had been celebrated throughout the nation for its victory. Perhaps Hedges had left Buffaloe Creek for Washington. Perhaps, the thought stung her, he had fallen in action on the western frontier. She shrugged and took a last sip of wine. Loyal, obedient and strong, Joel Kipp would bring a welcome change to Claverack. She called Hilda and prepared for bed.

That night her dreams were filled with Daniel Hedges. She dreamed of him aboard his *Silver Pearl* as she'd imagined years before. She dreamed of him as a babe, borne away in the arms of dark heathens into a land of wolves and wildcats. She dreamed of him as the lanky westerner she had first met at General Van Rensselaer's ball. She awoke at sunrise and felt refreshed. She stretched lazily as the cocks were crowing, and hugged her pillows. Only Daniel could stir such passion, and the effect was immediate and strong.

"Hilda! Hilda! Prepare a bath. And tell Samuel to saddle Hecate. I will ride also."

Hilda had yet to learn unquestioning obedience. "Why not bathe after you return from riding?"

"The bath, Hilda. When I wish to bathe, I wish to bathe." The flustered girl left and Eleanora peered into the mirror. She saw new energy and hope in her face.

As the weeks passed, the change in the household was so dramatic even the servants began to wonder how it had come about. New furnishings replaced old. Menus and gatherings were planned. New wall hangings, carpets, chaise lounges and sofas replaced those used for three decades. The exterior trim of the mansion was painted. A landscape gardener changed the approach to the house, laid out new flower gardens with two new fountains, and planted evergreens, Japanese maples and shrubs. Nothing had been done to the mansion since Jacob's death, and now within a year Claverack's dilapidated aspect gave way to a modern, handsome and cultivated charm.

Nor was the change wholly physical. Eleanora hired a new chef from France whose sauces and pastries were celebrated throughout the county. No longer was her door only opened to landed gentry. Now, heeding Joel's counsel, she invited certain of her more prosperous tenants to her table. The effect on her people was remarkable. Flattered that they had been recognized, seeing what changes were taking place at the mansion, they too improved the appearance of their holdings. The bickering between farmers and the miller and the smith, and between the tavern keepers and their customers, all grew far less frequent and far less intense.

Late in the spring, a spirited horse with an expert horsemen trotted up the drive. The tall rider dismounted and stepped up the three stairs to the new veranda that looked favorably over the Berkshires. He took in the view before knocking.

In her counting room, Eleánora was projecting when the schoolhouse could be built as Hilda appeared at the door.

"Gentleman by the name of Clinton, ma'am."

"I'll receive him in the parlor, Hilda. Please escort him in."

Eleanora darted up the back staircase to her room, and quickly combed her hair, applied a touch of rouge and slipped into an informal gown of Chinese silk. She had not seen Clinton for a year, and he had appeared unannounced. Given that his every move was calculated, there was surely something behind this visit.

"Eleanora, you look wonderful." He placed a kiss on her cheek and led her to the sofa. "A year has brought many changes, all for the better." He looked approvingly around the drawing room.

"Thank you. We've been working hard to rebuild, DeWitt. Please, sit down."

"Ah, the spirit is everywhere." Clinton ignored the invitation and began to pace. "People have put the war behind them, and are seizing every opportunity. Our unexpected victory over Britain gives us ambition to build. And we must harness this energy. You heard they ousted me as mayor again?" Eleanora nodded. "That Tammany crew! They play such cynical games with the rank and file. Nevertheless, my freedom from the mayor's duties gives me time for grander things."

"DeWitt, sit down! Please!"

He lowered his brow at her directness but did take a seat on a divan. "I have come to ask for your help."

"The canal again?"

"Of course."

"I wonder whether such projects aren't beyond me now."

"Beyond you?" He scoffed. "Never! You have always been up to it."

"But the war taught me a great deal. I have changed. I no longer think in such grand terms. Instead, I concentrate on the people close to me. And you yourself have remarked on the results. I truly don't see how I can help you now."

Clinton brightened – she was not outright refusing.

"I am organizing a meeting of the first citizens of New York City on December 30 at the City Hotel. We'll form a committee to revive the canal both in the public mind and in the legislature. I have received many favorable responses so far. Speculators see fortunes to be made in selling land out West. Legislators see many votes to be won in promoting such a bold project and current landowners see the value of their property rising. Everyone I speak with sees immense benefits to our state, and I must use this support before it dissipates. You can help vastly with your charm and your quick pen."

"I don't know. I truly believe I've lost all that."

"Oh, nonsense! You were born for it!" His voice changed key. "Won't you come this winter? I'm sure life up here must get tedious that time of year, and there are so many diversions in New York."

Eleanora laughed and folded her hands in front of her lips, considering. Her eyes moved back and forth looking for an excuse. Finding none, she threw up her hands. "Your sneak attack has worked, DeWitt. You don't give me time to find a reason not to, so I guess I must."

"Wonderful!" He clapped his hands. "The enthusiasm we once knew has redoubled since the war. Certainly the war has taught us all many lessons. Even those who preferred war to the canal three years ago acknowledge the convenience it would have provided in shipping men and munitions to the Canadian frontier. Now there will be no stopping until we finish. We are on the verge of a new era. For all its hell and horror, the war has drawn us together, and shown us that we need fear nothing." He raised his index finger. "One task I'd like you to do first."

"Yes?"

"Have you been in touch with that surveyor fellow?" Clinton certainly remembered his name and his oblique reference irritated Eleanora.

"Daniel Hedges?"

"Yes, yes, do you know where he is?"

"No, I don't. The last time I saw him was in Washington with you, three years ago."

"Could you contact him? We'll need him in New York."

"Is that appropriate? Wouldn't it be better if the commission notified him?"

Clinton shook his head, "No, Eleanora. I doubt he'd respond to them. But I believe he'll respond if you ask. See if you can reach him. Ask him to join us in New York late in December. Tell him his expertise is essential and that he will be well compensated."

"I'll try to reach him, but I can make no promise."

"Good," Clinton stood. "Keep me abreast of any development. If you haven't heard from him by October 1, let me know and we'll try something else."

As she stood on her porch, watching Clinton ride westward toward the capital, she folded her arms and sighed. "So, DeWitt thinks to employ me as a siren song to lure bold

Ulysses." And she turned to go inside, fearing that Hedges would not respond to her letter, and then fearing he would.

~

Daniel Hedges weathered the winter on his mountain peak, but after the ice broke, he journeyed down to the lowlands. He had no money and only some dried venison strips for food. People noticed and feared his wild appearance even in the remotest settlements. He offered labor here and there, and he slept in barns and haystacks and abandoned cabins, wherever he ended up at night.

Traveling from village to village that summer, it slowly came to him that he must go West. Solitude and independence had spoiled him for living among men – he had to strike out into the virgin territories and leave behind all his old memories and ghosts.

Hedges entered Buffaloe Creek in late August, 1815. He had been away sixteen months and the village had fully recovered and even grown. New buildings stood on old foundations and new names hung on the signs of stores and taverns. New ships rode at anchor in the harbor.

At the site of his home, squatters had built a one-story structure above his old foundation. He saw children in the yard. He had no desire to identify himself and lay claim to the land. There was plenty of land to be had in the West. He ambled down the path to the waterfront, and booked passage on a shining new sloop for Sandusky.

Because the sloop left in three days, he took a room in the new Hickey's Inn, paying for his lodging by chopping wood. In the evening, he sat alone by the taproom hearth, listening to the men's talk, hoping he'd not be recognized.

They discussed commerce and the price of real estate. There was some talk about the canal, but it was very speculative and the project depended a great deal on what the legislature did next session. One vocal critic of politicians stated that the canal had merely been a pre-war fantasy and was now abandoned. Hedges said nothing.

On his last night in Buffaloe Creek, he sat an extra hour at the hearth, and just as he was rising to go upstairs to bed, the door burst open and in stumbled a drunken threesome shouting for whiskey punch. "Keep 'em coming, lassie, till I drop," one man said. Daniel recognized the voice of Lester Frye.

Daniel walked over and extended his hand. "Lester?" The man had nearly doubled in size and his face was a florid red. He scowled. "I know the voice, man, but not the cuts of ye. Who is it?"

"Danny! Your captain. Daniel Hedges!"

Lester looked him over from the crown of his shaggy head of hair and his long knotted beard down to his moccasins.

"No, you ain't!"

"Yes, Lester, it's me, Danny!"

Lester scowled and tipped a lamp into his face. "The eyes are his, but . . ."

This was the first time Daniel had considered or taken any notice of his own appearance. He hung his head.

"By the cuts of ye, Danny, looks as though you come back from the dead. Why I wouldn't recognize you in a month of gazing. Will ye have a drink?"

"Sure."

Lester hammered his palm on the table. "Lassie! Another tankard of punch and step smart." He turned to Hedges. "Where have you been?"

Hedges' answer was hesitant and evasive so Lester turned to his two friends as the girl brought the tankards and set them down. "Do you know who this is? Why, it's Danny Hedges, best ship's captain on the lake. 'Course you'd have to cut back the brush a bit to see him. Was Danny and me what captured Jack Layland the pirate, and 'twas Danny and me what captured the *Caledonia* during the war. Danny here built the fleet for Perry and served in the battle. A real honest-to-God hero, though he's too modest and would never own it."

The serving girl looked keenly at Daniel and the other men turned to scrutinize him. Hedges drank his punch.

"You look prosperous," he said to Lester to draw the attention away from himself.

"Aye, I'm a rich man now. The money we made together," he winked, "helped me buy land when it was cheaper than week-old fish." Lester described some of the real estate he had bought after the British invasion when people needed cash, and how valuable those holdings were now. "Ye've got to come and join me, Danny! I've got an opening for a man with your skills. You always were one who could drive a deal."

"No, thank you."

"It'd be like old times."

"No, Lester. I have other plans."

"Aw, Danny!" Then Lester regaled the others with smuggling stories. Hedges quickly drained off his punch.

"Was nice seeing you, old friend." He shook the fat man's hand. "I hope our paths cross again soon." Lester responded with four or five questions about where he was going and what he was going to do, but Hedges evaded them and left to go upstairs. The tavern girl stopped him in the kitchen.

"You don't remember me?"

He looked closely at her. "No."

"Edna McKay, Captain Hedges. You rescued me long ago from a British ship and kept me out of the prison camp." Daniel squinted, then saw it was the young girl who had been cabined with the British commander. She had grown up in three years. He bit his lip.

"Yes?"

She dropped her eyes. "I came to the American side as soon as the treaty was signed, and I asked about you. I heard your wife and children were murdered by the British, and I searched far and wide for you. No one knew where you'd gone. I wanted . . . I wanted to thank you."

Daniel nodded noncommittally. He turned away and started toward the stairs.

"Captain Hedges!" She followed him. "Even if, even if you don't wish to . . . I thought you should know that Oliver Forward, the postmaster, stopped by last week. He has a letter for you, but no one had seen you."

He looked into her eyes.

"I wonder, Captain . . ." A faraway look came into her face. He gently placed his hand on her arm.

"I'm sorry. No. But thank you."

Next day Hedges breathed more freely knowing he was to set sail. It was a crisp, clear September morning, the lake gleaming, gulls squawking and a full breeze in the pines. On his way to the sloop, Daniel stopped by the post office.

An old woman sat behind the counter and riffled through a packet of envelopes for his letter. He groaned when he recognized the handwriting and the return address: "E.L. Van Rensselaer, Claverack."

"Is something the matter, sir?"

"No, ma'am. That's correct. Thanking you."

He walked down to the waterfront and sat for half an hour wondering if he should open it. The return address and the handwriting brought back many memories. He watched the sloop being loaded, and he dangled his legs over the water. No harm could come of just reading it, so he tore open the envelope.

August 12, 1815

Mr. Daniel Hedges
Buffaloe Creek

Dear Mr. Hedges,

Mr. Clinton requested specifically that I write to ask if you would do him the valuable service of attending a meeting at the City Hotel, Broadway, New York City, on December 30 this year. He has secured the support of many influential men and believes that after the lapse due to war, the canal project can again be undertaken. Your expertise in these matters is valued and needed.

I will be attending as well. I hope that you weathered the war as I understand from the supervisor of my estate who fought in Niagara that it was particularly severe on the frontier. I look forward to renewing our acquaintance, and have much to discuss with you.

Please make every effort to join us then. Hoping that you will respond at your earliest convenience. I remain,

Your humble svt.,
E.L. Van Rensselaer

Now, here was a predicament. From the civilized east, a grand lady had summoned him. Daniel sought solitude and independence and she wanted him again employed on behalf of the canal. Why should he return to be manipulated by them? He held the letter gingerly above the water. If he let it slip away, forgotten, the uncharted lands explored by Lewis and Clark would open to him.

But then her image was before him, her aristocratic bearing, her long imperious neck, the inner pride, her dark, rich hair, long and fragrant, her brown eyes and full lips. The ship was nearly loaded. He was all packed and ready. And he was no longer married so he might court her openly now. He re-read the letter.

"I look forward to renewing our acquaintance and have much to discuss with you." He glanced back at the ship. Over the water before him lay a vast wilderness to explore, but back in the east was Eleanora.

Hedges read the letter a third time, and with each word his certainty grew until he wondered how he could've had any doubt. He walked to the sloop and accepted half of his fare as a refund. Then, whistling and light of step, he returned to the village to find a barber and a bathtub.

CHAPTER 18

*M*artin Van Buren knocked at the door of the hovel, but it seemed unlikely "the Master," as O'Hanlon referred to him, would inhabit such a low place that made one fear for his linen! It was a one story shack, long and narrow, and the rest of the lot was filled with rusted iron, slag and wooden crates. A beautiful black-haired girl opened the door.

"Sir?"

"This is Colonel Burr's home?"

"Yes, sir. May I tell him who's calling?"

Van Buren was all charm. Though he currently held both a judgeship and a seat in the state senate, he said simply, "Martin Van Buren."

She closed the door. Van Buren looked with dismay around him. What possible alignment of stars could reduce a man to living so? The duel with Hamilton, the conspiracy in the southwest and trial for treason, the betrayal of friends and backers led to this door. With a courteous smile, the girl returned, held up a lamp and said, "Please follow me." He compressed himself in the narrow hallway to avoid the soot and cobwebs and walked behind her until she stepped aside and opened the door to a narrow chamber where a small slender man with graying hair sat on a bench before a table loaded with law books. A roaring fire burned in the grate making the room hot and close. The man looked up.

"Judge! Judge! So good of you to come!"

Van Buren was taken aback by his friendliness. "Sir?"

"Ah," 'the Master' rose and stepped around the desk, extending his hand, "It's been an age since I've seen you. You have done well! Sit down, son, sit down!" The man motioned him to the only chair in the room. Van Buren complied. "Perceive life," Burr waved theatrically at the squalor, "when things go awry."

Awry. Van Buren nodded while Burr scrutinized his features closely. To this remarkable man whose mind ran in terms of duels, conspiracies, empires, dark plots, armies of Spaniards and natives, wooing beautiful women (many of them), treason and exile, a man who came within a hair's breadth of winning the presidency and then was nearly executed for treason, a man whose only child perished at sea, things simply went "awry?" Van Buren was immediately charmed.

"O'Hanlon said I should call on you."

"O'Hanlon's a whore," Burr said candidly. "But he's our whore. Do you owe him anything?"

Van Buren smiled at Burr's directness. He preferred to approach things a bit more obliquely. "No, sir, I don't believe so."

"Good. Good. You know how valuable it is to keep people in your debt. That is as it should be." Suddenly his expression changed to woe. "Poor, poor Theodosia! She wrote me of you and of your accomplishments. May I call you Matty?"

"Of course!"

"Since returning I've inquired into your whereabouts. Billy Van Ness trained you well and you demonstrate great ability. If we work together, you shall pluck the golden apple." He pulled an imaginary apple out of the air. His eyes were luminous and his voice husky. "The presidency."

"I only had the pleasure of meeting Theodosia once."

"And yet your generosity to me in my time of need will never be forgotten."

"I imposed the condition of anonymity. She told you?"

"There were never secrets between the two of us," Burr said, and the way he raised his left eyebrow made Van Buren feel uncomfortable. "Twenty-five dollars, and you with a young wife and babies. Well, it provided many a warm fire that November, and some vintage claret, and a good many bouquets for the wenches." Burr fixed him with a penetrating gaze. "And now I mean to help you."

"Sir?"

"Behold this wreck of an old man! Behold how I live. You would not think it, but the golden apple was once within my grasp," he reached up again, "yet alas, it slipped from me. I knew so little then. But now . . ." His eyes grew narrow and sly, "You shall have it in my stead. You shall be president, Matty, and vindicate, for this poor old man, his years of disgrace and exile."

"You flatter me, sir."

"Nonsense. Your abilities precede you. I want only to keep you from repeating my mistakes."

"Well, then, how stands the game?"

"Ah, ha," Burr cackled. "Yes," and he rubbed his hands together. "The game! Yes. Of course! Let's lay it out like a lawsuit, my boy!"

Van Buren's lips pressed together imperceptibly at the appellation "boy."

"You recognize the three ways to gain power – inherit it, build it or steal it?" Van Buren nodded. "Well, Clinton inherited power, and is expanding it statewide even though he was ousted from the mayor's office. His followers are legion. Masons! They're thicker than the forty thieves.

Without connections or fortune, you have no choice. You must seize power, and who better to seize it from than Clinton? Therefore, Clinton must fall. *Quod erat demonstrandum.* We will bury him in that ditch, his own political grave. O'Hanlon and the Tammany rabble plan a demonstration for the night he tries to sell this canal project to our merchants and financiers. Tammany will be yours, and you should keep them close to you. What better way than having them show their strength in the street? That is what they do best, bless their innocent hearts. Our plan, yours and mine, shall be discreet, behind the scenes. The imperious, aristocratic Clinton! Madison and the Virginians trumped his cards, but he could very well pluck the golden apple if we don't intervene."

Van Buren was instantly persuaded: "How do we proceed, sir?"

Burr tapped his graying temple. "Wisely." He then asked a series of questions, elicited responses, interpreted the information, translated it into directions, suggestions and strategies to be followed. At one point he noted, "We can also attack him through his advisors. Whom does he trust?"

Van Buren placed his fingertips together. "Very few. Clinton keeps his own counsel. There is one, though, a woman, a widow."

Burr's eyebrows raised at this news. "Ahhhhhh!"

"No, I've inquired. It's platonic."

"Doubtless, knowing him. But would an accusation stick?"

"I doubt it. She's rather adept in politics, intelligent, beautiful and extraordinarily charming, she lends a certain perspective, a humanity to his visions and his projects. She is unrivaled in communicating with the folk, for she loves and helps her tenants considerably on her estate which lies in my county. I don't believe she herself understands how vital she is in his undertakings."

"So much the better," Burr said. "But let me caution you,

Matty, never underestimate women! When they are wise, they are far wiser than men. Ahhhh! My poor Theodosia."

"I shan't. But if I could cut her away from him, I believe it would effectively cut away what gives Clinton's politics flesh and blood."

"What is her name?"

"Eleanora Livingston Van Rensselaer."

A smile spread across Colonel Burr's face, and he nodded. "About twenty-seven, twenty-eight? Handsome woman? Auburn hair? Plays the harp like a seraphim?"

Van Buren nodded. "Why, yes."

"And she married Jacob Van Rensselaer, the general's nephew?"

"You do astonish me, sir."

"And the young man had peculiar tastes, liked Latin and Greek and other scholars who shared his interests, *male* scholars?"

"The same."

"The Livingstons are a black-hearted clan, my boy. They rival the Clintons for lying and double-dealing. Mark my words, this woman, if she is as close to Clinton as you say, can be his Achilles heel. Aim an arrow there. Not only is that spot unguarded, it begs for a wound. What of her, her," his right hand circled in the air, "her appetite?"

"She is chaste, I believe."

Colonel Burr laughed and shook his head. "No one, Matty, is chaste. Chastity is not a natural condition. Some people are simply good liars. Find out what stallion rides this mare and you will undo her."

"I hardly think for having an affair . . . ?"

"No, for breaching a condition in a deed, the deed from the Van Rensselaers." He nodded at a perplexed Van Buren. "Yes. Before I left in haste, I was consulted about an agreement, a covenant the families were framing. The Van Rensselaers knew Jacob would never produce an heir and knew that the woman would bear fruit only if a colt jumped the corral. The Van Rensselaers are not in the business of parting with land, and so to the happy couple was conveyed the vast estate named Claverack, Van Rensselaer land of six or seven thousand acres, to which the Livingstons joined the girl's dowry of four or five thousand, with one simple and unalterable condition." He raised his finger instructively. "Old Van Rensselaer required them to agree that if his son died, the girl could possess and draw income from the entire estate only so long as she remained a widow. If she remarried, she would be dispossessed of all lands, including the right of dower, and the entire estate would revert to the Van Rensselaers."

This small bit of news magnified very quickly in its usefulness as Van Buren considered. "But I know of no impending wedding," Van Buren said.

"Hmmm! I would be interesting, though, to see what a judge might hold in the event of conduct unbecoming of a widow."

"And I could very well be that judge!" Van Buren nodded at the simple beauty of the plan.

"Precisely."

"And then who would take possession?"

"Ah," Burr said with a gleam in his eye, "the remainderman? A philosophic question that underlies every negotiation! Who takes? Indeed! Find him. Have him perform the more unsavory work. Nothing spurs a man like informed self-interest! He will dog her and spy on her and then bring the case to you. Play Iago, Matty. Whisper in his ear that this woman has a lover, for she must, my boy, she must! Tell him that they plan to wed secretly, to have children in violation of the covenant, make up the details. Land! That's what all men want. He will not sit long on his rights. It is a most handsome estate as I recall. And when he begins to hound her, the girl will hold nothing else in her mind but how to keep her property and will not have a thought for Clinton or his causes. That, my boy, if what you tell me is true, could very well be the breach in Clinton's wall. Make the passage but a little wider and his whole lofty edifice will tumble."

"Brilliant!"

"But of course!" He bowed theatrically. "And all the better since neither she nor Clinton will suspect you are the unseen hand."

"It is a decided pleasure, sir." Van Buren reached for his hand to shake. Burr extended his in the frilled sleeve. Their eyes met.

"The pleasure is all mine, I assure you."

CHAPTER 19

$\mathcal{A}$fter a long, tooth-rattling stagecoach journey along the icebound Hudson, Daniel Hedges reached the metropolis Christmas Day. A light snow had fallen and he walked the streets, the quiet broken only by bells from churches and sleighs. Hedges enjoyed walking New York's streets alone in the snow because he felt anonymous. The air was crisp and cold, and the snow softened the harsher edges and eased memories of past Christmases.

Although Eleanora had already checked into the lavish City Hotel, she was spending Christmas at Clinton's mansion in Flushing. Daniel's room was connected to a living room shared by Eleanora. He heard noises in that room when he awoke next morning. He quickly shaved and dressed and knocked on the hallway door. He did not presume the connecting door would be unlocked. A tall, pale young man answered. "Yes?"

"Is Mrs. Van Rensselaer receiving callers?"

"And who be you?"

"Daniel Hedges. I was a surveyor for the canal commission."

Joel Kipp closed the door. Daniel leaned back and waited. Soon the door opened again.

"She'll see you," Joel said curtly and Daniel brushed past him through the anteroom and into the parlor. The room was high, bright and airy, sunlight reflecting on the new snow through the tall latticed windows.

"Ah! Mr. Hedges! So wonderful to see you again!" Eleanora rose and extended both her hands. "It's been far too long." She kissed him on the cheek. Hedges held her at an arm's length. She wore a pink morning dress and slippers of silver brocade. She looked casual, fresh and well-rested. "You must tell me simply everything," she said excitedly, and she sat and folded her hands in her lap. Hedges glanced toward her attendant. She nodded.

"Joel, please go help Clinton's men in the ballroom. And Hilda should accompany you."

"Very well, ma'am." Kipp bowed from the room and closed the door. Daniel and Eleanora stared intensely at each other for a very long moment.

"The war was difficult along the Niagara frontier."

"And for us. I lost my maid, Kate, when the British burned Washington. We were captured and held in a prison ship. It was horrible. This past year I did not want to emerge from my estate. But DeWitt is nothing if not persuasive."

Daniel nodded, and after a long pause: "I lost my family."

She leaned closer and reached for his hand. "Your babies?"

"My wife and my little ones." He tried to appear nonchalant and stoic. "They were murdered by the British as we fled the burning of Buffaloe two years back. Christmas is not my favorite holiday."

"Oh, Daniel, I'm so sorry!"

"Yes, the war rearranged many lives." He shrugged.

"Everyone suffered lost. Joel too." She indicated the door where Joel had left. "He was captured by the British and held in a camp and nearly starved. His wife was my girl, the girl who died. I took him in because of her. He's extremely capable and he protects me."

"Protects you . . . from what?"

She smiled. Her fear, brought on by the capture, seemed excessive now in peacetime. "Often from myself."

"I was glad to receive your letter, quite by accident too. I was leaving to go west, to begin a new life. I see now that we may do that here, . . . build for the future . . . after the war."

"And the canal project proves even more exciting now than before." Smoothly she deflected their talk into discussion of the canal, listing recent developments, and then she said, "Let's get down to business."

For three days Eleanora and Daniel pored over newspapers, pamphlets, speeches, maps, geologic surveys, commerce predictions, altitude measurements, figures for tonnage of goods and produce shipped and population – digesting all that had been written about the canal and the canal route. Each evening, they met with Clinton who had spent the day calling on influential people, gathering up their questions and persuading them to support the project. He posed questions he had heard that day, questions about the survey and engineering to Daniel, questions about public sentiment to Eleanora. By the day of the mass meeting, they had viewed the issue from every possible angle, and Clinton felt confident discussing it in depth in public.

The noisy, smoky ballroom filled with applause as Mr. and Mrs. DeWitt Clinton, Eleanora Van Rensselaer and Daniel Hedges entered with the canal commissioners. Clinton raised his hands to quell the clapping and cheers, but it only grew louder as he ascended to the rostrum.

"Ladies and gentlemen of the great State of New York,"

Clinton cried, his hands spread wide. "The war is behind us. A new age has dawned. Tonight we begin again that great work that will open the gates of our bountiful West, and will raise New York up to become an empire state, with the great western territories its vassals!"

More applause and Clinton waited, motioning for silence. He delivered the speech Eleanora had written. Again and again applause erupted, again and again Clinton paused and motioned for quiet.

"And in the weeks and months to come," he concluded, "I encourage you to contact your legislators. Each vote will be critical to secure the necessary funds. We have not a moment to lose. If the funds are forthcoming, digging will begin this summer. With East linked to West, West to East, the great City of New York will be the fairest port in the world!"

The crowd was on its feet. Landowners, manufacturers, shippers, merchants and gentlemen clapped and whistled and cheered, anticipating vast gains. But as Clinton was stepping down, a stone shattered the window behind the dais and the loud crash brought silence. Men and women stood still in stunned alarm. Despite the freezing temperature, Clinton ordered three men to open the French windows to a balcony. "There's a mob in the street!" one man cried. Stepping up on the sill, Clinton looked down to see fifteen hundred men with torches in the snowy street, and they carried signs reading: "Stop the Canal" and "No Ditch!" Clinton started to climb out on the balcony.

"Don't go out there," Eleanora implored him, tugging at his sleeve. "They'll heckle and ridicule you."

Clinton paused and stepped back to the rostrum. "Ladies and gentlemen, every cause has its opponents, and the leaders of this mob are ours. Why? Not because they object to the canal! No. We encourage divergent opinions. Divergent opinions help us see any flaws in our reasoning. They are our enemies because they want to reduce the canal to a partisan issue. They don't understand that the canal will benefit all New Yorkers, even them. We must keep this project above party politics. No mob will undo what we've done tonight. I shall reason with them and send them home."

He motioned for Eleanora and whispered, "That's the police chief yonder. Tell him to collect some men in the lobby and stay there until I call for him."

Clinton stepped through the window and was met by boos and catcalls. The steam of his breath encircled his head as he raised his arms. "People of New York!" A loud jeer met his words.

"Listen to me! Compare what I say with what your leaders tell you! I am calling on you, as I called on those inside, to join with me in our great effort that will build our city and our state and will put money in each and every pocket."

"It's a conspiracy!" a heckler called. "Immigrants want our jobs!"

"The canal's only for the farmers!"

"Gentlemen! Gentlemen!" Clinton called. "I ask the Sons of Tammany, who have long led this great city in making reforms, to help me now. I do not ask to forget your frustrations or criticisms, but to vent them in a proper forum. This destruction of property and hazard to life and limb," he waved to the broken window, "serves no one, and only defeats your purpose."

"Only the rich will benefit!"

"No tax for a ditch!"

"I ask you as a fellow New Yorker not to go home and forget, but to meet among yourselves. Return to Martling's Tavern. Organize. Appoint five delegates to meet with us tomorrow. We shall discuss our project and listen to your concerns. This canal is not proposed to benefit any one segment of our state, but to benefit all."

"Liar! We know different!"

Another brick sailed out of the crowd. Clinton ducked and it flew through the window. Clinton was furious. "I will not respond to heckling or to force. If there's a man present in your cowardly mob, prevail on your friends. I have made my offer and I will receive five of you tomorrow for as long as you wish to talk. Tomorrow, peaceably, reasonably, we shall resolve our differences by discussion, not by violence tonight in the street."

Then Clinton climbed back through the window to the resounding applause of those at the banquet, and held up his hands to quiet them. "We welcome divergent opinions, but we will not countenance mobocracy!" Again wild applause during which Clinton leaned over to Eleanora and Daniel and said: "Get ready to flee if they invade."

"They wouldn't dare!"

Clinton rolled his eyes. "You can never tell."

But the mob did not invade. Confronted by Clinton himself when they expected him to huddle in fear, invited to discuss their differences, the crowd lost its spirit. Many went back to Martling's Tavern with words of admiration for Clinton's courage.

In the ballroom, the orchestra had begun and men at nearby tables expressed their respect and admiration for Clinton in endless toasts. But Clinton was impatient, and as soon as he could, he summoned Eleanora and Daniel to his suite on the fourth floor.

"This is precisely what we must not have," he said when the door was closed. He paced the floor. "Controversy! A torchlight mob in the street!"

"You handled it marvelously, DeWitt." Eleanora's excitement had not abated. "You advanced our cause by five years tonight! You stood up to them and reasoned with them!"

"But I despise their tactics. I see someone's hand in this and it troubles me. O'Hanlon is surely involved, but he's just a stooge. Possibly Van Buren. I hear he secretly opposes us." Then Clinton's expression grew very grave. "But possibly someone else, too."

"Who?"

Clinton paused and looked from Daniel to Eleanora, then back. "Aaron Burr."

"Burr?" Eleanora seemed puzzled. "Why would he be involved? His political career is long over."

"That is precisely why. He cannot keep out of it, and not being able to involve himself directly, he works through others, minions and surrogates. I hear he has taken Van Buren as his protégé."

"But why?"

"Burr misses it. Power is his game. He wants it back, and Van Buren thinks as he does. If Burr cannot have it himself, he can live vicariously through Van Buren. He was always close to Tammany. A mob in the streets! I haven't seen that tactic in years. Burr will oppose us with all the guile of the devil himself. He wants revenge for the disgrace he's suffered. He and the Clinton family have always been opponents." Clinton nodded. "We must get to him and back him off. But how can you hurt a man who has nothing to lose?" Then Clinton cleared his throat and looked up at the two of them. "But Burr and Van Buren are my problems, and need not concern you."

They discussed a "Memorial," an essay they could publish in newspapers across the state. For Eleanora, Clinton sketched the broad political outlines, the arguments he wished to explore. He discussed with Hedges what engineering details were necessary. "Take all the technical mystery out of it. Make it so simple that a father could build one for his child, or better yet, the child could build it for the father. See if you can have a draft for me by morning."

"By morning?" Eleanora was surprised. Clinton simply turned and looked at her and she was silent. As he reiterated a few points, a knock sounded at the door.

"Four farmers from Brooklyn, sir," a young man said. "They have a contribution, and they would appreciate a word."

"Very well," Clinton dismissed Eleanora and Daniel. "I will see you at breakfast. Nine o'clock."

They left the room and passed the four farmers waiting to speak with the great man. They went down the stairs to Eleanora's suite and she told Hilda and Joel she'd need them no longer that night. She and Daniel began at ten o'clock while a riotous canal party celebrated Clinton's triumph over the Tammany mob below in the ballroom.

Four hours later they had twelve pages of persuasive text that Eleanora delivered to a scrivener for copying. "Are you tired, Daniel, or shall I send down for champagne?"

"I'm all right. The excitement's stirred me up."

Eleanora sent for the champagne and it came in a silver bucket filled with snow. Hedges opened it and poured.

"To the canal," Eleanora held up her glass, "on the night of its rebirth."

"To us," Hedges replied.

She smiled. "You, myself and DeWitt."

Daniel nodded.

They discussed the arguments they'd refined that evening. Then Eleanora said, "DeWitt admires your capacities. I watch him watch you."

"I admire his," Hedges returned.

"He has all sorts of engineers feeding him all manner of technical details and other men promoting inventions of all kind to him. Yet when you speak, he listens."

"Well," Daniel tossed off his wine and stood. "That is what we're both doing here, isn't it? Helping him?"

She looked down at her finger holding the stem of her glass. Then she looked up, and the soft expression of her lips, the depth of her eyes surprised him. "For the most part." She waited for him to say or ask something, but he did not. He set his glass down and looked into her eyes again.

"I should get some sleep."

"So should I, but not just yet. Sit by me, Daniel." She placed her glass on the cluttered table. Daniel crossed the room and sat next to her. Her voice grew husky. "I have often thought of the night we spent together. In those horrible times in the prison ship . . . and afterward . . . I remembered, and wished I'd known the feeling of love . . ." she reached for his hand and held it, "with you."

He gently touched her ear and her cheek and looked into her eyes. In those eyes he saw her vast intelligence, the depth of their sorrow, but tonight there was something else. Excitement, yes, but also joy. He leaned over and kissed her and her lips were delicious with champagne.

"I lived as a hermit for a year, alone on a mountain peak, looking into my fire every night and also out into the sky and the stars. I thought of you. I remembered how you carried yourself, gliding through rooms of men and women, how these eyes look out on the world with trust and hope and joy. And I tried to find all that within myself."

Eleanora kissed him passionately, and looked up into his eyes. "Oh, Daniel!" He pulled away. She swallowed and struggled for control. "I know that without a wife you have no need for, for *discretion*. You have no reason to keep silent about our, our *association*."

Daniel cringed. "Association?"

She suddenly looked unbearably sad. "See how guarded I must be!"

"I love you," he said softly. His eyes searched hers. "I have no difficulty in telling you or in telling the world."

"And I love you." She sighed, the admission relieving some of her anxiety. "But I must ask a favor, an enormous favor that you could very well refuse me. Can you promise you will never discuss our time together? Never tell another about our love?" She looked down.

Daniel saw sorrow and also fear in her. "If that's what you wish, of course." He wanted to ask why, yet he didn't. She nodded and tears welled in her eyes.

"I am sorry, but I must ask this of you. You don't know, and you never will know what it is like for me." She reached for him, pulled him toward her and kissed him with desperation. "I love you, oh, Daniel, I love you so! Forgive me! Promise me! Ours shall be a secret love! Only we can know of it! And it shall be even more sacred because we do not profane it to others."

He nodded. "And this reason, this cause for our silence, it can never be removed?"

"Never!" she cried, "And that's what makes it so horrible." She leaned into him and wept. Daniel felt her warm tears on his neck, and he lifted her chin and kissed them away.

"I guess if you could tell me the reason you would."

Slowly he stood and lifted her from the love seat and carried her through the door into the darkened chamber. He lay her on the bed, and lay down beside her. "The secret," he said, then corrected himself, "*our* secret will be kept."

"Oh, my love!" she moaned, and tangling her fingers in his hair, she encircled him with her arms and kissed him passionately.

Comforted by the sound of his breathing, Eleanora drifted into a contented sleep and her dreams were happy and bright.

That night she slept in the deepest slumber she'd enjoyed since before her capture. But when she heard a door close outside the room, she bolted upright. Daniel was still beside her. Sunlight streamed in the tall windows and sleigh bells jingled below in the street.

"Daniel," she whispered, "you must go."

She watched him awaken, as he registered where he was, and then as he looked at her.

"Good morning," he said easily, drifting back to sleep.

"Good morning," she answered. His ease calmed her. The situation was comic enough. "You've got to find a way out of here unseen."

He opened his eyes a second time. Far off a church bell rang eight times, muffled by the snow.

"We're late! We're supposed to meet DeWitt at nine. I must dress. I'm sure I look a fright."

He leaned his head back and opened his eyes and gently stroked her hair. "You are beautiful." Their eyes met and they kissed.

They went down separately to breakfast. Clinton had read their draft and he praised much of it, criticized some and suggested changes. As he finished discussing it, he reached out and took Daniel's hand in his left, Eleanora's in his right.

"I know in the hurly-burly of this we sometimes lose sight of our overall objective." He smiled warmly to each. "A man could never ask for two wiser, more loyal, more capable allies than you. Last night, we built a firm foundation for our effort to reach the public, and we learned a great deal, including about how the project will be exploited by our enemies. When this Memorial is finished, and three or four more drafts should suffice, I'd like both of you to travel across the state together to promote our cause in villages and townships. We need to put pressure on all our legislators, and the best way to reach them is through the people." Clinton grasped both of their hands firmly. "This will be our triumvirate. Let us go forward together, and together we shall accomplish what small minds and timid hearts now consider impossible."

Clinton placed their hands back on the linen. "Now I must meet with O'Hanlon and the Tammany Bucktails. I'm sure it will be a charming soiree." He stood and left quickly.

Still glowing from their night of intimacy, Daniel and Eleanora gazed into each other's eyes.

"We have so much to celebrate at the New Year's Ball tonight," Eleanora said.

"Eleanora, I still don't know how to dance."

A hundred couples had been invited, but so great was the positive reaction to the canal project that seventy more appeared uninvited. Clinton stood at the door, greeting each couple and wishing them a happy New Year. The orchestra played lively new waltzes. The wives of the men of wealth and power had dressed in the sheerest Parisian gowns and the dancers swirled gracefully, bathed in candlelight. Displays set out around the ballroom included a birch bark canoe, a stuffed wildcat, a wooden native in buckskin, a Durham salt boat and one of Oliver Perry's cannon. When all the guests and uninvited guests were assembled, Clinton gave a short address, then left his wife with Eleanora and Daniel and hurried to a private room adjoining the first floor bar.

Martin Van Buren had been waiting impatiently for half an hour. "I was about to leave," the small man announced from the table where he sat. Light from the hearth fire glowed on his reddish blond hair. "I thought you'd forgotten me."

Clinton ignored this. "I asked for a meeting to reconcile our views about the canal. Thank you for coming."

Van Buren inclined his head slightly, a faint smile playing at his lips.

"I spoke with O'Hanlon and four Tammany leaders this morning.

They oppose the project and will fight it in the legislature," Clinton sat. "They are short-sighted and cannot see the great effect it will have for the Port of New York. They see all sorts of conspiracies and menaces that simply do not exist. Where do you stand on the issue, Judge?"

"I remain curious, open-minded." Van Buren inclined his head thoughtfully. "I need to know more before making up my mind."

"My people will give you all the information we have."

"I endeavor to collect information, sir, slightly less biased." This annoyed Clinton. He glared at Van Buren for a full minute. The little man stared directly back, again a sly smile on his lips.

"What exactly are your reservations?"

"I want to determine the canal's popularity."

"Popularity?" Clinton demanded. "It will be popular if we make it popular. The canal will be the single most important issue in New York for the next decade!"

Van Buren smiled and looked down at the table. "Perhaps there are men who look beyond your promises, Mr. Clinton. You assume state government should engage itself in building a waterway. I don't know if a majority of the people agree with you, at least a majority of those who vote. Many believe private companies are better suited since they must turn a profit at what they undertake and so there is an incentive."

"No such company has come forth. No such company is large enough for the undertaking."

"The Manhattan Water and Canal Company may be interested."

"Burr's people? Never. He's far too slippery. Even Ellicott and the Holland Land people have washed their hands of Burr."

Van Buren shrugged. "Well, then, some other company perhaps."

"We don't need a private firm!" Clinton grew impatient. "All benefits will accrue to this state and to the public at large, so it is only right that the cost should be borne by the public. No private firm has sufficient capital."

Van Buren shook his head. "This obligation could very well bankrupt the state for a generation. Six to seven millions! Without a more positive showing, I am afraid I cannot support it."

"And so you and Tammany will obstruct a funding bill to begin the digging?"

"Unless you can satisfy me the project is sound and the people want it. My associates and I will need more than letters in the newspapers and speeches, and," he nodded toward the door, "New Year's Eve parties. While a certain visionary capacity is to be admired in leaders, particularly religious leaders, prudence and caution are far more important in public men."

"So you hang back as the voice of prudence and caution?"

Van Buren smiled and nodded. "Precisely."

"Therefore we must convince you and yours that it is prudent to proceed?"

Van Buren spread his arms in candor. "That is all we ask."

"Very well," Clinton said abruptly, extending his hand for Van Buren to shake. "I just hope you don't someday regret not joining us sooner." And he turned from the small man, opened the door and left.

Van Buren waited with a bemused smile. Seeing Clinton lose his composure was pleasurable. And yet the night could bring more pleasant news. Within five minutes a knock sounded at the door and a thickly-built Loyal Son of Tammany entered. "Yes?"

"Your suspicion was right. A surveyor feller. Name's

Hedges. Their rooms are connected by a door. Uh, Mr. Van Buren, sir, I, uh, I had to bribe a chambermaid."

"Sure, my good man," and Van Buren fished in his pocket and slipped him a golden eagle.

"The arrogant little upstart!" Clinton thundered to Eleanora and Hedges in the privacy of his suite. "How can the bastard son of an innkeeper hold our canal in his waistcoat pocket? I loathe these politics. Madison was bad enough. Van Buren is intolerable! I see Burr's treachery behind this! Burr is ever the schemer, a spider spinning his web. Before he is done there will be many more ruined lives. Now Van Buren postures himself as the protector of the public purse. He's only waiting to see if the canal can help his career, and when it does, he will fall in step with us. He and Burr are doubtless one in their thinking, both have such voracious appetites for gaining political offices, but none of the integrity needed to execute them."

"His colleagues always vote in a bloc," Eleanora observed. "He has the votes needed to push or obstruct any legislation. Of course, bribery and blackmail are always at his disposal, too."

"Yes," Clinton set his jaw, "and Tammany supports him to a man. But we shall have the people on our side. The people." Clinton thought a moment. "We must appeal directly to them, energetically and soon." He warmed to a new idea. "We shall hunt that little fox of Kinderhook. You and Hedges make arrangements to travel through every crossroads hamlet in this state and stir up enthusiasm to send a clear message to Albany. Speak in farmers' markets, churches, taverns, wherever four or five voters congregate. Carry our message to the hustings. The good work you've done here will serve you well. We shall ignite such a canal fever, that Van Buren would sooner seek to halt the advancing tide."

There was a knock at the door. A waiter entered with a tray of glasses and champagne in a silver bucket. Hedges passed out the glasses as the waiter removed the cork with a pop and poured the wine.

"I propose a toast for the New Year," Clinton said. "To our association, the three of us. May success be ours together."

"Together," Daniel smiled at Eleanora.

"Together," she lifted her glass and clinked it with DeWitt's and then with Daniel's, her eyes ablaze with joy.

CHAPTER 20

Returning to Hudson, Martin Van Buren asked his clerk to find deeds for the Claverack conveyance. Locating them in Dirk Vonderdonk's office, the clerk produced two parchment indentures with red seals. Van Buren perused them. Set forth in the twin conveyances, both dated 1806, the date of Eleanora's wedding, were the metes and bounds of two large tracts, one Livingston and the other Van Rensselaer. Each parcel was conveyed to "Jacob Van Rensselaer and Eleanora Livingston Van Rensselaer, his wife, and upon the death of either, if there be no issue, an estate for life in the survivor so long as that survivor shall not marry, thence by descent."

"That's odd," Van Buren scratched his head. "In the normal course, if the husband dies without children, the remainderman enters into possession, and the wife only gets dower, one-third income for life, one-half if there are no children. My good Henry, you've been clerk for twenty years. Why would both families create a full life estate to terminate upon remarriage?"

Henry frowned, then smiled. "I do recall now. It was widely believed there'd be no children to the union."

"The husband, right?"

"Yes. 'Twas thought he was not disposed to perform his husbandly duties."

"Physical impairment?"

"No, Judge. He more enjoyed the company of men than women."

"Ah, I see." Van Buren smiled. "The weakening blood of our landed gentry."

"After entail was abolished in 1782, the 'landed gentry,' as you call them, sir, still desired to restrain alienation. Rather than allow the Livingston portion to slip back to those Scots, the Van Rensselaers devised this arrangement to keep it all. They knew, of course, there'd be no children, so they held out for merger, reversion and descent through their line in the event of the inevitable – her death or her remarriage, or indeed, any 'unwidowlike conduct,' as the cases hold. In return, they gave her a life estate – all of the income instead of mere dower."

"Did the Livingstons know about Jacob's proclivities?"

"It is doubtful, sir. Jacob married the poor lass under false pretenses. She was much taken with music and poetry, as I recall, and he was publishing verses regularly. She was only eighteen or so and smitten with his talent. He was thirty-seven. Even knowing his son's bent in life, Jacob's father hoped to produce an heir, so fair and regal was the girl – and she still is, sir –"

"I know the woman! She is as you describe."

"If she could not lure Jacob from his carousing to bear a child, then more likely than not she'd seek love after his death."

"Well, other lands, the lands of a new husband would be settled on her!"

The clerk shook his head in mock sorrow. "But any prospective husband would find her far less attractive when he found that re-marriage extinguished her estate. The lands of Claverack would vanish, *poof!* as in a dream."

"So the woman has a Hobson's choice! Chastity or poverty! This is good, Henry. And how did Jacob perish?"

"Drowned, sir. He was cavorting with some companions in the dark on Kinderhook Lake and they found him the next morning. It was all kept quiet."

"Foul play?"

"Only as foul as such play is to nature, sir."

"Well put, Henry."

"Thank you, sir."

"One last matter, my good Henry. If she forfeits, who takes?"

Henry peered through the spectacles at the end of his nose. "Let's see! Let's see! By descent. Where the conveyance terminates, it would be the next oldest brother who would be the remainderman. There were three sons, Master Jacob, Master Edward and Master Randolph. Master Edward died in the war without issue. Master Randolph, it seems."

"Where might I find him?"

"Oh, he's a young man of low habits. He's always at the Burgomaster – a tavern at the docks – with a pretty hard crew."

"For your efforts."

Henry accepted a five dollar gold piece. "Thank you, your honor. It's noon now, he shouldn't be too drunk yet."

Van Buren left immediately for the Hudson docks where two whaling ships in dry dock towered above the frozen river. The inland port seemed more like a Cape Cod harbor than a bay on the Hudson River. New England warehouses, salt-boxes, shops and houses lined the shore, built inland by whaling captains transplanted from Nantucket. Van Buren stepped brightly along in his plumed tri-cornered hat. The irony of his plan pleased him. Landed aristocrats used such deeds and wills and covenants to consolidate their wealth and power. Now he would use their own instruments of conveyance to divide and conquer.

He located the Burgomaster Tavern and asked for Randolph Van Rensselaer.

"Randy? Why, he's over there." The bartender nodded with disgust in his eye.

Van Buren crossed the low, dingy room to a thin man sitting at the cold hearth with a shock of red hair dangling in his eyes. "Mr. Van Rensselaer?" He wasn't as young up close as he was at a distance.

The man's startled expression turned to anger. "Whatever you're peddling, I don't need none."

"On the contrary, sir, you will be very interested in what I have to say." He introduced himself, then sat down. "I'll come directly to the point. You stand to inherit your brother's estate of Claverack if you can demonstrate certain conduct in its current occupant."

Randolph scowled. "I'll be dead before I see that. Father gave them the home and lands. Then Jake died, leaving that barren bitch in the house! It's a disgrace." He swigged from his pewter tankard, licked his lips and asked. "What's it to you?"

"Are you aware that if she remarries, she forfeits Claverack and it becomes yours?"

Years of drink and smoky taprooms gave Randolph's skin a sallow cast, and it wrinkled as he scowled again. "No."

Van Buren's eyes twinkled. "Yes," he nodded, "yes."

"Ah, but she won't re-marry. Who'd want her if she has no lands? Besides she knows what she'd lose and she's a sly bitch, that one. She caught hold of Jacob, didn't she, when he never looked at women."

Van Buren raised his finger instructively. "I hear she is secretly seeing a man, and has plans to marry."

"Fine!" Randolph grew surly. "When she does, I'll eject her."

"But they plan to be secretly wed. Your father is gone, and both your brothers are dead without issue. She need only wait until you are dead. Then your claim will be moot and she can announce her married status."

"Stop the doubletalk, man!" Randolph narrowed his eyes unpleasantly. "Do I have a claim or not?"

Van Buren backed up. "As a judge I cannot practice law, but I'd suggest you look into the matter. I don't think you'd have much of a problem."

Randolph's eyes brightened, and he took another swig of punch. "What do you gain by all this?"

"The pleasure of seeing the estate returned to its rightful owner." He smiled. "And your perpetual friendship."

"Who is the man she's seeing?"

"That will be for you to determine, but I suspect it is a surveyor of this canal project we read so much about. Daniel Hedges is his name." Van Buren stood. "I cannot be involved, you understand. And I trust you will keep this conversation confidential."

Randolph nodded. "Want a drink?"

"No, but thank you."

Randolph smiled. "I never thought this day would come but oh, how I've been hoping for it!" The judge doffed his hat and left the tavern.

"Ah," Van Buren said to himself as he pushed into the fresh sunlight, "Informed self-interest. As dependable as gravity."

And it was. The change in Randolph Van Rensselaer was profound. Before a slovenly drunk, he now hired a valet, bought new clothes and trimmed his shaggy hair. With a walking stick and a feathered tri-cornered hat, almost overnight he affected the air of a landed gentleman. He talked to anyone who'd listen about his windfall, referring to the current occupant in words that were less than civil, indeed, crude and unwarranted.

Eleanora never suspected. Returning from New York City, she unpacked then re-packed a traveling trunk and left immediately on a journey across the state. She traveled with Joel Kipp, Hilda and Daniel Hedges. Armed with copies of the printed Memorial, they went westward in three large sleighs to Schenectady, Rome, Utica, Oswego, Salina, a cluster of buildings huddled on the Genesee called Rochesterville, and then along the Ridge Road to Black Rock and Buffaloe Creek. Joel secured their lodging in each place, and they met local officials and major property owners to discuss face-to-face what the canal would accomplish.

Usually the evening they arrived, Joel tacked up broadsides in the taverns and post office that a public meeting would be held the following night at an inn or a church. By nightfall of the next day, a curious throng had assembled. Daniel and Eleanora allowed local officials to share the dais, and after some introductory remarks, the mayor or town justice introduced Eleanora.

The men and women who came were surprised that a woman took the rostrum, yet because it was a woman, they listened more attentively. Eleanora described how funds would be raised and spent, what the project would cost, how long the canal would take to dig, then what benefits would accompany its completion: larger cities, greater wealth, schools for the children, expanded industries with the opening markets, and the access to manufactured goods from Europe and the Far East.

"In the words of Mr. Clinton," she concluded, holding up the pamphlet she and Daniel had written, "'It remains for a free state to create a new era in history, and to erect a work more magnificent and more beneficial than has ever been achieved by the human race.'"

She sat to their resounding applause. Daniel followed. He identified himself as a ship captain from Lake Erie and used a map to show how without the canal, trade generated in the

Ohio Valley, the Great Lakes territories and beyond would naturally flow either down the Mississippi to New Orleans or down the St. Lawrence to Montreal.

"Like many of you," he lowered his voice, "I fought in the war to defend my home. My house was burned, my wife and children massacred. Why? Because the government in Washington could not defend the frontier. A cannon costing four hundred dollars to cast in West Troy cost two thousand dollars to ship to Niagara! An eight dollar barrel of pork for the men cost a hundred dollars to ship to them! This canal will channel commerce through our state, but more importantly it will help prevent another invasion from Canada."

He then described the canal's dimensions and explained how a lock lifted boats, how aqueducts would carry the canal over rivers and creeks, and how the towpath would accommodate teams going in both directions. His final point usually piqued local curiosity. "Now as to the men needed to dig, we'll be using local contractors mostly. You have plows and teams and picks and shovels. You know where granite and limestone may be quarried, where oak for the lock gates and scaffolding can be cut. When the funds are approved by the legislature, a state agent will contact you to see who is willing to work. This agent's strongbox will be filled with silver and gold. If some of you want to subcontract, you may dig two or three miles of the canal according to our specifications. The money you earn may build you a new home, buy livestock or tools, or purchase new fields and pastures. From the day the legislature passes this act, all will benefit."

Daniel sat to polite applause, then Eleanora urged the people to contact their legislators to demand a favorable vote, and requested that they sign a petition. During this western sweep, three ledgers were filled with over ten thousand signatures.

A rivalry had arisen between Black Rock and Buffaloe Creek as to where the canal would enter Lake Erie. Without making commitments to Joseph Ellicott, whose old feud with Buffaloe Creek and his vast holdings in Black Rock caused him to want it there, or to Lester Frye who favored Buffalo, as it was now being called, Daniel and Eleanora channeled the furious enthusiasm into letters and petition signatures. To celebrate their most promising meeting yet, they decided to remain a day longer at Buffalo. It was the first of May, a glorious sunny day, and tender green buds of unfolding leaves stood out against the deep green of the pine forest.

"Will you show me where you lived?" Eleanora asked brightly at breakfast. "I want to see everything you have told me about."

"Everything's changed."

"Good morning, Mr. Hedges," Daniel heard at his back, and he turned to see a pretty young woman. "I attended your lecture last night and I thought you and the lady were wonderful!"

Daniel then recognized her. "This is Edna McKay," he said, "Edna, Eleanora Van Rensselaer." Edna curtseyed.

"So nice to meet you. If there's anything I can do to make your stay more comfortable, please let me know. I have been promoted to head chambermaid."

Daniel congratulated her, and she left. Before he could explain how he saved her during the war and how she located Eleanora's letter that sent him east instead of west, Eleanora smiled roguishly: "I see some things haven't changed."

They walked out together in the clean spring sun. Eleanora wore a beautiful gown of yellow saffron and carried a small parasol. Daniel described how the village looked before its burning, what sort of goods had lined the docks and where he moored his *Silver Pearl*. He told her about how they'd ignored the embargo and used moonless nights to smuggle deep within the coves and bays of the Canadian side and to Pennsylvania and Ohio. They paused at a small shack whose chimney belched wood smoke into the morning air. "What is this?"

"This is where my home stood." He looked on the site with dismay. "It was a large house, a fine home for raising children. The British burned it."

"Who owns the land now?"

"Why, I do. They're squatters."

"Then you must evict them! This is valuable property and its value will increase a hundredfold once the canal is dug." She stared disgustedly at the shack. "Property, Daniel, property is something you must seize and hold, else it will slip through your fingers."

"They have children," he pointed to a clothesline. "I can't do that."

"But they will perfect title if they remain long enough."

Daniel shrugged. "It doesn't mean that much to me." He led her into the woods a distance until the overgrown path disappeared among the briars. "I own this land as well. Twenty acres or so. We, uh, I built a cabin, and our children were born here."

"I should so like to see it!"

"But your dress!" He did not want to admit there were other reasons for keeping her away from the cabin. He and Carrie had been so happy. Then he looked into Eleanora's eyes and saw her empathy for his loss. "Very well. Come along." He started into the briars, parting them for her.

The cabin still stood, rough-hewn logs and clay chinking, but the roof was partially caved in. The yard was completely overgrown with saplings and fern. They walked around the cabin, then paused at the doorway. Daniel took Eleanora's hand. She slowly put her arms around his neck and stepped up and kissed him on the lips.

"Oh, Daniel," she murmured close to his ear, "it is so beautiful here! A man and a woman could imagine they were beginning the human race again, free of all its mistakes." She kissed him again, more passionately this time. Daniel responded, and when they parted, Eleanora asked: "Are we desecrating her memory?"

"No," he shook his head. "Carrie loved life so very much, and she showed others how to love it too. She was never petty or jealous."

"And yet so many seek to control us from the grave."

"Well, they can't if we don't let them."

"Oh, I feel so free here!"

He led her inside. The place looked very much the same as when he had stripped it of its furnishings the day they moved. The caved-in roof had deposited a heap of pine needles on the floor. After peering here and there, Daniel crossed the room. From a high shelf he took a small toy boat, a model of the *Silver Pearl*. "This was my son's." He put it back. "It's cold in here, Eleanora. Come outside. I know another place." He led her through the chirping forest to a mossy glade by a stream. The ground was elevated and from the bed of moss they could see down to the village and the harbor beyond where ships rode in the breeze. Daniel covered the moss with his coat, and they lay back on it looking toward the lake.

"It is so serene!" she sighed. "Ah, Daniel!" her eyes grew misty. "I could be so happy here!"

"If only . . ." he began to say, but he stopped himself. He was about to mention the strange promise she'd extracted from him.

"Yes, if only!" she sighed, and she added, "It feels so wonderful to be out of doors."

"It could be like this always."

"If only it could!" Her tone ended that subject. Daniel watched the high, fleecy clouds, and the sailboats tacking out on the lake. He thought momentarily of the war, of Oliver Perry and the battle, then he bolted up: "Let's go sailing!"

"Oh, yes, let's do!"

"I'll show you how I used to make my living."

They rose quickly and returned to town. At a dock in the harbor he rented a small sailboat while Eleanora fetched a coat from the inn and soon they were out on the lake tacking in the brisk breeze. The tight little boat responded to his hand, and they reached ten knots.

Eleanora lay back, watching the wind in his hair and the sun and shade on his face as they tacked, listening to his calm, mellow voice describe what he was doing, and how it affected the boat, and she thought, "He is the finest man I've ever known." The wind blew her hair and kissed her cheek. "I love it here!" she cried, throwing back her head.

Daniel smiled, watching the wind in her hair and taking in how she held her face proudly into the wind. The sun sparkled gloriously on the water, and silhouetted against it, Eleanora seemed more beautiful than he had ever seen her. This, he told himself, was his happiest day since the massacre, sorrow slipping behind into the boat's wake as the wind propelled the leaning sail ever forward. He regretted the sun's passing across the sky, and the moment arrived when he said, "We should start back."

As he came about, the setting sun lit Eleanora with a deep rose color. Paying out the line, Daniel ran before the wind, and with no skippering to be done, he sat beside her, the line in his hands.

He watched her for a long moment, then, believing the time to be right, he spoke: "This journey with you has made so many things clear." Eleanora nodded and smiled. She did not want to speak now. "I'd be honored if you'd become my wife."

"Oh, Daniel!" She gave him an immediate look of radiant love and joy, but then turned her head and looked as though she felt a stabbing pain. He reached out and touched her cheek, and she smiled and dropped her eyes.

"Can you give me some time to answer you?"

"Of course! I just . . . I just wanted to tell you . . ."

"I'm sorry. There are other considerations."

"What considerations? What can there be? I'm a man, you're a woman! We love each other. What can stand between us?"

"You'd think less of me if I told you."

"No, my darling, please. Don't keep anything from me. There is no problem we cannot solve! I can help you!"

"It is my own affair, Daniel, one I must live with, alone. I do not wish to burden you with it, and you only add to my sorrow when you pressure me."

"I don't mean to do that."

"I cannot read the future. Perhaps there'll come a day when I can explain, but I don't want to promise what may never be. Please trust me." She placed her delicate white hand on his strong calloused hand, so comfortable on the tiller.

He squinted into the sparkling waves. "Of course," he said, his steady hand guiding the boat as the wind blew them eastward toward the harbor.

CHAPTER 21

*W*hile Daniel and Eleanora promoted the canal in the western territories, DeWitt Clinton politicked in the river counties of Albany, Rensselaer, Columbia, Greene, Ulster, Dutchess, Putnam, Rockland, Westchester and his native Orange. Van Buren and the Tammany crew were campaigning too, preying on fear that western produce shipped by canal would flood the local markets and lower prices, and also that tenant farmers would leave the large estates for more fertile bottom land they might own for themselves. The legislative session would be the battle ground among the various interests.

"But how do you know you can trust Mr. Burr?" Hannah Van Buren lay across the bed watching her husband adjust his silk cravat in the mirror.

"He has nothing to gain or lose."

"But why is he offering you all this help?"

Van Buren turned and flashed her a boyish smile. "It's the nature of the game, my dear. No one retires from politics, they are forced out."

"But why did he pick you?"

"We think alike. He understands and admires my methods. I consider myself brighter than he, surely more agile and less extreme in my methods. He gets too involved in plots and conspiracies and revenge, but he is useful." Van Buren turned back to the mirror. "I genuinely like him, too."

"But if it should become public that you're involved with a traitor!"

"He's discreet. While there are excesses, and sometimes he seems a bit unhinged, mad even, for the most part his advice is sound." He faced her. "Don't worry. Although he considers me his avenging angel, I keep my own counsel. I'll ride with him only so far as he drives in my direction." Van Buren crossed the room and kissed Hannah's forehead. "Only so long as he benefits me and my family."

With the legislators in town, Albany was ablaze with canal fever. Debate about canal funding dominated the last two weeks of the 1816 session. The night before the vote, Clinton staged a torchlight parade through Albany's streets to show public support. With trumpets blaring, a bass drum pounding and thousands shouting and cheering, the parade passed through the street by a hotel where two men stood at a window watching.

"Nice effect," Aaron Burr dropped the heavy velvet curtain of his window and turned to Martin Van Buren. "The mob. *Coriolanus* and the Roman mob. Voracious beast, never satisfied."

"Clinton has much support." Van Buren didn't like to admit that he didn't recognize literary allusions.

"Never rely on the mob, Matty. No one can control it. Rely only on men who hold office. Once you give a dog his dish, you can easily slip the leash about his neck."

"But Clinton has the mob on his side."

"We will turn it on him. The mob will always turn given

the proper provocation." He held up his hand in its ruffled sleeve. "Patience. You'll have a good floor fight tomorrow. Are your votes firmly committed?"

"We'll see tomorrow."

"Just keep to the high ground. You may have to retreat once or twice as the battle heats up. Speak sparingly. Watch where your support erodes. If you've prepared your troops sufficiently, you'll know what arguments to use in swaying the weaker ones to stand and not fall back."

"Clinton's people have been working, too."

"Yes, I hear from an old ally in the Holland Land Company that the Van Rensselaer woman's oratory and wit, not to mention her extraordinary beauty, have garnered quite a bit of support in the western counties. Have you done anything to neutralize her?"

"Randolph Van Rensselaer has been gathering evidence, but his attorney doesn't believe they have enough yet to bring an action for ejectment."

"My friend told me she was cavorting rather openly with the surveyor in Buffalo." Burr winked. "Tie those two together, and Clinton's little triumvirate will blow sky-high."

"Van Rensselaer's agent is checking registry books at the inns to see if they ever signed as man and wife. But the woman is cautious. She keeps a young man as bodyguard and a maid as chaperone. We need to be patient."

"A few gold coins in the proper hands could get you the evidence you need. How about a town justice swearing he performed a wedding ceremony?"

Van Buren just smiled. The renegade was up to his old tricks. "No need for perjury, sir. Not yet at least. We'll uncover something."

∾

At Eleanora's Albany townhouse that same evening, Clinton, Hedges and four senators from the north, south, central and western portions of the state were finishing dinner.

"We shall waste no time. Immediately after the appropriation is voted," Clinton turned to Daniel, "you should travel to Rome and begin hiring contractors. If all goes well, thirty or forty miles of the canal may be dug by the first frost."

The senators present had assured Clinton they had the necessary votes for victory on the appropriation bill. They asked questions of Hedges, and projected the benefits flowing immediately to their constituents.

"It's essential we proceed quickly," Clinton led the way to the drawing room for brandy and cigars. "With the public on our side, the clamoring of that Tammany mob will seem mere whining, and once the digging begins, people will flock to our cause."

As he and Eleanora had prearranged, Daniel left the dinner party first. At his rooming house he changed clothes, waited half an hour, then returned to the townhouse. Satisfied that everyone had departed, he walked up the alley to the gate of her small flower garden. He paused. He noticed a man slouched against the stable door. The man was watching him.

Boldly Hedges crossed the alley to confront him, but seeing that he was noticed, the man turned his face from the light and bolted up the alley. Daniel looked around warily but saw no one else.

Unlatching the gate, he saw the candle in the window, their signal.

He let himself in and forgot about the loiterer.

Next morning, the steps to the Capitol were crowded with politicians holding last minute conferences and newspaper reporters straining to overhear. The senate convened at ten. In the high hall with green velvet curtains and oak desks, debate raged between Henry Yates, Clinton's ally from central New York, and Henry Seymour, a Van Buren follower from Utica.

For three hours, the other thirty senators sat, weighing, evaluating and considering the arguments. Van Buren watched the proceeding warily. He did not wish to cast himself and his followers as obstructionists.

DeWitt Clinton, as lieutenant governor, presided over the senate. He was pleased to recognize one of his allies on the floor who called the previous question. A majority vote was needed to close debate and bring the issue immediately to a vote. With sixteen to sixteen, Clinton might break the tie with a casting vote, yet only fifteen "Ayes" were tallied. The motion failed, and discussion continued, splintering Clinton's solid support.

"Mr. Chairman, may I have the floor?"

"The chair recognizes the senator from Columbia County. Mr. Van Buren, you have the floor."

Van Buren stood. He was not a good orator. His voice was reedy and thin. At first, he seemed nervous; yet soon his logic overcame any lack in oratory.

"Even conceding that this project should be undertaken at all, must we proceed blindly? Should we levy a tax of five dollars on every man, woman and child of this state to conduct an experiment? The canal commission has explored many possibilities as to how and where it should be built, yes. And yes, the people have expressed a desire for the canal. Surveys have been made and engineering studies done. But is there one conclusive fact before us that such a project can be built? No. It is too speculative at present to warrant funding.

"Consider, gentlemen. The canal commission has sought to retain noted engineers from England and France at seven thousand dollars a year, a princely sum. Has anyone accepted? No. They say the project is impossible. Do we have an engineer? Perhaps. The names of Benjamin Wright, Canvass White and Daniel Hedges have been mentioned.

"But they are surveyors, not engineers!" Van Buren spread his arms at the absurdity.

Sitting together in the gallery, Eleanora clasped Daniel's arm.

"Have they ever built anything like this before? No. And who will dig the ditch? Where will the men, the horses, the oxen come from? Mr. Yates, my colleague from Madison County, says the work will be contracted out to local inhabitants, but he must know there are vast tracts of unsettled wilderness. Will the canal simply end at a cliff or a forest or a swamp? As for the canal route, where will it be? There haven't even been stakes driven to show farmers where their fields will be crossed. How long will the digging take? No one knows. Nothing like this has ever been attempted. Five years? Ten years? Twenty? And each year will they come back for more money to save their foundering project? And will we pour more money into this misconceived ditch after what has been wasted already? I say, no, gentlemen. No."

Van Buren shook his head. "We have given this canal project a great deal of attention. I move we call the previous question and vote immediately on this construction appropriation."

The chamber gasped at Van Buren's audacity. He had held out so he could have the last word. Now, his vote and the votes of his allies would provide enough to put it to the test while his arguments were fresh in the legislators' minds. And on the appropriation, a two-thirds vote was needed. With Van Buren's men voting "Nay," a two-thirds vote was impossible.

"Secretary," Clinton hammered the gavel. "Call the roll."

Exactly twenty-two ayes supported Van Buren's motion. The floor of the Senate buzzed with excitement. The appropriation bill would be voted on without further debate. Clinton hammered the gavel again: "Bill before the senate: Whether to appropriate funds for canal construction, amount to be set if two-thirds approve, those in favor say 'aye,' opposed, 'nay.'"

Eleanora gripped Daniel's arm even more tightly. He

looked at the politicians disdainfully. "We need to get twenty-two," she whispered. One by one, the votes were counted, and the chamber gasped at each.

"Twenty ayes," the clerk called. "Twelve nays."

"The appropriation is lost," Clinton cried and hammered down the gavel. The place exploded. Seasoned senators leapt up sputtering, pointing fingers at those who did not vote yes. Furiously Clinton hammered his gavel, crying "Order! Order!" And while shouts and recriminations filled the chamber, Clinton glared down from the desk at Van Buren, and the Fox of Kinderhook inclined his head ever so slightly and smiled.

That evening Clinton stormed into Eleanora's parlor, took a chair and glanced from her to Daniel. He deliberately folded his hands and sat stock still, striving for control.

"What was the telling blow?" she asked.

"Not driving stakes into the ground to mark the route." He rolled his eyes. "No wonder they call him the Little Magician. He defeated our motion to call an immediate vote, got his arguments before the chamber, then succeeded in passing his own motion to call a vote after the fence-sitters decided to be cautious and side with him. He is a master of the game! We knew he had nine, but he picked up three additional votes. I'd like to learn what he promised them in return."

"It's madness how he opposes us," Daniel said.

"Mad and shrewd. He builds his power by tearing our support apart." Clinton raised an eyebrow. "He's an anarchist, profiting from confusion, and he's an accomplished demagogue. Today, he has emerged as the leader of the canal opposition. He has positioned himself as the single vote we must win over and keep if we're to function." Clinton shook his head in disgust.

"Now what?" Eleanora asked.

"I have spent the day regrouping. Adversity must only make us stronger. We have a year to prepare for the next battle, and then the fair-haired boy from Kinderhook will learn how to swallow defeat. I have dispatched young Canvass White to England to study and make drawings of canals and locks, and also to hire diggers. Napoleon's defeat has left many English military engineers idle. And Mr. Wright will build a workable lock so our doubters can see how it will raise and lower boats."

"They are very able," Daniel agreed. "White surveyed much of the central section, and Wright has done the eastern. Have you plans for me?"

Clinton nodded. "I want you to begin at Buffalo and survey the western course of the canal for the last time, hopefully, every inch of ground to the Irondequoit. Others will do the same for the central and eastern sections. We'll need altitudes, soil composition, ownership of the land, the depth of gullies and streams to be crossed, as well as sites for aqueducts and culverts and locks." Clinton gently pounded his fist on the arm of the chair. "By next year, we shall have the most exhaustive survey of any strip of land ever conducted. Let Van Buren oppose us then."

"And I?" Eleanora asked.

"I ask a special effort of you, my dear Eleanora. In this state, hundreds now languish in prison for debt and other petty offenses. We should turn their idleness into productive labor. We could allow them to work on the canal until their sentence has run, and pay them the same wage as other men. I have attorneys looking into the constitutionality of clemency. You should visit the prisons in the guise of a reformer and look into conditions there. The legislature will need a report about using prison labor as well." Eleanora nodded.

"Well, it would be much easier if I were a dictator," Clinton said with levity, "but the people have spoken through their representatives, and we must speak back." He lightly tapped the arms of the chair. "The canal lost a year today, but let us put this setback behind us quickly." He stood and shook

Daniel's hand heartily. "Let us prepare for the next session and we shall prevail." He kissed Eleanora on the cheek, shook Hedges' hand again, and walked from the room.

They sat and stared into each other's eyes for a long moment. Eleanor spoke first. "And so we must part again?"

Daniel nodded and set his jaw.

"Oh, Daniel, will it always be this way?"

"Only so long as the canal is all we share." He stood.

"You're not leaving?"

"Yes, I am. I'm tired and I have a lot of thinking to do. These damnable politicians and their trickery and deceit."

"Please, Daniel, we can't part this way! We can't! I won't see you for six months." Her eyes darted back and forth. "I have a plan that occurred to me this morning when Van Buren was speaking. We'll appoint you chief engineer for the actual digging. You can manage the work, I know." She was clasping his arm, staring with anxious hope into his eyes. "That's what we'll do. DeWitt will do it for me . . . for you . . . for us."

Daniel looked down at her. "Let's take the path a step at a time. We trip over ourselves when we think too far in advance." He turned to go.

"You'll not part from me this way?"

"No. I'll call tomorrow before I leave."

He kissed her gently and she backed away from him. After the door closed, she threw herself on the love seat sobbing. "Oh, this wretched, wretched business."

Across the city, Van Buren and his supporters were celebrating Clinton's defeat and their own rise to power as an independent force allied with Tammany.

"Today we demonstrated," Van Buren said, raising a glass of claret high into the candlelight, "what may be accomplished when we vote together. Today marks the beginning of a new era in state politics. Yes, gentlemen, we in this room," he looked slowly around at the twenty-three assembled, "will shortly control all offices of this state. I christen us 'The Albany Regency' and we shall win the admiration and respect we deserve."

"Here, here!" the others cried in unison.

As Van Buren moved around the room talking with each man individually, a waiter approached him and whispered in his ear. "Yes," Van Buren said, "I'll be up presently." Excusing himself then, he proceeded upstairs to a private room. Aaron Burr was seated on an ottoman, a fire blazing in the hearth despite the warm summer weather.

"Come in, my boy. I hear the most glowing accounts of your speech in the Senate this morning. I quite regret I could not attend."

"You do me great honor, sir."

"You play the game extraordinarily well, turning the tables so quickly on your opposition. You have raised yourself up as the leader of a powerful faction which Clinton will have to reckon with soon. You must get on the Council of Appointment. Then you shall control the offices dispensed in every county of this state!" Burr chuckled, then narrowed his eye.

"You have learned much from watching others. Now learn from one old man. You have an able enemy in Clinton, and the farther you push him and all of his people down, the higher you will rise. But Clinton has a great following, as did General Hamilton. Use Clinton as you will," he raised an instructive finger, "but take care how you dispose of him."

"Dueling is no longer in fashion." Van Buren was still cocky from the day's victory. "I shall employ other means."

Burr grew gravely serious. "Yes, Matty, but remember that in politics you can kill a man, but you can't mutilate his memory. You can strip him of power but not his reputation, for to be deposed is one thing, dishonored is another. His followers will rise and stalk you all your days."

"I learn from your example, sir, and am flattered by your attention."

Burr nodded at the homage. "You offer me the chance to rectify many of my mistakes, as if I had a son. Now," Burr grew more cheerful, "be off with you to enjoy the praise you have earned. There be many setbacks to offset your victory tonight, so savor it deeply. Leave an old man alone to reminisce about his own past victories."

CHAPTER 22

*H*edges rode back across the state to measure and survey the western course of the canal for the legislature. He finished by winter and decided to remain in Buffalo. He repaired the roof of his old cabin, and on his land between the Seneca reservation and the village he hunted for his meat. The solitude pleased him, and when he gazed into the fire on winter nights he remembered the sweet life with Carrie in the cabin and the joy of his children. He also thought of Eleanora.

Occasionally Daniel strolled past his lot in town and looked at the squatter's cottage and the children in the yard. One afternoon early in March, Daniel saw a woman leave the hut. She barely glanced at him, but he recognized her. "Miss McKay?" She turned. "Edna?"

"Captain Hedges?"

"You live here?"

"Why, yes."

"And these are your children?"

"Yes."

"I didn't know you were married."

"A woman scarcely needs a husband for that."

"Quite so." Her saucy expression made her quite pretty. "May I walk you to the tavern?"

She nodded and her eyes bored into his: "If you do not mind being seen with me." She kept talk to neutral topics, about what had brought him back to Buffalo and how long he would be staying. As they parted at the inn, Edna extended her hand, "I hope we shall speak again, Mr. Hedges."

"I'd like that."

He had seen for the first time how pretty she was. Every other time he had been distracted by something else, the raging battle, Lester Frye or Eleanora. Now here was a dilemma. He pondered it long and hard for a week. Three hundred and fifty miles separated him from the woman he loved, a woman who would not publicly acknowledge him. Here at hand was a most attractive woman he'd rescued years before, who had children he might help raise, who even lived on his property! It would be practical indeed to court Edna McKay. But as Daniel reflected, he cursed the perversity of human nature that made men always want what they cannot have and the more unattainable, the greater the desire.

But although he avoided courting Edna and watched for her children each time he passed the lot, his letters to Eleanora, both to Claverack and to the Albany townhouse, went unanswered.

There was good reason why she didn't write back. After touring Sing Sing, the Tombs and Newgate, Eleanora returned to her estate, but the solitude she usually enjoyed at Claverack was shattered in mid-September. Alone in the candlelight of her drawing room, she was playing a wistful Mozart prelude on the pianoforte when Hilda burst in. "Ma'am, Joel's here and he's in a powerful upset state, asking to see you, he is."

"Well, show him in."

Joel's eyes smoldered and he trembled with rage. "Beggin' your pardon to call at such an unreasonable hour, ma'am, but

I just come from the Chatham Inn, and a scoundrel named Gleason taunted me terrible." She looked up and frowned. "No, I didn't brawl with the red-nosed Irish bast –, beggin' your pardon, ma'am, but on your account I should have splayed his nose across his miserable face!"

"What was it about? I don't know the man." She arose and moved the candelabra to a side table and motioned Joel to a chair.

"Well, he railed on and on about the estate and about you, ma'am. He called you names I ain't heard since the prison camp. It was more than I could stomach, so I told him to be still. Well, an Irishman can't keep still even when he's stone cold sober, and that certainly warn't the case here. So he turns on me and says that he and his master will be running you and me off Claverack before long because of your, er, your *friend-ship* with Mr. Hedges."

Eleanora's heart missed a beat. "Hilda, bring two glasses of brandy." She fought for control, attempted to appear cool and indifferent. The brandy provided a welcome interruption, and she sipped it slowly. "Did he mention who his master might be?"

"Yes'm. Randolph Van Rensselaer, that rum-soaked drunk out of Hudson."

"Jacob's brother!"

"Yes. Gleason said he's been surveilling you on your 'jaunts,' as he called them, and he's kept a watch outside the house in Albany, and that they have enough to run you clean off your land right now." Joel poured his brandy off in one gulp. "Evil business, it is, sure enough, mum."

Eleanora was silent. Joel was curious and he summoned his courage and asked:

"Would there be any truth to what he said about running us out of Claverack?"

Eleanora tried to smile. "Of course not! Randolph has elevated delusions of grandeur to an art form."

"Aye, he surely puts on airs. I encountered him Saturday at market. He's strutting the streets of Hudson with new clothing, trussed up like a peacock. There's a suspiciously smug look to him these days."

"Pay no attention to it," she said off-handedly, but her voice wavered, and she saw that Joel noticed. Her hand was trembling, too, as she reached for the glass.

They then discussed back rents and Claverack's mills and the carding house and Joel left. For half an hour, Eleanora gazed into the candlelight, hardly breathing. Stretched out before her she saw only sordid name-calling, endless court battles and vicious, greedy grasping for her land. Until now she had stood above it all, a lady, a woman of property, deserving of respect. Now she would be dragged down in the eyes of her peers, her tenants, her friends, family and society at large for allowing herself the simple, all too human pleasure of loving a man. "How could I be so stupid?" she asked herself endlessly.

She did not sleep that night. She paced the room like a caged beast. Whom could she tell? No one. Admitting her love for Daniel Hedges could forfeit her this land. She paused at the window. The fields and barns were bathed in moonlight, and the answer seemed to hover in the moonglow above the rooftops and weathervanes. She did not love him any less, but the consequences! Eleanora closed her eyes, slumped to the floor and stretched full length on the cool oak. It soothed her cheek she rolled over to press her breasts, hips, arms and thighs against its cool, polished smoothness. This land, this house, this estate was hers and it was as much a part of her as her name. But tonight she felt a kinship with the wretched prisoners she had seen. She must fight for these lands, and she must avoid Daniel at all costs. She regretted that she couldn't tell him why, yet she must not. No one must know and he would think less of her. "The dead hand," she murmured in the darkness, her brow pressed to the floorboards.

~

That December, Clinton summoned her to Albany. "You look pale and thin," he observed as he kissed her cheek. "But never mind. Tompkins is resigning and I am running for governor in a special election on the popularity of the canal. Our work will put the roses back in your cheeks." He described the tremendous support he'd received for the canal project and for a gubernatorial campaign. "It seems as though we've been working on this forever, dear Eleanora. Hedges' final study will be presented next week and we will call Van Buren's bluff. What possible objection can he raise now?"

"I see none." The mention of Hedges affected her noticeably.

"Canvass White, our engineering genius, has returned from England with drawings of canals, towpaths, locks, bridges and canal boats. He brought an Irishman back with him, J.J. McShane, a hardy, unlettered fellow who shows precisely the muscle we'll need for the digging. How did you fare at the state prisons?"

"Oh, DeWitt, what a pitiful lot! Nowhere but in Dante have I encountered such horrors, such despair. The cells are only four feet wide and ten long and the men are stacked to the ceiling on wooden slabs as if in bookcases, two or three to a cell. They sleep on moldy hay in the most unbelievable stench, and the cells crawl with insects and rats."

Clinton nodded gravely. "And many are there simply because they can't pay their debts. We'll screen out the violent felons and offer the others this work."

"They didn't look human! Their heads were shaved to prevent lice. They shuffled around in chains with their eyes cast down."

"I can't imagine any of them opting to stay in prison if they could be in the open air digging." Clinton considered. "I was impressed with that Irishman McShane. Immigrants from

Ireland are pouring into Manhattan, and the great proportion of our prisoners are Irish. McShane seems just the man to keep them in line. We'll use work gangs – immigrants and prisoners – to dig where private contractors have not bid the job."

"I assume this young man White will oversee the contractors, then?"

"No," Clinton shook his head. "He will certainly be invaluable as an engineer, and I must keep him free to travel. I want to hire Hedges to oversee the construction gangs. He performed valuable service for Commodore Perry during the war, getting men to work together and work hard. I'll put McShane under him."

At the mention of Daniel's name she involuntarily looked away. "I see."

Clinton scrutinized her. "Have you any objection?"

"No." Still she looked away. She felt faint.

"You have no objection?" Clinton asked again.

"No," she said, failing in her attempt at nonchalance.

"I thought you enjoyed the man's company."

"I, I do. And yet, and yet," she was losing her composure in front of a man who'd risen to power reading the truth in people's faces.

"You don't think him competent?"

"Of course he's competent!"

"What is the difficulty, then?"

"Something personal."

"Something personal!" Clinton exclaimed in exasperation. "I knew it! I told you at the outset that personal feelings must not interfere with our great work, and you agreed, and now . . . something personal . . ." His voice trailed off.

Eleanora was silent, but her face flushed red. She felt as though she had betrayed him.

"What am I to do?" he demanded of her. "I must rely on both of you. I *need* both of you."

She stared back silently. Her own embarrassment and sorrow far surpassed any damage to Clinton, but she couldn't tell him. Clinton and his damned canal!

"I will be governor of this state!" Clinton held his hand out as if striving to grasp something intangible. "The state, Eleanora, *this* state of New York is the repository of all our hopes and dreams and gives us our identity as a people. The state provides the justice and protection from fear that we enjoy. Men put their trust into the state, and from the state they take direction in leading their lives. And to rule the state nothing, *nothing* personal can stand in the way of guarding men's interests in liberty and property."

"Is that one of your Masonic ideals?"

He ignored the jibe. "I cannot afford to have personal issues in my way, particularly when they can be avoided with a little self-control."

Eleanora flinched at his lecture. *Self-control!* She considered an angry rejoinder, but knew it would accomplish nothing except make her look foolish and defensive. Clinton saw her expression and his voice softened.

"You have been by my side, Eleanora, in so many under-takings. How many times have we been to Washington? Above all our other efforts, Eleanora, this canal will change the thinking of men. Until now, wealth has been measured largely by land-holdings. Soon trade will replace that and a whole new class of leaders will arise, merchants and manufacturers, raised up by the riches and the high accomplishment our canal brings us.

"The completion of this canal will be the greatest hour, not only for New York, but for our nation. It will show the world the best that liberty and our system of government can accomplish. You have been my most helpful ally from its inception. Hedges has been invaluable since we began looking past political issues toward the actual digging. We cannot afford to splinter apart. That is exactly what Van Buren wants."

He reached down and she placed her hand in his. Slowly she looked up into his eyes. "And so I must ask you to put aside any feeling you may have for the man. Work with him as another man might. Our success is far more important than our personal concerns and only together will we succeed. Apart, we all shall fail and fail miserably."

"Of course, DeWitt," she bowed her head with respect, "it will be done."

"Then contact him and set up a meeting. Use a subordinate if you must. We should meet soon after my election to orchestrate our drive for funds this year in the legislature."

"I will do so directly."

Clinton showed himself out. Eleanora sat for the better part of an hour, her mind in hot confusion. Of course she must never tell Daniel any of this! But when he tries to re-establish intimacy, she must fend him off and return their association to one of strictly business. She'd deal with Daniel through Joel Kipp. Let Randolph Van Rensselaer and Gleason make innuendos, they would never have proof.

CHAPTER 23

*A*pril's special election swept DeWitt Clinton into the governor's chair, 43,000 votes to 1,500, a staggering mandate to proceed with the canal. As they traveled by sleigh toward the inauguration, Clinton remarked to Eleanora, "Now let Van Buren obstruct us."

The *Albany Argus*, usually a Van Buren mouthpiece, editorialized that the canal's time had come, and urged a speedy passage of the funding bill. Daniel Hedges entered Albany on inauguration day 1817 on a rented horse. The ale houses, hotels and streets were filled with drunken crowds cheering Clinton and the new age he'd usher in. Hedges proceeded to Mrs. Pratt's, but it was full and he had to ask at five others until he found a room.

"'Tis a grand eve, sir," the innkeeper remarked as he opened a dusty room up under the eaves.

"Yes, but crowds have a habit of turning, and I wouldn't want this one against me."

"But there's no effigies burning tonight. Everyone's of one mind."

The innkeeper was correct. Martin Van Buren had not even complained.

Indeed, earlier that morning, Van Buren had met with Aaron Burr.

"Now, my boy, is the time to show your statesmanship," Burr said, rubbing his hands together and cackling at the notion of statesmanship. "You must show you're bigger than their petty politics. You alone listen to the people and proceed cautiously."

"I will proceed cautiously because today it's Clinton's mob."

"It is never wise to ignore the mob. Like a baby wailing, there's often more wisdom in what it says than in all of our philosophy."

"Yes, for a time I must support the canal."

"But cautiously, Matty, cautiously." Burr tapped his temple. "In politics you should never close all the doors behind you for eventually you'll need an escape."

Van Buren was busy that day throughout Albany responding to Clinton's swearing in and what many considered a telling defeat. He returned at six to his new home on State Street for his usual change of linen.

"Everyone tells me that Clinton has bested you, dear." Hannah selected a shirt for him.

"Ah, love," Van Buren removed wrinkled shirt, "issues in politics are like these shirts. You wear them until they're soiled, then you change. Last year, we were merely asking for more information. They complied. Now we can support the project."

Hannah shook her head. "Politics is second only to law in utterly confounding me."

Meeting with the members of his Regency, Van Buren found them less likely to change their shirts. During the evening caucus, Van Buren pleaded with them to give in.

"We will seem inconsistent and weak!" George Marshall complained.

"Clinton will carry the day with or without us," Van Buren predicted.

"But our position will erode!"

"Our position is untenable," Van Buren said quietly, his pale eyes quickly darting about. "As for consistency, the only consistency I care for is to be on the right side of this issue."

Still the men protested, venting frustration that Tammany would object to their changing their votes, and because Clinton was governor, many relatives and friends would lose their jobs. They also protested that if they didn't continue their opposition, the canal would be dug and their former votes would seem short-sighted. Van Buren watched them, listened to them and smiled to himself, for he knew that by persistence and persuasion eventually he'd have his way.

Daniel Hedges passed through the streets feeling as if he'd awakened in Bedlam. Drunken men capered on roofs howling and screaming; they leapt off wagons and danced in the streets while tavern doors flew open, spewing ragged songs and streams of revelers from their smoky taprooms.

He was glad to see lights in the windows of Eleanora's townhouse. He stepped up the stairs, rang the bell and noticed a curtain sway in an upper window. The door was a long time in being answered.

"Yes?" It was Joel Kipp, and he wasn't friendly.

"Joel!" Daniel said with familiarity.

"What do you want?"

"Why, to see Eleanora, of course."

"Lady Van Rensselaer's receiving no one," Joel said flatly.

"Is she ill?"

"Yes," Joel snapped, patently lying, "she's ill."

Daniel paused, looked down, then back up. Joel's expression was inscrutable. "Well, then, tell her I called and that I hope she is feeling better."

"Yes, Mr. Hedges, I'll do that." Abruptly he closed the door. Hedges paused on the porch, and saw the window curtain above sway again.

Everything seemed topsy-turvy tonight, a night they should be celebrating. Daniel stepped to the street, shoved his hands deep into his pockets and ambled back to his room.

For the next two days Albany buzzed with anticipation over the canal bill vote. If approved, funds would at last be set aside for digging. The Tammany crew was unalterably opposed, but Van Buren had mollified his voting bloc into keeping an open mind.

The vote came on the last day of session. In the gallery, newly sworn Governor Clinton and Eleanora hoped for passage, but steadied themselves for defeat.

"There's Hedges," Clinton pointed. Eleanora seemed startled as Daniel turned and waved. She nodded and looked away.

Four times through the morning the bill was shuffled from the Senate to the Assembly for modifications. The tall clock read 11:45, only fifteen minutes remained until adjournment. "Damn them," Clinton muttered. "They'll defeat us with their delay and their procedures." Eleanora placed her hand over his and she stole a look at Daniel. He sat in a relaxed posture, indifferent to the goings-on. She felt a stab of sadness. The excitement, the disappointment, the nearness of Daniel, but the distance she must maintain, all of it made her feel that she would burst into tears. Then Van Buren asked for the floor, and the Senate chamber grew very quiet.

"Now we're undone," she whispered and threw up her hands.

Clinton looked down dejectedly. Van Buren would filibuster until the clock ran out, and another year would pass before they could begin digging.

"Gentlemen of the Senate," the little man spoke, "we were asked to consider such funding last year, and before us now this bill returns."

"The *coup de grace*," Clinton muttered. "He's despicable!"

"I have studied what our able surveyors have compiled for us, and I am staggered by the enormity of the project, and the size of the financial commitment we are being asked to underwrite. Nowhere has any state built a public work of this scale."

"Why won't he thrust in his sword and have done with it?" Clinton said through clenched teeth. He rapped his walking stick impatiently on the floor.

"Last year we asked for this additional information to be made available for us to make an informed decision. This year we can make that informed decision."

The clock read 11:51. In despair, Eleanora looked at Daniel, but he still viewed the debate dispassionately.

"The minor adjustments we have made over the last three weeks allow me, gentlemen, to stand before you this morning and say . . . I believe the time for the canal has come."

Pandemonium erupted. Four justices in the gallery, canal opponents and intimates of Van Buren, nearly tumbled over the railing. Clinton's mouth dropped. Again, again, and again the new lieutenant governor rapped his gavel. "Order! Order!"

Van Buren raised his hands for quiet.

"I have heard a great deal about the Fox of Kinderhook," Clinton whispered. "He is the ablest politician I have seen." He nodded to the clock. "He has just become the savior of the canal, the champion of this year's session."

"Yes," Van Buren called. "We have ample findings here to commit state money for one year of digging."

Instantly Clinton was on his feet and down the stairs. He passed the sergeant-at-arms and joined Van Buren on the

Senate floor. Many cheered seeing the two together, and Clinton shook Van Buren's hand warmly to signal to his allies that they should follow Van Buren's lead. "You have shown yourself a statesman this morning," Clinton was flushed and enthusiastic, towering over the smaller man.

"It will be a pleasure to unite for the good of all," Van Buren said.

Waving to his cheering supporters, Clinton left the floor for the final vote. The appropriation bill, needing two-thirds, passed by one vote – Van Buren's – and the chamber erupted again with applause as the clock rang twelve times and on motion the lieutenant governor adjourned. Eleanora looked at Daniel Hedges, and he was staring at her.

"Decisive vote! Decisive vote!" The canal supporters flocked to Van Buren and escorted him from the chamber. But when he reached the sunlight outside and the crowd thinned, Van Buren replied to a friend's question: "Yes, we've given Clinton the money to dig his ditch. One year's worth, and then we'll bury him in it."

Hedges vowed to see Eleanora that night. The streets were loud and joyous, drunken songs spilling out of sawdust saloons, and coaches careening through the streets as he walked along, but an ominous feeling beset him. Again the lights were on in her townhouse. Hedges rang the bell and waited. The door was opened again by Joel Kipp.

"Sir?"

"Please announce me to Eleanora."

"I'm sorry, she's receiving no visitors."

"Please announce me." Daniel glared at the young man. "Allow her to make her own decision."

Joel paused, closed the door, was gone just a moment, then

returned. "I'm sorry, sir, Mrs. Van Rensselaer is receiving no one."

Daniel grew impatient. "I don't believe you!"

"She told me she would talk with you tomorrow at the canal board meeting."

"I don't believe she said that at all! I must insist that I ask her myself."

"Sir, you should go."

"No. I will not. I saw Mrs. Van Rensselaer this morning, and I want to discuss an important matter with her."

Joel looked over Daniel's shoulder and nodded. Daniel turned and saw a man slouching against a house across the street. He thought this was a diversionary tactic. "Announce me at once!"

Joel stammered something behind the door, then the door opened fully, revealing Eleanora behind it, listening to them. Hedges was shocked and silenced.

"Why won't you believe my servant, Mr. Hedges? He speaks for me."

"I didn't believe he told you what I said."

"So, you see you were mistaken. My servants obey me. I have implicit trust in Joel, and you should as well."

Angry, embarrassed and bewildered, Hedges bowed and muttered, "I am sorry to have upset your household."

"Good night, Mr. Hedges," she said with icy formality, and slowly but emphatically she closed the door.

When Daniel left, Eleanora dashed up the stairs. Joel watched, not understanding what had happened. She ripped open the bedroom door, slammed it behind her and threw herself on the bed. She tried desperately not to remember, but it all came back, the night he visited her in this very room and the tenderness of his lips, his touch, the joy in his face, the tour across the state, the visit to Buffalo. Now, four walls and an empty bed. No, she told herself with clenched teeth, she must not descend into self-pity, but even as she vowed not to, sobs and hot tears came. Oh, how she loved him! And she could never tell him why she could not declare it!

Meanwhile, smarting from the rebuff, Daniel turned and stepped to the street. As he started on his way, the man in the shadow of the doorway across the street came to life: "Care for a pint of ale?" He fell in step with Daniel. "Name's Gleason."

"Hedges," Daniel shook his hand. "Daniel Hedges."

Hedges accompanied Gleason to a warehouse on the riverbank. Inside, planks on sawhorses made a bar, and in the center of the floor a boxing ring had been roped off and marked by lines on the sawdust floor. Everyone spoke in Irish brogues. The crowd pressed up to the ring, cheering the boxers. In the ring, two large bare-chested men, sweating, hairy and brawny, were parading before the loud, applauding crowd, holding their fists in the air.

"She's a game lassie, though?" Gleason leered. Daniel ignored him and ordered two tankards of ale.

"Could you imagine returning home to that each evening?" Gleason smacked his lips and winked. Daniel paid for the ale. The roar of the crowd signaled one of the boxers was knocked unconscious. The bookmakers chalked odds on their slates.

"So," Gleason licked foam from his lips, "how well do you know her?"

"Not well. We work together on the canal project. That's all."

"Aye." Gleason saw Daniel's irritation and fell quiet.

"And now," the referee cried, "from County Cork by way of Liverpool, that battlin' brawlin' son of old Erin – John Joseph McShane!" Boos and catcalls filled the air.

Into the ring stepped a wide, barrel-chested man of forty. He raised his clenched fists defiantly and strutted around the ring.

"And opposin' McShane, gentlemen, five times champion

at Hannigan's Saloon, Irish Sean Malloy!" The place went berserk over the local Albany favorite. A slimmer, younger man pranced into the ring, punching and feinting and dancing with fancy footwork. Bookies chalked their odds and betting began. Soon the odds were four-to-one against McShane.

"Let's get on with it, Paddy!" McShane called impatiently. The referee discussed rules, the bell rang to start the fight and the bare-fisted fighters came from their corners. The bookies continued to erase and scribble. Malloy staggered McShane with a punch, and McShane seemed red-faced, out of breath.

"Are ye a bettin' man?" Gleason asked Daniel.

"Not usually, but perhaps tonight. Five dollars on the older fellow."

"He won't last three rounds!"

"But Malloy has no odds. It ain't worth risking my coin."

Gleason shrugged, took the five dollar goldpiece from Hedges and placed two bets.

Like a lumbering bear, J.J. McShane groped around the ring. The younger man danced and jabbed and ducked and circled. Tempers rose and men screamed. When the odds reached eight-to-one a bookmaker called: "Bets are closed, gentlemen."

Now a change came over McShane. His chest expanded, his legs grew limber, a keen defiant look flashed in his eye. He danced and feinted and jabbed at Malloy who had tired himself out. Each of McShane's punches was well-placed and shook Malloy to his frame, body shot after body shot. Men pressed closer to the ring, crying desperately for Malloy to guard, to hit back, to duck. McShane's withering blows rained on the younger man despite his fancy footwork. "Your boy's in the winnin'," Gleason cried. Daniel nodded.

Malloy's face was a bloody mess, blood smeared down his arms and chest when one of McShane's shattering punches sent him to the sawdust. He lay there, trying to rise, sawdust clinging to the blood. The referee asked if he would return to the fight. He shook his head. As McShane crossed the ring, he bent over and helped Malloy up. A small group of men who'd been standing together, McShane's crew, cashed their bets.

"Looks like you won," Gleason told Hedges. "Yes, I won big tonight."

"Shall I collect your winnings?"

"By all means," Daniel said, motioning him toward the bookmakers. Gleason returned with forty dollars in gold. Daniel watched McShane accept congratulations from the small group of men who had won by betting on him.

"We thought you were done this time," one said. "You waited long enough."

"Only till they closed the books," McShane said, toweling himself off. "We got enough for a round of whiskeys and some rooms with lassies? I'm tired of sleeping on the floor."

"Aye, J.J. Enough for two weeks of both."

"Then let's have a drink!" The Irishmen cried and moved to the bar. Four whiskey bottles appeared, and without glasses they swigged and passed them man-to-man.

"Good boys," Gleason observed. "Just off the boat. Probably left wives and gals back home whilst they seek their fortune in the New World." He squinted at Daniel. "You married?"

"No," Daniel said flatly.

"Do you fancy the lady?"

Daniel looked Gleason squarely in the eye. "Even if I did, what would she ever see in me?" The question hung unanswered for a full minute.

"You're right."

"Well, Gleason, time I get some sleep." He clinked down ten dollars. "Buy those Irish boys a drink."

"See you again?"

Hedges nodded, pulled on his hat and left the tavern. The air off the river was cool. He paused and looked, thinking. The river ran smooth and still and dark beneath the pilings of the piers. Why had Gleason been outside Eleanora's house? Then he thought of McShane. The fighter pleased him, how he had played the crowd and milked their bets. Daniel thought of the deck of the *Lawrence*, red with blood after battle. He remembered how he felt that day when Perry left, and how he felt tonight as Eleanora turned him away. Tonight it made him feel good to watch one man beat another into a bloody pulp.

He slept well and awoke refreshed. Lying in bed, he thought about what he would do now that Eleanora had rejected him. Ellicott had been right so long ago. Perhaps the canal commissioners needed something else; if not, he should return to Buffalo and build another ship. Edna was there and no doubt her offer stood. She was more like him, common and easygoing. He'd wasted his time by waiting for Eleanora. The future was refreshingly open to him now. He would enjoy turning in his surveyor's notebooks, collecting his salary and being done with the canal. Then he would owe no one anything, and he might leave Albany forever. Joseph was in town, and they could ride home together.

Dressed in buckskin, Hedges attended the commissioners' meeting the next morning. Uncomfortably he, Simeon DeWitt and five canal commissioners waited for the governor. In the dusty office they discussed geology and topography until a clerk announced Clinton's coach. Hedges watched through the window as Clinton helped Eleanora down and escorted her up the steps to the Capitol. Daniel noted that they made a fine couple as they entered the room, a suspicion suggested by her smile.

"Thank you for coming," Clinton said. Eleanora sat regally, her eyes fixed with admiration for her governor. Daniel watched Eleanora, but she did not turn his way. He thought he saw the game. Today Clinton spoke with new authority. Like a military commander he gave orders as if he were deploying troops.

"And to superintend the digging, I have carefully considered this appointment." Daniel watched Eleanora. How inscrutable she seemed! "You'll all be pleased, as will the public, when I give this to the press. Daniel Hedges will superintend the digging of the first phase of the canal."

Daniel started to clap, then Ellicott nudged him. All eyes were on him. He heard the words echo, then he looked at Clinton in disbelief. The great man was clapping his hands and nodding at him. Eleanora smiled evenly and clapped her gloved hands. Ellicott was beaming congratulations.

"Speech! Speech!" they demanded of him.

"I'd be honored," Daniel stammered at their applause.

"And to help with the first stretch," Clinton motioned to one of the lads and the young man opened the door. Bruised and smiling, J.J. McShane stepped in, folded his arms and gazed around. "I present to you Mr. J.J. McShane who has emigrated from Liverpool with valuable experience in digging canals."

"County Cork originally," McShane nodded.

"Mr. McShane and his Irishmen will accompany Mr. Hedges to Rome where he will help get the digging underway this summer." McShane waved to them, then left the room. As a last item, Clinton set the official opening ceremony for July 4th.

As they adjourned, Daniel watched Eleanora. She brushed past him, murmuring, "Excuse me, Mr. Hedges."

Daniel met McShane in the hall.

"I saw your fight last night," he told the big man. McShane had a shock of red hair and heavily freckled skin.

"Didn't lose no money, did ye?" He winked. Daniel shook his head. "Good. Always bet on J.J., Mr. Hedges. Me and the boys were a wee bit short of capital being new to America and all, and that's the handiest way of raising the scratch."

Together he and Hedges walked outside. Daniel listened to his account of the voyage, trying desperately not to watch the slender form in a burgundy gown and parasol helped into Clinton's carriage.

"Ah," McShane said, filling his lungs with fresh spring air, "ye've got the sweetest air on earth, Mr. Hedges. America! You can smell it, laced with the perfume of freedom, it is."

"Call me 'Daniel,' please, McShane."

"Aye, 'Dan-o' then it is."

"We've got a lot of work ahead of us." Daniel watched the carriage pull away, and the woman sit back in its shade and close her parasol.

Again McShane breathed deeply, "Aye, it's a new era being born, Dan-o, a new era indeed."

Daniel nodded. "So it is."

CHAPTER 24

*A*s the sun rose that Fourth of July, a small cluster of men stood in a meadow outside the ruins of Fort Stanwix. Along the flat plain to the east, and the plain of rich dark soil to the west, a line of stakes had been driven. Men talked in low voices.

Dressed in woolen trousers, shirt sleeves and a beaver hat, Governor Clinton smoked a cigar. "Gentlemen, today we realize the fruit of many years' labor. We have triumphed over the disbelievers, nay-sayers and politicians. Forty-one years ago today, a courageous group of men put their signatures to the Declaration of Independence and gave birth to our nation, but we must remember that the Declaration only signaled the beginning of a bloody seven years' war. We are beginning a great undertaking, and now we must level hills, bridge streams, scale heights and cut through mountains to join Lake Erie to the Hudson River and the Atlantic."

Nearby, a mule hitched to an upright plow flicked its tail and a blue jay screamed across the sky. Hedges scanned the serious faces of the other men, farmers and merchants from Rome along with Clinton's brethren from the Masonic temple. Eleanora had not attended the ceremony. He looked to the east where the stakes disappeared over the horizon, then to the west. This small informal ceremony pleased him.

Clinton continued: "At last we have the funds to dig, and we shall dig as much as possible this year. Yet we must not forget that our project has its enemies, able enemies. Funds may very well dry up before we dig much farther. So let us work vigorously to show the world what a free people with vision can accomplish."

Clapping sounded light in the open air.

"Let us then proceed." Clinton threw down his cigar and took the handles of the plow. "Giddyap!" The mule awoke, pulled the reins taut, and the plow sank into the rich black soil and turned up the first furrow of the canal.

Daniel shook McShane's hand. "We've got a lot of digging to do, my friend!"

"Aye, Dan-o. So let's get on with it."

BOOK IV
INTO THE WESTERN
REACHES

Office of the Holland Land Company, Batavia.

CHAPTER 25

*B*y September the great work was well underway as contractors ripped through forty miles of virgin soil. These yeomen hired out their teams of horses, mules and oxen and also hired out their own brawny backs and arms and those of their sons. Along the staked-out route, they stripped trees and brush, dragging out stumps and primordial root systems. They grubbed and furrowed the land with teams and plows, back and forth, then hauled loose earth to the sides to form embankments. Forty feet wide at its lip and sloping to a width of twenty-eight feet at bottom, the ditch was a modest four feet deep. The sloping sides formed a prism, with a berm on the south side and a towpath on the north. Horses and oxen plodding back and forth packed the banks firmly.

Only three locks were needed along the level ground, the bed of an ancient lake, between Rome and Salina. Canvass White carefully designed the locks from sketches drawn in England and he scouted with local farmers for suitable granite to quarry. White experimented until he found limestone with the proper chemical composition to make hydraulic cement, a mortar that hardened further the longer it was exposed to water.

Daniel Hedges traveled back and forth along the canal bed that summer and fall supervising the dig, measuring to assure the prism was uniform and paying the contractors in coin from a strongbox in his buckboard. He enjoyed the supervising. He understood these pioneer contractors. They were honest, direct, simple men who welcomed the chance to link their hamlets and farms with the markets and factories of the east. From Oliver Perry he'd learned how to command, but his style was never arrogant. He paused with each contractor as if visiting, asked about difficulties encountered, made suggestions, then offered them a swig of corn liquor from a jug.

Soon McShane had his forty-five Irish mates quarrying, cutting and dressing granite blocks. They hauled the huge granite blocks along the towpath on rollers, and measuring and checking levels, they built the first twin lock chamber, one for eastbound and one for westbound traffic. McShane caulked the lock gates made of white oak with tarred hempen rope, then hung the gates and fixed levers to open and close them from drawings in the sketch books of Canvass White. By mid-October the first lock and fifteen miles of canal were ready for water. The testing of the ditch and lock drew a thousand people. At a signal from a cannon, the dams of feeder canals were opened and water poured into the canal ditch. A resounding cheer rose from men and women, squeals of delight from children.

Just south of Salina, J.J.'s natural showman's flair came out as he tested the Milan lock. With a flourish of his arm he commanded the down-water gates be closed and the up-water gates be opened. Water poured into the lock chamber and lifted a boat on which he had placed three children. The children's fear turned to delight as the boat rose, and the crowd applauded wildly until the boat was eight feet above its former level and the gate opened and a team of mules towed it eastward.

Praise for this small stretch of canal was universal. Hedges found the digging immensely rewarding compared to the endless haggling of politics. "Now it's something a man can get his hands around," he explained, "not like the endless wrangling before." In his tent late at night, Daniel often thought of Eleanora. He remembered, as he balanced his books, how happy they had been on their tour across the state, and as he blew out the lamp and lay down on his cot, he felt an emptiness that no amount of work or success could ease.

Eleanora's problems deepened. One muggy August afternoon, Joel announced the Columbia County sheriff. "And he's got some paper, some order with him, too."

As she swept into the foyer to meet him, the sheriff doffed his hat. "Sorry, Mizz Van Rensselaer, but I got these papers to serve from the court."

"What are they?"

"An order of ejectment."

"Ejectment?" Joel demanded, advancing on the man. "I'll show you ejectment."

"Joel!" Eleanora said, then extended her hand for the papers. "Very well, Sheriff. I'll take it."

"Sorry, ma'am." He fumbled with his hat, glared at Joel, then left.

"But why?" Joel asked in disbelief.

"This is a matter for lawyers and courts. Don't concern yourself. I will attend to it." After dismissing Joel, she went upstairs and took an iron box from a secret compartment in her bedstead. The box held her mother's jewelry, twenty-three thousand dollars in gold, and a copy of the deeds to the Claverack estate from the Livingstons and the Van Rensselaers. Eleanora removed the deeds, replaced the box, threw on her riding clothes and went to the stables.

"Saddle Arabel," she told the stable boy. He led the chestnut mare out and as he was pulling tightly on the cinch, Joel Kipp appeared.

"Let me accompany you."

"No," Eleanora said firmly. "I will ride alone."

The mere taste of owning land had replaced his fondness for drink, and Randolph Van Rensselaer aggressively applied himself to advancing his claim. Though Gleason had seen Daniel Hedges enter the back door of Eleanora's townhouse only once, and though Gleason had been unable to draw Daniel out during the night of drinking and betting on the prizefight, he had returned from the west with depositions that the couple had shared a room nine times. "Cousin" Randolph, as Eleanora called him, didn't bother to ask whether the witnesses could be produced, or indeed if the evidence were truthful, and neither did the judge when issuing his order.

"Please, calm yourself, Lady Van Rensselaer." Alan Van Zandt escorted her to a chair. "You may challenge this, certainly." A florid man of fifty with great shocks of white hair, Van Zandt motioned for the documents and spent half an hour poring over the deeds, murmuring, "Hmm!" and "I see." He looked up. "Very interesting case, most interesting indeed." Nervously, Eleanora adjusted herself in the chair. "Have you read these deeds lately?" he asked.

"I'm afraid none of it makes much sense to me."

"The deeds are good and legally signed and sealed, but a clause significantly modifies your right of occupancy." Eleanora suddenly felt faint. "Are you all right?"

"It's the heat."

Van Zandt poured a glass of water and she sipped it. "There's one very troublesome phrase," he scanned the parchment again. "In the event Jacob died, you were granted a life estate, that is, possession of all of Claverack with rents and tenements, unless and until you remarry." Van Zandt looked up. "Some of the cases hold that any 'unwidowlike conduct' can also result in forfeiture as well to prevent a so-called 'common law' marriage from circumventing the prohibition."

Van Zandt raised his eyebrows. "Don't underestimate the Van Rensselaers. They do not lose or give their property away. They foresaw the possibility of Jacob predeceasing you. Of course," he peered over the edge of his spectacles, "he was quite a bit older than you, but the question is, does this clause forbid an affair of the heart?" Eleanora's cheeks flushed a brilliant red. "Certainly in your wedding vows you promised to be faithful, but that promise extends only till death of one party. On Jacob's death that condition was fulfilled, and, I would submit, you are released. What now? Interesting, most interesting case." Eleanora sat with folded hands and lowered eyes while he read the documents again.

"Mr. Van Zandt, will you represent me?"

"Why the Livingstons – your cousins! – have the finest legal minds in the state."

"But the chancellor helped draft that clause, apparently," she pointed, "and you see how troublesome it is. In any case, I consider the whole affair too delicate for my family to become involved."

Van Zandt scrutinized her. "Does Randolph have any case?"

"Meaning what?"

"Meaning have the usual standards of widowhood been breached?"

"Of course not!" Eleanora said with indignance.

Van Zandt nodded, bowed his head and then looked up under his bushy eyebrows at her with guile. "Then the case will hinge on the strength of their proof. I had a case of this sort regarding the custody of a child. They found the poor mother, only a girl herself, had taken a lover, and they subpoenaed him, gave him the oath. Unfortunately she wasn't frank with me. His testimony undid her. She lost the child to her in-laws. Terribly messy when people lie." Van Zandt peered deeply into her eyes, and she felt he could read her heart. "Nothing of the sort?"

"Nothing at all." She stared back at him. "So you will file the appropriate papers to challenge this ejectment, and I can ignore it?"

"Yes. You have not remarried, you are not pregnant and you have no lover. I will suggest the delicacy of the situation to the judge and try to get a proffer of Randolph's evidence. Unless he has something substantial, and we both know he cannot prove what never happened, that will be the end of it."

"Very good."

"You might also consider a journey. If you travel beyond the state, your absence will delay the day of reckoning after I challenge the writ successfully. We needn't rush into a trial."

"I'll consider it," she said.

As her horse ambled homeward, Eleanora imagined the disgrace of a public trial, the humiliation of being stripped of her lands, her dignity, of being dispossessed and pauperized. Though she appeared to have wealth and status, she was as much a slave to these laws as any indentured servant or African sold at auction. She imagined Daniel in the witness box testifying. How could he or she describe their love to twelve yeoman jurors?

And why should they have the right to judge her? It was a private affair. How could she ever face Daniel again? Yet as she rode, Eleanora knew she would do it again, and her weakness shamed her. Daniel wasn't suffering. He had no inkling of this horrible affair. She envied his easy acceptance of life. She wanted to weep, but when the gables of Claverack rose into view around a stand of pine, she was filled with resolve and she spurred the horse into a trot. She must take a journey out of the state. Europe would be a suitable place to hide for a few months, perhaps a year. She would write immediately to Washington Irving in London – he'd been encouraging her to visit for years – and she decided to sail from New York or Boston in the next few weeks.

CHAPTER 26

*I*n October, after the cold hand of frost gripped the land, the canal commissioners met in the governor's executive chamber to discuss the first construction season.

"Quite an elegant change, General," Simeon DeWitt observed of the new velvet drapes and Persian carpet.

"Yes," Van Rensselaer said. "It reflects the majesty Mr. Clinton brings to office."

Clinton emerged from his private office with Eleanora Van Rensselaer. Hedges involuntarily turned away but then caught himself and turned back. He was so accustomed to the drab labor camps and the companionship of men and she was a vision of grace and beauty. A diamond pendant gleamed above her deep russet gown and her quick dark eyes looked from man to man until they rested on him. She inclined her head inquisitively and a smile quivered on her lip before she moved along to Ellicott.

"Thank you all for coming," Governor Clinton sat. "We have much to discuss this morning, so let us begin."

At his allotted time, Hedges showed the commissioners on a map how fifty-two miles of canal were under construction since July, and that fifteen miles and two locks were completed.

He described McShane's work crew and offered his book of disbursements.

"Thank you, Mr. Hedges," Clinton folded his hands and slowly looked around the table. "I think we're all of one mind, gentlemen, that progress is far too slow." The others nodded seriously. "Our powerful adversaries in the legislature will fasten on these paltry fifteen miles to suggest it will take twenty years to complete the project. Should construction lag next year as badly, our defeat is certain."

Hedges had expected praise, and he was annoyed. Others responded with suggestions for speeding the dig. Clinton turned to Daniel. "What do you say, Mr. Hedges?"

He glanced at Eleanora, and she smiled radiantly. He turned back to Clinton. "We started late this year, July 4th, yet we soon had fifty miles under contract. While private contractors can supplement the digging, I believe we need a large, reliable, permanent workforce."

Eleanora encouraged him. "You need an army, Mr. Hedges, an army of men who will dig."

"Yes. Send me a thousand, two thousand men and our progress will surprise even the most optimistic." Other commissioners murmured that his idea was far-fetched, an army of men digging. Then Clinton recognized Eleanora.

"I have visited the prisons, gentlemen, and there are seven or eight hundred able-bodied men languishing in cells for minor, non-violent crimes, mostly for not paying their debts. We could use them in the digging until their sentences expire."

"We have considered that," Clinton nodded, "but to use my clemency power I need assurance they won't escape."

"Hire guards," General Van Rensselaer suggested.

"Too cumbersome. We need someone who will control and work them."

"We have such a man in J.J. McShane," Hedges offered.

"The Irishman?"

"Yes. He can do it."

"Most of the prisoners are Irish," Eleanora noted.

Clinton considered. Discussion followed, and the others, seeing Clinton warming to the idea, warmed to it themselves. They began to support it, even push it.

"Then let's proceed with the convicts," Clinton concluded. "And with the Irish pouring in through New York harbor, Let us hire recruiters to sign them up to work as soon as they step off the ships."

The commissioners discussed some logistics and then Clinton left for an appointment. As the meeting broke up, Daniel noticed Eleanora staring at him and, to his surprise, suddenly she smiled, walked around the conference table and stood behind his chair.

"Why, Mr. Hedges and Mr. Ellicott! It has been a long time indeed." Both men returned the greeting, and Ellicott excused himself.

"You look well," Daniel said. Eleanora's eyes sparkled and a mischievous smile played at her lip.

"I am. I am journeying. I leave next week for Boston, then for London."

"How nice." Daniel nodded, considered this news, then his eyes met hers. "Would it be possible to see you before then?"

Eleanora glanced left then right and gave an embarrassed laugh. "Would that be wise?"

Daniel nodded. "London, eh?"

"Yes. Kind Mr. Irving has invited me to enjoy his literary circles there and I find life tiresome here now that the digging is actually underway."

"Tiresome? There are plenty of challenges at the dig."

"I'm sure you're equal to them, Mr. Hedges."

"You should visit us sometime."

"I'd like that. After London." Then she leaned closer and whispered "I'll send word tomorrow night."

Returning from the dinner the legislators held that

evening, Joseph and Daniel talked of Eleanora. Only men had been invited to the dinner, but her name came up repeatedly. Joseph was feeling his champagne.

"I thought that after Carrie died you would make a bid for Eleanora. You're the sort of man who needs a wife."

"She's too unpredictable. So warm sometimes, then she suddenly turns cold."

Ellicott laughed. "All women do. That's why I am a bachelor."

"Carrie didn't."

"Eleanora's an aristocrat. You can never understand that. She will have things her way always and everywhere. To her, people are objects moved about like pieces on a chess board."

"But she is so far superior to other women!"

"So much so, she's unattainable." Again Ellicott slapped him on the back. "Forget about her, Danny. Find yourself a woman of your station in life and get married again."

Daniel thought of Edna McKay. "Unfortunately I measure every woman against Eleanora, and they all come up wanting."

"Don't aim so high and you'll hit your mark. Forget her. Get on with your life."

Daniel did not answer.

The next day Daniel was so evasive about his evening plans that eventually Joseph went out alone. Daniel waited for word as the church bells rang eight o'clock, then eight-thirty, then nine o'clock, then nine-thirty. When the bells rang ten he put aside the drawings and geological text he was studying, stood, stretched and started for the bedroom. At that moment he heard a faint tap on his door and, opening it, he saw Joel Kipp.

"Come quickly."

Seizing his coat, Hedges followed Joel down the back stairs to a waiting carriage. Quietly they passed through the streets in the moonlight, only the sound of the wheels on the stones, then north along the riverbank, past the general's gracious manor house. A mile farther they halted at a small cottage by the river.

"I'll return in three hours," Joel said.

The moon was nearly full as Daniel crossed the frozen yard and knocked on the double Dutch door. Eleanora opened it. She was dressed in ordinary homespun. A fire was burning in the hearth and there was a warm glow to the simple home. Hedges folded his arms and admired the effect. The warmth and comfort of the cottage pleased him, and it amused him to see Eleanora Van Rensselaer dressed as a simple housewife.

"The house belongs to my maid's sister," she explained. "Come in."

"And the clothing?"

"A disguise for me to get here unnoticed."

"A disguise."

Eleanora took a small pot from the hearth and poured hot chocolate into two clay cups. "I'm afraid I'm not very good at this."

Daniel took one. "Neither am I . . . at hiding and skulking about.

"Why must we go through all this?"

"Please, Daniel, let us just be together tonight. I'm leaving for Europe. Let's not quarrel."

But after being rebuffed so often, he meant to be heard. "I want to know why you turned me away last spring. All summer I slogged through the rain and mud, haggling with woodsmen and farmers, watching over the birth of our canal, the project that you and I and Clinton worked so hard to realize, and I resented being there. I despised the slowness of its progress, the sweat and the strain of cutting through forests, the plodding oxen and mules.

"Now you're leaving it all behind. Our great vision can easily be lost in the rain and mud and mosquitoes, which are still far easier to cope with than the politicians of Albany. It makes no sense for me to be digging a ditch through the forest when the money may dry up, especially after you stopped loving me."

"Stopped loving you?" she cried. "Oh, Daniel, don't ever think that!"

"Your words and actions are not consistent. Why can't we be seen together? Why must we hide from the world?"

"I've told you that you must trust me. There are reasons, good reasons why we must not just now. I cannot explain beyond that."

"Very well." Daniel stood to go.

"Joel won't be back . . ."

"I'll walk."

"Can't you trust me? Won't you?" She stood and went to him. "What do you think this separation does to me? Night after night I must lay there alone, thinking of you, dreaming of those precious few times we've been together. Then I awaken to the four walls of my chamber. Life mocks me. I, mistress of all I see, envy my tenants their children, my mares their foals."

"But why don't you do something about it?"

She sobbed and embraced him, and he held her.

"What is the huge mystery, woman?"

"Oh, Daniel, I love you, I love you so very, very much. But I cannot tell you. You must trust me. You must!" She pulled away from him and her eyes were wet with tears. "Let us be together, tonight, now!"

She led him to the recessed bed closet near the hearth. Daniel reached down and swept her up and she parted the curtain and he lay her on the quilt. Instantly he was beside her, and she outlined his face with the tips of her fingers.

"Oh, my darling!" she sighed. "I want nothing but to be with you always, yet I must deny us both. I've been so foolish, and I'll not be back for a year or more . . ."

"All those nights on the dig . . ."

He tenderly brushed a strand of her hair aside and touched her lips gently with a kiss.

"Oh, Daniel," she sobbed.

He kissed her slowly but insistently and she responded.

Afterward she sighed sleepily, "If it could only be like this always."

Daniel did not say what he thought. They lay sleeping in each other's arms for a time, then awoke. Outside, a horse was jingling in its traces.

"Daniel? It is time for you to go."

"Yes."

"Oh, my love, I envy you so. You live among the stars and the rock, the forests and the water, the forces of earth and air. And I have only my four walls. I sit alone at night and dream of your digging and your commanding the men."

"You must visit us on your return. Wear the clothes you wore tonight. Be that woman, Eleanora."

She smiled and kissed him. The horse whinnied outside and Daniel sat up. They heard boots on the gravel. Daniel swung his legs out of the bed closet by the hearth as a knock sounded on the door.

"I must go."

"I love you, Daniel, and I shall miss you."

"Until your return." He kissed her again, adjusted his garments and pulled on his coat. Outside it was raining furiously and the horses hung their heads, waiting to pull the carriage. Hedges paused on the threshold and gazed back into the warm light of the cottage. Then he pulled on his hat, raised his collar and walked with Joel through the rain.

"You'll be home soon enough, sir," Joel said with encouragement.

"Home." He settled into the carriage seat and stared out at the rain on the wet, barren trees, and at the river that flowed silently and dark.

Eleanora awoke with a start. Gray light seeped in through the bed curtains and she sat bolt upright, forgetting momentarily where she was. Memories of the night returned then and she sobbed and hugged her pillow. When at last she arose and crossed to the washstand, she looked into the glass. She saw new lines along the corners of her mouth and wrinkles in her forehead that made her look older. She scrutinized her eyes. They seemed cold and sinister this morning.

Her imminent departure for London had made her adventurous with Daniel, but now, in the cold light she heard his plea for their togetherness and had a horrible thought.

"Oh, you fool!" she chided her reflection. "What if you are pregnant? You perfect fool."

CHAPTER 27

*D*aniel sat in his tent reviewing maps of the work. It was March and frost was still in the ground. The fifty-two miles under contract were alternating strips of finished stretches, land scarred by a few passes of the plow, land barely cleared of brush and stumps, and occasional rock outcrops yet to be blasted. He heard J.J. call out and he stepped outside to see the first group of convicts arrive.

"So, ye've been sprung by the guv'ner to dig his ditch, and yer heads are all filled with dreams of whiskey and women, eh?" As J.J. circled the group, it huddled closer together. "Ye didn't know there's a lot of backbreakin', soul-splittin' work to be done, nor did you counter on not having a place to sleep tonight. But first things must always come first, so send out the toughest man among ye, and I'll meet him presently."

J.J. walked over to Daniel. "Hard cases, eh?" Their heads were shaved, their striped canvas prison clothing filthy and ill-fitting. Some were barefoot on the cold mud. Daniel nodded. "Yet most are good Irish lads, Dan-o. Ye'll be surprised at the spirit I'll get out of them. First, though, I must slip the bit between their teeth. Pity it's always got to be this way, but that's their nature." J.J. shrugged and walked back to the group shaking his head.

From out of the group a great hulk of a man stepped. He towered over McShane. His fists were the size of hams, his forehead low, his jaw immense and his shoulders massive knots of muscle.

J.J. put his hands on his hips. "You're the toughest of the lot?"

The man sneered. "Shamus Fitzgibbon's a name you won't be forgettin', I'm sure."

"Well, well, well, Shamus Fitzgibbon, welcome to the canal. Here we work from sunup till sundown. You'll have four meals a day soon's we get the cookhouse built. You'll get a pint of whiskey spaced out in fifth-gill shots during the day and forty cents wages. Now, there ain't no walls, for this ain't no prison. This is the frontier. Ain't nothin' in them woods but wildcats and wolves and maybe some crazy Injuns left who'll scalp you worse'n you already been in the slammer. Do you see that man?" J.J. pointed at Daniel Hedges. The group nodded.

"His word is law. He is sheriff, judge and jury out here. He's the one what can land you back in prison to start serving your sentences from day one. And me – I'm the one what enforces his law."

So saying, J.J. sucker-punched the big man with an uppercut that sent him reeling backward. Shamus was shocked, then pained, then furious. He snorted and wiped blood from his nose, then crouched and ran at McShane. McShane stepped aside, grabbed Shamus by the collar, rolled onto his back pulling the big man down, set his feet in Shamus' groin, then spun him over in the air. Shamus did a complete flip and landed on the frozen mud. Dazed, he struggled to his feet, growled and advanced again. He dealt J.J. a withering blow to the stomach, and J.J. countered with a punch to the man's jaw that nearly broke his fist. Shamus squeezed J.J.'s neck, and it looked like he would simply pluck J.J.'s head off his shoulders until J.J. buried his heel in the man's instep, then sank his knee in the man's groin. Shamus expelled a loud rush of air, his eyes rolled back into his head, and J.J. reached up striving on the bald head to find hair to pull. Then he grabbed Shamus' ears and brought his face down on his upraised knee four times.

As Shamus struggled to stand, J.J. hauled back and with all his might landed a blow on his nose. Shamus fell back, sprawling in the mud and melting snow, and after a meager attempt to rise, just sighed and lay still and bleeding.

"Now that we understand each other," McShane said, catching his breath, "we'll begin by building you boys a camp so's you won't be sleeping under the stars." He reached down and helped Fitzgibbon up. "But first, I know you've been languishing in state's prison, so let's have a drink."

A cheer went up. J.J. rolled a whiskey keg from his tent, and the men clustered about it, eagerly drinking with their hands and with a tin dipper and the few tin cups he handed around. Hedges returned to his maps and drawings.

Soon the woods behind his tent were ringing with whoops and the blows of axes felling trees. For an hour they worked and sang and shouted. Suddenly the men were screaming wildly and a pistol shot rang out.

"'Tis only a snake, lads," J.J. called. "When St. Paddy drove them from the holy ground, why, like you they come slitherin' across-t to the New World. Sure, and if the land hereabouts ain't crawling with snakes, but take heart, only the poison ones can hurt ye."

"But will we survive the Irish?" Daniel mused.

His fears were allayed, though, when he saw them dig. Energetic, fond of laughter and song, the Irish sprang to the digging each morning. They joked and dug and drank their ration of whiskey, and ate their four meals with abandon. Many had been bogtrotters and peat cutters in the old country, others had raised horses and therefore showed great prowess with the teams.

Clinton granted hundreds of prisoners clemency because he knew the canal's future depended on the 1818 digging season. Agents along the New York City docks signed Irish immigrants as soon as they stepped down the ramps from the coffin ships to "come and earn a steady wage." They arrived on the frontier in waves, trudging in gangs over the turnpike and towpath. McShane devised an organizational structure as new camps sprang up along the staked-out course of the canal. He searched for physical toughness, for lieutenants who commanded respect. According to his merit system, if another man "whupped" his boss in a fight over an issue considered fair in J.J.'s judicial opinion, he would be promoted to gang boss, and the unfortunate loser was demoted or moved to another crew.

"New blood, Dan-o, we always need new blood. If they believe they'll advance, they'll work and fight like dogs. And that's the secret, for every Irishman's a king in his heart. So long as an Irishman believes he's his own master, there's nothing he won't do to further his interest. But cage him up, cut off the hope that tomorrow will be better, and he becomes a vile, nasty customer."

J.J. imposed the routine and the canal steadily crept westward. He kept a sharp eye on the lines of the berm, the prism and the towpath to assure they were true. Rarely did he bother Hedges with questions. For days at a time, Hedges and Canvass White left the dig to ride westward and prepare the route for autumn and the following spring. Five locks would be needed to drop the canal into the dreaded Montezuma Swamp, then nine or ten more to lift it to high ground farther west. They took borings at each lock site to find bedrock, and they scouted out likely quarries for granite and limestone, and stands of white oak for lock gates.

By late summer, three thousand Irish immigrants and

convicts were working along a hundred miles of canal. They returned each night to bunkhouses clustered together in shanty towns where they collapsed and snored soundly on slabs of pine.

As he moved his tent and belongings westward to keep on the forefront of the dig, Hedges became friendly with many of the workers. When the leaves blazed and frost again gripped the earth, he moved his tent to Montezuma to survey a course through the swamp. On a warm Sunday morning during Indian summer, he and J.J. walked down to the edge of the Cayuga Marsh.

"Aye, but 'tis a foreboding place, Dan-o. I shan't be too keen on working through this next spring."

Behind them on the hill the trees were gold and crimson. Before them lay a morass of tangled roots and dead trees, as if the very life of the trees had been sucked down into the black water.

"There's fever lurking in there, J.J."

"Aye. We'll lose many of the boys."

"Mr. White is trying to design a way to dig in that soft ground. We'll need to race through as quickly as possible."

"Aye, but it'll take a season at least."

They scaled the hill and left the swamp behind. "I say, Dan-o, autumn makes the heart sad, don't it?"

"I suppose." Daniel had asked J.J. many questions about England and London, and he used these descriptions as back-drops for imagining Eleanora's travels. From the camp across the meadow came a melodic lilt of the Irish elbow pipes and the scratch of a fiddle. The resplendent sky, the brilliant leaves, and the sad sweet Celtic melody caused Daniel to ask: "What is that tune, J.J.?"

"Ye have a fine ear, Dan-o. *Carrickfergus*. An ancient air that come down from heaven on the wings of an angel, to be sure. Did you ever have a wife?"

Daniel was startled by the abrupt question, but then he saw J.J. was remembering his own lost love.

"Yes, yes, I did. A wife and two babies. They were killed by the British during the war."

"I'm sorry, Dan-o. And since then, lad, has there been anyone?"

"Just one, but she couldn't decide whether to wed, so it came to nothing. You?"

"Aye," J.J. shook his head. "I made the great mistake. Turned a sweet milkmaid into a mean old shrew. Astonishing how they change! Bare me two sons and a daughter, she did, before she left. I was in Liverpool. She returned to her da in County Mayo. Took me wee ones too. Ah, I was hard at the liquor for a while over that, but me mates brought me about. Wasn't too long afterward old Canvass came snoopin' about with his spectacles and sketch book, and I'd heard stories about American woman." He spread his arms in the sunshine. "So I'm here. But where are they?"

"What did you hear about American women?"

"That they're independent and saucy."

Daniel smiled as he applied those epithets to Eleanora.

"'Course it wouldn't do just now to involve meself with a woman. Got to stay lean and mean and on me toes. There's many of the men itching to knock down the straw boss and take the job. But when the diggin's done, then I might look about for a wife."

They drew near the shantytown named "Kilkenny" by the men, and heard a tin whistle, fiddle and Irish pipes send sweet notes quivering high into the brilliant sunshine among the gold and crimson leaves.

"Whatever is that tune now? It's so sweet and haunting!"

"'Tis an old air about a sailor who fears he'll never see his true love no more."

Daniel listened to the music. He was a sailor in his heart, lured inland by Eleanora, trying with sweat and strain to link the landlocked lake with the sea. The song conjured up emotions only a sailor could know, the endless rolling of the waves beneath the stars, a wind propelling him onward.

J.J. threw his arm over Daniel's shoulder.

"I suppose you and me are a dying breed, eh? Let's not get glum and moody, Dan-o. We'll have Jimmy strike up a rouser, and I'll demonstrate a few jigs."

They entered the camp. The melody that had tinged the afternoon with a lovely sadness wafted off into silence, and the men called out for more. J.J. filled two tin cups at the whiskey cask. Hedges felt uncomfortable among this wild and motley group. He listened to a few songs, shared the whiskey, then returned to his tent.

At sunset Hedges lay on his cot. He thought of Eleanora and he remembered the night she had dressed as a simple Dutch wife. Her elegance, her grace, her passion made such a simple presence sublime. It was impossible for him to favor another woman, and the ineffable sadness of the Irish pipes gave this feeling a voice. Especially that one lovely Irish air, quivering high in the autumn sun. But soon the music ended, the men clapped and drank whiskey and cried for more lively tunes, and his precious moment of insight was trampled beneath jigging, roughshod boots.

Daniel Hedges closed his eyes that night and dreamt, not of bright autumn leaves, the bright skies of Indian summer, or sweet Irish airs, but of the foul, murky swamp that lay before him.

CHAPTER 28

*E*leanora Van Rensselaer booked passage aboard the
Ariel and left Boston Harbor in early March. She
stood at the railing in a beautiful sealskin coat watching the
land recede behind cold gray swells. Exhilarated by the ocean
air, she fondly remembered the afternoon on Lake Erie with
Daniel, and she longed to be with him, working along the
canal. This trip, this hiatus was necessary, she told herself in
the stiff wind, to throw off her pursuers and retain her lands.

A month later the Isle of Wight hove into view, and the
Ariel soon passed on to Southhampton. As the ship was
moored, Eleanora saw Irving among the crowd and she gaily
waved her scarf. She hurried down the gangplank and he met
her at the bottom with a kiss. He seemed far older than the
last time she'd seen him, older and heavier. Gray streaked his
hair, and his skin was sallow from too little sun.

"You look ravishing, Eleanora!" He held her at an arm's
length. "You don't know how ecstatic I was when you wrote.
How long can you stay?"

"As long as I'm welcome." She kissed him on the cheek.

"Then you shall never leave!" Arm-in-arm he led her
along the quay to an inn where he'd secured lodging for the

night. Over dinner that evening – "English food is so very bland, they steam and boil the flavor out so you need to spice it up with ale" – Eleanora relayed news of Clinton and Van Buren, the politics and the canal.

"Forgive me for thinking this way," Irving said, "but I cannot see how anyone could take that seriously."

"The canal will bring wonderful prosperity to our state!"

"I'm quite sure it will. But all the strategies, the thrusts and the parries. I find it irksome. And, dear Eleanora, what is won when the shouting and the smoke clear? Headaches and responsibilities that you never bargained for, and the awful midnight fear that someone else will take away your power. No," he shook his head and held up his tankard for a refill, "political office is not worth the price it exacts."

"And yet I remember a certain author who befriended the Madisons to seek an appointment."

Irving shook his head sadly. "That was shortly after poor Matilda died. I sought an ambassador's post in vain. Ah! Heartbreak!" he sighed, looked away and seemed about to weep. He swigged his ale. "This world is too cruel to allow such beauty to survive. Why, we should be absolutely frantic, dear Eleanora, if anything happened to you!"

"We? You and who else?"

"Why, me and my characters. I have been incredibly prolific these days!" He grew excited again. "Last autumn I visited the great man himself, Walter Scott at Abbotsford. He had read a few of my sketches, and was so encouraging! He said that in my work, America had produced a new voice and a new sort of literature, and he told me I must keep writing."

"Well of course you must. Walter Scott! How wonderful."

"To write accurately about America, I'm convinced, one must be an expatriate." He finished his ale and ordered another. "I've got some sketches for you to read, sketches about the Hudson Valley. I've developed the most charming characters from folk tales you and I heard as children. I hope to publish them next year. But you must be kind in your criticism. They're not quite finished."

"Of course, of course."

They talked awhile longer, then Eleanora went upstairs leaving him glassy-eyed, gazing into the hearth, ordering yet another mug of ale. In her room, Eleanora was saddened by her first encounter with Irving. He seemed defeated, resigned, his "sketches" as much an escape as the ale.

They hired a coach next day to carry them up to London. As excited as a schoolboy, Irving pointed out everything he could along the way. A gray sky hung over the green land, and when Eleanora remarked about this, Irving said: "It is always so. You must go to Italy or Spain for sun."

"It seems rather melancholy."

"No, my dear, thoughtful. 'Thoughtful' is a better word." They stopped for dinner in Winchester and Irving led her through the sanctified cloisters of the cathedral where the moody gray light softly infused the stained glass. A choir practiced an intricate hymn and the young boys' voices rose like the singing of angels in the dim gothic vaults.

"Imagine the legions of nameless, faceless laborers who worked on scaffolding generation upon generation to raise up this house of worship," Irving whispered. "Some of them carved their own faces and faces of their wives and children high in the arches. Sort of like my elves and sprites."

"What faith and dedication! It is so inspiring. How different from our stern faith."

"Our modern era offers nothing to compare."

But Eleanora didn't entirely agree. As they strolled through the dim, echoing cloisters and chapels, she saw a parallel, but she didn't relate it to Irving because she knew he would scoff. She saw the great canal as a modern day effort, motivated not by religious faith, but by the desire for commerce and prosperity, trade, progress and growth. While it was practical and without artistic beauty, surely it was on the scale of this cathedral, a colossal public work, an embodiment of a people. And Daniel Hedges was one of its architects and builders. Clinton's efforts were to crown himself king by undertaking the great project. Irving's works were mere embellishments, gargoyles. Of them all, she admired Hedges' work the most.

London enchanted Eleanora: the crowded, jostling streets, the lavish hotels, the theaters, the gracious restaurants and taverns, the teeming riverfront, the wide and noble squares and the grand townhouses and public buildings. Since Waterloo, an energetic spirit filled the city. As the empire expanded, prosperity and pride were infusing the English with hope and joy. So, too, would New York State be, Eleanora reflected, when the canal was finished.

Because Irving was a literary celebrity, invitations were frequent.

When she asked if the social whirl ever stopped, he said, "I try to keep amused." And he did. He danced, he applauded from his theater box, traded *bon mots* with witty young playwrights, flirted with duchesses and dowagers, and he drank constantly. He drank ale for breakfast, Madeira at dinner, whiskey at tea, claret or Chablis at supper, champagne at parties. Eleanora was alarmed. When she mentioned it, he only shrugged. She tried to ignore it after that, but she saw his talent being dissipated, and it saddened her.

True, he masked his darker feelings with happy, sentimental prose, doggerel and gay laughter. True, his expatriate swagger gave him an objective view of his homeland. True, he was well-regarded. Yet beneath it all as the weeks wore into a month, and the single month wore into two, Eleanora sensed his profound sorrow. Whether caused by the death of his beloved Matilda, or his absence from his brothers and sisters, sadness had conquered him and he drank it into dullness, with no effort to be rid of it.

She saw, too, that although he was invited everywhere,

Irving was only on the periphery of the city's and the empire's life. The royalty and the nobility made the policies that expanded the empire. They ordered troops to the field, the navy to the seas. Irving was merely an artist. Eleanora longed to involve herself in a far greater enterprise than the pursuit of pleasure. She missed the tenacity of Clinton and the quiet competence of Hedges. As primitive as they were by comparison with this sophisticated land, they were building something new and different, something based on merit, not heredity or privilege. At the end of three months she knew she must return to America.

Their farewell was painful. For three days after Eleanora announced she wished to return to America, Irving stayed blind drunk. He only wept in private. She told him he talked "sweet nonsense" when he said that of all the women he had ever met she alone had the will, the integrity and maturity he admired. She booked her passage. Still he was determined to change her mind. He hired a private dining room at Gray's Inn and instructed the cook to prepare a savory roast mutton. He had champagne brought up, and under the guise of a farewell dinner, he toasted Eleanora. "My dear," he said during the soup course, "a plan has been forming itself in my head of late."

"Another plot, new characters?"

"Yes." He sipped the wine and warmed to the idea. "Absolutely!

You and I, Eleanora, we're not what anyone would call young . . ."

She knew what was coming. "I'm terribly flattered," she tried to head him off, "but I cannot remain. Oh, Washington. I never knew you felt so."

He took her hand. "Stay, Eleanora! Stay here! London is the place for you, not the wildernesses of Albany and the West. Your spirit needs gaiety, the finer things, civilization. Our mutual regard over the last decade has matured. If you prefer, we might live as brother and sister. Just allow me the smallest chance that we might marry – no, no, no, you needn't decide tonight! I'd rather you took time for mature reflection. I merely want to open up the possibility for you."

"I'm very touched, my dear, dear friend." Eleanora saw his loneliness laid bare, and it greatly depressed her, for she saw her own reflected in it. "You have been so very kind these last three months, but I'm afraid I shall live and die an old maid."

He quaffed his wine and poured another. "Was, was your life with Jacob so very rich you can't bear another?"

"Partly," she lied.

"Please, Eleanora, I beg you, don't dismiss the idea out of hand. Think on it. I shall write. Answer my letters. Perhaps in a year or so?"

"I am rather set in my ways."

"Oh, I can accommodate that! I will accommodate anything for you! But," he said then with false nonchalance, "let us discuss the matter no further tonight. I only wanted to acquaint you with a thought that's been nagging at me." Thus he shrugged off her refusal and plunged into the next course and the next bottle of wine.

A week later, Eleanora watched the Isle of Wight recede behind the gray-green seas. Gulls screamed and banked sharply and the bright August wind snapped the colorful ensign.

"I forgot others had heavier burdens," she murmured, and she made up her mind, as the sunset burnished the cold waves of the North Atlantic, that she'd put her life in order, resolve the property dispute, see the canal finished and come to some sort of understanding with Daniel.

On reaching New York that September, she learned Clinton was at his Flushing estate. She also learned that Maria, his wife of twenty years, had died. Immediately she ferried across to Brooklyn, hired a coach and rode out to his mansion.

Black crepe still hung limp and stained from the windows and the doors of the great house. "I'll tell the governor you have come," old William showed her to a parlor. "Things, as you may understand, are not as they once were."

In a few minutes, a door opened and Clinton limped in, hunched over a cane. "It's good of you to visit." He looked pale and weak.

"Oh, DeWitt! I just heard about Maria! I'm so very sorry." She offered him her hand and then her cheek.

"Come in, come in," he ushered her into a large rear parlor where a chilly gloom was not relieved by the small fire in the grate. Eleanora asked many questions. Maria had died of consumption in late summer. "Three of the boys were with me at her bedside, and of course Sadie." He sighed. "Not long after the funeral, I fell off Zephyr while riding to the hounds. I have been as you perceive me, a cripple in body, heart and soul."

"Oh, DeWitt!"

"It wouldn't be so bad for me now she's gone, Eleanora, if I hadn't neglected her so these last fifteen years." The over-whelming grief and guilt that she saw in his face quite shocked her.

"Everything came before Maria. My Masonic brethren, politics, scientific research, the canal, the war, the smallest, most tedious affairs of state, and she, kind heart, bore it all happily, patiently. She'd not see me for months at a time, and when I returned, worn down from an expedition or throttled by a debate or a series of newspaper editorials, she'd sit in my lap like Sadie does now, and she'd hold me. 'At least we have this time together,' she'd say. 'You make me so very proud and happy.'"

He cradled his forehead in his right hand. "To forget my grief for an afternoon, I agreed to go fox-hunting and I fell off the mildest mount in my stables!" There was a long silence as the large man gazed into the fire. "I have never fallen off a horse in my life."

"May I stay with you awhile?"

He looked up, surprised. He squinted as though he had just noticed her. "Why, of course, as long as you wish. I don't need to be in Albany until session begins after the New Year. Stay with me until then."

"I'd like that." She went to him and entwined his strong fingers in her own. "I'd like that very much."

Clinton sighed, patted her hand. "Good, kind Eleanora. We must build up the fire, warm up the place for you. I'll call William." Stiffly he started to rise.

"Now, just sit there. I'll see to everything. We've worked so hard, you and I. Let us gather our energies for the coming year."

"You are as wise as you are beautiful."

CHAPTER 29

*T*he 1818 digging season was an unqualified success. Sixty-two miles of canal were open, greatly reducing shipping costs from central New York to the Mohawk Valley. Still, only five of sixty locks had been built, and the canal threaded through relatively flat lands. The engineers still faced enormous challenges – rivers to be bridged, cliffs to be scaled, three hundred miles yet to be dug. The greatest immediate problem was the Montezuma Swamp.

"Aye, Dan-o, I worked the peat bogs as a lad. Tough duty, t'be sure, but nothing like what's waitin' for us come summer."

Daniel and J.J. were riding through the snow with their yearly report for the canal commission. Daniel was absorbed in other thoughts. Ellicott told him that Eleanora had returned from England and was staying in New York City. Three days ago a whiskey merchant told him the governor's wife had passed away. Daniel drew an obvious conclusion.

"We'll need more men and teams. A pity we can't work the lads all winter. They'll be like an army itching for combat by spring."

"Yes," Daniel agreed, "the waiting is always hardest."

After delivering his report to Clinton and the commissioners at the Capitol, Hedges paused on the landing while Clinton limped down the icy steps on a cane. A coach-and-four drove up State Street and stopped. When the door opened, he saw Eleanora inside. Nearby, two of the canal commissioners gossiped:

"She's been living with him since before last autumn. Shameful. His wife wasn't cold in the ground, and he took up with the Van Rensselaer widow."

"Oh," said the other. "They've been carrying on secretly for years. Everyone knows that."

Daniel turned.

"She's a spirited one, they say. Uses her widowhood to conceal her affairs. Be interesting to see if she can get Clinton to the altar now." Hedges was stupefied with rage. Just then he saw J.J. coming to meet him.

"How did it go, Dan-o?"

"Well enough, well enough."

"You don't look like it did."

Daniel glared at him. "I can't get away from here fast enough."

"Well, Dan-o, there's a lot of good whiskey to be drunk tonight, and if there's any left in Albany when the sun rises tomorry, it won't be the fault of J.J. McShane!"

He led Daniel to a tavern. They spent the afternoon in waterfront bars. For sport J.J. battled a hefty stevedore and won a fifty dollar prize. They drank poteen and ale and corn liquor, and J.J. sang and danced Irish jigs along with men playing fiddles and squeezeboxes.

Daniel awoke in a room that reeked of perfume and he saw a tussled head in the bed next to him. He moved to rise, and the woman turned, clacked her tongue and opened her eyes. She was an Irish beauty with dark hair and deep violet eyes. "Leavin', love?"

"Yes." Daniel was mortified he couldn't remember what had happened.

"Well, do come again." She laughed lasciviously. He saw silver coins on the bureau, and he dug into his pocket and left a gold piece too. "Now ain't you the sweetest?"

Downstairs, Daniel discovered they were in a fancy bordello, and McShane sat on a sofa talking with disheveled girls as if he were the owner. "Top o' the marnin', Dan-o. Sleep well, did ye?"

Daniel muttered something in reply.

"Katie here's from County Kerry, Jane from Cork, and the twins," he snapped his fingers, "ah, the twins, they're from Dublin City."

"Let's go."

"Sure, Dan-o, sure." Promising to return, J.J. bid farewell. In the morning light Daniel remembered what he had seen yesterday, and what he'd been trying to forget all night. "We start back this afternoon."

"Ah, Dan-o! Sure, but 'tis a long, long year on the dig. Another day, a coupla more women . . ." but McShane fell quiet at Daniel's sharp glance.

In the governor's suite farther up the hill, Eleanora had arrived from her townhouse for breakfast. Clinton was in an unusually happy mood.

"You seem awfully cheerful today," she remarked.

"I am." He showed her to the table and they began a breakfast of kippered herring, eggs and toast. "I've made a great decision, a wonderful, earth-shattering decision."

"Why does that make today different from any other?"

"Quite," he glowed with joy and pride. "I'm going to remarry."

Eleanora nearly choked on the herring.

"You must be happy for me."

"I am, I am! Who, pray tell, will be the new Mrs. Clinton?"

He saw her dismay and he reached across the table. "You are to be the first to know, Eleanora, because I need to share my joy with my dearest, closest friend. I must pledge you to secrecy until the formal announcement. Catherine Jones."

"I know Kitty. I'm very happy for both of you."

"We must wait until the legislative session is far along so the wedding will not energize my enemies or distract the public from the issues."

"Of course." Her appetite flagged. "Isn't this rather sudden?"

"Oh, we've been keeping company since Maria passed away." Eleanora frown. She believed she knew Clinton before but apparently she now knew him better. She had been at his side for two months and never suspected this romance. Catherine's father was a banker and would be useful in financing another presidential bid.

"I wanted her to join us for breakfast today, but she preferred I tell you alone."

"Oh, she's in Albany?" Eleanora stared at him. So he had been using her as his decoy for two months – allowing people to see them together while he'd been carrying on this affair!

"I have often wondered why you did not remarry," he said. She glared at his impertinence. "I simply cannot get along without someone sharing my life." He regarded her. "Life is far too short to forego such intimacy and companionship."

"I would rather you spared me this sermon!" She was indignant, angry, bitter. Tears pressed at her eyes. She abruptly threw down her napkin, rose from the table, and realizing she could not very well flee, went to the window, breathing deeply to calm herself.

"I'm sorry," Clinton was at her back, his hand on her shoulder. "Please forgive me. I am too often insensitive to the feelings of others." She turned to face him. He looked sympathetic. "Your feelings have not been altogether platonic?"

"Yes, DeWitt, yes, of course they have. I have enjoyed our companionship these last few months and I regret it will end."

"Why do you not find someone?" he asked. "Why not remarry?"

She shuddered at the idea. "I cannot."

"Why, of course you can!"

"No, DeWitt. I cannot."

"But why?"

She turned away from him and leaned her hands on the windowsill. "When I was betrothed there were negotiations between my family and the Van Rensselaers regarding Claverack. It was agreed on the eve of the wedding that I might keep all of the estate in the event of Jacob's death only if I agreed never to remarry. A future marriage would mean I'd forfeit everything. I have school friends who are spinsters without property. I have seen how they live."

"But that's absurd. Even if you gave up Claverack, you still have the right of dower, one-half of its income since there were no children."

"No, we bartered that away."

"You did?"

"Well, my father and uncle did. They wrote up the deeds. You know what a woman's rights are worth. Without a father or a husband, she has no rights at all."

"So you have a life estate then, which exceeds the right of dower."

"So long as I don't marry."

"What happens if you do?"

"The lands revert to the Van Rensselaer family. I lose all." Eleanora turned and stared at him for a long moment. "The next in line to Claverack, Randolph Van Rensselaer, has brought an ejectment action to dispossess me, and I have consulted a lawyer."

"A lawyer? Eleanora! I'm the governor!" Clinton held her by the shoulders.

"It seemed so hopeless and so . . . so shameful. The marriage to Jacob was a disaster, and then to live under the threat of losing my lands!"

"But you would have dower. What have you lost? Nothing."

"Nothing," Eleanora whispered. "More than a decade of my life. All that time, DeWitt, time that cannot be recovered, I have lived as a widow because of the law."

Clinton shrugged. "I can't speak for your families, but don't blame the law. It will be that very law that will save you, and obtain at least your dower's interest. Why didn't you consult me about this before?"

"I wanted to keep it secret, DeWitt. They are hanging their case on my, my, indiscretions." She dropped her eyes. "And there has been one."

"The surveyor?"

Slowly she nodded.

"He shows a certain nobility, it's true, but he's hardly worthy of you."

"Let's not evaluate that aspect of each other's lives." Eleanora's tart response indicated she held little respect for Catherine Jones.

He nodded. "But the legalities must still be sorted out. I shall call the judge."

"Please don't involve yourself."

"Nonsense. Your rights are guaranteed by the laws of this state, and you must get what you're entitled to. Let me talk to the judge, Judge Edmonds isn't it?"

She nodded, then dropped her eyes. "I thank you for your interest, but if the law is as clear as you say, I won't need your help."

"Never mind, never mind, just let me take care of everything." It was Clinton's way to make amends and he embraced her. "It's a grand day for us both, isn't it?"

"Yes." And she surrendered to the safety of the great man's arms.

~

Daniel Hedges returned to the work with a hollow sense of duty. The Montezuma Swamp lay before them stagnant and foul, its muck offering small promise for a channel or a firm berm or a towpath. He ordered the convicts and Irish out of winter quarters while the ground was frozen to fell stands of oak, and he constructed a sawmill to cut the logs into piles and planks. Only by driving piles and building a wall could they keep the muck shoveled out from oozing back. Nor were his spirits lifted by the news from Senator Harley of Oneida that Clinton was remarrying. This shocked and hurt him. "She has loved Clinton all along," he told himself. He felt foolish and used. Work was his only comfort now, the canal his only mistress, and so he worked feverishly.

Ice was on the fetid water when they began digging that year. Frost reached three feet into the ground, and the congealed muck made easy digging, yet the sloppy last foot of black slime showed them what they would be encountering all summer. One by one, Daniel built five camps through the swamp on what high ground he could find. The men nailed up their shanties and bunks and their cookhouses, but the swamp prohibited a connecting roadway.

"Only way out of here is to dig," J.J. told the work gangs he led in. "So let's get on with it." The men responded and the ditch progressed rapidly.

"Dan-o, Dan-o," J.J. said one afternoon as Daniel poled a barge out of the swamp to the lumber dock for another load. "Ye've got to slow down, lad. Your second trip today. Leave it for the men. Won't do to get yourself sick."

"We must make progress before the mosquitoes rise. You've never seen the malaria."

"Aye, but take precautions so you ain't the one what gets it. Leave the barge. My man Feeney'll pole it back to them. Come dine with me tonight. I have a fine bottle of the Irish."

Hedges accepted. In the six weeks of digging, he'd taken great comfort in J.J.'s expansive good nature. At an old camp-site overlooking the swamp, J.J. built a fire and fried trout and bass with potatoes and onions, and they drank the Irish whiskey.

"Ye've seemed sad recently, Dan-o."

"It'll pass, J.J. It'll pass."

"Progress is good so far and I heard tell Ben Wright is opening twelve miles to traffic next week." J.J. waved his arm toward the setting sun. "Now ain't that a sight?"

The sky was a fiery lake as storm clouds massed in the west. The sun reflected in the water of the canal, smooth and straight, illuminating it as if a roadway of red gold.

"I used to sail on the lake; now I pole a barge in a swamp," Hedges observed. "I made much more in the lake trade, and I was free."

"Aye, but now we work for the love it, eh, Dan-o?"

"Love?" Daniel waved the neck of the bottle at the canal. He was feeling the liquor. "Behold what one man has done for the love of a woman."

"Aye. Built her a highway of gold."

"Yes," Daniel nodded and swigged the liquor, "straight into a swamp."

Governor DeWitt Clinton presided over the Council of Appointment, the body which appointed all state officers, judges included. Power had see-sawed on the council between Clinton's faction and the Tammany Bucktails. Tammany needed one of Clinton's men to secure an appointment, and they had succeeded in turning one back in 1816 to get Martin Van Buren appointed attorney general. When Van Buren resigned his judgeship and left Hudson to reside in Albany, the council appointed Nathaniel Edmonds to succeed Van Buren as surrogate Judge. Edmonds knew what hand fed him, so when Clinton summoned him to Albany, a sense of gloom descended. Tammany had put him in office, but he mustn't irritate Clinton. He hated politics but immensely enjoyed wearing the black robes.

Clinton, though, was affable and relaxed, not at all testy as Edmonds entered the executive suite. "So kind of you to come, Judge." He asked about the judge's family, and they talked about the weather. Obliquely Clinton asked:

"Are you aware of an action for ejectment pending against Jacob Van Rensselaer's widow?"

"Why, yes, I am, Governor. A magistrate issued the order and I've been asked to interpret the will."

"What do you see as the merits of the case?"

"It is highly irregular, if not unethical to . . ."

"Of course, of course. But you understand the petitioner has a heavy burden to bear in proving his case."

"Quite."

"My interest, Judge, is simple curiosity. I assume the losing party will appeal to the chancellor in equity, but the plaintiff's claim appears to have so little merit, while its potential damage to a woman's property interests and reputation would be grave. Do you agree?"

"Quite right, Governor. I agree fully."

"Good, Judge. I'm so glad you were able to attend today." Clinton abruptly stood, signaling the meeting was over. "Let me stress again, Judge, my interest is only that of curiosity, yet any leeway you may extend will be noticed, rest assured."

"The matter will receive my most careful scrutiny." Edmonds shook his hand and left the Capitol relieved. A simple ejectment! The triviality of it made him laugh and in high cheer he strolled down the broad thoroughfare of State Street. Then his eye caught a lawyer's shingle: "Martin Van Buren, Esq." He tapped his cane and decided to visit his old friend.

Van Buren's clerk answered the door, and the senator happened to be home. Van Buren bustled out from the back room, his eyes a-sparkle and he pumped Edmond's hand with vigor. "What brings you to the capital?"

"Why, the funniest thing," Edmonds scratched his head. "I was summoned by Governor Clinton over an ejectment proceeding."

"You don't say," Van Buren directed him to his office, "Come in, do come in."

Immediately Van Buren whispered to certain gossip-mongers that DeWitt Clinton was tampering with the courts, and a week later a letter to the editor ran in the *Albany Argus:*

> SIR:
>
> A matter of burning importance concerns me today.
>
> QUERY: What state official recently met with the Columbia County Surrogate Judge threatening to rescind his appointment if a case was not decided in a particular way?
>
> ANSWER: An official wishing to help a widow keep lands she occupies wrongfully. This high official, influential with the Council of Appointment, believes he is above the law. Such blatant court-fixing offends every citizen of this state and cries out for an investigation. At the very least we should closely watch the calendar of the Columbia County Surrogate Court.
>
> CATALINE

"This is abhorrent!" Clinton raged, hurling the paper into

the love seat in the parlor of Eleanora's townhouse. "I made it exceedingly clear to that oaf Edmonds that I took only a passing interest in your case!"

"But when you spoke you were robed with the power of your office, and the judge interpreted it so." It quite upset Eleanora to see her case in the press. A profound weariness came over her. She'd planned to leave for Claverack to consult with Van Zandt, but Clinton had just arrived unannounced and was beside himself with anger. "I urged you not to become involved, DeWitt! I knew this could happen."

He glared at her, first angry she could think her judgment superior to his, then outraged that her case had generated such publicity.

"It's Van Buren," the governor said hoarsely. "That snake. I can read it in his methods." Clinton held up a clenched fist. "How do you cripple a snake? You cut of its head. I will strip that snake of every office he enjoys. He won't be attorney general past tomorrow."

"Why does he do this?" Eleanora asked with exasperation. "I've seen politics played many ways, but never like this before."

"He's an anarchist. He'll set a building on fire and scream 'Fire! Fire!' and then take credit for saving lives by sounding the alarm. Burr used the same tactic. People admire men who seem to predict events, never suspecting they cause them. Van Buren wants to keep us on the defensive so we'll be so busy tending to our affairs that we cannot undo him, and so he may strengthen his Regency in perfect security."

"So, what can we do now?"

"Delay," Clinton said. "We must rely on the shortness of people's memories. We must postpone your suit at least until my reelection next year. If the matter should come to bar, we will lose either way. If you're dispossessed, I'll be criticized for meddling; if you win, the public will howl for my blood."

"I've already postponed it a year. Randolph grows impatient."

"It can't be helped. We must for the good of our undertaking."

"But what of the progress of the canal? That will surely offset people's acrimony."

"Ah, Hedges and his Irish are the brightest lights that shine today. But it's a sad truth in politics, the smallest personal benefit discredits everything else you've done. The evil that men do lives after them; the good is interred with their bones. Given the envy that power always generates, people recall only the missteps of their public men."

"And that applies four-fold to women."

CHAPTER 30

*B*lack flies rose suddenly in clouds one overcast day in June. Till then the men dug methodically, cranes and massive stones on ropes driving piles into the soft earth, workers then connecting the piles with planks. Diggers scooped up the muck and threw it beyond the wall on each side of the channel. Black flies ended all that. They flew into the men's ears and eyes and noses and throats, and coated their brawny arms and shoulders and necks. Worst of all they swarmed into their eyes.

"Aye, lads," J.J. McShane called. "Clothe your naked parts now. Rig up a hood when you got the cloth to spare." Yet before they could blink, or between blinks, three, five, eight flies attacked.

Night was worse. The flies swarmed into the rude shanties, and the exhausted men, usually sprawled snoring on planks of pine, now cursed and spun and swatted them. For two weeks, the men arose from sleepless beds and fled into the open air only to be assaulted by the rising orange sun and new legions of flies. Suddenly the flies were gone.

"Like Moses' plague on the Pharaoh. Gone."

"Other plagues will follow."

337

"What will there be?"

"Besides leeches and black flies and water snakes? Only the worst – mosquitoes. Swamp fever. Malaria."

"Aye, 'tis a hellish place they send us."

Hedges looked up to the barren limbs of dead trees that writhed toward low gray clouds. "It's flat, sure, and the best course for the canal, but those that will use it later aren't the ones that dig it, and that, J.J., is a mighty difference."

With the black flies' disappearance on the westerly wind, the men's temperament improved. Knee and thigh and waist-deep in the muck, hurling the black slime over the wooden barrier, they joked and laughed and sang. But this good humor was soon to end.

Eleanora returned to Claverack confused and depressed. Clinton had succeeded only in drawing universal public attention to her case. He despised her now because disgrace and criticism had followed. He was getting married, he didn't need her advice and she sensed Kitty, his fiancée, jealously questioned her presence in his life. Eleanora despised him, too. He had acted so high-handed with her sisterly affections, using her as a decoy to draw attention away from an affair that possibly was going on before Maria's death.

Van Zandt notified Eleanora, and she met him in his office so her farmers and servants would learn nothing of the matter. He informed her the case was on the court calendar for September.

"Is it possible to delay?"

"Perhaps. For how long?"

"A year."

Van Zandt frowned. "Considering its publicity, Edmonds might not be willing to do that."

"Well, don't you attorneys have tricks to stall? I need the case delayed at least a year."

"You wish to be hanging in the balance for that long?" She did not respond. "You may be accountable for the rents you collect during that time if we lose."

"A year," she repeated. "I need a year."

Outside his office, her face burned with indignation. A year! She was reduced to begging time from an attorney! She rode home in the sunshine and the bright cheery day thrust her spirits even lower. Like those poor convicts she had visited, she could do nothing except wait for her freedom. But rebellion was fomenting within her.

On the solitary ride home she considered her predicament from all sides. Clinton wanted her to place a year of her life as a sacrifice on the altar of his political ambition. For what? The canal was being dug. Daniel was seeing to that. Indeed, she had brought Daniel to the project. This request for a delay offended her, but she acknowledged that she had asked the same of Daniel Hedges, to put his life aside for her. Why? So she might keep her property. Why did people need to extract such a price from each other? What right did they have?

She considered Washington Irving and how he'd tried to lay claim to her future. She marveled at this revelation, how friends and lovers sought control just as the dead hand of a property conveyance even now controlled her. A subversive thought she'd had before occurred to her now, and this time she didn't repress it. Why not throw the whole thing off? Why not give up Claverack? Go West, live with Daniel? The happiest days of her life were those times they'd politicked together across the state. She spurred Arabel into a trot. Giving up Claverack was far different from having it taken away.

The logic of it rolled out quickly. What did Clinton want her to be? A confidential secretary. What had Washington Irving wanted? A mother. And what had Jacob wanted? She

339

clenched her teeth because it infuriated her. He wanted a decoy, too, a woman to live in his house, to be beautiful and accomplished, to keep up appearances while he went off with his young friends. She had served them all. She had gone to each of those men and after helping them, had nothing for herself.

How different Daniel was! He wanted her only to be a woman, nothing more . . . and nothing less. Daniel cherished her for who she was. He wasn't frightened or envious or domineering. He loved her. Right now, he was literally moving mountains for her, and she had been too blind to see. More than that, this . . . this was what the canal was all about, a new life and hope in the vast western lands beyond her pastoral Hudson Valley that beckoned men and women of imagination and purpose. A year to sit here at home and wait? Wait for what? The inevitable?

And the cavalier way Clinton asked for that time! He expected it, took it for granted. She might conceive and bear a child in less time. Her thirty-second year was approaching. She couldn't wait another. Certainly the suit could be delayed that long, but she needn't live in its shadow. Let the property look after itself. If it was hers after the suit, so be it. If not, what had she lost?

She looked around her in the radiant sunshine. So that was what she'd do! She'd go west and find Daniel Hedges and cast off this apprehension, this fear that had paralyzed her for so long. The air tasted sweeter already. She spurred Arabel into a canter. With the decision made, it was as if she'd reclaimed that year. The strong muscles of the horse's neck, the rich red mane, the clouds above and the streaming sun, suddenly she was happy! Yes, happy because she knew then she would go to Daniel on the western dig, and he would not seek to control her. She was sure of his love because she knew him, and she trusted him, and above all she loved him.

Eleanora rode hard until the gables of Claverack came

into view. She left Arabel with the groom to be cooled down, and walked to the house flicking the riding crop on her thigh.

～

Late June brought mosquitoes. They attacked the men in relentless swarms and with diabolical accuracy, stinging tender flesh, siphoning blood, and injecting the deadly malaria. Order broke down and the digging slowed.

The disease announced itself with a shiver of cold sweat. Disregarding it, the men continued to dig. Many hung smoke pots around their necks and in these earthenware cups on rawhide cords they burned green sticks. But smoke was a poor substitute for air in their lungs, and the mosquitoes clung to their backs. Fever raced through the work gangs, chills and shakes laid the men low until the shanties were groaning hells as the stricken men lay shaking and moaning.

J.J. McShane walked a blessed path. He had found a rag of cheesecloth and draped it over his broad-brimmed hat to keep the insects out. In his leather coat and blacksmith's gloves, he lumbered through the dwindling crews like a faceless gladiator encouraging the men to dig, watching closely for deserters. And they deserted in droves. The convicts knew the cool breezes of Lake Ontario sparkled only twenty-five miles to the north and offered safety from the disease, and possible escape to Canada and freedom. McShane alerted the gang bosses to prevent workers from using the canal bed as an escape route. Still, many fled into the wilderness and perished among the snakes, turtles and swarms of mosquitoes. Some reached Canada. But most of the three thousand men remained at the dig, mingling their groans and delirious rantings with the croaking of bullfrogs.

A doctor rode between work camps, but he could do little else than give the men feverwort, green pigweed and snakeroot. Nothing abated the plague. In a matter of days able-bodied laborers fell where they dug, groaned and twitched in the bunkhouses, then were carried to a common grave. As the weeks wore on, men died by the hundreds and the work soon came to a standstill.

"We've only got a hundred men and four teams on this stretch, and the piledrivers hang limp," Daniel complained to J.J. one August morning. "How many behind and how many up front?"

"Four hundred up in front and eight behind, one here. Thirteen hundred still working, Dan-o, but they're weak and slow. The lads have lost their spunk."

"It's a sorry time for us all."

Daniel protected himself with tight clothes and gloves and a cheesecloth veil hung from his hat brim. He attended the mass burials out of duty, never considering he'd succumb.

He tried to ignore the first shiver.

"J.J.," he called with a wave of his hand, "I'll be in my tent."

He rode fast and hard along the towpath, hoping that a sweat would carry the poison out of his body. The second shiver lasted a long and alarming minute and he knew he was ill. He rode hard, clinging to the horse's neck, five miles along the towpath back to his tent. By the time he arrived, he was shaking and sweating and he lay on his cot certain he would die.

Water snakes whipped through the green scum, hungry mosquitoes sucked at his blood, leeches clung to his thighs and genitals, and the swollen red sun grew larger and larger until it filled up the sky and the whole vast jumble of rock and swamp and forest seemed to be falling into a fiery lake. He cried out for water, but his parched throat cracked and no sound came out.

Suddenly it was quiet and cold. His sweat made him shiver. He was so very cold and wet. He huddled in wet blankets on a bed of ice. In barren crystal trees four white wolves sat, their yellow eyes peering at him from a silver mist in the dark. The warmth drained from his body into the cold empty night. His teeth were chattering.

He heard voices echo during the fevers and chills, disembodied voices, and his wife and children seemed to float in a circle just beyond his sight and hearing. When he burned again, he sensed that a cool benevolent hand touched his face and forehead. Cool waves passed through his flesh and his burning thirst was slaked. He wept. His mind was playing tricks. He ground his teeth together and pressed his eyes tightly shut, then with an extreme effort, he threw them open.

Light blinded him. Far above him he saw her face. Her rich brown hair was tied back and her brown eyes looked kindly down on him. "Daniel?"

He clenched his teeth even harder and wept, despising the trick his delirium was playing.

"Daniel?"

The voice was sweeter than any melody. He opened his eyes again and saw her.

"Daniel!" She smiled. "Your fever has broken." He blinked, licked his parched, cracked lips. He tried to speak, but his voice caught in his throat. He reached out and touched her hand.

"Eleanora!"

"Yes. I am here." She pressed his hand between hers, and they were cool. "I won't leave you."

And he turned on the bed, pressed his face into the damp sheets, *sheets!* and he wept. "Oh, at last!"

As a convalescent, Daniel was impatient. He longed to get back to the digging and push forward, but Eleanora stood firm. He must rest in order to be of use to anyone. She told him days later of the harrowing week she had spent trying to locate him, how she and Joel Kipp had ridden west on the turnpikes and along the towpath only to find a plague among the workers. Albany knew nothing of it, it was all kept secret to forestall political opposition.

"At the first work camp all we could hear was groaning. The men's teeth chattered, and they shivered in their bunks with chills. Joel approached a man sitting alone with flies buzzing around him. He was dead. Everywhere dead men lay as we pressed farther into the swamp, their stomachs bloated from the heat and decomposition. The stench! When we asked why they weren't buried, we were told no one was well enough to lift a shovel."

She told him how they had discovered him shivering in his tent and had rescued him in a buckboard, hired a spacious stone farmhouse and carried him there. "As soon as I saw the fever," she held up a bottle. "I sent a rider to New York City, and he returned in a week with it." She held up a bottle. "They call it 'Jesuit bark' and it seems to work. Bark from a South American tree. That's what brought you around."

"If only we had more."

"Most are beyond help." Then she mentioned Van Buren and frustrations with the digging.

"No talk of politicians, please! Tell me of J.J."

"Joel says he is impervious to the illness. Nothing bothers him." She described how he tried to maintain order.

"I have to return!"

"Of course, and I will tell you when that day arrives."

Despite his impatience, Daniel enjoyed how she doted on him. For hours at a time she sat at his bedside reading and talking and singing. She dressed as a woman of the land – homespun skirt, loose woolen blouse, a wide black belt and simple boots. She let her hair fall free. Daniel lay in his bed and luxuriated in the aroma of baking bread. The farm fields had been planted by the owner and soon workers were harvesting.

"What about your obligations?" he asked one morning in late September.

"What obligations?"

"Your estate and the matters before the legislature and . . . and Clinton." He spun his hand in the air as if the list were endless.

"I have only one obligation now," she smiled, "and you keep me busy enough."

The leaves were turning when Daniel could walk outside. He walked with her in the pastures and meadows. They picnicked during the warm, sunny Indian summer. For two weeks their lives were bliss. Then one evening Daniel announced they would dig all through the winter.

"It was a mistake going into that swamp in summer. Cold congeals the earth, and makes it easier to dig. We'll work all winter and be through the swamp by the first thaw."

Eleanora said nothing.

"What is the matter?"

She paused in their stroll, took his arm and looked up sadly. "What about me?"

He scratched his head. "Haven't you always made your own decisions?"

"Yes, and now I shall!" She lay her head on his shoulder. "I'll stay here, where I belong."

Daniel reached down and kissed her. The delicious scent of harvest was in the air and birds screamed across the bright autumn sky.

"I am so very happy." He kissed her again.

"I love you, Daniel."

CHAPTER 31

*C*linton's marriage pleased New York society. The
handsome, energetic governor could not have chosen
a more beautiful or accomplished wife than Kitty Jones. Her
father's banking connections would someday finance DeWitt
Clinton's successful presidential bid, they speculated, and then
all of New York society would benefit.

Immediately after the letter in the newspaper, Clinton
convened the Council of Appointment and ousted Van Buren
from the attorney general post. Now Van Buren only held his
state senate seat, but his Albany Regency was a powerful political machine, the critical voting bloc that passed or obstructed
laws and budget bills. And soon afterward, when a New York
seat fell vacant in the United States Senate, Van Buren took
the legislative appointment and left for Washington.

"He has a voracious appetite for political office," Clinton
observed to his wife. "The result, I suppose, of his low birth."

"We should pity the less fortunate."

"Not in politics. He has single-handedly cost our state
years of work and progress on the canal to advance his selfish
political ends."

Van Buren thought otherwise, naturally. By championing

347

the cause of those who hated Clinton, he had built a reliable power base.

"Ah, Matty," Burr was fond of saying, "power is like fire, it consumes what it feeds on, and requires more and more to burn brighter, higher and hotter." Van Buren soon discovered new fuel in the malaria epidemic and the dire financial Panic of 1819. If he could blame all the negative aspects on Clinton, Clinton's political funeral pyre would blaze into the sky.

Van Buren asked his Regency to get a death count from the canal commission and the commission duly sent Daniel Hedges a letter requesting the information.

"Have you counted the dead, J.J.?" Hedges asked his foreman.

"For them politicians? They sit comfortable in Albany with their tarts and their dinners and their chessboard games, why don't they just let us get on with the diggin'?"

"How many died, J.J.?"

"All of 'em, Dan-o. Tell the sons o' whores that. All of 'em."

Daniel modified this response to the commission: "Too many. I was one of the few who recovered. Many fled into the forests and perished there. An accurate count is impossible." Not wanting to open the issue, the canal commission forwarded Van Buren a letter saying it hadn't kept count. Van Buren then focused on the Panic of 1819 to impede the canal's progress by citing the expense. He couldn't blame Clinton for the recession, but he might use it to dry up the money.

Another summer and autumn passed quietly along the course of the canal. Daniel and Eleanora lived in the stone house with a panoramic view of the glacial valleys. Though in Albany it would be highly disgraceful, frontiersmen paid little attention to church weddings, so they lived openly together. She told him nothing about her pending lawsuit, but harbored a defiance toward matrimony that Daniel found puzzling.

"Why should the state invade our lives and tell us we cannot live such as this?" They lay together in bed. Dying embers took the edge off the October chill. "Why can't we live as man and woman? Why must it be man and *wife*, with the woman nothing more than a man's property?"

"Ah, my love, who cares? I never think of such things. I'm happier now than I can remember."

"But it's infuriating! Even now I suppose there are rumors rampant in Albany about us."

"Let them squawk. We can't hear them out here. It won't get the ditch dug any quicker."

"But we must think about Albany because we have been summoned there."

Eleanora held up a letter.

Daniel moaned. "Not again!"

"DeWitt has a problem with funds for next year's digging."

Daniel's fist clenched. "Goddamn them!"

"You don't understand."

"No, Eleanora," he pointed his finger at her. "I do understand. We have been dying out here, hundreds of men, perhaps a thousand, laying them in unmarked graves while these petty politicians play their games and are now threatening to cut off the money! Our diggers must not have died in vain! We must finish this, if only for them."

"But the legislature makes the decisions."

"And you understand all that far better than I ever want to. I am going to work these men through the winter again – why? To keep them warm, to keep them busy, to keep the canal progressing. What will the politicians be doing? Drinking and wenching. I'd put the young boys who run whiskey on my mudline against those politicians any day, and they'd be favored by the comparison."

"Be reasonable."

"Reasonable? What else have I been for years? I have done their bidding. I understand their troubles. I don't even care if

349

they understand mine, but if Clinton calls us, you go, I won't. And you tell him how I feel." Angrily he rose.

Eleanora pulled the quilt up about her neck. "Daniel, please." He stood tall in the firelight and pointed his thumb eastward.

"Right now they're worried about what they're going to have for breakfast, if their wives will catch them fornicating, how many votes they can steal. They have no courage, no honesty. Give me J.J. McShane over them anytime because McShane is a man of his word."

"Daniel!"

"No," he cried, "don't pretend with me that they are more important to this work than we are. I would have died if it hadn't been for you. I owe you my life, but I owe them nothing. All debts have been paid in full. Let Clinton find some way or another to keep the money flowing so I can pay my men. He's never shy about taking all the credit for the work."

Daniel threw on his clothes and left to exhale his frustrations in the frosty moonlight.

Clinton did do something. He planned a celebration in late October to open the finished portion of the canal from Utica to Rome. The ceremony, replete with a brass band aboard a canal boat, politicians praising each other in endless speeches and gun salutes, greatly impressed the locals. But the *Albany Argus* complained that at such a rate the canal would require twenty years for completion and would surely bankrupt the state. The newspaper continued its charge of judge-fixing. Clinton was fighting for his political survival as the recession plunged merchants into bankruptcy, forced freeholders off the land as banks foreclosed, and then ran those very banks into oblivion.

Yet with a stroke of genius, Clinton turned the panic to his advantage. He appeared personally before the legislature and urged passage of a funding bill to allow the state to pay farmer contractors a higher wage. This wage, in turn, would allow them to pay their mortgages and thus pull the economy of the central and western part of the state up by its bootstraps. The bill passed in both houses.

Despite this ingenious plan, ugly rumors persisted, rumors about his reclusive ways, his drinking habits, his new wife's control over policy. Even though ninety miles of canal connected Rome with the Seneca River by July 4, Clinton squeaked through the election with less than a one-percent margin.

"I grow weary of it all," Clinton confessed to Kitty. She peered up from her novel. "I wonder sometimes why I have worked so hard."

"So do I," Kitty agreed. "Why can't we leave Albany? This is a horrid little place, so small and dull. I don't care in the least whether some woodsman can ship his lumber or furs more cheaply to market. You've done more for these people than they deserve. Let us return to New York. You have holdings, and Papa will help us get started. You'd make a perfect bank's attorney."

"We shall see, my dear." And while her plea had not fallen on deaf ears, Clinton watched her return to her novel and measured her unfavorably against Eleanora.

CHAPTER 32

*J*oel Kipp brought the news. Eleanora read on his face that she had lost the suit. With the funds at last approved, Daniel and the crews had dug all through the winter of 1820-21, and as the canal proceeded out of the swamp, Hedges had gone west for three days to scout the Irondequoit Valley and the turbulent Genesee.

"I was in that courtroom, ma'am, and I listened to them." Joel shook his head. "Van Zandt made all manner of excuses for you not appearing, but you could tell it angered Judge Edmonds. The judge said there were some irregularities alleged in your, your, ah, *conduct*, that Van Zandt did not dispute. The judge kept saying 'acquiescence' and that you 'acquiesced' and so forfeited Claverack."

"I simply could not appear." She dropped her eyes to the simple dress she wore, and looked around the kitchen and into the fieldstone hearth. "It would have been humiliating, and would not have helped the case."

"Van Zandt agreed." Joel handed her a letter. She focused on this passage:

The court held that by the deeds your father and Jacob VR Sr. conditioned the conveyance and that they might impose any conditions they desired. I argued that 'Till death do us part' was a condition subsequent and Jacob's death released you from any and all obligation. Thus, you might comport yourself as you saw fit and could retain your lands so long as you did not marry. Yet the judge looked at the parties' intent. Plaintiff's proof as to midnight liaisons and your current living arrangement was damning. Your non-appearance was considered acquiescence on your part and fatal to your claim. The application for ejectment was approved and sent to the magistrate. Still, I suggest we appeal to chancery for reinstatement of your dower right.

Inasmuch as his claim was granted, plaintiff Randolph VR now requests you remove all personal property from both the Claverack house and from the Albany townhouse by September 1, 1821. Any personalty left after that date will be sold at public auction.

Eleanora sighed and lay the letter on the table. "And now we must find you a position, Joel."

"Why? After I look to your effects and all this is settled, I'll just work here, on the dig."

She nodded. "Daniel is due home this evening. Put up at the inn in Pittsford. I want to tell him in my own way."

"I'll stop tomorrow before I return to Albany."

Daniel arrived at sunset excited by what he had accomplished. "We took soundings in the streambed of the Genesee and the bedrock is only five feet beneath the gravel and silt. We'll begin laying the footings in August when the water is low. J.J. and I have devised a way to bridge the Irondequoit, too." He squinted, noticing her quiet. "Is there something wrong?"

"Yes." She fought back a sob. "Something terrible happened to me."

He clasped her hands and held her to him. "What is it?"

"Oh, I cannot hope that you will marry me now!"

"But you have always railed against the notion of marriage." He scowled. "What is it?" She held him and wept on his shoulder.

"I so much, so very much wanted to be your wife!"

He held her, repeating over and over, "It's all right, it's all right."

When she had calmed, he helped her to a seat. "What makes you think I'd let you get away this time?" She looked up into his broad smile and sparkling eyes and she smiled faintly.

"I have nothing. I have lost my estate and the home in Albany attached to it. I've lost my station in life. Everything. I'm destitute."

"How?"

"There was a condition in the deed with Jacob that I did not fulfill."

Daniel nodded, his eyes grew wide and he whispered with sudden revelation: "They prevented you from remarrying! That's it! That's what it has always been!"

"Yes." She turned away, ashamed. "And now you must believe that my lands were more important to me than my love for you. But that wasn't it. My beautiful Claverack, my home, the land and the people that I loved. I couldn't abandon it until I saw that fighting for it meant hurting us. Until I came west, the deed prevented my remarriage. Now, now my poverty does. You're all I have, and I don't even know if you'll have me."

"Eleanora," he whispered, sitting on the hearth beside her chair, "you saved my life! I knew there was a reason you would not acknowledge us to the world. Why didn't you tell me?"

"I couldn't! The shame of being destitute! I couldn't!"

"I thought it was love for another, Clinton perhaps. Or

355

that it was my lower station in life, who I was, where I came from."

She looked at him with tears streaking her face. "Oh, no, my love. From the first I loved you, your wisdom, your courage, your quiet competence. I couldn't show it. I fought it. I tried to deny and forget it, but I couldn't, and I felt so foolish, so torn. I believed the dead hand of my father controlled me, yet in you I saw such life, such love, such hope. Before I met you, I lived alone, chasing after things like poetry and politics, believing, hoping they would acquire value for me. When we were together, though, I felt love. I knew I could love, I *must* love, but I still wouldn't accept it, not until this evil business began. I came west because I couldn't drag us, drag you through public rebuke, the newspapers, the gossip-mongers, the screaming of DeWitt's enemies. It could have been such a scandal! They would have swept aside all the fine work you've done. I had to be with you. I *have* to be with you!"

"Then I bless the day this evil business began! I am grateful to Clinton's enemies!"

"But I can bring nothing to our union. I am a pauper."

He laughed and reached for her. "We don't need anything. We have each other! Let them have Claverack. We'll build a new life, a happier life in Buffalo." He pulled her to her feet, lifted her off the floor and spun her around. "This is the happiest day of my life! What children we shall have!"

"Children?"

"Of course. I've dreamed about this day for years. What a mother you will make!"

"I'm quite . . . I'm quite . . ."

He kissed her passionately and held her tightly.

"What about supper?" she asked.

"It can wait." And he carried her up to the bedroom.

BOOK V
UP THE ESCARPMENT TO THE LAKE

CHAPTER 33

*a*fter the court decision, Eleanora Van Rensselaer felt and acted like a different woman. The worst had happened and she awoke from the curse of her long-standing fear to accept her new life. Freed from worrying about what people thought, she adopted the western pioneer attitude and set out to earn her happiness.

She sewed trousers and a jacket for herself, and announced to Daniel: "I'd like to do something useful. Can I command a group of the diggers?"

Unfortunately this request ignored J.J. McShane's manner of discovering and promoting gang leaders – those who beat the boss in a fair fight won control of the gang.

"I don't think the men would respond to you," Daniel said.

But she was not to be rebuffed. As J.J. began the mile-long earthworks necessary to carry the canal eighty feet above the Irondequoit Valley, Eleanora asked Daniel if she could assist in setting up the three new workers' camps. He agreed to that and detailed some older workers to her.

Before, not much thought had gone into building the work camps and most of the thought about provisions concerned whiskey. The men's fare was usually stew – boiled salt pork or beef or fresh game with whatever carrots, potatoes, turnips and onions could be bought from neighboring farmers – the stew and biscuit washed down with coffee and whiskey. The lanes of the work camp were ankle-deep in mud and smelled, after a rain, of sewage as the jakes overflowed. Rude bunk houses held only wooden shelves where the men collapsed after sixteen or eighteen hours of digging.

"With a little planning we can greatly improve the accommodations," she observed to Daniel. He authorized her to build new camps. At three sites, each near a bright spring, she laid out compounds two hundred feet square and marked out bunkhouse sites at each corner. Instead of rude, overflowing ditches for latrines, Eleanora had four-holed privies built farther down slope. She left nothing to the judgment of carpenters, but designed on paper a new spacious bunkhouse floor plan that centered around a hearth and sitting area, with the bunks set off from the central area by panels.

She journeyed to Rochesterville and arranged with a merchant for a shipment of blankets and towels, barrels of flour and yeast. Budgeting the limited funds, she bought cattle, swine and sheep. She hired a boy for each work camp to graze the cattle on the central green, and had pens built for the pigs. She arranged for a special meal each Sunday of roast beef, pork or mutton. She showed the mess hands how to bake bread in Dutch ovens, and the fresh bread each night alone won her universal acclaim from the men. She added cake and pastry occasionally when sugar or molasses could be obtained in quantity. The men responded. Each Sunday they held prize fights, "sings," cock fights and even rat races on the greens.

"She's a rare angel," J.J. told Daniel. "The men love her. I believe if anyone was to lay a hand on her, why, he'd find a Dublin blade between the ribs. Aye, Dan-o, I'm getting half again as much work out of the boys, and miracle to end miracles, the whiskey rations have gone down!"

"But she grows impatient since that work's done, J.J. She needs a new challenge. I've been thinking of giving her command of a gang."

J.J. shook his head. "No again, Dan-o. The men would resent taking orders from a female no matter she don't wear skirts. Would upset the dig, y'see? Why not give her five or six men and have them spur along private contractors who're slacking off?"

This appealed to Daniel and soon he dispatched Eleanora with three men to report on progress, and also to seek contractors for any stretches not yet being dug.

Daniel worked and reworked the aqueduct plans with architect Canvass White to span the Genesee River. During the low water season in August, they diverted the turbulent river at Rochesterville first to the east and then to the west in order to sink massive footings through the riverbed to the bedrock, footings to support eleven fifty-foot arches. As the pilings rose and the aqueduct was becoming a reality, so did the confidence and spirit of the men.

However, harmony and enterprise were not universal. The vicious battle between Black Rock and Buffalo for the western terminus became still more bitter. With his longstanding feud and his land holdings in Buffalo sold, Joseph Ellicott argued Black Rock's advantages: a shorter distance to dig and a wider harbor. Clinton opposed him, though, opting for Buffalo with the more southern entrance into the lake. In disgust and frustration, Ellicott resigned from the canal commission.

Seeing this rift, Van Buren conferred with Aaron Burr, and the senator then discussed with Ellicott ways to turn Holland Land Company farmers against the governor. Here, there and everywhere, using every means at his disposal, Van Buren eroded Clinton's popularity and support. He saw that his long years of plotting and building an organization based on patronage would bear fruit if the powerful Clinton were gone. Van Buren then approached Ellicott directly.

"Perhaps you might share your dissatisfaction with the western counties?" the senator, home from Washington, suggested over dinner in an Albany tavern.

"Clinton's flaw is that he won't compromise! I've been loyal to him for twelve years, but once you fall afoul of him, you're finished." Ellicott shook his head. "You can never again get near him no matter how close you were before. He's intractable."

"And we both know," Van Buren said with a smile and flourish of his hand, "that public men must be flexible if nothing else. I can help you if you help me."

"Consider it done," Ellicott said.

As the construction season of 1821 ended, Daniel and Eleanora set up housekeeping near Rochester. Only a cluster of homes with a mill until the year before, the village had suddenly become a boom-town, and dropped the "ville" from its name. Land doubled and quadrupled in value. Foundations were laid for homes and warehouses as merchants saw that the canal would soon link Rochester with the Hudson River and New York City.

Eleanora's help and enthusiasm this season had been extraordinary. The invigorating outdoor life tanned her skin and lightened her hair, putting a new sparkle in her eye.

"We do make quite a pair," Daniel said one day after regaling her about a man's astonishment at seeing a woman in trousers.

"Yes, and beyond the bit of gossip from churchgoing women, it's surprising how few people notice our living arrangement."

"Does this mean you don't want a wedding?"

"Not at all," she said coyly. "In fact, we should probably plan it soon."

"I thought you wanted to wait until the canal is complete."

"I thought so too, but what if we were to be blessed with a baby?"

"You're not . . .?" Daniel's eyes lit up.

"No," she laughed, "no, I'm not. But it might happen, especially during the winter when we're so idle."

"Next week, then?"

"No, I think we should let DeWitt know. He brought us together. He'll certainly want to attend."

"Clinton, eh?"

"Oh, yes! If it weren't for him . . ."

"If it weren't for him, you'd still be comfortable and wealthy on your estate."

"Yes, but I wouldn't be happy." And she lay her head on his shoulder.

"All right. Make the arrangements."

Eleanora wrote Clinton and he wrote back that he'd be visiting on a campaign swing while he was securing his party's nomination. She indicated they would wait for his visit. But he did not come that winter because his political support for the 1822 election was eroding in the lower Hudson counties and he needed to campaign vigorously to shore up his base. In February, they set the day for late March, just before the party would select its candidate.

In mid-March Daniel journeyed to the western escarpment to take further measurements of the canal's last great obstacle. This cliff, home to eagles and rattlesnakes, would require a flight of five twin locks, a grand staircase of water, each lock spilling into the one below, one side to lift boats, the other to let them down.

Through the winter, J.J. and the men had quarried stone for the Rochester aqueduct. After blasting with black powder or cracking stone with water poured into bored holes for the frost to expand, the men dressed the blocks and dragged them to the river bank over an icy chute on oxen-drawn sleds. All lay ready the day Daniel returned, March 18. The men who had celebrated the feast of their patron St. Patrick lay hungover in the work camps. Daniel and J.J. discussed his wedding ceremony, and how work would begin the day after as Daniel and Eleanora left for their honeymoon.

Returning home that night, Daniel was surprised that no lights were on. Inside he found only a note:

March 16, 1822

Dearest Daniel:

A very important matter compels me to go to Albany. I hope you understand. I will write at my earliest convenience.

Love,
Eleanora

At his first reading, Daniel shrugged and considered that he could get along alone for the month. Then, with a start, he remembered their wedding was set for the 24th. The next day, he told J.J. the wedding would be delayed and that work should start immediately.

"What is it, Dan-o?"

"Pressing business drew her away."

"Aye. Pressing business, is it?" J.J. asked nothing further, but Daniel could see McShane didn't approve of Eleanora's conduct. He didn't approve himself. He drove the men harder than usual, working by sun and by torchlight to dress and haul granite blocks for the aqueduct.

But Eleanora's journey was hardly for pleasure. A week before she had met Assemblyman Atwater in Rochester and he triumphantly announced that Clinton was not seeking re-election. Eleanora thought he was joking until she consulted the state senator. "No," Senator Clayburn said, "he's not running this year. The party won't give him the nomination. Van Buren's faction has denyied him that."

Daniel wouldn't return for two days. Eleanora felt

stunned: this devastating blow, the canal project and her impending marriage hit her all at once. She immediately packed, left her terse note and boarded the stagecoach to Lauraville. From there, she traveled in a passenger boat day and night until she reached Rome. By day she sat on deck, marveling at the landscape passing by, and at night she slept on a closed bed shelf, the boat filled with men's snoring. At Rome, she boarded a stagecoach and set off along the gravel turnpike. By the morning of the third day she was in Albany. Calling at the governor's mansion, she found to her dismay Clinton had left for New York City the day before.

With her townhouse gone, Eleanora stayed at Gray's Hotel that night, then she caught Fulton's North River Steamboat in the morning. Within a week of her departure she was at Clinton's house in Flushing. When the butler announced Eleanora, Kitty swept down the stairway.

"Oh, Eleanora, it's so good to see you! I'm glad you have come!" But the alarm she heard in the socialite's voice was foreboding. "DeWitt is not himself. Perhaps you should spend the night elsewhere and speak with him in the morning."

"I heard he is not standing for office this year and I find that incomprehensible! I must speak with him."

A loud cry in the back of the house and a crashing of glass interrupted them. Kitty looked in horror toward the sound.

"Please," Kitty pressed Eleanora's hand between hers. "I think you had better go. There's lodging at the Peacock Inn. George, our footman, will escort you over and see to your comfort." Another groan and a crashing sound startled them.

"Kitty, I must see him."

"He is in no condition to entertain."

"I regret that I must insist." Eleanora glared at her until Kitty spun about and went to the back of the house, then returned. "He will see you, but please, please don't press him. He's been through a terrible ordeal."

Eleanora followed her. The rear parlor was dark except for

two candles. Six empty wine bottles stood on the table. Another one lay in pieces on the floor and the wall and the carpet were stained red.

Clinton stood in the middle of the room, an impotent giant, snorting in rage. He worked to focus his eyes. "It is you. Eleanora. You have come. That is good."

"She'll be stopping at the inn tonight," Kitty said primly.

"Leave us, Catherine!" Clinton commanded, pointing to the door. Both women were surprised by the force of his command, and as Kitty left, Clinton looked at Eleanora with a cruel sidelong glance. "So, you have come."

"I heard you weren't running for governor, and I had to talk with you."

"Glass of wine?" He poured himself another tumbler. "My only solace these days." He drank it quickly and poured another.

"Yes. I'll have one with you." She accepted it. "You look terrible, DeWitt. You need sleep."

"Sleep? Sleep is the one thing I've forgotten how to do." He struggled to focus and to speak. "It is true . . . what you heard . . . that I'm not running . . . but it's not my decision. The party . . . the party refuses to back me."

"But why? The canal progresses so well."

"Why?" he whispered hoarsely. "Van Buren! That's why! That little snake has made my re-election impossible. While I've been devoting my time to serving the people, he's been consolidating his power within the party."

"Surely you overestimate him, *they* overestimate him."

"No!" Clinton bellowed. "No! That was our mistake all along. We underestimated him. While we've been building the eighth wonder of the world, he's been building a party structure. That bastard son of an innkeeper. God! Is there no justice?"

Eleanora had never seen him so. The sight of this massive man howling like a wounded beast frightened her.

"He's everywhere. He called a convention and rewrote our state constitution to abolish my powers on the Council of Appointment. So now the men I've put in office, the men I've fed for a decade, all have turned against me and turned to *him*. My own men eating out of his hand!"

"But it's not that hopeless," she pleaded. "His trickery, his deceit will undo him. The people of this state . . ."

"The people?" Clinton cried. "What do they know? They cannot see into men's hearts as we can and read the ambition in men's dark deeds. Their sight is clouded and their memories short. They believe the damned newspapers, and the editors believe Van Buren. I am undone!" Clinton's eyes grew wide and his voice was insidious, a theatrical whisper. "'Soft you, a word or two before you go.' Shakespeare's moor, Othello – 'I have done the state some service, and they know it. No more of that. I pray you, in your letters, when you shall these unlucky deeds relate, speak of me as I am. Nothing extenuate, nor set down aught in malice.'" Now his voice dripped with sarcasm. "'Then, then must you speak of one that ruled not wisely, but too well!'"

"DeWitt!" she scolded him.

"You have never suffered political exile, woman. You do not know how it is to be stripped of the robes of office and turned out. Tiresias the beggar, limping, vilified by men who once genuflected before you." He thumped his chest. "I do! I was twice turned out as mayor. Now I'm turned out as governor."

She paused, sipped the wine, and then spoke softly. "No, my dear friend, you forget. I have been publicly dispossessed of my estate and turned out with nothing but the clothes on my back."

He looked up. "Ah," he quaffed his wine and poured more, "fortune plays the whore with us both."

"Yes, but tomorrow is another day. I shall talk to you when your senses have returned. But know this, DeWitt, I have never been happier since I lost my lands. And you must get control of yourself. Kitty will find me a room in this drafty house of yours. Be kind to her, she is not the cause." Eleanora turned and walked from the room leaving Clinton looking down at his wineglass as if he just noticed it in his hand. "How long has he been this way?" Eleanora asked Catherine who had been eavesdropping in the hall.

"Two days. It terrifies me."

"He'll be better in the morning."

In the morning, the governor joined them in the airy planetarium for breakfast, a trifle haggard but in far better spirits.

"Eleanora, I have never seen you look so well! You glow like a country wench. You're positively robust!" He kissed her. "Good morning, Kitty." He kissed his wife and signaled for the servant to bring cider and cocoa. "It must be that Hedges fellow you're marrying. Lucky man, lucky man. One can always tell when a woman's in love."

"Yes, it is due to him, partly, but I've also been working on the canal and I feel so . . . *useful*. If our lazy class would only do something physical they should all be the better off for it. He who humbles himself shall be exalted. Truly, since I lost my estate, I have never felt so free."

"You must appeal to Chancery. Equity would never allow a woman to be cheated of her dower."

"No, DeWitt, I'm happy now. I don't need to challenge that."

"I'll have the attorney general look into it personally and confer with your lawyer. I may as well use the office I hold for as long as I hold it. Now tell me about building the great pyramid, my 'political tomb' as the newspapers call it."

She regaled him with stories of the contractors, the hard-drinking, brawling Irish and the constant migration of people to western lands for farm and trade. She described the elephantine pilings that would carry the canal over the Genesee, and the mammoth excavations needed up the escarpment farther west.

After breakfast, Clinton asked her to join him in his library. "I'm sorry about my behavior last night. I cannot believe what is happening to me, Eleanora. It's reprehensible."

"The tide will turn," she said brightly.

"I am so weary of the conspiracies of men! Like hounds dragging down the stag, they set on me from every side."

"You must forget them. If you are not running this year, so be it. But do not resign yourself to anonymity. Come west with me and see the awe that our canal awakens. It is more than a highway for transporting people and goods. It is a phenomenon of ingenuity and raw perseverance. Yours. That's what captures imaginations!"

He nodded. "Your enthusiasm is welcome."

"You must come out and view the great work and accept the tribute and accolades of a thankful people. Forget Van Buren and his pack of dogs. The canal is a thing of surpassing beauty. Westward, beyond the river is a land where no possibility is limited, and ambition and enterprise are all that matter. I have never felt freer, happier, more useful since I have lived out there. Visit us this summer. You'll draw surprising strength from it."

"Perhaps, perhaps."

"Daniel will show you the marvels that he and McShane have worked in earth and stone."

Clinton gave a laugh. "Rumors abound about your scandalous lifestyle."

"Oh, yes." She agreed. "Nowhere is the difference between east and west more apparent than in that attitude toward a man and a woman. In the west men and women join together often without a ceremony because they face a struggle for survival. They build a cabin, clear the land, plant their crops and raise their children. Cruel nature is our enemy, not any conception of evil or sin."

"When will your wedding be?"

"You've delayed it twice. We were going ahead without you and scheduled it for . . . well, for today, actually."

"Today? What are you doing here?"

"I heard you weren't running, and I had to come. I know you far too well. I knew how you would react and I was correct. Daniel will understand. Another few weeks won't hurt anything." An idea occurred to her. "Why don't we postpone our wedding until your visit?"

"So I could attend?"

"No," she smiled broadly, "so you can perform it. Who has more authority to join man and wife in this state than the governor?"

"I would be flattered. I have always admired Hedges. He's intelligent and steady. His efforts have kept the construction on course. If I had five men like him, I'd be president by now."

"Wonderful!" She clapped her hands. "Then it's settled. I shall write him directly. Oh, this is an unexpected joy! Daniel will be immensely pleased!"

But Daniel was far from pleased. He missed her badly and waited for some further explanation. Occasionally he occupied his evenings at a Rochester tavern with J.J. McShane, but he always returned to the empty house and stared at her chair by the cold hearth. He was finally relieved when a letter arrived:

Flushing,
March 24, 1822

My Dearest Daniel:

I am staying with DeWitt and Kitty another two days, and then I shall return. Please know that my immediate action has helped our project immeasurably. Soon we will have DeWitt's personal attention. He has agreed to view the work in June, and he will perform our wedding ceremony!

I go to sleep each night with thoughts of you, my beloved, and I miss you so very much. Thank you for your understanding, and know that I love you.

Your own,
Eleanora

"Clinton," he muttered, "again, Clinton." He slapped the letter in his hand.

CHAPTER 34

One mild June afternoon, work ceased early on the Rochester aqueduct. Blocks of granite hung idle from cranes above the massive stone arches that marched across the foaming river with Roman determination. In this frontier hamlet of woodsmen, trappers, river boatmen, traders, farmers, a doctor, two attorneys and their wives and children, the townspeople often paused to contemplate the aqueduct and how it symbolized a great age of commerce and civilization flowing into their midst. Today, everyone paused together, even the workers.

On the western side a large crowd was gathered, a hundred and seventy workers, eighty-five townspeople and a rustic band of diggers that played Irish elbow pipes, a tin whistle, a squeezebox, a fiddle and a drum. They played jigs and reels and the men sipped freely from a whiskey keg. A tall man in a dark suit stood near the unfinished bed of the bridge lined with oak planks that soon would be filled with water. Governor Clinton was waiting for the ceremony to begin.

A whoop went up among the men as the door to the foreman's cabin opened and a young girl in a yellow gown stepped out, green ribbons fluttering in her hair. She was followed by

Eleanora Van Rensselaer in a flowing white wedding dress. Many of the men had only seen her in woolen trousers and a buckskin jacket. An awed hush fell on the assembled. As she moved into the sunlight, her dark hair was accentuated by the pure white of the veil. Judge Nathaniel Rochester, the town's founder and father of the maid of honor, took Eleanora's arm to escort her.

Near the governor, Daniel Hedges stood in a dark suit, and at his side, tugging at the high uncomfortable collar, was best man J.J. McShane. The crowd fell back, and Eleanora gracefully bowed, scanned the great stone breastwork, and then looked at Daniel. They exchanged nervous smiles.

As the squeezebox, pipes and fiddle played a wedding march, the judge solemnly escorted her to Daniel, and he bowed. Daniel returned the bow, looked into Eleanora's eyes and his nervousness disappeared. The slightest smile curled her lips, and her eyes were misty.

"Who gives this woman in matrimony?" Governor Clinton asked.

"I do, sir," Judge Rochester said, then he bowed and stepped aside.

Eleanora glided to Daniel and stood facing the governor. Clinton bowed, then he took out a small book. He welcomed them informally: "It is fitting you have chosen to sanctify this grand work that joins east to west. You both have worked so long with me, with these men and with the people of our state. Eleanora, Daniel," here Clinton's voice broke, "you have helped give birth to what was once only a dream, but is quickly becoming a new age for all of us. Generations of New Yorkers will be in your debt. I am grateful, and deeply humbled by the honor you do me to say these few words that will join you together as man and wife."

Men cleared their throats and women sniffed into hand-kerchiefs. "Daniel Hedges, do you take this woman, Eleanora Livingston Van Rensselaer, as your lawfully wedded wife, to love, honor and cherish from this day forward, in sickness and in health till death do you part?"

Daniel looked into her eyes. "I do."

"And do you, Eleanora, take this man, Daniel Hedges, as your lawfully wedded husband to love, honor and obey from this day forward, in sickness and in health, till death do you part?"

Eleanora smiled. "I do."

"If you would place the ring on her finger, Daniel." Daniel looked to J.J., and the Irishman was so taken up with the formality he went blank.

"The rings, J.J." The Irishman patted his waistcoat, produced a small jeweler's box and handed it to Daniel. Daniel opened it, removed the smaller gold ring and took up Eleanora's small hand. He placed the ring on her finger and repeated the pledge Clinton recited. Then Eleanora took the larger ring, placed it on Daniel's finger, and gazing into his eyes, made her pledge.

Clinton spoke in a deep, official voice. "With the authority vested in me as governor of the State of New York, I now pronounce you man and wife."

They kissed. The words were no sooner uttered and the kiss exchanged when a deafening holler erupted from the men, the band struck up, and the Irishmen, whiskey in their veins, linked arms and jigged.

"Congratulations," Clinton clasped both their arms. "I wish you all the best." He waved his arm at the great aqueduct, gleaming in the early summer sun.

"Thank you, Governor." Daniel shook his hand warmly.

Eleanora kissed him on the cheek. "Today I know at last what happiness is, and you shall know it too, DeWitt, the day the canal is open."

The crowd converged on them. Judge and Mrs. Rochester congratulated them warmly. J.J. McShane embraced Daniel and gave a shy kiss to the back of Eleanora's hand. The gang leaders were next. Each one advanced to deliver his good wishes. Then workmen pressed forward and they started in a procession, the young Rochester girl strewing flowers on the road, back to the tavern for a reception.

The governor did not participate in the festivities. He walked back and forth along the width of the aqueduct, then the length, as if on a rampart, admiring from every angle its straight clean lines. He leaned over the side and watched the water swiftly flowing. "That was perhaps the last good thing I'll do in office," he spoke to the foaming water. Remembering a tale Daniel told him long ago about a native chief swept over Niagara Falls, Clinton returned to his lodgings.

The wedding reception brought out the gaiety and festiveness of the Irish. "Aye, Dan-o, there's nothin' more to an Irishman's liking than a wake or wedding."

"I'm happy we chose the latter."

The celebration demonstrated to Daniel how tightly knit a team J.J. had forged. The band played all afternoon, and the men danced strenuous jigs and reels. A ring was set up in the tavern yard and boxing matches brought the clamoring, gambling men to wager on two giants who mauled and gouged each other untill they couldn't stand. Whiskey and porter flowed freely, and barroom choruses shook the rafters.

The couple departed in a carriage early in the evening. Already men were snoring in corners of the tavern, and the maid who'd caught the bouquet was dancing barefoot on the village green with her friends.

Daniel had secured a cabin downriver near Carthage. It was a log cabin, built in a tall stand of pine just back from the river and the rushing water and wind in the pines lent a happy peace to the evening. Eleanora sighed contentedly as they sat together in candlelight where a moth circled: "Tonight," she whispered, "we could be the only man and woman in the world."

After lighting a fire and drinking a glass of champagne, they lay together in the big featherbed.

"Oh, Daniel," she sighed, afterward, catching her breath. She stroked his cheek gently and looked into his eyes, "I am so very happy."

He smiled at her. "And I'm the luckiest man alive."

They slept holding each other, content and perfectly at peace.

On waking, Eleanora stretched and yawned and looked outside. Daniel was standing knee-deep in the river with a fishing pole. She called to him. Outlined by the sun sparkling on the water, he turned and waved.

"I've caught breakfast. Put the skillet on the coals."

They ate outside, trout, eggs and fried potatoes. The larder Mrs. Rochester provided included a round loaf of Irish soda bread, and Daniel cut and buttered slices. They ate heartily, and lingered over coffee.

"Three years ago I would have said this was impossible." She looked around. Birds called in the forest and the sunlight slanted down through the canopy of pine. "I thought losing my estate would be the end of my life." She laughed. "I knew from the first time you came to my home, perhaps the day after the general's ball, that if I could get you involved, perhaps my dream would come true."

"You don't know how many nights I lay awake wondering why I was digging a ditch to connect my lake to your river and the sea beyond. Yes, I'd remember sailing in my *Silver Pearl*, and I'd think of leaving this work, of building another brig and returning to the lake trade. Certainly it wasn't the salary. My old first mate now owns half the lakefront in Buffalo. I thought many times, too, that you were just using me to help Clinton and that your true affections lay with him."

"With DeWitt?" Eleanora feigned shock.

"Yes. You were always together. He saw more of you than

he did his wife. His wishes always came first. Even this March."

"Daniel!" she scolded. "One thing about DeWitt you have seen, no doubt, is that he needs steady attention, acclaim and admiration. That was difficult for me at first, almost as if he had no self-confidence. I don't admire weakness. Sometimes he acts like a prideful child. That offends me. But I see another side to his genius, a tender side. He spends so much time reading and pondering, politicking and planning, that when he awakens from those long spells of concentration, he needs people he can trust. He needs to be reminded that he is as mortal and as ordinary as everyone else. He only asks that people understand and appreciate his effort."

"You must love him very much."

"I do. He is a remarkable man, but he is also a distant man, cold and often bitterly cynical. He lapses into depressions gloomier than the Cayuga swamp, and when the rage he strives to control erupts, only I can reason with him. He trusts no one. Both his wives have been simple, beautiful girls who bore his children, kept his house, and allowed him his way."

Hedges nodded. "I thought you'd marry him when his first wife died."

She gave a short laugh. "Many people did. How far appearance is from reality! I could never live with DeWitt. He is far too demanding. After you told me about losing your parents in a massacre, I saw you as quiet and stoic, a welcome change from the men of privilege I knew."

Eleanora sighed with contentment and listened to the rushing water. She gazed up at the sun shining through the fragrant pine needles.

"This is nice." He nodded at the woodland around them.

"Yes," she said. "Our wedding reception was a far cry from my first. Aristocrats in powdered wigs, dowagers in brocade gowns, an orchestra that filled Clermont with waltzes, and Jacob . . ." her voice trailed off.

"Today was far different than my first marriage, too." Daniel thought back.

"Let's go inside," she whispered.

"Inside? On a beautiful morning like this? How can you think of it? Now," he cast a glance into the forest, "I bet we can find a sunny bed of moss if we were to walk along the river."

"Oh, yes," she grew excited and clasped his arm. "Let's go!"

They stood and kissed, and he led her hand-in-hand into the forest where the morning sun slanted majestically. Soon the birds, chipmunks and squirrels came out of hiding for their breakfast scraps.

CHAPTER 35

*A*ll too soon their honeymoon ended. A new enthusiasm filled the work crews. As flooring was laid for the channel and towpath on the great Genesee aqueduct, Daniel put contracts out to bid for the next big push, along the ridge. He wanted to spend time with his wife, so Canvass White took charge of the cut through the great cliff seventeen miles east of Niagara Falls, a place they were already calling "Lockport." Daniel and Eleanora left the digging and boated eastward to tour what had been completed, giving a final inspection to the portion soon to open.

In August, Eleanora visited the Holland Land Company farmers who contracted to work, and she gave them each one-mile lengths while Daniel and J.J. rode to Buffalo. From the back of his horse, Daniel pointed out the wide harbor. He described his capture of the British vessels during the war, and how he had built Perry's fleet.

"Aye, Dan-o, them Brits are nasty sods, truth to tell. Once you Yanks beat the tar out of them, why, says half the Irish population, America's the land for me."

"What will you do when we finish the digging?"

"Find me another canal to work on, sure enough. What

else can a great bellowin' buck like me do? 'Tis certain I'm getting too old for prize-fighting."

"Look over Buffalo. It could be to your liking."

"Ah," he said disgustedly, "I ain't the kind to be settling down, Dan-o. Ain't in my blood." He clucked at the horse, gave a tug to the rein and they ambled along.

Lodging at the renamed Eagle Tavern, Daniel invited Lester Frye to dine with them.

"Only luck, Danny, only luck pulled me through them tough times," Lester observed soberly. "I come in after the war and bought up frontage for a song. So convinced was everyone that the British would capture us, they sold and fled." He grinned at J.J. "Me and Danny was in business together, see? Anyways, them pair of villains, Ellicott and Porter, why they're trying to steal the western port of our canal for Black Rock, and that's what's got me concerned." J.J. nodded. "Now they're boasting how they run Dee-Witt Clinton himself out of office over that there tug o' war. Oh-ho, Danny and me seen some high old times, we did. We made this area what it is today. Them johnny-come-latelies trying to cash in, why, Mr. McShane, it's downright disgusting."

With an appropriate look of disgust, Lester buried his red face in his tankard of ale and emerged with foam on his lips. "Didn't tell you, Danny, that I got something of yours. Sold what was left of the *Pearl*."

Daniel glared at him. "The *Pearl*?"

"Yep. Sold her to some salvagers. You were nowheres around and after she burnt there weren't much left of her but the hull and some fixtures. They inquired of me, so I up and sold her."

"And what did you do with the money?"

"Invested it, Danny-boy. Been keeping it for you. All safe and secure. In fact," he leaned across the table, "I got a wharf that's yours I been keeping. You throw up a warehouse and get a boat and you're in business again. The future, Danny, got to protect your investments for the future."

The waitress brought another round of ale. She bent down and whispered in J.J.'s ear, then left.

"You own a wharf here in Buffalo – prime dockage," Lester told him, "– and if the canal winds up terminating here, why, we'll both be rich."

"How much did you get for the *Pearl*?"

"Three hundred. She took a lot of punishment."

"And the dock? How much did it cost?"

"It's worth about . . ."

"Not what it's worth. What did you pay?"

"Two-fifty." Lester reached into his vest. "Here," and he slapped fifty dollars in gold on the table. "That's the balance, and you've got good title to the wharf."

"Say, Dan-o," J.J. said, "all this talk of finances makes me a wee thirsty. I'll be in the taproom awhile and if I'm gone when you get there, why, I'll see you tomorry."

Daniel turned and saw Edna McKay removing her apron and glancing their way.

"Till tomorrow, J.J."

"So," Lester resumed, "don't mourn the loss of the *Pearl*. We'll build a whole fleet of vessels. This place is exploding with opportunity. When they hear the canal is definitely coming to Buffalo, and you can deliver the news to me whenever you know for sure, the building spree will be crazy." Lester leaned closer, licked his lip and winked. "But you can tell your old mate, can't you?"

"I'll do what I can."

"Your word is like the jingle of coin in my pocket." He pushed the gold pieces nearer Daniel and Daniel picked them up and put them in his vest.

"Which wharf?"

"End of Washington Street."

"Thanks, Lester." Abruptly Daniel rose from the table, leaving Lester with the bill.

He walked through the streets of Buffalo, and he remembered back when the village was a frontier outpost. He remembered Carrie and Rachel and Eli, and he remembered the peace of mind he felt each morning when he walked down to the harbor to board his *Silver Pearl* and sail on the lake. He smelled the wind, and the clean lake air beckoned him to be sailing again. He walked out on the pier at the foot of Washington Street. Clearly Lester was trying to bribe him for a favorable decision, but he was inept even at that. Daniel decided he'd accept the wharf. He reached the end of the pier.

The lake lay black and silent, gently rising and falling on the pilings. Instinctively he reached into his pocket, and clutched the ten gold pieces. He used to moor his *Silver Pearl* out there and her trim lines and her speed on the lake had made him proud. "I'll build another," he said. "I'm not meant to be on land." He took the fifty dollars from his pocket, considered hurling it into the water as a proper farewell but then slipped the coins back into his pocket. They'd make an initial payment on materials for a new brig.

The next day, Daniel walked his property with J.J. "I'll build a house on this rise," he scanned the shore of the lake.

"There's a good stand of timber," J.J. pointed.

"No," Daniel said. "Stone, it will be built of stone. I had a wooden house before, and I had a wooden ship. This will be a house of stone."

"The lass, Edna, she told me something about you rescuing her."

"The war was difficult out here. I found her in a compromising situation, and I helped her out. That's all."

"Aye," J.J. said, "she's a game lassie." Together they scanned the lake. Daniel saw it with new eyes today, planning for his wife and a new family. Returning home, J.J. rattled on.

"I'll tell you, though, Dan-o, it's been a while since I've been with a woman, but she was sweet, sweeter than the liquor that drips into the jug. She weren't no female with a whine in every word, but she ain't no breezy day neither." He spat, then turned to Daniel. "I'm getting old, mate. She showed a rare ability last night. I've been thinking of settling down."

"Ah, ha!" Daniel slapped J.J. on the back. "As soon as the canal is completed, we'll be partners."

"Nay, Dan-o. I meant the settlin' to be a state of mind, not a location. I must keep moving." And J.J. looked into the clouds above the lake. "As life gets shorter, Dan-o, I grow philosophic. 'Tis a grand canal we've dug, and few men can boast such a friend as you."

"I own the site where Edna lives," Daniel said. "I'll deed it to you if you're of a mind to remain."

"Can't do it, Dan-o. There's a canal madness over the land. They are seeing what we've done, all over, in every state, and I'm heading down Philadelphia-way after we're through." He laughed. "This lake's mighty sweet, but I need to be nearer the sea."

"Have you asked Edna if she'll accompany you?"

"No!" J.J. was shocked. "Never give a woman such a say!"

"Now there you're wrong. Women are wiser than we'll ever be. Talk to her. If you decide you want to stay, the site of the house is yours."

J.J. turned to him and reached out his hand. "You're a good man, Dan-o. I did promise her I'd stop by this evening, so can we tarry here till tomorry?"

"Absolutely."

Freed from his gubernatorial duties, DeWitt Clinton spent the summer of 1823 on the canal. He took an obsessive personal interest in the great work. He dressed in the casual clothes of a gentleman farmer, corduroy trousers, wool coat, slouch hat, and he moved among the men with an encouraging word and handshake. He appeared more relaxed, but when caught in thoughtful moments, he seemed sad and defeated.

"Ah, Hedges, it's like myself being ripped up," he sighed one day as they looked down on the massive blasting and earthworks at the deep cut. Cranes hung above the cut, swinging baskets of rubble up and out. "Politics!"

"You give the men great encouragement with your interest in their work," Daniel remarked.

"That's Eleanora's doing. She wouldn't allow me to sit in New York brooding. She loves this work, and the change in her is astonishing. She looks so much younger and livelier since your wedding."

"She certainly prefers married life to politics."

"Ah, Hedges, but it's hell to be out of power."

"Surely you'll rise again!"

"Surely? There's nothing sure in politics. That reptile Van Buren is consolidating power day and night, purging my name from people's memories, taking credit for all we've done."

"What drives a man like that? Has he no sense of justice?"

"Ambition. He's ruthless and expert at seizing power. He'll take credit for the canal. I'll be a private citizen when it opens, and he'll bask in glory for all the work we've done. Ah, the people are a fickle mob. Deep appetite and shallow memory."

"I have more confidence in the people. Yours is simply a temporary setback."

Clinton ignored the optimism. "You Hedges," he waved his arm over the furious activity spread below them, "you have done the best of the three of us since the war. Eleanora has been run off her lands, and I've been run out of office. But you . . . you're our engineer and you have the lovely Eleano-ra." Daniel saw a gleam of admiration in the great man's eye.

"But you're still on the canal commission!"

"For how long? My term ends next year."

"They would never remove you from that!"

"Never say 'never' in politics. The impossible can and usually does happen. In any event, I have some news for Eleanora about her chancery suit, promising news."

"Let's find her."

"You're a lucky man, Hedges."

"We both are," Daniel answered.

In Clinton's honor, Eleanora was laying out a picnic luncheon of cold ham, chicken, Canadian cheddar, fresh bread, pie and coffee.

They sat at a rustic table in the shade of an ancient chestnut tree. Over lunch Clinton talked about the new sense of energy and enterprise along the canal, and about festivities planned for the fall. "I've come to ask you if you both would accompany me when the canal opens and accept some of the praise."

"You didn't tell him?" Eleanora asked. Daniel shook his head. She turned to Clinton. "We'd love to, DeWitt, but I'm five months with child and that will be my time for lying in."

"Why, my goodness, congratulations!" Clinton circled the table and embraced her. "I'm so very happy for both of you. What an unexpected joy!"

"Yes, and if it is a boy, his name will be 'Daniel Clinton Hedges.'"

Clinton's eyes filled. "You do me great honor. And yet," he tried to hide his emotion, "I bring you good news, Eleanora. Your suit has been heard in chancery. While the court upheld Randolph Van Rensselaer's claim to Claverack because you acquiesced, it also awarded you dower. While the life estate terminated at your remarriage, the court held that there was no such limit on your right to dower, and without a specific limitation in the conveyance it would be awarded. With no children, you'll get a life income equal to one-half the rents and tenements Jacob held while you were married. This works in your favor. As long as you remained at Claverack, the 1787 statute limited your right to income from that estate. Now you may collect income from everything Jacob held, and his holdings in Manhattan were vast. Your attorney Van Zandt is now seeking an accounting, and you'll get arrearages back to the date you were first ejected. Since Claverack was only one-quarter of Jacob's property, you'll realize substantially more than all you were earning when you held the estate."

"That all seems so long ago and far away," Eleanora said. "It is good news, DeWitt. Thank you for looking into it."

"Yes, it will be welcome with a baby, particularly when your husband works for such a meager wage."

"I'll correct that presently, just as soon as I retire from state service," Daniel said. "Opportunity knows no bounds in Buffalo today."

"I should consider that. I'll be retiring soon."

"Retiring?" both cried.

"Yes." Clinton nodded emphatically.

"Nonsense. Just you wait until this is completed. You alone will be the hero of a grateful people."

"The people," he scoffed. "We shall see."

Construction was hectic that year as work gangs blasted a mile and a half through solid rock. The men could almost smell the end. Daniel had delegated most of the work so he could build a home in Buffalo for himself and Eleanora. She went into labor in mid-October. Daniel brought old Doc Barnes to attend her. The labor was long and difficult and Daniel sat at her bedside applying cold compresses to her forehead for thirty hours.

When the baby was born and Doc Barnes whispered hoarsely, "It's a boy," Hedges accepted him in the blanket, walked out into the light of an autumn morning and held him to the sun. He murmured an Iroquois prayer, lowered the babe to his cheek, and as little Daniel Clinton Hedges began to wail, he murmured, "My son! My beautiful boy!" His heart swelled with love and pride and he held the baby and looked into the forest and then far out over the lake before returning him to his mother. Then together the happy parents gazed into each other's eyes as their miracle lay between them.

CHAPTER 36

"*A* grave mistake, Matty," Aaron Burr said when Van Buren revealed the plan he had just set into motion. They were sitting in Burr's hotel room before a low fire. "You overplayed your hand. If you have any power to stop it, do so."

"Too extreme?"

"As I've told you before, in politics you can kill a man, but you must never mutilate the corpse. For six years, you've eroded Clinton's support and you have succeeded in undoing him. But this, this will humiliate him, and given the progress of the ditch, the public will react with anger."

"The Regency supported it to a man."

"The Regency is not infallible. Driving Clinton from the canal commission will prove to the people that he has been a victim of political intrigue all along. Yes, we harried him about his damned ditch, but boats are passing from Rochester to Albany in days, and the big cut is nearly complete all the way to Lake Erie. He was right and the nay-sayers were wrong. This plan – you say Judge Skinner proposed it? – it will backfire. Too harsh. You must distance yourself from the Regency's vote."

"But I am their leader!"

Burr winked. "Only when it serves your interests, Matty. Say you were busy with federal issues, that you support Clinton's reappointment. Better yet, get out of town."

"But they've got the votes to oust him – downstate, the mid-Hudson counties, and Ellicott worked for us in the western counties."

"Votes mean nothing to an angry mob. And that's what you will have." He held up his index finger. "I learned the inescapable truth of political assassination the hard way. Was my duel with Hamilton merely the settling of a private grudge? I thought so. But nothing is private with public men. I brought down the wrath of the American people on my head and won a place in infamy. They hounded me, tried me and exiled me. And in those hovels in London and Paris I saw Hamilton nightly, bleeding and groaning, stalking like Banquo's ghost through my dreams. Let us leave town together tonight. Sometimes retreat is the best and only alternative."

"There is no honor to be had in this?"

"None whatsoever. Believe a man who has seen too much."

"Very well, I shall call on you at six in the morning."

"I hope Mr. Fulton's engines are repaired. If we hadn't had to stop at Kingston on the way up, I would have been here to avert this debacle."

In addition to the transport of goods, the canal speeded the transmission of news. Hedges first heard of this latest political outrage two days after the April 12 legislative vote ousting Clinton from the commission. Hedges was inspecting the blasting operation at Lockport, and Clinton was due at the site that morning.

"Guess I'll have to break the news to him, J.J."

The Irishman was begrimed with soot from the blasting powder. "'Tis a sorry business, Dan-o."

"They'll be here about noon."

Just after the dinner bell had rung, horses and mules threaded down the path toward waiting canal boats. Clinton was to journey east to Schenectady on a triumphant inspection tour. A similar cut in the east was descending the cliff face at Cohoes Falls.

Daniel approached him and they found privacy in a construction shack. "I have some very bad news, Governor."

"I am used to it, Hedges, tell me."

"The legislature voted to remove you from the canal commission."

"What?" Clinton knit his brow.

"They voted to take away your last public office, sir, to remove you from the commission."

Clinton shook his head. "They can't do that!"

"I am sorry to say it, sir, but they have already done it. Your appointment expired and they filled it with Senator Barker from Little Falls."

"No," Clinton said impatiently. "They have the power to do it, of course, but they can't do it politically."

"Well, sir, they've done it." For the first time in their long association Hedges considered Clinton obtuse. When Clinton then rose, shook his hand and laughed out loud, Daniel believed he'd come unhinged.

"This is the happiest day of my life!" Clinton cried, throwing his arms out to the sides. "The fools!" And he laughed and laughed.

"I'm afraid I don't understand, sir."

"Did your man tell you what happened immediately on the heels of the vote?"

"Why there was a torchlight parade protesting it, sir. But a mob can't reinstate you."

"Ah, but it can, Hedges. It can, and it will. You and Eleanora have been telling me to trust the people. You should have counseled me instead to trust Van Buren's stupidity and arrogance. Oh," he clenched his hands at his temples, "this is hardly to be believed. I didn't have the power to call a coach or get my boots blackened. The fools! The pack of fools! By taking away my last office they have in essence given me back all that I lost. I was going east today. Let us instead ride west to inform Eleanora. I'll stay with you until the resentment builds to a crescendo, then I shall progress triumphantly across the state and allow the people to summon me back as their leader."

"We won't reach Buffalo till dawn."

"Let us set out now. Eleanora deserves to share in this and I need a quiet place to stay for a day or two. Have they champagne in Buffalo?"

"If they do, I'll find it."

"Before we start, Hedges," Clinton reached for Daniel's hand, "I don't tell you this often enough. You have been a source of strength for me during all of this. Now things have come full circle. Let me tell you before the riotous clamor begins. The only way that I could negotiate and fight down in Albany was because of my certainty that your work out here on the line was steady and sure. Often your achievements were all that went as planned."

"We have been honored to work with you," Daniel said. "Eleanora will be happy to see you thus. I'll have my man find mounts and ask him to tell your party to go east without you."

Clinton clapped his hands and laughed, relishing the irony of it all. Soon they were riding toward Buffalo as the spring sun set. "Tell me, Hedges, how fast could you finish the deep cut and these twenty-odd miles?"

"Two years."

"Could the work be speeded up?"

"With more men and more money."

"I am going to run for governor this year, and I'd like to see the work completed by 'twenty-five."

"So would I. I'm anxious to get back into the lake trade. When the canal is completed, there will be tremendous opportunities for making money and now there's a great incentive," he turned and looked at Clinton, "I have a family to support."

"But you could finish so soon?"

"If you say it must be done, it will. Direction from Albany under this current governor has been less than inspiring."

"Well, then, my good man, we shall finish in 'twenty-five, and we shall show the world what my enterprising leadership can do. Ah ha! Onward!"

They rode through the sunset and the darkness and reached Daniel's large stone house in Buffalo at sunrise. Already up with the baby, Eleanora heard their horses and appeared on the porch. She waved and smiled, the babe in her arms. "Now there's a sight!" Daniel said, spurring his horse into a gallop.

"I didn't expect you till Friday!" She handed Daniel the baby. "And DeWitt! Heavens! What a lovely surprise. You two must be famished. I'll have Hilda fix breakfast."

They sat in the clean, spacious kitchen while Hilda bustled about frying bacon and sausage, eggs and fish.

"Have you heard what has happened in Albany?" Daniel asked. Eleanora shook her head. "The politicians removed DeWitt from his post on the canal commission."

"Impossible!"

Clinton nodded and smiled.

"Where will it end?" she asked.

"Right here and right now," Clinton said, accepting the baby from Daniel. "Already there are riots in Albany against Van Buren and his cynics." Clinton bounced his little namesake on his knee. Soon Hilda had the breakfast ready. Eleanora set out cups and poured coffee.

"Ah, little man," Clinton said to the baby, "it's a grand life you're beginning. Your papa and mama and I have struggled through so much together."

He looked around the kitchen with satisfaction. "If I have one regret, it is that I chose a public life over a private one. I paid so little attention to my wife and family. There are few rewards in public life beyond the revenge I'm now enjoying, and so many sacrifices. Perhaps it is my nature and yet beyond his family and a few close friends, a man has little else to hold dear."

He cradled the infant awhile, then handed him back to his mother. Eleanora took the babe who bore both their names back to the bedroom to nurse.

The reaction was even more dramatic than Clinton predicted. Immediately after the vote that ousted him, an angry mob rushed through Albany to the hotels and rooming houses of Regency members and clamored for an explanation. Aboard the North River Steamboat, Burr and Van Buren were enjoying a gentleman's game of whist and admiring the majestic Catskills.

By nightfall the news had reached Troy, Schenectady and Kingston. Throngs turned out in the streets that night, angry faces burning in the ruddy glow of torches to march in protest to what the legislature had done. Word reached New York City, already reaping benefits from the canal, and swept through Utica, Rome, the fledgling village of Syracuse near Salina, and then Rochester, Black Rock and Buffalo.

Editorials deplored the petty political move, and praised Clinton for withstanding a decade of hostile political attacks. When the people of Buffalo learned Clinton was at Hedges' home, they assembled in a joyous crowd, marched there and called him out.

"And now the backlash begins," Clinton remarked as he

prepared to go out on the porch to address them. "I'm off across the state on our waterway!"

"At last," Eleanora said, "the conquering hero."

"Best of luck," Daniel slapped him on the back. Clinton opened the door and stepped out with raised arms to the rousing applause.

Clinton's triumphal journey across the state sent Van Buren to Washington and his faction into hiding. A grateful people demonstrated its regard in banquets, parades, receptions and interminable speeches. That spring, Clinton was the unanimous choice of the Democratic-Republicans, and he was re-elected to the governor's office by a landslide. His clear mandate from the people was to finish the canal.

J.J. McShane finally completed the mile and a half blast through the deep cut during the summer of 1825. "Sixteen miles still separate me from Buffalo, and the arms of my Edna," he sang. "So let's get digging, you lazy Irish luggers!"

J.J. devised an ingenious way to encourage his men. At intervals he placed casks of whiskey, and as the men reached each cask, they were allowed fifteen minutes' rest to drink. His Irishmen dug furiously and neither the prism, the berm or the towpath suffered for their imbibing.

That summer, the Marquis de Lafayette, the famed Revolutionary War hero and survivor of the French Revolution, visited the canal on his tour to see how the American "experiment" in democracy was progressing forty years later. In flowery speeches he heralded the canal as proof of what men could accomplish untrammeled by a monarchy and ruling class, in a free land where ingenuity was motivated only by self-interest and free enterprise.

Hedges still visited the dig, but his skills were no longer required. During the summer he rented a berth in the shipyard, and with a hand-picked crew he built a brig according to an old plan, and he named this ship the *Silver Pearl*. He constructed a warehouse at the wharf, hired Joel Kipp to manage the land side of his enterprise and he began reestablishing himself in the lake trade.

Clinton scheduled the opening ceremony for October 26, 1825, just before winter would seal the canal with ice. Along its length, towns were booming, buildings rising day by day as a steady stream of commerce flowed from Detroit and Cleveland toward New York Harbor and the sea. The celebration committee planned events and spectacles from Buffalo to New York, ending in a splendid fireworks display among the tall-masted ships in New York harbor. When Daniel and Eleanora received their invitation to accompany the party, they discussed whether to journey to the metropolis.

"Clinton will expect us to share this moment with him," Daniel said. "We can't refuse."

"But the work is all done," Eleanora protested. "I see no use in going. And what would we do about Danny?"

"Truthfully I don't want to go either. The nay-sayers will be out slapping each other on the back, everyone taking credit for what they didn't do."

"Well, then, let's tell DeWitt we'd be honored if he'd stay with us here before he starts, but that we won't be accompanying him."

Eleanora used her most persuasive arguments and finally warmed Clinton up to the idea that he and Kitty should lodge with them before setting out on the opening tour. Clinton didn't "want to be a bother," and had booked rooms at the commodious new Eagle Hotel. Yet Eleanora prevailed, and he and Catherine arrived as the brilliant leaves were falling from the trees. They spent an agreeable three days with the Hedges while all along the three hundred-and-sixty-three miles of the canal preparations went forward.

Daniel had laid in special cuts of meat and imported wines. Although at first Catherine seemed apprehensive of frontier life, Daniel's easy manner soon charmed her. At dinner on the eve of the opening, Clinton proposed a toast:

"Let us drink to Daniel and Eleanora, who helped transform my dream into a highway of the future for all New York. May this household be blessed, and may they prosper with many more children."

They drank and then Daniel stood.

"When I first heard about your canal, I was curious. And in the last ten years I've done my best to meet the impossible challenge you set for us, to make water run uphill."

"Here, here!" Clinton cried.

"There's nothing else to say. We have completed the great work. I have married the fairest lady of the land, and the future lies before us. I raise my glass, then, and simply say to you, and to my lovely Eleanora, we did it."

"Yes! Yes, we did!"

"Together," Eleanora said quietly.

In the candlelight, they all clinked their glasses.

At the tavern in the Eagle Hotel a United States senator was causing local people to stare. Martin Van Buren, the man who approved the first resolution to fund the canal, was enjoying the glow of popularity with his entourage of four. Already he had made arrangements for a canal boat to carry him in the triumphal party the five hundred miles to New York harbor. He had pondered on what to name his boat, and decided to keep it simple: *The Senator.*

"Those people don't look normal," a waitress remarked to Edna McKay.

"They're daft," Edna replied. "From Washington, you know."

"Let me get the table," the waitress said, "you've got a big day tomorrow, and then a big night." She winked. Edna and J.J. were to be married after the opening celebration the next day, and this was Edna's last night of work.

"No," Edna said, "I'll get it. I'd better get used to their sort as J.J. wants to move to Philadelphia now."

She found Senator Van Buren affable and gentlemanly, and he left her a very large tip. As she crawled into bed with J.J. McShane for their last night of pre-nuptial bliss, she told him she'd waited on Van Buren.

"Van Buren?" J.J. bolted upright. "Are you sure 'twas him?"

"Why, yes, he's in room twelve."

"*Martin* Van Buren? The senator?"

"The very man."

"But what could he be doing in Buff'lo?"

"The celebration. The canal was his idea, wasn't it?"

"Oh," J.J. said, folding his arms behind his head. "I see."

"J.J.? What's the matter? Don't think about him! Lie down! Lie down! Oh, I wish I hadn't mentioned it! Tomorrow we'll be man and wife. J.J.? What's the matter?"

"Leave off! I'm considering, woman, I'm considering."

The next morning at seven, as Martin Van Buren breakfasted with his companions, a pretty waitress whispered that DeWitt Clinton wished to speak with him privately to discuss moving his boat up toward the front in the official flotilla.

"Very well." Van Buren folded his napkin meticulously, and looked smugly at his companions. "I shall be back presently." The senator adjusted his coat and stepped outside. A coach waited for him, and he smiled as he stepped inside. This was a sign they might at last make peace. "Drive on!"

"Very well, sir." The whip cracked, the horses' traces jingled and groaned and the coach was moving. Van Buren considered how sweet it was being summoned to his adversary. He wanted something, no doubt, Clinton always wanted something. The senator had heard he was lodging with the Van Rensselaer woman and her husband, the engineer. He enjoyed the rustic scenery but after they had driven for half an hour, he rapped on the trap door with his cane.

"Where are we going?"

"Few more minutes, sir."

Van Buren opened and closed his watch and settled into his seat. A canal across the state, surely an extraordinary feat. He would make amends with Clinton, but he'd extract a full price for his presence in the flotilla. Another half hour passed and he rapped on the door.

"My good man, you must have taken a wrong turn."

"Oh, no, sir. A mile and a half ahead."

The canal boats would be boarding at nine and it was after eight now.

"Take me to the canal at once!" Van Buren commanded.

"Yes, sir, right away." But still the driver did not change course. The sun was out the right window so they were going north. Impatiently Van Buren pounded his walking stick into the floor.

"Man!" he called. No answer. "Sirrah!" He pounded his cane on the trapdoor. No answer. "I demand as a United States senator to know where I'm being kidnaped!" No answer.

Van Buren looked out at the passing forest and panicked.

"I *demand*, sir, that you stop this coach."

Miraculously the driver reined the horses, but they turned left until the driver backed up the coach, then pulled forward. He opened the hatch and looked down at Van Buren. "Yes, sir?"

"Where are we?"

"We've reached our destination, sir." The driver leaned back, then produced two pistols. "Get out."

Van Buren's eyes opened wide with shock and indignation. "What?"

"Get out."

"But you don't know who I am!"

A deafening explosion sounded as the driver shot into the sky. Van Buren senator laughed uneasily, "This is a fine game, driver, now take me to the ceremony."

The lad lowered his other pistol, sighting it on Van Buren's nose. "Get out!"

Van Buren looked this way and that, then he opened the door and stepped to the roadway. "Do you know who I am?" He pulled out his purse to offer a bribe. "I am a United States senator. How much to take me back?"

The lad flicked his whip and the horses sprang again in the traces.

"Wait!" Van Buren cried. "Wait!" He started to follow, his arms out imploringly as the coach wheels picked up speed.

"Don't you know who I am?" Van Buren cried with outstretched arms. "I'm a United States senator! I demand you return!" But the Irish lad never looked back.

The United States senator looked around him and saw he was deep in a forest where no one knew or cared who he was. He uttered an uncharacteristic curse, brushed off his sleeves and began the long trek back to Buffalo.

Daniel, Eleanora and Daniel Clinton Hedges escorted DeWitt and Kitty through the clamoring village of Buffalo to their boat, the *Seneca Chief*. It was barely nine o'clock when they boarded, yet both sides of the canal were lined as far as sight could see with well-wishers. All cheered as Clinton and Kitty waved from the deck. The governor raised his hand for silence.

"As we go east we'll be swamped with odes and bombast, so I'll not engage in any of that now."

The crowd cheered.

"I congratulate the citizens of Buffalo today. I assure them their community will grow and prosper and will soon become a foremost city in this land. Let me also recognize your own son, Daniel Hedges, who built much of this great work, and I'll doff my hat to your lady, Eleanora Livingston Van Rensselaer Hedges." He tipped his hat to Eleanora. The crowd cheered wildly.

"Well, we mustn't keep the rest of this great State of New York waiting. Thank you for the support you have given us, people of Buffalo. May you thrive and prosper, and may God bless you and your descendants who today inherit a new and blessed land." Clinton gave a signal and a cannon blast startled the assembled.

The people cheered wildly and the small bell in the church tower rang as the brass band struck up a marching tune. Clinton winked at Daniel, and blew a kiss to Eleanora and the baby. The barefoot boy on the towpath flicked his switch at the white horses' flanks and the team began to pull. The rope's slack lessened until it gently jerked the *Seneca Chief* ahead in the water. Far off, another cannon exploded, then in the distance, another.

"J.J.'s wedding is at two," Daniel took Eleanora's hand.

"We have time," she said.

"Time?"

"Yes." Eleanora bent down and kissed little Daniel Clinton. "Time for our own celebration." Eleanora set the boy down. "There now, Danny, you're going to play with Miss Hilda while papa and I go to a wedding."

"Miss Hilda?" the two-year-old asked. He nodded and ran to the maid.

"You know, my love," Eleanora said. "that Daniel Clinton mustn't be an only child."

"No," Daniel smiled, "we'd better do something about that."

"I love you," she said, reaching for his hand.

"And I love you." He slipped his arm around her waist and drew her to him, and together they watched the canal boats recede northward toward Black Rock. Holding hands as young lovers do, they walked along the waterfront talking as the canal boats proceeded to their feasts and speeches and fireworks.

In the distance, like far-off thunder, another cannon boomed. In a relay the cannon blasts would progress eastward to Troy, then south to New York where the guns of the Battery would respond, then the relay would return the five hundred miles to Buffalo. "We'll be asleep in each other's arms by the time that cannon shot returns," Daniel said.

"Yes," she smiled and kissed him again and wove her fingers into his calloused hand. "Oh, yes!"

To them the world had never looked quite so pure and new and they turned again to view the boats between the green hills, and the sunshine and the bounteous blue of the sky reflected in the great waterway.

Meanwhile, all down the canal, the cannon shot was quickly relayed from emplacement to emplacement. Many of Oliver Perry's cannon had been used in the West. The shot sounded down the flight at Lockport, over the great aqueduct at Rochester, through the foul stagnant air of the Montezuma swamp, echoing across Onondaga and Oneida Lakes, ancient haunts of the Iroquois, then down the Mohawk Valley past Schenectady. The cannon of French and British and American wars were called into service on battlements in old forts farther east.

At Troy, the cannon relay turned southward. By a prearranged signal the shot in Albany set all the church bells ringing. "It's open!" joyous crowds on the Capitol steps cheered. "It's open!" Down the meandering Hudson, echoing through the Catskills and the sleepy Dutch villages where descendants of Washington Irving's characters paused to listen. Down through Tappan Zee and below the Jersey Palisades it rolled until crowds on Manhattan docks cheered wildly. "It's coming!! It's coming!!"

Cannon aboard warships in New York harbor answered with deafening roars, then a fusillade from the Battery signaled that the Atlantic coast had been reached. The relay had taken an hour and a half. Now it turned back and its answer raced up the Hudson and out along the route of the canal. Clinton's flotilla was well on the way to the flight at Lockport when the cannon shot returned.

And farther west, in the master bedroom of their great stone house overlooking Lake Erie, Daniel and Eleanora slept in each other's arms.

EPILOGUE

WEDDING OF THE WATERS

*A*t every township along the canal the *Seneca Chief* paused to greet grateful New Yorkers now joined by a ribbon of water to the ports of the world. The locals lavished Clinton and the flotilla with feasts, toasts, speeches, songs, dances, odes and ballads, gun salutes, cannon salvos and fireworks displays. No superlative was left slumbering. Eastward to greater and greater celebrations the boats were towed, boats that carried barrels of Erie lake water, deer, bear cubs, raccoons, birds, logs of red cedar and birds-eye maple to be fashioned into commemorative boxes, boats that carried canal commissioners, legislators, engineers and foremen.

The flotilla reached Albany Wednesday, November 2. There the greatest celebration so far began with a twenty-four gun salute and in a rapture of balls and banquets, speeches and odes, the capital city welcomed its hero. Three portraits were hung in the Assembly Chamber: America's first president, George Washington, New York's first governor, George Clinton, and New York's first son, DeWitt Clinton.

Martin Van Buren, who insisted on passing the celebration party in a closed boat, reached Albany two days before Clinton. Despite McShane's practical joke, one that Van Buren ever after ascribed to Clinton, the senator took the dais at a formal state dinner honoring the governor and praised his foresight and his overriding will.

Steamboats towed the canal boats down the Hudson next day, and the flotilla reached New York harbor Friday, November 4, dwarfed there by tall-masted ships from Europe and the Orient. New York City's ecstatic celebration outstripped all the others together. Fireworks, balls, banquets, illuminations, parades and speeches kept the city awake the entire weekend and all but obscured the simple ceremony that Clinton performed – a "Wedding of the Waters."

To join the waters of Lake Erie with the Atlantic, Clinton had his boat towed to Sandy Hook and he poured a barrel of Lake Erie water into the sea. This simple wedding, like another he'd performed on the Rochester aqueduct, marked the beginning of a new era.

Immediately New York State reaped untold riches from commerce flowing along the thin artery between the heartland and the sea. Tolls soon paid back the seven million dollars in construction costs and revenue filled the state coffers. Cities grew from villages and boom towns along its route: Troy, Schenectady, Utica, Rome, Syracuse, Rochester, and Buffalo. So effectively did the canal tap into the vast landlocked territories of the Great Lakes, drawing commerce from Cleveland and Detroit, produce from the farmers of Ohio, Pennsylvania, Indiana, Illinois, Wisconsin, and Michigan, that New York was dubbed "The Empire State" and New York City, the maritime port, became the nation's first harbor and financial center.

DeWitt Clinton, who foresaw such immeasurable prosperity and employed his keen political skill and unyielding will for a decade and a half to achieve it, realized few personal benefits. Returned again to the governor's office in 1826 by a grateful populace, he died suddenly in his Albany home in 1828 before revisiting his national ambitions. A legal judgment against his estate forced the sale of his house, belongings and holdings and pauperized Catherine and their four young children. Over fierce objections from Van Buren's Regency, the state legislature finally settled an annual income of $10,000 on his widow.

Martin Van Buren delivered a touching eulogy at Clinton's funeral, and with Tammany's support and Burr in the background, he succeeded Clinton as governor. But he served only three months, preferring to return to Washington society where President Andrew Jackson soon appointed him secretary of state. The "Fox of Kinderhook" quickly became the most influential member of Jackson's cabinet, and with Jackson's support, Van Buren finally plucked "the golden apple." He was elected eighth president of the United States in 1836, the year Aaron Burr passed on, perhaps to advise the greatest schemer of all.

Van Buren's political skills far surpassed his statesmanship. Tensions between North and South and the Financial Panic of 1837 plagued his administration and he lost his bid for a second term to General William Henry Harrison, the frontier fighter who once supplied Kentucky riflemen to Oliver Hazard Perry. Van Buren retired to his Columbia County estate, "Lindenwald," and despite a few unsuccessful attempts to re-emerge, he never again held public office.

J.J. McShane declined Daniel's offer of the property on Washington Street in Buffalo, and he and Edna followed the canal craze into Pennsylvania. Accustomed to the exclusive company of men, J.J. was blessed with five daughters and he returned each night from his labors to a happy hearth. Joel Kipp proved a loyal and capable agent for the Daniel Hedges Shipping Co. He married again and raised his family in the burgeoning city of Buffalo.

Lester Frye grew both immensely wealthy and immensely fat. He made two unsuccessful attempts to be elected mayor of Buffalo, a city that soon became the second largest in the state. Lester always credited Daniel Hedges with giving him his start, the "two hunnerd dollars" on the whiskey run as his first investment. Though he urged Daniel to involve himself in municipal concerns, Daniel preferred a very guarded private life.

As far as life will allow two people, Daniel and Eleanora did live happily ever after. Little Daniel Clinton Hedges had two brothers and a sister. He followed his father into the lake trade, then entered public life and was elected to Congress from Erie County for three terms. His brother Edward spent a restless youth in Nevada mining camps before joining the army. He fell during the Battle of Gettysburg, fighting for the Union. John Hedges, the youngest and most beloved by his father, named after the burly Irishman J.J. McShane, attended Rensselaer Institute, a school founded on the riverbank by Stephen Van Rensselaer during the final year of canal construction to teach civil engineering and the practical sciences, and he turned his talents to surveying and building the transcontinental railroad.

It was on their daughter that Eleanora placed her hope for women of the next generation. Eleanora settled the restored dower income on Lorraine and sent her to Emma Willard's Troy Female Seminary to develop her passion for learning. Lorraine worked for a time with Elizabeth Cady Stanton and Susan B. Anthony from Seneca Falls to secure women the right to vote and the right to own property.

When a wealthy brewer, Matthew Vassar, endowed an institution for higher learning for women, Lorraine accepted a professorship at Vassar College in the Hudson Valley town of Poughkeepsie. In her thirty-third year she married a worthy sea captain who had made his fortune in the China trade. They lived on his estate in Dutchess County and Lorraine involved herself extensively in the education of Vassar women.

As the nation grew from childhood to adolescence, Daniel and Eleanora lived happily in their big stone house overlooking Buffalo and the lake, watching sunsets and thunder-storms and the sails of many ships blow eastward toward the canal. And on clear days, as they walk hand-in-hand along their grand waterway, the words Eleanora once spoke to Clinton seem to echo: Together they created a thing of surpassing beauty.

ALSO BY JACK CASEY

Hamilton's Choice

The Trial of Bat Shea

Lily of the Mohawks *(coming soon!)*

ABOUT THE AUTHOR

Jack Casey studied literature at Yale, Edinburgh and Cambridge Universities. He writes novels about his native New York State and practices law in Troy, NY. Recently married, he and Victoria make their home in Troy and in Raleigh, NC.

Connect with Jack at JackCasey.com and on Facebook at JackCaseyAuthor.

Made in the USA
Coppell, TX
30 September 2022

83832230R00247